THE FOXGLOVE KILLINGS

THE FOXGLOVE KILLINGS

TARA KELLY

Entangled Publishing, LLC
2614 South Timberline Road
Suite 109
Fort Collins, CO 80525

Entangled Teen is an imprint of Entangled Publishing, LLC.

Visit our website at www.entangledpublishing.com.

Edited by Alycia Tornetta
Cover design by LJ Anderson
Photography credit (c) Pablos33/Shutterstock
Interior design by Jeremy Howland

Print ISBN 978-1-63375-165-1
Ebook ISBN 978-1-63375-166-8

Manufactured in the United States of America

First Edition September 2015

10 9 8 7 6 5 4 3 2 1

FRIDAY, JUNE 20

I still smell the blood. It doesn't matter how many times I shower. How many times I wash my hands. It's still there. Warm and sticky. The smell caught in the back of my throat. I didn't think I could do it. I didn't want to do it. But I did it. I looked right into those scared brown eyes and something took over. I stopped feeling. I stopped seeing. I disappeared.

You think you know me. You think I'm weak. You think I'm nothing. You're wrong.

CHAPTER ONE

Alex saw it first.

We were cutting through Neahkahnie Park, the morning sun warm on our backs. I was telling him we should take his grandpa's El Camino SS and drive down the coast to California for the summer.

"He left that car to you," I said. "You know he did." I reached over to muss his light brown hair. It always stood straight up afterward, as if he'd been electrocuted.

"We can't, Nova. I—" He stopped walking, his eyes widening at the playground.

Clumps of fur blew across the grass, like the cotton blooms did in July. I didn't think it was real at first. Some kid's stuffed animal, maybe.

But the stench was unmistakable. I'd practically been raised in my grandpa's diner. I knew the smell of meat past its prime. Raw. Metallic. Even a little sweet.

A deer's carcass was a twisted heap in the playground, its legs jutting out like winter branches. Bits of flesh, ranging in color from pink to dark red, were strewn across the wood chips. The head of the deer sat on the middle bucket swing. A misty film covered its eyes, and its mouth was open, as if it were gasping for air.

My stomach muscles began to knot.

I saw a dog get hit by a semi once. The scene replayed in my mind for months. The *thud* of the impact, the way he'd yelped. The last second of that dog's life seemed to echo forever.

This was worse. Someone planned this. Put it on display, like it was entertainment.

"What the hell…" Alex said, his voice barely above a whisper.

"Don't look."

Alex had been on an animal-saving crusade since birth. He'd tried to bring a rabbit back to life the day I met him. In fifth grade he'd called the police on his neighbor for yelling at her cat.

This wasn't something he could handle. Especially not now.

"There's nothing you can do," I said, the words slipping out automatically.

"I know. I'm not nine anymore." He glanced down at his busted Vans. Years of skateboarding had turned them from black to gray.

"I didn't mean it like that."

"Yeah, you did." He held my gaze this time. His eyes looked almost yellow in the dull light. Usually they were green.

I knew whatever came out of my mouth wouldn't be the right thing to say. He'd been so weird since his grandpa died last month. Happy one minute. Pissed off the next. Sometimes he didn't talk at all.

I slowly moved toward the deer, wishing I could ignore its vacant eyes, the drone of the flies pecking at its belly. My gramps used to clean up crime scenes back in the day. He swore by downing a few dozen peppermint Tic Tacs, claiming it obliterated his sense of smell. He was also a chain smoker…

A handful of mints wouldn't take this image out of my head. Nothing would.

"We should call someone," Alex said behind me.

Neither of us had a cell phone. He couldn't afford one, and my mom thought they caused brain cancer.

I held my breath, trying not to gag. If I wanted to be a detective one day, this was the crazy shit I'd be dealing with. Too bad I'd inherited my mom's weak stomach.

Something bright purple sat on top of the deer's limp tongue. Darker spots peppered the inside, like a rash.

As I leaned closer, I realized it was a wilted foxglove. Or deadmen's bells, as Mom called them. They were bell-shaped flowers that grew all over coastal Oregon. When I was little, she told me not to eat them or I'd end up like Sleeping Beauty. I used to think they belonged to the fairies. The evil ones, anyway.

A chill swept across my skin, the kind that came from inside.

Laughter echoed from the hiking trail that led out of the woods. Matt Delgado and Jenika Shaw emerged from the shadows of the trees, shoving each other playfully. I could already smell Jenika's cheap off-brand cigarettes.

They were probably on their way to the first day of summer school. Jenika and Matt cut so much school they always had to make up a class or two.

"You think they did this?" I asked Alex.

"I don't know…"

Emerald Cove bragged about its low crime rate, but that could be said for the entire Oregon coast, since it was 363 miles of boondocks. My gramps said this area was cursed, a magnet for psychos and other things that went bump in the night.

Jenika, Matt, and their friends wreaked their share of havoc around here. They were all about destroying property and beating up the "cakes," what us locals called the rich kids who lived and partied here every summer. But animal mutilation didn't seem like their style. Most of their destruction had some message about "sticking it to the man." They grew up together in the Pacific View trailer park—same as Alex and his sister. But unlike Alex, they thought the world owed them an apology for it.

"What's up?" Matt called out. His cowboy hat hid his dark eyes, but his wide smile was unmistakable. The silver rings around his bottom lip made it appear to glow.

"Let's get out of here," I told Alex, not in the mood for Jenika's shit. I was already late for my morning shift at the diner—we could call the cops from there.

Alex kept his gaze on the deer's head, like he was in a trance.

"Quack, quack," Jenika said.

One day she'd decided I looked like a duck and never got over it. Even so, her dumb insults still got to me. "Find a new line, Jenika."

She scanned me from head to toe, that slow, icy drink girls seemed to pull off so well. "Lookin' more like Mom every day."

My skin was darker, like my father's, but I was almost a mirror image of my mother. Thick brown hair. Deep-set hazel eyes. Overly plump lips and a cleft chin. But that wasn't what she meant.

In her mind, I was my mother.

Jenika had been out for my blood since second grade—the year her dad moved in with my mom and me.

"What the fuck…" Matt gaped at the deer's remains, one foot behind him as if he wasn't sure he wanted to get closer.

Jenika walked right up to it like she couldn't wait to inspect the carnage. And knowing Jenika, she couldn't.

She fished through her ratty old military backpack and pulled out the 35mm camera Eric, her dad, gave her. She took that thing everywhere, like he used to. It was the only part of him she wanted anything to do with.

She tossed her backpack on the grass, near where Matt was standing, and squatted in front of the swings. The heel of her left boot sank into a piece of flesh, but she either didn't notice or care.

Most people never saw her coming. Petite. Doe eyes and delicate features. Before she hacked off all her blond hair last summer, she kind of looked like a Russian doll. But she sure knew how to throw down. Almost broke my nose once with a single punch.

"You're twisted, Jen." Matt laughed, shaking his head.

Jenika took the lens cap off her camera and leaned closer, studying the deer's face. As if she was plotting the perfect angle.

"You need help, you know that?" I said. I'd never seen her feel bad about anything. Not even the time she wished her dad dead to his face.

"Nobody cares what you think." She paused, aiming the lens right between the deer's lips.

Matt remained on the edge of the grass, his arms folded. He wasn't watching her, though. He was watching me.

I shivered inside, trying to block out the night I fell apart last summer. The night I let him touch me. His rough lips, the bitter smell of vodka. His hands, cold and completely wrong, underneath my shirt.

I'd never live that night down.

Matt turned his attention to the swings now, his lips parted.

"That's messed up."

Jenika's finger hovered over the shutter button. "No shit."

"Did they glue the head or what?" he asked.

Nobody answered. I didn't *want* to know.

"Anything for a little attention, right, Jenika?" Alex asked, coming up behind her. He was careful where he stepped.

"Shut up, Boy Scout," she said, lowering her camera.

Alex leaned into her ear, his lips curling up the slightest bit.

"What are you doing, Alex…" I said under my breath.

Jenika didn't let him finish whatever he was saying. She shoved him away from her.

Alex put his hands up, backing away onto the grass.

"What'd he say?" Matt dropped his backpack and moved between Alex and me.

Jenika didn't answer. She continued to glare at Alex, her entire body tense. "He's just talking shit," she said, finally, turning her attention back to the deer.

I didn't believe her. And I was pretty sure Matt didn't either, from the way he was squinting, his dark brows pinching together. He took a step toward Alex, but I blocked his path.

"Back off," I said.

Matt stared down at me—it seemed like he was ten feet tall. I was pretty strong for a girl, but he outweighed me by at least fifty pounds.

He leaned closer, lowering his voice. "What's your problem with me?"

He was there. And I was stupid. Now the whole school whispered *skank* and *smells like trout* when I walked by. That was my problem.

Alex wedged himself between us. "Leave her alone, all right?"

Matt moved closer, getting right in his face. But Alex didn't budge. His fingers clenched at his sides.

"What happened?" Matt asked, smiling. "You finally hit puberty?"

Alex shoved him. Matt staggered and fell right onto his butt with his mouth agape, that cocky grin wiped right off. I wanted to laugh, but I couldn't.

Alex used to look away and mumble an apology to avoid *any* confrontation with Matt. But now he just stood there, his expression unreadable. He had to have been freaking out on the inside.

Matt scrambled up, wiping his jeans. "Cheap shot, little man."

But he wasn't so little anymore. There was barely a couple inches difference between them.

"You're one to talk," Alex said.

Redness inched up Matt's neck, like it always did when he was pissed.

"Stop it," I mouthed to Alex. Matt always fought dirty, and Jenika would have no problem jumping in.

"Boob just rolled up," Jenika said, stomping out her newly lit cigarette.

She meant Officer Bube, the youngest and newest cop in Emerald Cove's police department. His last name was actually pronounced "Buh-be," but Boob was what stuck. His biggest accomplishment was busting some poor granny for having a pipe in her glove box—it turned out to be her grandson's. Polite locals called him overeager. Most people called him a douche.

"Watch your back, Pace," Matt said.

Alex watched him, like a silent challenge. I finally let myself breathe, even if the stench of rot and copper in the air made me queasy.

Bube slammed his door shut and walked toward us, talking into his radio. A staticky voice replied, but all I could make out were numbers. Codes.

"What's going on?" he asked, giving each of us a quick once-over. He was short, but built like a linebacker.

"Nothing," Matt said, picking up his backpack. "We're going to class."

Bube cocked his head toward the deer. "You know anything about that?"

We shook our heads or muttered no.

"It happened hours ago," I said, wincing as soon as the words escaped my mouth.

"Really?" Bube took a step toward me. "How do you know that?"

"It's obvious."

His lips ticked upward. "You a medical examiner?"

Someone snorted. Probably Matt.

"You think this is funny?" Bube asked.

Matt shook his head, failing to hold back a smile.

"There's nothing funny about that." Bube jabbed his thumb toward the swings. "Absolutely nothing. You hearin' me?"

Matt nodded, keeping his eyes downcast.

Another police car pulled in behind Bube's car, and Officer Mackey got out. She'd transferred here a couple months ago from some town in Nevada—which didn't make her too popular. Locals didn't trust new blood, especially if it was from out of state.

"Turn around," Bube said as Officer Mackey approached. "All of you."

"What for?" I asked.

"Do it!" he shouted.

I was terrified they were going to try to pin this on all of us to have a quick and easy culprit. I'd been interrogated more times than I could count, just for walking around past 9:00 p.m. They didn't want tourists to be turned off by us "seedy-looking" locals.

Gramps said the heart of the town was destroyed when the fishing industry died, making our survival completely dependent on tourism. Then Steve De Luca arrived from California and decided it was the perfect place for his world-class golf resort, the Inn. His next mission was to turn Emerald Cove into Laguna Beach. Minus the sun. And decent surfing. And, well, everything else.

"You're Sam Morgan's granddaughter, right?" Officer Mackey asked me. "Nova?"

I nodded. Everyone in town ate at my grandpa's diner, the Emerald Spoon. They called him a crazy hippie and raved about his food in the same breath.

"Hold your arms out and to the side," Officer Mackey said.

Bube had already started patting Alex down, paying extra attention to the pockets of his jeans.

I obeyed, wishing I had the guts to ask them if they had reasonable cause. But that would just make me a target. I was tired of being a target.

"I'm checking for weapons, okay?" Mackey patted the sides of the army jacket I'd stolen from Alex. "You got anything sharp on you?"

"No." I'd stopped smoking pot a few months ago, mostly because all it did was make me sleep. Suddenly I was real glad.

"Take your coat off, please."

Damp air crawled up my bare arms as I let the army jacket and purse fall to the ground. I fought the urge to hug myself.

Summer didn't get here until after the Fourth of July, if it showed up at all. "Me and Alex had nothing to do with this."

"Yeah? Why didn't you call the police?"

"I don't have a—"

"Too busy gawking and taking pictures, huh?" Bube said as he moved from Alex to Matt.

I bit my tongue. Maybe remaining silent was the best choice here.

"And if the devil is six, then God is seven…" Officer Mackey read off the back of my Pixies shirt. "What's that mean?"

Alex gave me a side glance and smirked.

"It's a song." It never ceased to amaze me when adults weren't familiar with big singles from *their* generation, even cult hits.

"Huh." Mackey finished checking the outside of my jeans. "Mind if I check your bag?" She motioned to my black crochet bag on the ground.

Yes, I wanted to say. That's what my mom and Gramps would do. They'd tell me not to give up my rights. But I had nothing to hide. "Go ahead."

It didn't take her long to pull out my wallet, my ancient MP3 player, a compact, a tube of mascara, lip gloss, and my Emerald Spoon T-shirt. She unraveled the shirt, staring at the green spoon on the back.

"Your grandpa makes a killer salmon scramble," she said before handing me everything.

I smiled, not sure how I was supposed to respond to that. The last thing on my mind right now was food.

Bube rummaged through Matt's backpack, probably hoping to make his ultimate bust. If you wanted pot or Adderall, Matt or Jenika were supposedly the people to hit up. Where they got it or how they'd never gotten caught was a mystery, though.

Bube only came up with a Zippo. "What's this for?"

"It generates a flame, sir," Matt said without a twitch.

They stared each other down for what seemed like minutes before Bube turned his attention to Jenika and Officer Mackey.

"Are me and Alex free to go?" I asked. "I'm late for my shift at the diner."

Bube opened his mouth, but Mackey beat him to the punch. "Yes."

"Thanks," I said. I couldn't get out of there fast enough.

"Can we go, too?" Jenika asked as we walked away.

"Not yet," Bube said.

Jenika said something that sounded like a protest, but her voice faded as we crossed the street.

"What were you *thinking*?" I asked Alex. "Matt's got it in for you now."

"Then he can bring it on."

I touched his arm. "You don't mean that."

His muscles tensed for a second. "I'm not afraid of him, Nova."

I wasn't convinced.

We walked to the diner in silence, an overwhelming sense of dread growing inside me. Just knowing there was someone in town capable of gutting a deer and staging its corpse kept me looking over my shoulder. People that unhinged didn't stop with one act.

CHAPTER TWO

The Emerald Spoon sat on the corner of First Avenue and Beach, right in the heart of the downtown, but it was nothing to look at. Moss and grime dulled the bright green paint, and the neon spoon in the window didn't light up anymore. Tourism had been down for the last three years. We were lucky to still be open.

Steve De Luca implied it was an eyesore every time he stopped in to eat. It didn't match the utopia he was trying to build around here. The decorative crosswalks and sunshine-colored flower beds on Beach Street. The fountain on Second. New paint slapped on decaying buildings.

Gramps said it was like someone gave the town a sponge bath and some lipstick. Emerald Cove was basically made up of four sections, with downtown and the Inn in the middle. The north side, where I lived, was known as the Green Rock neighborhood. Nobody seemed to have any idea who came up with the name — probably someone who got tired of naming things. It was a nest of small houses built in the early 1900s. The east side, along Highway 101, was known as "tweakerville," and it included Alex's trailer park, the Hemlock Tavern, a couple cheap motels, and your run-of-the-mill hermit shacks.

The south side was higher in elevation. It had been built up over the last twenty years, when all the retirees from California started moving here. Vacation homes, perched on jagged cliffs, overlooked the ocean—and the rest of us. That was where most of the cakes spent their summers.

Grease thickened the hot air inside the diner, but there were also hints of cinnamon, sugar, and fresh apples—my favorite pancakes. Only about a quarter of the green booths were occupied, and Gramps's girlfriend, Rhonda, had those covered. Weekend mornings were a whole different story. We got tourists of all kinds—truckers, ghost chasers, photographers, musicians, newlyweds, bikers, and a ton of Canadians, just to name a few.

Rhonda gave me the stink-eye as she walked by with plates of pancakes and eggs. Her way of telling me I was late—she could be a real hard-ass about that, even when there was nobody for me to serve.

She was good for Gramps, though. Gave him the love he needed, but didn't take his crap. When it came to the ladies, he had always been a heartbreaker. Just ask my grandma in Phoenix—she called him Don *Not*.

Alex followed me through the swinging doors, into the kitchen, which hopefully meant he was sticking around. He used to hang out here all the time during my shifts, but lately he'd been staying home.

Gramps smiled at us before turning his attention back to a sizzling ham-and-cheese omelet. His assistant buzzed around him, juggling eggs and tins of fruit. But Gramps was a statue with a black and silver ponytail. His big hands moved with grace and control.

"I'm going to take a ten," his assistant said before heading out the back door. His twitching fingers made it clear he was ripe for a smoke.

"You get a good look at that deer?" Gramps asked, his dark eyes focused on me.

"How did…" I trailed off when a sharp radio voice echoed across the kitchen. Gramps's clunky old police scanner was back on top of the fridge. "I thought you were going to give that thing a rest."

"I will"—he pointed his spatula at Alex—"when he gives me something decent to listen to."

"I got something." Alex unzipped his black backpack and took out a blank CD case. "If you don't like this, you're a lost cause." After turning off the scanner, he reached for the boom box that shared a shelf with retired bottles of ketchup Gramps insisted on collecting.

Alex burned CDs for Gramps all the time to prove that good music was made after 1990. Gramps hated MP3s, calling the quality "chicken scratch." Those two could never agree on anything music-wise, and they'd go on for *days* about it, if allowed.

"What are these jokers called?" Gramps asked, sliding a steaming plate of eggs and sausage out for Rhonda to take.

"The Gutter Twins," Alex said.

"Oh." His eyebrows rose, and his lips curved up. "Well, *that* sounds promising."

The singer had a rough baritone voice, the voice of a haunted man. When he started singing about the rapture, all I could see were the glassy eyes of that deer.

Gramps shook his head. "It's a wonder you get out of bed in the morning. Would it kill you to listen to something…happy?"

Alex leaned against the metal fridge, folding his arms. "Probably."

"How'd you know we were at the park?" I asked Gramps.

"Did they say our names?"

"Nope. They mentioned four juveniles at the scene. And that one had quite a mouth on her." He smirked.

"They did not."

"So, the deer's head was on a swing?" Gramps asked. "Is that right?"

I nodded, folding my arms. I could still smell the decay. That wrong kind of sweet. "Someone stuffed a foxglove in its mouth. It was just sitting there on its tongue." Like it was being served.

Gramps ran his hands up and down his white apron, his eyes scanning the walls, as if he heard or saw something we couldn't. He did this whenever his wheels started turning. I used to think he was searching for ghosts.

"Was it male or female?" he asked.

I hadn't even noticed if it had antlers or not. Some detective I was.

"Female," Alex said.

"Hmm." Gramps's thick brows pinched together as he mixed the batter for his infamous black raspberry pancakes.

"Why's that matter?" I asked.

"Everything matters," Gramps said without looking up. "You know that."

Rhonda shoved the swinging doors open, reminding me I wasn't even in my uniform yet. "You comin' out or do I need to drag you out?"

"Sorry," I said. "It's been one of those mornings."

Rhonda put her hands on her square hips, a smile flickering across her lips. "Clearly."

"Be right back." I hustled to the bathroom to change. I'd give anything to assist Gramps in the kitchen rather than grin and serve, but we'd lose all our customers. Destroying perfectly good food was my specialty.

Rhonda had me work the counter until more people came in. The tips were crappy, but I actually preferred being there to the tables. It let me eavesdrop without being obvious about it, and I got to hear all kinds of dirt. That was the thing about most customers, even the locals. They didn't give a damn what I heard—I was invisible until they wanted something.

Betty, the ancient owner of the salon across the street, sat at one end of the counter, talking away on her cell. "All the money he dumped into that park," she said, adjusting the green rhinestone bird clip in her hair. "What a waste. Who's going to go there now?"

Steve De Luca donated money to replace all the equipment in Neahkahnie Park six months ago. He said he wanted it to be *safer* for the kids, as if there were that many. Most of the population here was over sixty.

"They should've taken out those trees years ago," she continued. "Too many places to hide." Her blue eyes flickered up to mine. "We can thank all the busybody tree huggers."

You sure love your tree hugger *banana cream pie*, I wanted to say. Instead I turned and made a new pot of coffee, gritting my teeth.

Around eleven, other locals started showing up at the counter, most of them taking their lunch break. Everyone was talking about the deer mutilation, speculating who'd done it. Jenika and her friends came up a lot. So did a guy who was diagnosed with paranoid schizophrenia last year.

We had some petty theft around here. Plenty of drunks. The occasional drug bust. But nothing like this—at least not recently.

Nobody was asking why or what it meant. If it would happen again.

That was all I could think about.

Alex's little sister, Megan, showed up just in time for my lunch break. She slowly weaved her way toward the counter, tangled blond hair hiding her face, arms crossed. Given the time, she should've come straight from summer school, but she didn't have her backpack with her—which meant one of two things. She either didn't get up in time or got halfway there before realizing she forgot her bag. Probably both. That girl would be late to her own funeral and forget her body, too.

Alex came out from the kitchen, clutching a dish tub. He insisted on busing tables in exchange for all the free meals he and his sister got here. We'd feed them regardless.

"You go to school today?" Alex asked Megan, squinting at her.

"Yes, Dad." She'd just turned fifteen, but she seemed younger in some ways.

They could almost be twins. Megan's face was heart-shaped, while Alex's was more angular, but they both had big green eyes rimmed with dark lashes and fine blond hair that curled up at the ends when it rained.

"Where's your backpack?" Alex pressed.

"Forgot it."

He exhaled, setting the dish tub down. "Megan..."

"Don't start," Megan said. "We weren't all born perfect little students." She gave me a look, urging me to agree with her.

I held up my hands. Joining *that* conversation never ended well. I'd be lying if I said I didn't envy Alex sometimes. Two hours of homework for me was one hour for him. He aced tests without even studying, and he was a master at bullshitting his way through essays, even when he didn't read the book.

Okay—maybe envy was an understatement. Sometimes I wanted to throw books at his head.

"Pick a booth, guys," I said. "You want the usual?"

They both nodded, still staring each other down.

After putting our order in and getting us drinks, I found them in the last booth by the window. They argued a lot, but they were almost inseparable. They'd lived in Reno with their mom and her ex-convict psycho boyfriend until Alex was in fourth grade. One day their mom dropped them off at their grandparents' mobile home here in Emerald Cove, promising she'd be back when she cleaned up.

She never did.

Now all they had was their grandma. She'd always been a fanatical Catholic and a little bit north of neurotic, but her drinking had gotten much worse since their grandpa died. His heart stopped. Just like that. I'd let someone break both my arms and legs if it meant things would get easier for them.

I set down our drinks and slid in the booth next to Alex. The cracks in the vinyl scraped at my jeans. These booths needed to be replaced years ago.

"I heard you guys found that deer at the park," Megan said.

"Did you see it?" I asked.

Her face crumpled a little as she sipped her root beer. "No. But people won't stop talking about it. Like, describing it. This guy in my class even drew a picture."

"Dick," Alex muttered.

"Did you guys hear what happened to Gabi?" Megan asked.

"Her dad bought her an island?" I asked.

Alex smiled at me.

Sadly, it wouldn't surprise me if Steve De Luca was in the

market for an island. Or the world.

"No. There was a dead raccoon on their porch this morning." Her green eyes widened. "Gabi said there was blood everywhere."

The muggy air turned cold against my skin. Steve De Luca had recently announced he was running for mayor next year, and he was always boasting about his love of hunting. Maybe someone was trying to send him a message.

"Did Gabi tell you this herself?" I asked. One bad thing happening in this town got a lot of people in the mood to tell stories. It was hard to tell what was true.

Megan nodded.

"You're still hanging out with her?" Alex asked.

She shrugged, watching a group of seven tourists try to fit into a sedan outside. Gabi De Luca didn't give anyone at our school the time of day except for her boy toy Brandon Koza— and now Megan. Not that I blamed her. People were nice to her face because her dad employed their parents, but most of them hated her.

Megan and Gabi were paired together in their creative writing class last semester. The thought of Gabi, Alex's only real competition for valedictorian, having to cowrite a short story with a slacker like Megan was actually pretty comical. But at some point they became friends.

The thing was…I didn't like it. Not because Gabi lived in a 6,000-square-foot house in the hills overlooking the Pacific or because of who her dad was—neither of which she had control over.

It was that—outside of Brandon—Gabi's only friends were the cakes. Most of them were rich kids from Vancouver BC, Seattle, or Portland. We weren't real people to them. We were slow, and weird, and undereducated.

We were something to laugh at.

"Isn't Gabi's house like a fortress?" I asked, breaking the heavy silence.

"Sort of," Megan said. "They've got a security gate."

"What about cameras?" I asked.

Megan shook her head. "Her dad thinks it's some animal rights activist trying to make a point."

"Uh, what point would that be? 'I love animals so much I'm willing to kill and maim them'?" I rolled my eyes. "Way to be a detective, Steve." Just about anyone in town had motive to mess with him.

I glanced over at Alex. He was staring off into space, like he wasn't even here. Usually he had plenty to say when it came to Steve De Luca.

"You should see their den, though." Megan's voice rose. "It's like a taxidermy museum."

I'd never understand people who thought the skin of dead animals was some kind of trophy. I was taught to believe animals had spirits. Good and bad. Just like us.

Rhonda walked by with a plate of burgers, the juicy aroma of the meat overwhelming. My stomach turned. Every sip of my strawberry lemonade had the aftertaste of rot. I swore that stench was stuck to me.

"Did Gabi say anything about a flower, like around the raccoon?" I asked Megan.

Her eyebrows rose.

"Can we change the subject?" Alex asked, piling sugar packets and knocking them down. "I don't want to see that shit in my head anymore."

"Sorry."

Megan tore the foil off a mini creamer and downed it like a shot.

"Is that my shirt?" Alex asked her.

Megan glanced down at the black In Flames shirt that hung on her like a nightgown. A smile flickered on her lips. "No."

"Stay out of my room."

"Why? You aren't going to wear it again."

"Would you like it if I snooped through your room and stole your crap?" Alex asked.

"Go ahead. I don't have anything interesting, anyway." Megan grinned. "Like condoms in my dresser."

"What?" I asked.

A pink flush rolled up Alex's pale cheeks.

I was the only girl—not blood related—who spent any time in Alex's room. And as far as I knew, he didn't see me that way.

"Explain." I punched him in the arm. "Now."

"No." He stirred his raspberry lemonade with his straw. "It's nobody's business but mine."

"The box wasn't opened," Megan said to me.

"Shut up." Alex glared at his sister.

I felt myself relax. The thought of Alex having some secret relationship made me a little sick. We told each other everything.

"Hey, guys." Gabi De Luca stood at the head of our table, looking like a fairy tale with her brown curls and Bambi eyes. Speak of the devil…

We all froze and stared at her. "Can I steal Megan for a sec?" she asked, unfazed by our silence.

"Yeah." Megan wiped her mouth with the back of her hand and let out a nervous laugh. "Be right back."

Megan followed Gabi to a booth on the other side of the diner. I held my breath at the sight of Christian Barnett in

Gabi's booth.

"Relax," Alex said. He put a hand on my shoulder, giving it a gentle squeeze. "He's not here."

But seeing Christian was bad enough. Everything I felt last summer came rushing back. The lump in my throat that wouldn't go away. How I could barely keep food down. The shame, even though I did *nothing* wrong.

Christian's dark blue eyes met mine. His blond hair was down to his shoulders now, and he looked even broader than last summer, but he still had that douchey smile. The one that said, *you're a joke to me.*

I shifted my gaze, my chest tightening with anger.

"Didn't Christian graduate this year?" Alex asked, his voice tense.

"He was supposed to."

Most of the cakes stopped coming to town with their parents when they graduated from high school. It was just like Christian to come back and haunt us for yet another summer.

Megan slid back into our booth with excited eyes.

"What was that about?" I asked.

She hesitated, her long fingers tangling with her hair. "Gabi invited me to the summer kickoff party at Winchester Beach. It's tomorrow night."

If I felt out of place with the cakes, it would be even worse for her. She'd never even been to a party.

"Why would you want to go?" Alex asked her.

She shrugged. "Just to see…"

"See what?" he asked. "A bunch of rich pricks throwing back Daddy's vodka?"

If Alex thought he was convincing her not to go, he was doing the opposite. Megan loved to buck him, even when she knew he was right.

"You don't belong with those people," Alex continued.

Her eyes narrowed at him. "Neither did Nova. They didn't care."

"Yes, they did," he muttered.

"Let's not go there." I knew where this conversation was heading, and I didn't want to talk about *him*.

"Look, I'm not even going to hang out with the cakes," Megan said. "I'm going to hang out with Gabi."

Getting invited to one of their parties felt a little like being invited to a secret society. You knew they were dicks, but it was hard to fight the curiosity.

Alex stirred his drink again. "How do you know Gabi isn't setting you up for something?"

"She wouldn't do that."

"Because you know her so well?"

"You're right." Her palms slapped the table. "I'm too much of a loser. It must be a joke."

Alex's expression softened. "That's not what I'm saying—"

"Hungry?" My mom stood in front of us, three plates on her arm. A large clip kept her dark hair piled on top of her head, which meant she hadn't showered yet.

"Hey, thanks. I could've gotten that," I said, taking my plate from her.

"You're on break, babe. Enjoy it."

"What are you doing here?" I asked her.

She exhaled. "Toilet in the men's bathroom broke. Waiting on the plumber."

"Sorry." It never failed. Something always broke when my mom finally decided to take a day off.

She pulled out a purple envelope from her apron pocket and dropped it in front of me. "This was in our mailbox—any idea what it is?"

"Not a clue." "Nova" was typed out on a white label and stuck to the front. No last name. No address. My first instinct was to throw it away.

But even my haters used the internet to insult me most of the time.

"Maybe you have a secret admirer." Mom winked and walked away. Leave it to her to ignore the creep factor and jump to romance.

"It looks like a birthday card," Megan commented, before taking a giant bite of her burger.

"Four months late…" I pinched the envelope, checking for lumps. There definitely wasn't a card inside. It felt empty.

"Want me to open it for you?" Alex asked, eyeing the envelope. It was my favorite shade of purple, dark and rich like a grape Popsicle.

"That's okay." I lifted it to my nose and inhaled, trying to catch a telltale scent. The smell of my mom's citrusy hand lotion and cigarette-stained fingertips overpowered everything.

I dug my finger underneath the lip, tearing the seal slowly. Opening this in private was probably a smarter move. But I couldn't wait. It would nag me all day otherwise. Besides, if anyone was watching, I didn't want to give them the satisfaction of thinking I was afraid.

A folded piece of printer paper sat inside, looking harmless. Too harmless. I pulled it out, my heart racing with my thoughts.

The paper unfolded itself, revealing a flash of blue. I froze. *Don't be a coward. Whatever it is, you can handle it.*

I unraveled the paper again. A vibrant blue wildflower had been flattened against the page, part of its stem still attached. An odor wafted up from it, a little sweet, a little smoky. Almost like incense.

There is so much I want to say to you, the letter read. **I'll start with this**... That was it—just one typed line. No further explanation.

"That's not creepy at all," I muttered. What the hell did it even mean?

"Let me see." Megan snatched the paper from me, causing the flower to drop right on top of my potato. Her nose crinkled. "Oops."

I pushed my plate toward the middle of the table and shook my head at Alex offering me his fries. "Lost my appetite."

"Seems kind of sweet to me." Megan passed the letter to Alex.

He scanned it, his mouth turning up a bit. "Bad call on the flower, huh?"

"Unless it's the same person," I said. *That* thought would keep me up at night.

"It's not," Alex said. "They're obviously gunning for the De Lucas. Why would they send you something?"

"Please tell me you did this." Since my birthday was on Valentine's Day, and I hated all things Valentine's Day, Alex liked to tease me by showing up with the cheesiest cards he could find.

"Why would I..." He paused, studying my face. "Okay, I did it."

"Seriously?"

He exhaled, placing his hand on top of mine. "I know we see each other every day, but there's so much I want to say to you." His lips twitched. "And I know flowers are the way to your heart."

Megan snorted.

I shoved his hand away, smiling despite myself. "Shut up. It's not funny."

If only he knew how I'd been feeling lately.

"It's a little weird. I'll give you that," Alex said, his voice softening. "But it's nothing to freak out over. Not yet, okay?"

"Sure…"

People did a lot of things when they thought you were a slut. They believed *all* the stories about you. How you slept with half the guys in town and smelled like fish. How your home-wrecker mom made you that way. Even the one where you gave some drunk a blowjob behind the Hemlock Tavern and charged him for it.

They wrote "ho'mobile" on your mom's misty car windows and talked about you in whispers. They sent anonymous emails, telling you how vile you were—all the things they didn't have the guts to say in person.

But *nobody* secretly admired me. That I knew for sure.

CHAPTER THREE

Alex and me lay cramped together in my twin bed, my blue flannel sheets tangled around our bare feet. We were listening to Catherine Wheel, one of our favorite '90s bands. They were hope and sorrow. A wall of distortion. A jaded voice that felt like home. Alex's Uncle Joel introduced us to the shoegaze subgenre the last time we visited him in Portland, and we were hooked. Somehow I knew, even when we moved on to a different genre obsession, shoegaze would always be a part of our soundtrack.

We'd made it back to my house without Alex getting jumped by Matt, but there would always be tomorrow. And the next day. Matt wasn't someone to forget and move on.

For now we were safe in the world we'd been building since we were little. A world with only us. Our stories. Our music. Lavender candles. Silence was okay here, too. Sometimes we wouldn't talk for hours.

I shifted closer to him to keep from sliding off the bed.

He curled his arm underneath me so my head was resting on his chest. "That better?"

He was so close. Too close. I could smell the grass on his shirt, the mix of soap and salt on his neck. "Sure, even though you reek."

"Shut up—I do not." He inhaled, like he was breathing me in. "But you do."

I elbowed him. "Nuh-uh."

His fingers traced circles against the bare skin of my arm. "You smell good. Like cherries or something."

"Okay, weirdo." Heat washed over me, even with the night breeze sneaking through a crack in my window frame.

I wondered if he'd ever thought about kissing me. What he'd do if I leaned in this very second and laid one on him, slid my hand underneath his shirt. God, I wanted to.

And I hated myself for it. It felt shameful. Completely wrong.

When you've been friends with someone for so long, they become like family. He'd seen me get a ring of chocolate ice cream around my mouth more times than I could count, a special talent of mine. When his favorite pajama bottoms got a hole in the ass, he still wore them around me…for an entire year. We used to have regular burping contests at two in the morning and write insults on each other's foreheads when one of us fell asleep first. Romance *never* came into the picture.

He did ask me to marry him once, the summer after fourth grade. We couldn't afford video games, and my mom never liked us in front of the TV too long, so we spent most of our time outside, inventing alternate worlds. We created our own tribe, the Tribe of Morgace—our last names, Morgan and Pace, put together.

Coming up with names wasn't our strong suit.

That summer, we kept finding dead birds in the woods, as if they'd fallen from the sky. We decided the culprit was a trickster coyote named Jenika (my idea, of course), and we needed to catch her before she killed all the animals in the forest. Alex dropped to one knee and asked me to marry him. Our "tribe" would be stronger with a king and queen, he'd said. I insisted that tribes didn't *have* kings and queens, but I gave in, anyway. He looked so sad when he thought I was going to say no.

A familiar melody bounced off my dark blue walls. The opening of "Crank" always gave me the chills. "I love this song."

"Me, too," he whispered.

Rain tapped against the roof, tiny *plink*s reminding us that spring wasn't over yet. I wanted the sky to open up and pound us like never before. Wash everything away. But chances were it would drizzle all night.

"I can't stop seeing that deer," I said.

"Me neither."

I'd been running possible "suspects" in my head all day, but I always came back to one person… "Do you think Jenika would go that far?" Matt might've helped, but it would've been her idea.

"Jenika isn't behind every bad thing that happens around here, Nova."

The accusation in his voice bugged me. "Who do you think it is, then?"

"It could be anyone," he said softly. "People snap all the time."

"That's dark."

"But true."

I tilted my head up to catch a glimpse of him. His eyes were closed, his lids fluttering as if he was holding his breath. Waiting. Wishing. Hoping like hell I'd change the subject, maybe.

I used to be able to predict almost every thought of his. Every reaction. Now it was more like fifty-fifty.

"You sure you don't want to steal the El Camino?" I asked. "We could disappear for the whole summer. Megan can come, too."

"Why do you want to disappear so bad?"

Did he even have to ask? Waiting on snippy tourists in a hot diner all summer. Watching the stupid turf wars between the locals and the cakes. The name-calling and the fistfights. All the trash baking in the sun. And now some psychopath gutting animals.

Living here year-round was bad, but summer was pure hell.

"Where're we going to run to, anyway?" Alex asked. "We don't have a hundred bucks saved between us."

I didn't want to think about the semantics. I wanted to go and figure out the rest later. "You didn't used to care…"

"My grandpa's Social Security benefits got cut. I need to find a job."

I closed my eyes, feeling like a jerk. "Gramps needs an extra server for the season. The job is yours, okay?"

"You know I suck with people."

I wanted to tell him this wasn't the time to be stubborn. "It's better than nothing."

He exhaled, his warm breath tickling my ear. "I need to tell you something."

I didn't like the hesitation in his voice. "Is it about those condoms in your drawer?"

"What?" His arm tensed around me. "No."

"Then I don't want to hear it." My heart sped up. I just had this feeling…

"Nova…"

"Is it going to make me upset?"

He touched my hair so softly I wasn't sure if it was actually happening. "Yeah."

"Tell me about your secret girlfriend first." I tickled his ribs.

His body jerked, and he breathed out a small laugh.

"Teasing isn't going to get you out of this."

I turned to face him and used both my hands, tickling his stomach, his sides, and under his arms. He arched his back, grinning wide and letting out the kind of laughter I hadn't heard from him in ages.

"Stop!" His eyes squeezed shut.

I sat up, folding my arms in my lap. "You've got five seconds to start talking."

He stared at me, the hardness back in his eyes again. "Why do you care so much?"

"No secrets. That's the rule."

"We're not little kids anymore, Nova."

"I told you when I…" My breath got caught in my throat. "Come on. You've never even kissed a girl. Don't you think you're getting a little ahead of yourself?" As soon as the words left my mouth, I wanted to take them back—joking or not.

Alex's lips parted, and I knew he was hurt. No matter how hard he tried to hide it. "Who says I haven't?"

"You would've told me…I hope."

He folded his hands behind his head, his gaze flickering up to the ceiling. "Zach's in town."

There it was. The name I never wanted to hear again. "Are you sure?"

"I talked to him."

He said he wasn't coming back. No, he didn't just say it. He *promised*. "What'd you say?"

Alex sat up, moving closer to me. "He asked how you were. I told him to go fuck himself. And then…" He hesitated, his eyes lifting to mine. "I punched him."

"What?"

His lips twitched up. "I'm kidding. But I wanted to."

I'd gotten over Zach West months ago, but not the

humiliation of thinking I was in love. And telling him that. He was my first kiss, my first boyfriend, my first…everything. It wasn't like I had anything to compare my feelings to.

What was he even doing here? He'd graduated this year, like his best friend, Christian. And he'd always said the first thing he wanted to do was go to Europe and check out every big music festival he could.

"Hey…" Alex whispered, wrapping his arms around me. I rested my cheek against his shoulder, my hands clenching in fists.

The day before Zach broke up with me, we'd spent the night together on the beach. My first time wasn't anything special. And despite what everyone in town thought, it was my *only* time—if two awkward and extremely painful minutes of him trying to get inside me counted.

It wasn't like I'd been holding out for love or the perfect moment. I wanted the experience to matter. And for it to matter, I needed it to be with someone I trusted.

I trusted Zach, completely.

I remember the way his lips lingered on mine when he said good-bye in the morning. He had to get home before his mom woke up. We were going to see Blue October in Portland that night.

He called me ten minutes before he was supposed to pick me up. It was raining, and I'd been fighting the waves in my hair.

"I can't do this," he said.

And I kept asking what "this" meant. He said things were getting too serious for him. It was too much. I was too much.

So I did the dumbest thing I could that night. I made out with Matt Delgado at Rainbow Creek Park. Because I was a mess. And Matt had a flask filled with three types of booze and all the right things to say.

By the next day, everyone was talking about how me and Matt had "done it," right on top of that mossy, bird shit–covered picnic table. How I'd slept around on Zach and smelled like trout.

I figured Matt was behind it, probably with a lot of help from Jenika.

He wasn't.

At the end of the summer, Zach wrote me an email— yes, an email—saying he was sorry for how *things went down between us*. He was sorry that Christian spread those rumors about me. But *someone* had seen me and Matt kissing in the park that night.

As if that justified everything.

"You okay?" Alex asked.

"Yeah."

The purple envelope on my nightstand caught my eye. I'd stuffed the note back inside, planning to throw it away…or burn it. Why hadn't I? For a brief second, I wondered if Zach wrote it—he always did like to hide behind the written word.

But mystery wasn't his style. He wasn't exactly the kind of guy to go hunting for wildflowers, either. The closest to nature he got or *wanted* to get was riding waves.

Movement in my peripheral vision turned my attention outside. A shadow darted across my white curtains, toward the bottom of my window. I held my breath, waiting. Only the hush of rain followed.

My curtains were parted just enough for someone to see inside. I imagined someone standing out there…looking right at us.

"Did you see that?" I whispered.

"Thought I imagined it…" Alex ripped the curtains open

and cracked the window, peering into the darkness. I thought about Matt telling Alex to watch his back. If Matt wanted to coax him outside, this was a great way to do it.

There was a rustling noise, but it was soft enough to be an animal or the wind blowing through the trees. A tingling sensation inched down the back of my neck. They say you could feel it when someone was watching you.

Alex glanced at me over his shoulder. "I don't see anything," he whispered. The glow of our neighbor's backyard lights was the only sign of life out there.

"Close the window." The damp breeze made me shiver. "Close it!"

"Okay, relax." He slammed it shut, flipping the lock. "It could've been anything."

I jerked the curtains together, leaving no tiny gaps to see through. "Yeah, right." My mind went back to that crushed blue flower. Those cryptic words.

We stared at each other in silence. My arms folded. His fingers tapping against his jeans.

"We should go to sleep," he said, finally. "It's almost three."

My heart was still pounding, but I nodded. We crawled into my bed and faced away from each other, back to back... like always. He pulled his shirt off and tossed it over me, onto the floor.

Usually his warmth comforted me as my eyes fluttered shut. But not tonight. I kept seeing that deer's head. The life gone from its face. Its last breath frozen in time.

Gramps always said you could tell when something bad was coming. The air felt different. Still and thick. The crickets and the birds would stop chirping, too.

I hadn't heard a cricket all night.

SATURDAY, JUNE 21

Sometimes I have this dream about setting people on fire and watching them burn. Their eyes go hollow. Their smiles melt away.

You're standing right next to me, your hand in mine. The sky is as black as the void inside me. The place I used to feel. The place I used to care. The pain you took away.

You saved me. You saved me. You saved me.

CHAPTER FOUR

"Nova!" Mom's husky voice woke me up. She pounded on my door. "Don't make me come in there."

I must've been in a deep sleep, because she didn't threaten to come in unless she'd tried knocking a few times.

"Give me a minute," I called, looking over at Alex. My arm was stiff and tingly from sleeping on it all night.

There was something about weekend mornings that made everyone want pancakes. They'd start trickling into the diner at 7:00 a.m., all bright-eyed and impatient.

"Fine. One minute," Mom said before padding into the kitchen. She got out a mug and poured her morning dose of caffeine. The fifty-year-old walls of our one-story house hid nothing.

My half brother, Gavin, made kissing sounds and laughed before slamming the bathroom door. He knew Alex was over and liked to tease us endlessly about being "secret" boyfriend-girlfriend. Eight-year-olds were easily amused.

Alex was wedged against my wall, his eyes shut tight. A beam of light took direct aim at his face, creating a halo along his cheek and jaw. He could sleep through a metal concert—and he did once. The Metallica show Mom dragged us to a couple years ago. Oh, how I envied him that night.

I studied his face, like I had more often than I'd care to admit. He looked so innocent. His slightly parted lips and the dark eyelashes against his cheeks. The way his nose scrunched into the pillow. And his hair, the color of wet sand, standing up at all angles.

I ran my fingers along the curve of his cheekbone. He didn't even twitch.

"Alex, wake up." I reached under my navy blue blanket, tickling his stomach.

His whole body jerked, and his face scrunched up. "Quit it."

"Make me." I traced a line along his ribs. Goose bumps followed my fingertips.

In one swift motion, he was on top of me, pinning my wrists to my pillow. The heat of his skin bled through my T-shirt, and his jeans scratched my bare legs. I didn't fight him, though. I didn't want to. Every inch of me seemed to buzz.

"Whoa, Alex…" It was about all I could get out.

His face lowered toward mine, and my heart hammered through my chest. I was sure he could feel it.

"There," he whispered with a smile, his lips inches from mine. "I made you." Then he rolled off and onto his back again.

It took me a few seconds to breathe.

My door flung open. Mom poked her head in, raising her dark eyebrows at us. She was already dressed in the diner uniform. "You guys are too old to be squeezing into that bed."

I sat up and threw my covers off. "How about getting me a new one?" I'd only had this bed since I was five.

Mom's maroon lips stretched into a grin. "How about you stop spending your tips on music downloads?"

I rolled my eyes at Alex. Mom wasn't strict about much,

but she was antitechnology. I wasn't allowed to have a cell phone until my eighteenth birthday because she thought the radiation would give me a brain tumor or alter my brain forever or something. Luckily Eric insisted on getting a laptop for Gavin and me to share.

"There's Cheerios, if you're hungry," Mom said. "Grandpa needs us there early—they're already filling up."

"I need a shower," I said.

"Not unless you want to start paying the water bill. I heard the shower running for a half hour last night." She grabbed my diner shirt out of the hamper and threw it at me. "Get moving."

"It's dirty..." I knew I forgot to do something last night.

"Told you to do the laundry yesterday. Twice!" Mom left and shut the door behind her.

Alex climbed out of bed and snatched his black Alice in Chains T-shirt off my cluttered floor. I found myself staring at him again, at his sinewy torso and the way his jeans slid low across his hips.

"What?" he asked, combing his messy hair back with his fingers.

"You look good." I smiled, trying to pass it off as a friendly comment.

The tips of his ears turned a familiar pink. "Um, thanks?"

I turned toward the mirror on my door and brushed my tangled locks into a bun. "Get out. I have to change."

His lips turned up a little, and he grabbed his skateboard and backpack off the floor. "I'm taking off anyway."

"At least stay for breakfast. Let us give you a ride home."

"I have to take Riff out before he wakes Grandma up." Alex brushed his fingers across my back as he passed me. "I'll be fine. It's seven thirty. Doubt Matt's awake." He pulled my curtains open and froze, his hands still holding the fabric.

WHOREHOUSE was written across my window in dark block letters. They'd painted the letters backward, just so I could get the message loud and clear from inside my room.

My mouth opened, and my face got hot. But I couldn't find the words. I just wanted it gone.

"Fuckers," Alex muttered, dropping his hands.

I yanked my door open and ran into the laundry closet, grabbing rags—clean, dirty, I didn't care. Then I ran into the kitchen to get some Windex.

"What are you doing?" Mom asked, her brow furrowed.

I didn't want to tell her. See that guilty look on her face. She thought my reputation was her fault. That I was paying for the choices she made with Eric.

"Just a spill," I mumbled, knowing she wouldn't buy it. I ran to my room and shut the door behind me, then locked it.

"Nova!" She knocked.

Alex was already outside. He squinted at the window, touching the letter *W* with his finger. I climbed out and joined him.

Most of the houses around here were too old to come with window screens, ours included. And every time Mom nagged Eric about getting some, he'd say he'd get them when they paid off their credit cards.

They never paid off their credit cards. There was always some emergency with the cars or the house or the diner that would run them back up again.

"I think it's barbecue sauce or something," Alex said. "At least in part."

I didn't want to know what it was. The color was foul—a sludgy brown with a reddish tint. It smelled like sugar. And smoke. And rot.

I sprayed the glass, holding my breath, and then started

scrubbing. The stuff was like glue. It crumbled in tiny bits.

"You have to let it soak first," Alex said.

I gritted my teeth and pressed harder.

"Nova...let me do it, all right?"

"You have to get home." I could hear Mom trying to pick the lock of my bedroom door.

Alex yanked the rag from my grip, holding it behind his back. "I'll do it."

"No. I need—"

"It'll be gone by the time you leave. I promise."

I thought about fighting him for it, but that would take too long. Instead I let him pull me into a hug. His hands ran up and down my back, making me relax a little.

"They're idiots," he whispered. "They don't matter."

I closed my eyes. This could've been the cakes. But the timing made me think of Jenika and Matt—vandalism was definitely their thing. And I knew Matt wasn't going to let Alex pick a fight and not want to finish it.

I heard my bedroom door open, which meant my mom saw the window. I cussed under my breath.

"Go on inside," Alex said. "I'll leave the stuff on your porch when I'm done."

I thanked him, opened the window, and hefted myself back into my room.

stirred my soggy Cheerios. Gavin was more interested in lifting his spoon and watching the milk dribble back into his bowl.

We were crammed together at what passed for our kitchen table, a round slab of wood as old as my grandpa and vinyl chairs that wobbled and squeaked.

Mom rested her chin in her hand, giving me one of her soul-piercing stares. She was big on thinking she could *read* people. And she was usually right…Gramps always said we were part Salish, part English, and a drop of "witch blood."

"You want to talk about it?" She meant later. We weren't going to have the *slut* conversation in front of Gavin.

"Not really," I said.

She cocked her head, her lips pursing. "Thank Alex for me. For taking care of that…"

I nodded, swallowing a mushy bite of cereal.

"Did you guys kiss yet?" Gavin asked with a big grin. He had Eric's blond hair and my mom's hazel eyes, but he smiled like Jenika. It was eerie sometimes.

"No, jerk. Eat your cereal." His teasing had gotten to me lately. I felt like me and Alex had done something, even though we hadn't.

"Why does he always sleep in your bed?" Gavin continued.

I ignored his question, but I could feel Mom's eyes drilling a hole into my forehead. She'd asked me to have Alex sleep on the couch numerous times, mostly because Eric didn't like the example it was setting for Gavin. But Eric was in Seattle, working a three-month contract job. He did software development, mostly, and he wanted to move us to Seattle so we could be together more and have steady income. But Mom hated big cities, and Gramps needed her help running the diner.

"Gramps still needs that extra server, right?" I asked, pushing my bowl away. "'Cause Alex needs a job."

"Oh…" Mom frowned. "Grandpa hired Brandon Koza yesterday. I'm sorry."

"Why?" Brandon didn't need a job. His dad was the only veterinarian for miles, and his mom was promoted to police chief last year. They lived in a cozy oceanfront house off Beach Street.

Mom's forehead crinkled. "Because he applied?"

"Brandon isn't dependable," I continued. "He slacks off at school all the time."

"And you don't?" Mom asked.

"You never do your homework," Gavin chimed in.

"Not my point." I actually only knew a couple things about Brandon. He always hung out with Gabi De Luca, he was one of the best sprinters in the state, and he fell asleep in class sometimes. I saw him with Gabi at a few cake parties last summer, but we'd only address each other with a smile or nod. We'd probably said five words to each other our entire lives.

"Go brush your teeth, Gavin," Mom said. "We need to leave soon."

"I'm not done," he said.

"Now."

Gavin glanced from Mom to me and let out a dramatic exhale. He was smart enough to know when he wasn't wanted. "Fine." He took his time shuffling off, letting his feet slide and squeak across the hardwood floor.

Mom drank the last bit of coffee out of her favorite mug. It had a picture of the trickster raven on it.

"Alex is turning into quite the looker," Mom said. "Those puppy-dog green eyes? Wow."

I suddenly found myself playing with my spoon.

"Don't go acting like you haven't noticed."

I glanced up at her knowing expression. "We're friends, Mom. That's it."

"Yeah? Can't say I ever crawl into bed with my friends."

The floor creaked down the hall, and there was the breath of a giggle.

"Gavin!" Mom called. "I don't hear any water running." She turned her attention back to me, lowering her voice. "If something like this happens again, leave it there. We'll try to get the cops out to look at it."

"They're not going to do crap, unless it's a threat. And even then…" They'd figure I did something to bring it on.

I got up and rinsed my bowl, turning the water on high. A couple years ago, Jenika slashed all of our tires. I knew it was her because she practically confessed to it at school.

"Car trouble?" she'd asked when I showed up to class late.

Officer Young, who should've retired his racist ass years ago, told us, "These things usually don't just happen randomly." I still remember his face as he said it, red-cheeked and smiling, like it was all a big joke. Afterward, he told us to "get a couple security cameras."

The cops didn't do anything when Anya, Jenika's mom, shoved my mom to the ground in the Emerald Market parking lot, either. It didn't help that none of the witnesses came forward. They all thought my mom deserved it—the whole town did. Eric may have done the leaving, but my mom was the one who got all the heat for it.

Mom joined me at the sink, giving me her mug. She put her hand on my back and leaned toward my ear. "Talk to me…"

I'd never hidden much from her, not even what happened with Zach or the stoner phase I went through afterward. But I didn't want to talk about the window. And I didn't want to talk about my feelings for Alex. That would only make them more real.

"I'm worried about Alex," I said finally. "He tried to pick a fight with Matt and Jenika yesterday."

"Well, you've always said you wished he'd stick up for himself more."

"Not like that. I've seen Matt fight. He doesn't let up. And Jenika's psychotic."

"She's just angry," Mom said, loading our bowls in the dishwasher.

Mom was always making excuses for her, maybe out of guilt. And I did feel bad about what happened to Anya. Her bipolar went even more out of control after Eric left—these days she never left their trailer. But it wasn't as if Eric stopped being Jenika's dad when he moved in with us. He called her all the time, tried to take her out places. She was the one who pushed him away.

"Her mom just gave up on life, you know?" Mom said.

"And that makes it okay for her to do whatever she wants?" I lowered my voice. "I know she wrote that crap on my window."

She stopped loading, her lips parting. "Did you see her do it?"

"Well, no. But—"

"Then we don't know. It could've been anyone. I mean, there's someone running around town mutilating animals."

"Also probably her…" I muttered.

Mom put the last bowl away, closing up the dishwasher. "You can't keep accusing her of things without proof. It upsets Eric." She dropped her voice to a whisper. "It makes Gavin ask a lot of questions."

"Fine. But we both know she's capable of it."

Mom didn't respond right away. She shook her head. Then she asked, "What would you have done if I fell apart after your dad left?"

"I don't know. I was two." I hated it when she called him my dad. He'd never been a dad. He'd moved back to Argentina, his home country, when I was four and never came back.

"What if you were older?" she asked.

"I'd be pissed. At *you*. Not the entire world." I dried my hands off. "Besides, *Esteban* did the same thing to us. I don't go hating on his wife or him."

Mom looked down at her dark purple fingernails, the fine lines around her mouth deepening. "You never talk to him."

"He calls once a year and asks the same three questions. I don't know what else to say…"

Mom sighed and grabbed her purse, which signaled that she was done with the conversation. She'd been in a few long-term relationships in her life, Esteban and Eric included. But she feared marriage. She thought of it as an archaic tradition that made people feel trapped. Most guys left her for that reason. But that wasn't the case with Esteban. He left because of me… I wasn't exactly planned.

There were times when I got a little curious, wondering what my life would be like if he were in it. If I knew my family in Argentina. My grandparents. My dad's three sisters and two brothers. Mom said he had a big family. Most of the time I tried not to think about it—because then I'd get angry. I'd probably never meet them, much less know them.

At least Jenika had the option of knowing her father if she wanted to.

"Gavin, let's go!" Mom said.

"Hang on," Gavin called back. "I need my Story Cubes." There was a clanking sound from his bedroom, as he was probably rushing to put them back in their box.

"Okay. We're leaving without you," I said, making exaggerated steps toward the back door and opening it.

"Don't!" More bangs echoed from his room.

"Nova…" Mom said, shaking her head. "You're so mean to him sometimes."

"You know he'll keep finding things to bring if we let him."

She exhaled softly. "So, what was in that purple envelope?"

"Nothing."

Her eyebrows rose. "Nothing? Yeah, I'm not buying that."

"It was just some prank. A bunch of cryptic nonsense." I wasn't going to mention the flower, because I knew she'd find some romantic explanation for it, her way of trying to cheer me up. And then I'd tell her she was wrong. And she'd tell me it wasn't good for me to always jump to the worst-case scenario.

But even my most rational voice told me there was nothing benign about that note.

CHAPTER FIVE

People were milling outside the diner when we pulled up in Mom's old blue Subaru.

"Crap." Mom yanked the keys out of the ignition and opened her squeaky door. "Grandpa and Rhonda are gonna kill us."

"Then they'd be screwed." I climbed out and helped Gavin untangle his seat belt from his arm. I didn't know how he managed it, but he always did.

We rushed in the back door and into the kitchen where Gramps and his two assistants were doing three things at once and trying not to run into one another. Gavin settled on top of an old barstool to watch them work.

"Take section two, Nova," Mom said, peeking out the small window on our swinging wooden doors. "Rhonda's probably dying out there."

I finished tying my apron and headed into the chaos. Rhonda made a beeline for me, coffee pitcher in hand. Her lips were pinched into an anxious pucker.

"Hit those obnoxious punks first," she whispered, nodding at our biggest booth.

My heart about stopped. There were familiar faces in that

booth. Christian. Gabi. Amber Connelly. And Zach himself. He had a hell of a lot of nerve coming in here.

Two days after we broke up, I saw him walking down First Avenue, holding hands with Amber. They'd gone out for almost two years before he broke up with her at the end of his junior year. She'd been trying to get him back ever since.

Guess they were still together.

"Goldilocks hasn't put that camera down for a second," Rhonda said, referencing Christian. "He's irritating folks."

"Great," I muttered.

"Use that pretty young thing persuasion." She elbowed me and trotted off.

Cakes like Christian couldn't be persuaded to do anything, unless it was money or their mom doing the talking. This town was like Vegas for them—what happened here stayed here.

I'd replayed this scene in my head a million different ways—seeing Zach again. Sometimes I ignored him. Sometimes I smiled real big and acted like I couldn't care less. My favorite idea was a chocolate cream pie right in his face. He hated chocolate.

Instead I stood there like a moron. His dark eyes met mine for the quickest second. I could've been anyone.

He'd cut off his long dark hair—it was spiked and messy now, as if he'd rolled out of bed. It probably meant he was playing guitar for a new band, a different genre, no doubt. He changed bands like underwear.

"Nova!" Rhonda called. "What are you doing? Get moving."

I needed a minute to become bulletproof. *Suck it up and smile, Nova. He's dead to you.*

If I were water, Amber's stare would've frozen me in my tracks. I swore she inched closer to Zach as I approached their table. Amber was never the prettiest girl in the room, but she knew how to work what she had. Thick red hair. Black eyeliner applied with precision around her close-set green eyes. And then there was her rack, a perky set of double Ds under a tight cami. That alone turned heads.

Christian peered at me through the viewfinder of his fancy camcorder. His blond hair looked like he hadn't combed it in a month, and his gray hoodie had been frayed in strategic places. I never understood shelling out hundreds of dollars to look unkempt. Why not skip doing laundry and not bathe for a few weeks?

The camera lens zoomed out, aiming at my chest. His lips curved up. "How've you been, Nova?"

Like he cared. "Great."

"*That* Nova?" a curly-haired guy I didn't recognize muttered.

He said "that" like I was the lowest form of life. Amber smirked, her chrome-colored nails drawing circles against the menu. It took everything I had to not flip them off.

"Know what you want?" I asked.

Zach studied the menu, even though I knew what he was getting. A stack of buttermilk pancakes and a side of bacon. Safe and boring.

"What's good here?" the curly-haired guy asked, eyeing me up and down.

"Anything," I said.

Christian finally put his camera down. His eyes were bloodshot and glassy. He probably hadn't been to bed yet. "What's in the avocado omelet?"

"Avocado." I stopped there since the ingredients were clearly listed on the menu. "We can add jalapenos for an extra fifty cents, if you can handle it." I knew Christian would take the bait.

He did. I wrote down his order with "+5" next to it. This told Grandpa to go hog wild with the jalapenos.

"And you?" I asked Curly.

"I'll have, um…" He flipped through the menu. "I don't know yet."

"Excuse me!" A woman two booths down waved her arms like she was on a deserted island and I was a helicopter. "We were here before them."

"Sorry, ma'am. I'll be right with you," I called over.

"What—she can't wait to grow another chin?" Christian asked, loud enough for the woman to hear.

Amber put her hand over her mouth, her eyes wide and smiling. Gabi had no reaction, like usual. Zach at least had the sense to look embarrassed.

"Do you guys need another minute?" I asked, trying to keep my tone even.

"Just order, dick," Christian said to his curly-haired friend.

"Fine, damn. I'll have…" Curly flipped through the menu again. "Chocolate chip pancakes. And a Coke."

Gabi smiled at me, but it didn't reach her eyes. "I'll have a veggie egg white omelette. No cheese. You probably can't steam it, right?"

Amber rolled her eyes at Zach.

"We're not set up for that," I said. I guess when you were rich enough to have a personal chef, you expected one everywhere you went.

"Can I get olive oil instead of butter then?" she asked.

"Sure."

"Hey!" Someone else called behind me. "Can we get some syrup?"

I squeezed my pen and counted to ten in my head as the others ordered. Neither Amber nor Zach looked me in the eye when they spoke. Cowards.

I grabbed their menus and turned, almost walking right into Brandon Koza. He was wearing a diner shirt and looking completely lost.

"Hey." He gave me one of his ready-for-TV smiles. With Eurasian features, black hair, and pale brown eyes, the guy had his share of fans at our whiter-than-white school where they thought he was "exotic." "Your mom told me to shadow you…"

The cakes whispered something behind us. Brandon glanced over at them, his smile fading. Amber laughed.

"Of course she did." I pointed to the table next to us. "Get them some syrup, will you? Thanks."

As soon as I got the chance, I asked Mom to cover my tables for a minute and made a beeline for the bathroom. Once locked behind the metal door of the handicapped stall, I exhaled, relieving the pressure in my chest. I used to get angry at girls who went to pieces over some jackass guy, thinking they were weak. The old me would've told myself to grow a pair. But right now I wanted to hide.

I slammed my knuckles into the divider, imagining Zach's face. All I got was a sore hand.

The door to the bathroom squeaked open, and heels clanked against the tile floor. I slowed my breaths, trying to regain my composure.

"I'm ready to kill someone. Stop me." Amber's Texas twang gave her away instantly. She was originally from Dallas, but she'd moved to Mercer Island, Washington, her freshman year. Her dad worked with Zach's mom at Microsoft. They'd met at one of their parents' parties and hit it off after they'd sneaked a bottle of wine into his room.

"Gabi," she continued. "She can't even eat a real meal."

Pause. "We're at the Spoon, which is beyond awkward. But of course Christian *had* to eat here."

I peeked through the crack in the door. She stood in front of the sink closest to me, her cell phone glued to her ear. I briefly considered jumping her, if only this wasn't my family's livelihood.

"She hasn't said a single word to me," Amber said. "Christian needs a drool bucket just to be near her. It's disgusting." She fished a brush out of her cloth bag. "Oh, but guess who works here now?" She paused again. "Brandon Koza."

Why was that so amusing?

"I wish you were, too. You keep me sane. My life sucks so bad right now." She let her friend talk for maybe ten seconds before diving in again. "Zach can't keep his eyes off Diner Skank. He thinks I don't notice. Asshole."

I prayed that she'd leave before I lost control and busted out of here.

"He's *still* defending her. I'm sick of it!"

What?

Amber raked the brush through her red curls. "You can't tell anyone this, okay?" Her voice got softer, but it was clearly something she was dying to spill. "I was pissed at Zach last night." She mumbled something I couldn't catch. "So me and Holly got really drunk. We started taking random stuff out of her fridge, blending it together, and daring each other to try it. Like barbecue sauce and eggs and jelly—I know!" She laughed. "We'd had, like, eight shots at that point. That's my excuse."

My heart was pounding now. I knew what was coming.

"Anyway, this stuff looked like blood. Holly wanted to write all over Zach's car with it. Then I thought, wait. He'd know it was us. But I know where Nova lives." Her voice softened to a gleeful whisper. "So, we get there at three in the morning and there's a *light* on." She got quiet for a few seconds. "Yep. With some guy in her bed. Big shock."

Did she not recognize Alex? She'd only made fun of him every summer since we were fourteen. That was the summer she'd invited Alex to Winchester Beach, pretty much hookup central around here. When Alex showed, Christian and his friends told him to strip or they'd destroy his skateboard, a board his Uncle Joel designed and made for him. He had to walk home naked.

Alex never went into much detail about what exactly happened, but Megan told me she heard him crying that night. He never cried, at least not in front of me.

My fingers reached for the lock, and I shoved the door open, letting it bang against the wall.

Amber jumped, eyes wide, mouth open. "I have to go," she said, hanging up.

I didn't say a word or move. I just stared her down. Sometimes saying nothing at all was best. It made people wonder what you'd do next.

But I wanted to slug her so bad my nails cut into my palms.

"Shit," she muttered before turning and leaving with her tail between her legs.

I wished I could say that was enough for me. But it wasn't. Not even close.

The diner didn't slow down until after two. We were down to a trucker and Matt and Jenika's friend Tyler's doting environmentalist mom who was talking away to Rhonda, using big hand gestures. Even she couldn't figure out how she produced Tyler.

Brandon was helping me wipe down the tables and refill the ketchup bottles. He'd been following me for the last several hours, silent and attentive. I felt kind of bad for snapping at him this morning.

"So, if you have any questions," I said, scrubbing down a particularly soiled booth, "this is about as quiet as it gets."

Brandon walked by with an armful of ketchup bottles. "Do Christian and his band of assholes come in a lot?"

"Aren't you kind of friends?"

"Not any more than you are."

"Huh." I gave the table one last wipe. "Gabi seems pretty tight with them."

"She is." He clanked down the last ketchup bottle. "Is it cool if I take a ten? I need a smoke."

If he was a smoker before, I hadn't noticed it. Not that I kept tabs on him. "Sure."

"Can I go out back? My mom drives by here a lot and…"

"Got it." I tried not to laugh. Having the chief of police for a mom had to suck, especially if she was as hard as she seemed. Of course she had to stand her ground with the racist old-timers in this town who thought a five-foot-two Filipina had no business running *their* police department.

"Mind if I join you?" I asked Brandon. "I could use the air." The sweat was eating through my shirt.

His eyes widened a little, but he nodded.

We leaned against the wall of the diner, the sour smell of the Dumpster all too close. Our view consisted of the small gravel lot Mom and Gramps parked in, a banged-up metal fence, and the abandoned Pacific Sunrise motel. The pink doors advertised that it hadn't been updated since the '70s.

Brandon lit a cigarette and offered one to me, but I shook

my head. I'd tried my mom's menthols when I was twelve. Alex completely flipped out and told me I was going to die. I smiled a little, remembering how he tried to flush the entire pack down the toilet.

"What'd they do to you—Christian and 'his band of assholes'?" I asked. Considering Amber said Brandon's name like some inside joke, it was clear he'd been ousted.

He shrugged, blowing the remnants of a drag toward the overcast sky. "Nothing like what Zach did to you."

"What do you mean?" I asked. Just about everyone outside Alex believed that I'd cheated on Zach. That he was right to dump me.

"Just all that stuff he said about you."

My skin went cold. "Like what?"

Brandon flicked his ashes, keeping his gaze on the ground. "You know. About you being…" He took that moment to take another drag.

"Spit it out."

"Skanky," he said. "The trout thing."

My stomach felt as if it was being turned inside out. "Christian started that rumor."

"I don't think so."

"Did you actually hear *Zach* say it?" I asked.

He finally glanced up at me, pity in his eyes. "Sorry. I thought you knew."

I wanted to scream Zach's secrets from the rooftops. That he was afraid of his mom. That he hated Christian, but he was too scared to stand up to him. Hell, Zach was afraid of the world.

Silence fell between us. The jittery kind where nobody knows what to say next. I felt this urge to let out my every hateful thought, but Brandon was only the messenger. Someone who barely knew me. What good would it do?

"I heard you found that deer," he said, finally. "It was pretty bad, huh?"

"Yeah…" Just when I'd managed to block out that image for an hour. "What the hell is going on?"

He shook his head. "No idea. But De Luca is all over my mom about it."

"Does she have any leads?"

"Nothing I can talk about."

"I can keep a secret."

He laughed, dropping his cigarette to the ground. "Nobody can keep a secret."

"There was a foxglove left with the raccoon, too, right? In its mouth?"

He cocked his head, squinting at me. "Where'd you hear that?"

"From a friend."

His lips turned up at the corners. "Gabi didn't waste any time…"

"Was she not supposed to talk about it?"

"My mom told them not to share the details right now." He shrugged. "I'm sure Gabi couldn't help herself."

I wanted to ask him what happened between him and Gabi, but I had a feeling he'd dodge that question, too.

"Well, to be fair, I guessed it was the same deal as the deer," I said.

His smile broadened. "Good work, Detective."

"One day, I hope."

"A cop—you? Really?"

"Like you know me well enough to be surprised."

His fingers drummed against the pockets of his jeans, as if he was thinking of the right thing to say.

"Don't tell me I don't seem like the type," I said. "I'll punch you."

He breathed out a laugh. "I believe it."

Brandon wasn't the first person to have that reaction. When I told Zach, he grinned and said, *you're too cute to be a cop.* It felt like a compliment at the time, like a lot of the things he said. He had a real knack for making insults feel good.

To most people around here, even before the rumors started, I was what Amber called me—Diner Skank. The cheap kind of pretty. Boobs too big for my frame, skinny legs, and what Josh Byers called *blow me* lips. He'd sit behind me in trig every day, whispering it over and over. I could still feel his hot breath on the back of my neck, his chewed-up pencil eraser poking at my spine.

I was that cliché girl destined to grow old waiting tables, hoping to catch some sugar daddy's eye.

Fuck that and fuck them. I was the girl destined to prove them all wrong.

"Isn't this how serial killers get their start?" I asked.

"Sometimes." Brandon fingered another cigarette in his pack. "You never know around here, right?"

"No kidding."

While Emerald Cove didn't see much action in the crime department, there was no shortage of weird. Not just here, but all up and down the Pacific Northwest coast. Shoes washing onshore with decayed feet inside. Decades of young girls disappearing. Group suicides nobody could explain.

Sometimes in the winter, when the fog rolled in and silenced the waves, it felt as if death had its fingers around my neck. Fingers like frostbitten twigs that made me ache inside. Naturally I passed the time by reading dozens of books about serial killers and cold cases. I'd looked into a lot of the local urban legends Gramps shared with me, about people who vanished one day or were supposedly murdered by vengeful spirits. Many of the legends had grown from true stories where the victim's loved ones were desperate for an answer. Any answer.

"So does Alex have a death wish?" Brandon asked, startling me.

"What do you mean?"

"Heard he's going to fight Matt today."

"*What?* From who?"

Brandon's eyebrows rose. "You don't know?"

"Who told you that?" I repeated, my pulse rising. So help me if Alex decided to do this without telling me…

"Haley St. James was here earlier. I heard her talking about it."

My fingers curled inside my palms. "Did she say when?"

"No… Are—"

I was already opening the back door before he could finish. The muscles in my legs tensed with adrenaline. I needed to get a hold of Alex. Talk him out of this stupidity.

I headed into our closet-sized office that actually *was* a closet at one time and picked up the old yellow phone on the wall, dialing Alex's house. "Please be there," I muttered, as each ring lasted an eternity.

"Hello?" Megan answered, sounding a bit out of breath.

"Hey—is Alex there?"

Silence.

"Megan?" I shut my eyes. She always lost the ability to speak when she was scared or upset. "What happened?"

"Matt showed up at our house with Jenika a minute ago and…" She paused. "Alex went with them."

"Where did they go?"

"The Deception Creek Trail. I was just about to leave—
follow them."

"Don't. I'll take care of it." I'd much rather they kicked the
crap out of me than Megan. She'd never even been in a fight.

"With what? A superpower?"

"Just stay there," I hissed into the phone before hanging
up.

The Deception Creek Trail was behind Alex's trailer park,
a half mile from here. I'd get there in three minutes, if I were
lucky.

"Gramps, tell Mom I'll be back as soon as I can," I said as
I passed him in the kitchen.

He opened his mouth to respond, but I didn't look back.

The Pacific View trailer park was silent, almost like a ghost
town. No blasting music or laughter. Nobody outside
drinking beer or watering plants. Just the sound of my breath,
each inhale quivering more than the last. My tennis shoes
dug into the gravel. I kept pushing myself harder and faster,
despite my burning thighs and calves.

Blooming maple trees draped over the DECEPTION CREEK
TRAIL sign, a dark and narrow trail that only locals knew
about. It was one of my favorite places to run on a normal
day. Rugged and unkempt, but always quiet. Now it seemed
sinister, like it might swallow me whole.

I ran past a tree Alex and I had carved one of our "magic"
symbols into when we were ten, and the lump in my throat
grew. We'd spent hours in these woods, pretending we were
fairies and tricksters.

The humid air clung to my skin, covering me in sweat.

I imagined Alex on the ground, curled up in a ball, like I'd found him once in seventh grade. I promised him I'd never let that happen again.

Finally I heard a voice, what sounded like a yell. The trail became a tunnel, blurred on the edges, but clear in the center. No matter how fast I moved, it wasn't fast enough.

I rounded the corner, preparing to see the worst. Alex on the ground. Matt, Jenika, and their friends kicking and stomping on him.

But that wasn't what I found.

Alex and Matt were on the ground, their arms making fast, jerking movements. But Alex had the edge.

"Alex!" I ran toward them.

"Stay back," he said just as Matt got him in the face. That's when he started whaling on Matt, punching him again and again. Matt ended up on his stomach, trying to get away, but Alex got up and kicked him in the side.

Matt half groaned, half grunted, his eyes squeezing shut. His fingers dug into the dirt, knuckles pale and shaking. Alex stood over him, a hint of a smile on his face.

He was enjoying this.

My pulse throbbed in my ears, and my mouth went dry. Jenika and her friends, Tyler Lovejoy and Haley St. James, were watching, their lips parted. Tyler was making punching motions, as if he were following some kind of video game. There wasn't a whole lot to do around here. Getting into fights, for the hell of it, seemed to be their favorite way to pass the time.

"You made your point!" I said to Alex.

He squatted down next to Matt, his fist balled up like he was planning on using it again. "That's it?"

Matt gritted his teeth, his neck and face bright red. "Fuck

you," he said. Spit and blood were running down his chin.

Alex rose and walked away then, rubbing his fingers against his knuckles. He didn't even look at me as he passed. His face was like stone, no hint of emotion.

Haley and Tyler were kneeling next to Matt now, helping him sit up. Jenika stared after Alex with an odd expression, shock maybe.

I followed Alex down the darkening trail, back toward the trailer park. Cold raindrops pinched my cheeks.

"Talk to me," I said, staying a couple feet behind him.

"You weren't supposed to be here," he said softly.

"Yeah, well. I am."

He stopped and turned, shoving his hands into the pockets of his shredded jeans. Blood had welled up under his nose. "I need to be alone right now. All right?"

I caught up to him. "At least let me—"

"I'm okay." He reached out, touching my arm. "Promise."

"But—"

"Nova…" he whispered, his face inching toward mine. His breath was quick and uneven.

I closed my eyes. A damp breeze lifted the hair away from my face.

His lips pressed against my forehead, lingering for only a second. "Let me go."

MONDAY, JUNE 23

You keep asking why you, like you're some kind of victim. You are not a victim.

You have everything, and you're still miserable. You think you're better than me. You're a shallow, petty bitch. You'll do anything to bring someone down. Even believe a half-baked story meant to get you alone.

Who's laughing now?

CHAPTER SIX

Mondays at the diner were unpredictable. It was either chaos or a graveyard, no in-between. But one thing was certain — Monday nights always brought in the worst kind of crazy.

Tonight that crazy came in the form of Paul Cross, town hermit. One of them, anyway. This *was* the Pacific Northwest.

Paul had five dogs and a whole lot of whiskey to keep him company. Sometimes his dogs got loose and roamed the town like a pack of thugs. That's when you knew he'd passed out and left his door open.

Alex was usually the one to round the dogs up and take them back to Paul's trailer — they lived right across from each other.

Paul was anxious tonight, more so than I'd ever seen him. He sat up at the counter, his blue eyes buggy and red-rimmed. Bits of banana cream pie were stuck in his gray beard.

I considered running to the back real quick and giving Alex a call. But I was the only person here, outside Gramps. Plus it never failed that someone came in right before closing.

Every time I called Alex's house he wasn't there. He didn't answer his email, either, but their computer was older than dirt, and his grandma was always clicking on bad links and giving it viruses. Megan told me she hadn't seen much of him, either, that he'd been out looking for a job.

The longest we'd ever gone without talking was seven days, after I'd started dating Zach. Alex saw it as a betrayal, even though Zach never did anything to him. He was still Christian's best friend, one of *them*. I didn't listen to Alex when he told me Zach wasn't any different from the rest. I should've.

"Hey." Paul Cross slapped the counter with his meaty palm. "Isabella!"

That was what he called me, despite being told my actual name a thousand times. The only explanation he ever gave was—*you should've been an Isabella.*

"What's up, Paul?" Unfortunately for me, he was the only one here. Usually he got bored and left when we were busy dealing with other customers.

"You were in my dream last night."

Oh, no. Not another one of his *psychic* dreams. Last month the mega-quake we'd all been waiting for was going to strike, and a tsunami like the world had never seen would wipe us out.

"How about another piece of pie?" I asked. "We've got triple berry."

"You died." He said it just like that. Deadpan.

"What?"

"Your eyes were wide open, just starin' up at me."

I shuddered, seeing that deer all over again. Paul had been spouting off doom and gloom since I could remember. He'd just never made it personal before.

He grabbed my hand, squeezing so tight my bones hurt. "I told him to look out for you."

"Who?" I yanked my hand out from his grasp.

He studied me like I was nothing he'd ever seen before.

Two middle-aged women came through the door, their heels clacking against the tile. They wanted to sit in a booth. Then they wanted to sit at the counter.

By the time I got their menus and came back, Paul was gone. He'd left five crumpled one-dollar bills and two pennies in his place.

"Can we get some coffee?" one of the women asked in an impatient tone.

I didn't know how long I'd been frozen, staring at Paul's empty stool. Apparently too long.

He was a crazy old man. It didn't mean anything.

"Sure thing," I said. But I still had goosebumps.

Both women looked like they ran in the same circles as Zach's mom. With their designer purses and two-toned hair, the styles just edgy enough to make them appear five years younger. In fact, I was pretty sure I'd seen them at Zach's house last summer.

"This place is such a hole," the blonde one whispered. "Great pie, though."

They both gave me quick, tight smiles as I set two coffees in front of them.

The brunette's phone vibrated. She looked at the caller ID and sighed. "It's Rose again." She lowered her voice as if *Rose* could hear her. "I have no idea what to say to her. It's killing me."

"Me neither." The blonde took a hesitant sip of her coffee.

"I'd go to pieces if Holly didn't come home one night."

"She and Amber are best friends, right?"

I grabbed some empty ketchup bottles and began refilling them. There weren't many Ambers or Hollys in this town.

"Yeah," the brunette said. Holly's mom, I assumed. "At

least they were this month. It changes."

"Sometimes I'm so glad I had boys."

One of them was tapping a spoon against her cup. It was incessant. Headache-inducing.

"I'm lucky, though. Holly tells me everything."

Did she tell you she got drunk and painted "whorehouse" on my window the other night?

"You know…" Holly's mom lowered her voice again. "Amber ran off last year with some guy she met at a concert. Holly said he was *twenty-five*."

I turned to face them, wiping away crumbs from Paul's pie.

The other woman exhaled. "I hate to say it, but she's always struck me as a little…"

Their elbows rested on the counter and their heads were bowed together, like a couple of teenagers. Clearly Amber's sex life was more interesting to them than the fact that she was apparently *missing*.

Maybe my mom was right. High school never really ended.

"I'm betting Zach knows where she is," the brunette said.

"He claims he doesn't. The thing is…those kids don't go a day without posting on SayIt and all that. She hasn't posted anything since Saturday." Holly's mom threw her hands up. "Nobody saw her leave the party. Nobody's seen her since? It's scary."

"Yeah, well, kids lie. Someone knows something."

The last time a teen girl went missing around here, they found her at the bottom of the cliff. She'd jumped.

But Amber didn't seem like the suicidal type.

"Rose is jumping to worst-case scenarios," Holly's mom continued. "I would be, too. It doesn't help that there's some psychopath chopping up animals."

"I heard about that!" The brunette glanced over at me,

finally taking note of my existence. She leaned closer to her friend, talking quieter. But not quiet enough. "This place breeds people who aren't right in the head. The isolation. No jobs. Just look at the meth problem."

The way summer residents and tourists talked, you'd think the entire town was filled with zombie tweakers. Sure, we had our share. But no more than a lot of other places.

I tuned them out after that. Listening to their ignorance did nothing but piss me off, and I wasn't too good at hiding it. Besides, all I could think about was Amber.

They were right about one thing—that girl *lived* on SayIt. Two days without posting was a long time for her. When Zach and I were going out, I'd look at her page all the time. Mostly because he was always replying to her, sharing memories and inside jokes. Alex told me I was torturing myself—and I knew I was—but I couldn't help it. My curiosity got the better of me every time.

The week after Zach broke up with me, she'd posted: Everything is right again.

Those words haunted me for too long.

When I got home, I took my laptop to bed and went to Amber's SayIt page for the first time since last summer. I half expected to go on and see her back and posting every hour as usual.

But the last post was still from Saturday night—It's over, it said.

It seemed manipulative to me, as if she'd put time and thought into those two little cryptic words. Or maybe that was my disdain for her talking.

Her earlier posts were completely different.

Christian and Ben killed our fire. She'd included a blurry and—thankfully—dark image of what appeared to be Christian and some other guy peeing on a fire.

I'm so buzzedd.

I love my HoHo! Amber and Holly were cheek to cheek, smiling wide for the phone cam.

Don't ever get a sunburn on the backs of your thighs. :(

SayIt had this uncanny ability to make people become caricatures of themselves. It seemed like everyone was afraid to post something real, something *worth* saying. Then again, talking about your innermost feelings on social media had its drawbacks. I learned that the hard way when I'd written cryptic lines about Zach last summer and people had re-posted them on his page, mocking me.

I scrolled through her posts for the last few days. I knew what she ate—she'd even posted pictures. What shoes she bought. Who she hung out with. The last movie she saw (she hated it). There was nothing that even hinted at her being unhappy. Except for that very last post. *It's over.*

What the hell happened at that party?

Something tapped against my window, just once. It was no louder than a gentle whisper. My lace curtains had somehow become parted again, letting a couple inches of darkness peek through.

Maybe it was in my head, a reaction to everything going on. But goose bumps erected every hair on my forearms.

I slid my computer off my lap and leaned toward my window to take a quick peek outside. A high-pitched scratching sound made me freeze. It was like a zipper or leaves brushing against the house.

Alex came to my window late at night sometimes, when

he didn't want to risk waking up my mom or Gavin. But he would've knocked by now.

I ripped the curtains open, revealing a square shadow in the center of the glass. Another envelope. I cracked the window, just enough to curl my arm underneath and reach around the outside. The dim light of the half moon showed only the top of our apple tree.

Someone could be using the dark for cover, quietly watching. Waiting to get off on my fear like a coward.

"If you've got something to say, say it to my face," I called out, ripping the envelope off the glass and tossing it on the lawn. I slammed the window shut, locked it, and pulled the curtains back together, my hands shaking.

For all I knew, it was Amber playing some sick game. She seemed to think Zach was still into me—maybe that was what *it's over* meant. Her and Zach. What if she'd completely lost it?

But vandalizing my house while drunk and bragging about it where I worked showed she was hardly a mastermind. These letters took planning. Patience. Someone who enjoyed the anonymity.

Or maybe I'd read too many psychopath biographies.

CHAPTER SEVEN

barely slept through the night, jolting awake at every sound, real or in my head. My gaze kept finding its way to the window, hunting for shadows.

I gave up tossing and turning around nine and parted my curtains, the pale yellow sunlight a welcome presence at first. But my throat tightened as my eyes adjusted to the light. Another purple envelope, or maybe the same one, was taped to the window.

I'd stayed awake for over an hour after turning out the light, hoping they'd take the bait. If they'd come back then, I would've heard them. Which meant they'd waited quite a while... Pretty dedicated for a prank.

A chill ran down my bare legs. I threw on an old pair of jeans and Alex's army jacket before grabbing a Ziploc bag and a pair of disposable rubber gloves from the kitchen. Gavin was in the living room, completely focused on his five hundredth viewing of the final Harry Potter movie. Mom's voice echoed from her bedroom, most likely on the phone with Eric. They talked at least three times a day.

I headed outside, shutting the back door softly behind me, and made my way over to my window.

The envelope I'd thrown on the ground last night was still in the grass, seemingly untouched. I slipped on the rubber gloves, ignoring how ridiculous I felt. Maybe the whole CSI thing was overkill. But what if this escalated? It'd be better to have at least one letter that didn't have my own fingerprints all over it.

I opened the envelope taped to my window first, carefully tearing the side. There was just a folded piece of paper this time—no surprises.

Not everyone is out to get you, it read.

The hairs on the back of my neck seemed to buzz, as if someone were sneaking up behind me. I whipped my head around, only to see our elderly neighbor, Mrs. Zimmerman, walking by our house with her white terrier. She kept her gaze straight ahead and her chin tilted up, as always. She'd only spoken to me once, the day Alex and I had found a stray kitten. We'd followed it into her front yard, a maze of rosebushes and summer shrubs.

"Stay out of my yard, please," she'd said from her porch. Her voice was calm, almost polite, but her eyes were icy blue slits. Witchy, I called them.

She was the kind of woman who took frequent peeks out her window, but I doubted she'd tell me if she saw anything last night.

The second envelope was soggy with dew, but there was a bulge inside. My breath froze in my throat as I opened it up and dumped out the contents.

A conch shell hit the grass with a soft *thud*. The inside had a pale blue tint, almost violet. Sand coated the outside, as if it had just been plucked from the beach.

I pulled out the typed note. *Someone once told me you can hear the ocean through this*, it read. *I still believe that. Do you?*

I did…it was one of the few bits of magic I still believed in.

Part of me wished these letters contained insults or obviously fake secret admirer proclamations. At least then I'd have a pretty good idea where they were coming from and how to react.

headed to Alex's after breakfast. He still hadn't called me back, and I'd gone from concerned to pissed. Maybe he didn't want to talk about the fight with Matt. Too bad. We were going to talk about it.

I found myself running, not out of urgency. Just to think. Sometimes it was the only way I could.

I took the Neahkahnie Park Trail, one of the more heavily used trails in town. It was all paved and pretty with those doggy waste stations, compliments of Steve De Luca. I preferred the softness of mud under my feet, the smell of wet leaves…the unknown. But right now I wanted to stick with the known.

Usually this trail was filled with older couples and people walking their dogs. Today it was quieter than a snowy night, not even a squirrel rustling leaves.

As I headed into the shade of evergreens, a prickling sensation inched between my shoulder blades. Every now and then I'd get this feeling of doom as I ran. Usually nothing happened. But one time I swore I heard humming, a soft female voice echoing all around me. I was sure it was the Shadow Lady.

Out of all the tales Gramps told me, her story scared me the most. She was a powerful healer who lived east of town, right on the Nehalem River. She fell in love with a white man, the son of a ship captain. They had to sneak around to be together. But his family found out. They convinced him that she was a dangerous witch. That she'd be the death of them if he didn't kill her. So…he did. He sneaked up behind her, whispered *I love you* in her ear, and slit her throat.

They say she haunts the woods around here, looking for someone with a weak heart. A coward, like her lover. If you see her shadow, it means she's marked you. And once she's inside you, there's no going back. You'll be forced to carry out her revenge again and again. Until she's done or you are. And she's never done.

A branch crunched behind me. There were definitely footsteps behind me now. Thick. Clunky. Getting louder by the second.

"Where're you going, bunny rabbit?" a familiar deep voice called. Matt.

"What do you want?" I didn't stop. He wouldn't be able to keep up forever.

"You ever going to talk to me?" He fell into step beside me. His fight with Alex was still evident on his face, from his discolored nose to the deep purple skin under his left eye.

There was a part of me that felt bad for avoiding him. After all, he *didn't* start that rumor. But he was still Jenika's best friend. I let him way too close to me that night. Said too much.

There was a time I thought he was a little sexy, not that I'd admit that to anyone. Ever. He had an odd mix of features—a wide nose and rough skin. Big brown eyes and blond curls. There was something about his voice, too. It was sleepy, like some fictional rock star. Throw in the whole bad-boy thing, and he didn't exactly have problems getting laid around here.

But that wasn't what drew me to him that night. It wasn't something I could explain…or even wanted to think about.

"What is it that I did to you?" he asked, his breath getting thicker.

"You tried to jump my best friend?"

Matt grabbed my arm, forcing me to stop. I jerked away from him, but his fingers dug into my skin.

"Alex started that fight," he said. His clothes smelled of burning leaves, just like before. I liked it then. Now it made my stomach turn.

Matt could be the stalker type. But I didn't see him writing letters, and I definitely didn't see him collecting flowers and seashells.

"Let go of me. Now." My fist balled up, preparing to give him a matching set of black eyes if I had to.

Matt dropped my arm and took a step back, holding his hands up. "You didn't really answer my question…"

I turned and walked away, hoping like hell he wouldn't follow. He didn't.

Alex's sky-blue double-wide wasn't as bright or alive as it once was. I remembered the day his grandpa painted it that color—we'd all helped. Alex wanted to paint a giant sun on the side, but Cindy, his grandma, said if we did, it'd be over her dead body.

The orange and yellow flowers on the stoop had turned brown and curled inside their pots. Even Megan's cactus looked pale and withdrawn. Their grandpa's moon and star chimes still made music, though. They gave me hope he was looking out for them, wherever he was now.

I tried knocking on Alex's window first, but there wasn't any answer. Cindy never liked me much, mainly because of my mom's lifestyle. She called us a riffraff family, as if she had room to talk. But lately she'd been downright hostile, so I tried to avoid seeing her whenever possible.

Megan answered the door, rubbing her eyes like she'd just woken up. And knowing her, she probably had. "Alex is out getting eggs," she said. "Grandma ran out."

I glanced over my shoulder, only just realizing their grandpa's El Camino was gone. It had almost become a fixture in their carport with its cherry paint and black racing stripes. "She let him take the car?"

Megan's eyes shifted down toward her feet. "He kind of just started taking it…" she mumbled. "It's not like she can drive it."

Cindy never got her license. She'd gotten accustomed to her husband driving her anywhere outside walking distance.

"I can't believe he didn't tell me," I said. He knew I was dying to take that first ride in it—even if it was just to the store.

"If you're selling something, we're not buying!" Cindy called out.

"It's me," I said.

"Oh," Cindy said, before mumbling something I was sure I didn't want to hear.

"What's she making this time?" I asked Megan.

Cindy had three types of days—bad, worse, and baking binges. The baking binges seemed to be happening more often, but that wasn't necessarily a good thing.

"Oatmeal cookies for the Saint Francis bake sale." Megan leaned toward the screen. "She's in one of her paranoid, shit-talking moods," she whispered.

"It's okay…let me in." It wasn't, really. But I was going to talk to Alex, even if it meant holding my tongue while I waited.

Cindy was one of those people who were racist without realizing it. One minute she'd be shaking her head at some hate crime on the news and saying "God loves people of every color" and the next she'd be talking about how certain "types" of people were driving the U.S. into the ground.

Then there was her son Joel, the only sane family member in Alex and Megan's life now. Cindy kept insisting that his attraction to guys was a phase—something he'd get over—despite his being thirty years old. She wouldn't even let Joel bring his boyfriend to his own father's funeral, claiming it was disrespectful. But Megan and Alex's grandpa would've wanted him there either way. He hadn't completely accepted Joel being gay, but he was at least *trying* to.

The musky smell of prayer candles smacked me in the face as soon as I stepped inside. Two sat on the kitchen table, one holder featuring a picture of Jesus, the other just a white candle in clear glass. The odor always made me queasy, reminding me of the one and only time I went to church with Alex. It was cold and dark. And I couldn't stop thinking about death.

Their home was always cramped, especially with three bedrooms in such a small living space, but I'd never seen it look this bad. Laundry took up the old red couch in the living room, and the plants on the coffee table had gone into eternal slumber. Empty bottles of blackberry brandy and whiskey covered the floor around their overflowing trash can.

"Hi, Nova," Cindy said, her pale blue eyes giving me the usual once-over. You'd think she'd be done sizing me up after eight years. "Haven't seen you in a while."

"It's busy season at the diner. Been working a lot."

It was hard seeing her now. Bags under her eyes, ruddy skin. It seemed like she'd aged about five years since the funeral.

She came out from behind their cracked plywood counter, which was covered in flour. "How's your family?"

"Good."

Riff, their black Lab, bounded up to me with a hearty bark. He sniffed around my legs and plopped down, staring up at me with wide brown eyes.

Cindy reached for what looked like a glass of pineapple juice, but chances were it was half whiskey. "Must be hard for Gavin. Having his dad away all the time."

"He deals," I said.

"He's a growing boy. He needs his daddy."

I nodded, folding my arms. We'd had this conversation before. There was no reasoning with her.

Cindy brushed Megan's hair out of her face. It wasn't a warm gesture, more rough and hurried. "Your hair looks terrible," she said. "Why don't you brush it more?"

Megan ducked away. "Stop."

Riff squeezed himself between them and barked up at Cindy.

"Oh, be quiet." Cindy nudged him with her slipper. "You've got such a pretty face," she continued, reaching toward Megan again. "Put it back in a ponytail, at least."

Megan turned away, closing her eyes. "I like it down," she said, softly.

"You kids dress like hobos." She took a sip from her glass, wincing the slightest bit. "That's why your brother can't find a job. You don't go asking for job applications wearin' a rock band T-shirt."

"Actually…" I began, aching to tell her it wasn't 1965 anymore. Even in Emerald Cove. There weren't any jobs to be had around here.

"You know what they've been telling him?" She talked over me. "They say, *We don't have any applications. You need to get one on the internet.* That's a line if I ever heard one."

"It's pretty common," I said. "Most people apply online now."

"Well, I shouldn't be surprised." Cindy shook her head. "You got Generation Lazy and Generation Lazier running things. Most of 'em grew up wrapped in cotton wool, completely reliant on computers. Something goes wrong and you're all gonna be running around like headless chickens." She pointed at Megan, her blue eyes going sharp. "Be thankful you were raised different."

If she meant how a Pace family vacation was survival camping in the Cascades, I doubted Megan or Alex would be thanking her anytime soon. They dreaded those trips, especially when their grandpa tried to teach them how to hunt.

The oven beeped. Cindy scurried back into the kitchen, nearly bumping into the counter.

We used that moment to escape down the hall. Riff trotted after us, his paws clicking against the vinyl floor.

"Don't disappear for too long, Megan!" Cindy called. "I need your help cleaning up."

"Okay!" she said. "Let's go in Alex's room. Mine's a mess."

"You just want an excuse to snoop again."

"Maybe..." She pushed open his chipped wooden door. It still had remnants of tape from their Uncle Joel's posters.

Everything looked the same. Alex's gray-and-blue plaid comforter and sheets were a twisted mess on his bed. Parts for a computer he never got around to building still cluttered the small desk he'd made out of reclaimed wood. The stout bookshelf in the corner overflowed with books on the quantum theory, his latest obsession.

But the air felt warmer than usual, even with the window cracked. And it smelled overwhelmingly sweet, like candy apples. I noticed a couple red candles next to his iPod speakers on the windowsill.

There was the hint of stale cigarettes, too, but the bikers next door were chain-smokers.

Megan wrinkled her nose. "Gross. It's like the Pottery Barn exploded in here." She opened the window wider.

"No kidding. What's up with that?" I sat on his bed. Riff hopped up and nuzzled next to me. I ran my fingers through his coarse black fur.

Megan opened his closet and knelt down, digging through a pile of clothes. "I'm guessing he hasn't called you back?"

"Nope."

"He's been weird since his fight with Matt. Hasn't really talked to me either."

"I'm sorry…" Alex ignoring me was bad enough, but Megan needed him more than ever. What the hell was going on with him?

She pulled a black shirt out of the pile. "I *knew* he stole this back. Liar."

"I'm worried about him."

"I know." Megan balled the T-shirt in her hand and stood, avoiding eye contact.

"You do?"

"Yeah, I mean…you always are." She plopped down in his computer chair and pulled her knees against her chest.

"He just seems so different…"

She yanked out threads from the hem of her jeans, not responding for a few seconds. "Did you hear about Amber?"

I nodded, not surprised by the subject change. That was her solution for every conversation that made her uncomfortable.

"You saw her at the party, right?"

"Yeah. She had a fight with Zach and then got *really* drunk."

I waited for her to say more, but she nibbled on her thumbnail. That had to be what *it's over* meant. She and Zach broke up. "What did they fight about?"

She shrugged. "They went off by themselves for a while. And then they split up when they came back. It was pretty obvious she'd been crying." Her brow crinkled. "She said some stuff about you."

"Like what?" I wasn't sure I wanted to hear it.

Megan gave me a look that confirmed I didn't. "She said you were spying on her in the diner bathroom. That you tried to attack her. I told them that didn't sound like you, and she was like, *were you there? No.*"

"If by 'attack' she means stood there and looked at her? Yeah. Guilty." Part of me didn't want Amber to come back. Not that I wanted her to be dead or anything. Just gone. Hell, I wanted all of them gone.

"Amber's a drama queen," Megan said. "Even her friends don't buy half the stuff she says."

"When was the last time you saw her at the party?"

"Well…" She blew out a breath. "Grandma sent Alex to pick me up. And by then Amber was wasted. She was, like, *Hey, where's your slut friend?*" She paused and waited for my reaction, as if she expected me to freak out.

"And?"

"Alex flipped her off. She called us dumb hicks." Megan looked down. "Then we left."

I wound my hair around my finger, pulling tight. "You think she ran away?"

"That's what some people think. She did once before, I

guess."

Girls like Amber didn't hit the road by themselves without somewhere to go and someone to go with. She wasn't exactly bred for the streets. "Wouldn't she have told someone? Like Holly?"

Megan shrugged. "How would I know?"

Maybe Holly was covering for her. Or she didn't want to be found. But why? What could be worth scaring the hell out of anyone who cared about her?

Then I had another thought. One that involved her walking down a dark road, drunk and alone. Some psycho following her.

"Amber asked me if I'd ever eaten deer meat," Megan continued. "Everyone else ignored me."

"It's what they do, babe. They're jerks."

"Gabi's not," she said. "You know she gave me some of her old clothes?"

If someone offered me their *old* clothes, I'd be insulted. Megan was poor, not homeless. "Just be careful, okay?"

She looked at me then, her eyes accusing. "Because she couldn't actually want to be my friend."

"That isn't it. I…" I wished I knew how to tell Megan I was afraid for her without pushing her away. Or making her feel like she wasn't good enough.

"I don't know why you guys are so against her," Megan said. "She's never done anything to you."

"It's not her. It's who she hangs out with." Somehow I doubted Gabi would have Megan's back if a situation called for it. And the cakes had a lot of situations.

I scanned the floor, my mind still focused on Amber. That's when I saw it. A torn shiny wrapper lying on the carpet behind Alex's trash can. My mind tried to make it into something else, anything else. But there was no missing the word "Trojan" across the top.

My mouth dropped open, and I stopped breathing. The candles, the disappearing act, his sketchy behavior—it all added up. Alex does have another girl in his life, a girl he's having *sex* with, and he didn't even tell me. He was going out of his way to hide it.

"Are you okay?" Megan asked.

My head jerked up. "I'm fine. I thought Alex was just going to get eggs."

"That's what he said." She craned her neck to see out the window, and her eyes widened.

"What?" I got up and looked outside. I'd heard the rumble of an engine, but I thought it was the neighbor's car idling. It wasn't.

The red El Camino sat at the end of their lane, the passenger door open. A girl with unevenly cropped blond hair climbed out and waved before walking in the opposite direction. Jenika. She glanced over her shoulder, as if she could sense me staring at her.

I moved back out of sight, my heart pounding. Megan watched Alex pull into the carport, but there wasn't a trace of surprise in her expression.

"How long have you known?" I asked.

Her gaze shifted from the window to the thumbnail she was still picking at. "Since last weekend… Grandma was at church and I heard laughing—I thought it was you. I came in here and Jenika was sitting on his window ledge."

Jenika had to be the girl he was hooking up with. Why else wouldn't he tell me?

"Are you mad at me?" Megan asked.

I shook my head, but I couldn't speak. There were too many thoughts running through my mind. My skin felt like it was on fire.

The front door closed.

"I saw that, Alex!" Cindy yelled.

His footsteps stopped. "Saw what?"

"You must think I'm blind and dumb," she continued. "I saw that girl getting out of my car."

"Her name is Jenika, and she needed a ride home."

Megan moved from the desk chair to the door, turning the knob slowly. Silently. She pulled the door open a crack, enough to hear better.

"When you hang out with lowlifes, you're seen as a lowlife," Cindy said. "Is that what you want when you're trying to find a job? It's bad enough you've got that black eye."

Alex mumbled something I couldn't make out. I joined Megan, pressing my back against the wall.

"What was that?" Cindy's voice rose.

"Nothing."

"That's funny. I saw your lips move."

Neither of them spoke for a few seconds.

"Are we done?" Alex asked.

Cindy's slippers padded across the floor. "Give me the keys. You're done going out for the day."

There was a pause, as if he hesitated.

"Now!"

"I did what you asked me to do. What's the problem?" Alex's words were followed by a jingling sound.

He never pushed things like this. Usually he did whatever she told him to do, just to shut her up.

"I see you with that girl again and these are gone for good." The keys clanged together. "You understand?"

"Yes, *ma'am*."

"Don't be smart with me. I'll slap you until you see stars."

"Is that what God would want you to do?" Alex's voice was low, amused. He didn't even sound like him.

I winced, expecting to hear the *smack* of her hand against his skin. It wouldn't be the first time.

"If you ever talk to me like that again..." She paused for what felt like forever. "I'll toss you right out that door. I won't give it a second thought."

Alex said something in a soft voice, almost a whisper. His footsteps headed down the hall. Megan and I backed away from the door.

Alex's eyes widened when he saw me standing by his bed. His lips parted, but he didn't speak. Megan ducked past him, mumbling something I couldn't make out.

"I sent you an email," Alex said, shutting the door. As if that were good enough. As if that were all I was worth to him.

I folded my arms, pulse rising, stomach twisting. "Yeah? Does it explain what I just saw?"

He sat on the foot of his bed, keeping his head down. His bangs fell below his cheekbones. I hadn't noticed how long his hair was getting until now. I hadn't noticed a lot of things...

I lowered myself onto the edge of his desk chair, keeping my distance. "What the hell is going on, Alex?"

He didn't answer right away. Time froze. It was as if he were at the end of a tunnel, growing more out of reach with every breath.

"Me and Jenika..." He paused, resting his hand against Riff's fur.

I looked away, willing myself to stay quiet, not say a bunch of things I might regret. I kept seeing them together. In his bed. The same bed we'd lie in for hours and talk about life on other planets. The same bed we'd made fun of Jenika on... countless times.

"We've been hanging out," he continued.

"Why?" My voice came out in a ragged whisper.

"I saw her at Grandpa's grave site, the day after we buried him," he said. "She had a bouquet of sunflowers."

His grandpa's favorite flower.

"I guess he used to help her and her mom out sometimes," he continued. "Fixed their car. Picked up some extra groceries when they needed them." His voice faltered a little, as if he was holding something back.

His grandpa wasn't perfect, but he cared about people. He always looked for the good, even if he didn't agree with how they lived their lives. "Did Cindy know?"

Disgust flashed in his eyes. "She would've freaked."

"So, you guys started talking?"

"A little. Mostly about him. It was pretty awkward."

"What's it like now?" My eyes went to the trash can again. I wasn't sure I wanted to know the answer.

"I guess we're friends."

"Really? You deserve an Oscar for that scene at the park, then."

He finally looked at me. "I wasn't acting. She does stupid shit for attention. It pisses me off."

My eyes stung. My throat was getting tighter. "Were you ever going to tell me?"

He hesitated. "I've been trying to…"

"Trying to? You don't *try* to tell someone something. You either do or you don't."

He went quiet for a few seconds. "You're right. I'm sorry."

"That's it?"

His eyes flickered up to mine, holding my gaze this time. "I know you, Nova. There's nothing I can say right now that's going to make this okay."

"How can you be friends with her? After everything."

"It wasn't planned, okay?" He let out a breath. "It was nice having…"

"Having what?"

"Someone else to talk to. She gets what I'm going through with…" He motioned toward his door. "You know what her mom is like."

Everyone in town knew Jenika's mom was bipolar and had an addiction to pain pills. She ended up in the hospital years ago when she added alcohol to the mix. Nearly died.

I wanted to tell him I *got it,* too, that he could always come to me. But I didn't get it. I hadn't lived it… My mom battled depression sometimes, but she'd always picked herself up.

"The fight with Matt. Was that about impressing her?"

"What? No." His forehead furrowed. "That was about getting him to leave me the fuck alone."

My fingers tapped against my forearm. The room suddenly felt a hundred degrees. "Does he know about you guys being… friends?"

"She told him after the fight." His voice lowered. "Figured it'd help us bury the hatchet, or something."

"Of course. You're good enough to be seen with *now.*" How could he be so gullible?

"It's not like that. She's not everything you think she is. I wish I could get you guys to—"

"Oh, yeah. That's going to happen."

"Things haven't changed between us, Nova." He leaned over and touched my knee briefly, but I jerked away. "You're still my—"

"We were supposed to take the El Camino out for the first time together. Remember? You were going to pick me up and…" It wasn't what I'd meant to say, and it sounded stupid, even to my own ears. But right now that car ride felt like everything.

"You were working. I needed it to job-hunt—the only jobs around here are at the Inn. And I'm not working for that fucker."

"Doesn't Jenika work there?" Last I heard she'd gotten a housekeeper job. Easy access to tourists that way. They didn't mind paying top dollar for mediocre pot.

He shook his head. "She works at Lucy's now, down in Tillamook."

Lucy's had been around since the beginning of time, famous for its meat loaf and mashed-potato casserole. "Is she asking Grandma and Grandpa if they'd like a side of weed with that?"

"She doesn't deal. That's a rumor."

"And you believe that?"

He studied my face, his right eye squinting a little. "You know people around here talk a lot of shit. And most of it isn't true."

I couldn't argue that, so I kept quiet. It didn't change the person she'd been since we were eight. The things she'd done. Like how she started calling him "bed wetter" in fifth grade and got half our school to believe it was true. Or how she'd mock him whenever he had to give an oral presentation in junior high. His paper would shake in his hands, and he'd speak so softly you could barely hear him. *Don't piss your pants,* she'd whisper. *Don't pass out.*

Did he forget that?

"She knows the manager at the Safeway in Tillamook," he went on. "She got me an interview with him. For a stock job."

"So, she hooks you up with an interview and all's forgiven?"

"I never said that."

Alex's door opened suddenly, making me jump. Cindy poked her head inside. "It's time for you to go home, Nova," she said.

"Can we have a second?" Alex asked, keeping his voice light.

She opened the door wider and glanced at me before disappearing into the shadows of the hallway.

Neither of us said anything for a minute. My heart kept beating faster, telling me to go. Go now. But I had to ask him.

I had to know.

"Are you working Saturday night?" Alex asked.

"No."

"Let's take a drive. Just you and me."

"Are you and Jenika…"

The muscle under his right eye twitched, like it always did when he was nervous. I had my answer.

"Alex!" Cindy called.

That was my cue. Before even thinking, I got up and snatched the condom wrapper off his floor, pinching the corner between my fingertips.

I let it fall into his lap, wishing I could've said something witty, as if I didn't care. Instead I said, "You missed the trash." I folded my arms to hide my trembling hands.

His eyes flickered up to mine, his cheeks flushing. "Nova…"

"It's not my business. We're not little kids anymore, right?" Whatever he said would make things worse. If he denied being with her, he was probably lying. If he didn't, it was true.

I started to walk out of the room, but the sound of his voice stopped me.

"We're not going out," he said. "We just messed around a couple times." He mumbled the last part, like he wasn't sure he wanted me to hear it.

I turned, my hand still on the doorknob. All I heard was "a couple times." *Times.*

He stared back at me, waiting.

"I feel like I don't even know you," I said, my voice barely above a whisper.

Then I bolted. Before he could respond. Before the lump in my throat exploded and my breath went jagged. Before I lost all ability to say anything at all.

FRIDAY, JUNE 27

You haven't stopped crying since you got here. You keep making this sound. This high-pitched whine, like a sick dog. You won't stop.

Make it stop. Make it stop.

Make it stop.

Make it stop.

Make it stop

Make it stop

MAKE IT STOP

CHAPTER EIGHT

They say you could know a psychopath your whole life and not realize it. Not all of them were killers or even criminals. Some ran companies, some were politicians, some were even doctors and cops. The one thing they had in common was their lack of empathy. They didn't let emotions make their decisions.

But they were pretty good at faking it, making us think they were someone else. I'd like to think I'd know the difference.

Sometimes I wondered if life would be easier without so many feelings. If being able to lock up my emotions would make me stronger, a better investigator one day. What if I lost the key? What if I *wanted* to lose the key?

Saturday marked a week since Amber went missing, and there still wasn't any sign of her. No cell phone. No witnesses. No tips on where she might've gone, at least nothing the cops were sharing. It was literally as if she'd evaporated on Winchester Beach that night.

She'd made the regional news: Seattle Teen Missing on Oregon Coast. Like always, Emerald Cove wasn't worthy enough to be in the headline. We were another stop along the way. As one tourist put it, "You've seen one coastal town, you've seen them all."

Next to the story was a picture of Amber smiling in front of a Christmas tree, her usual black eyeliner absent.

People talked about her in urgent voices now, their collective paranoia smothering the diner like a thick fog. A lot of them thought she was the latest victim of the infamous Highway 101 Killer. In the last eighty years, just over a dozen teen girls had gone missing from Astoria, Oregon, to Crescent City, California—all of them last seen in the vicinity of the highway. So far they'd only recovered three bodies.

The biggest question, of course, was how it could be the same killer. I mean, even if they got a really early start, they'd be close to a hundred by now. Some locals thought it was one family, carrying on their "tradition" from one generation to the next. And then there were the select few who thought the killer was some kind of immortal demon.

Most of us figured the more recent disappearances were the work of a copycat—maybe more than one. The Oregon coast had an untamable kind of beauty. Moody, raw, more than a little dangerous. Gramps said living in a place like this brought out the best or the worst in people. *Normal people can't hack it here,* he always joked.

Zach showed up toward the end of the breakfast rush. He was with Christian and some other guy I didn't recognize. Zach kept his head down as they came in the door, his hands shoved into his pockets.

I couldn't imagine what he was going through right now. It was one thing to go through a breakup. It was another for the person to just vanish. Unless he had something to do with it...

He'd be the first person I'd look at. But Zach didn't have a violent bone in that lanky body of his. He was the guy who yelped when he saw a spider and then asked his girlfriend to kill it. True story.

Christian's laughter carried across the diner, distinct and cutting like a brass instrument. Clearly Amber's disappearance hadn't slowed him down. Not that I was surprised.

Of course Rhonda sat them in my section. I'd told her not to if they came in, but she'd forget her purse half the time if Gramps didn't remind her to bring it.

"Uh, hello?" A girl about eleven waved at me. She was clutching an iPhone. Something I probably couldn't afford until I was thirty.

"Sorry. What was that?" I asked, my cheeks burning.

"Do you have any vegan pancakes?"

I shook my head. Her parents exchanged a look that said they weren't entirely sold on their daughter's diet.

"Bring her a fruit salad," her mom said.

I nodded and headed back to the kitchen. Someone lightly grabbed my arm as I passed the row of stools that led toward the swinging kitchen door. I hated it when customers got touchy, but I forced a helpful smile anyway.

Alex was sitting on the stool closest to the door. "Hey," he said.

He was wearing a frayed gray thermal underneath his uncle's old My Bloody Valentine T-shirt, something he'd worn a million times. But it was like I was seeing him for the first time. His face, all tension and sharp angles. His eyes, a darker green than they should've been.

The nausea I'd felt since Wednesday came inching back.

"What are you doing here?" I asked.

"You won't call me back."

"Because I don't really have anything to say."

Brandon came flying out of the kitchen, three plates balanced on one arm. I gave him a nod. He'd picked up the whole server thing pretty quick for a guy who'd never worked a day in his life before.

Alex kept his gaze on me, his lips turning up a little. "You always have something to say."

"It's a madhouse right now, Alex. Order something or get out."

"You know what I like."

I jotted down a veggie burger with jalapenos, but he touched my arm before I could leave. "I got that job at Safeway. Start Monday."

"That's great." I stared at my writing on the notepad. It was messier than usual, almost illegible.

"Pick you up at six?" he asked. "We'll go anywhere you want."

I backed away, out of his reach. "I don't get off until seven."

"Hey!" Christian walked toward us from the direction of the men's bathroom, his glare fixed on Alex. "You almost hit us out there."

"But I didn't," Alex said.

An older woman a couple stools down crinkled her brow at us before whispering to the guy next to her.

Christian studied Alex for a few seconds, his blue eyes narrowed. A slow grin erupted as he glanced between us.

I knew what was coming.

"What—you can't face me?" Christian moved closer. "You've gotta hide behind your big, bad *El Camino*?"

"Disappear," Alex muttered, turning his back to him.

"If you're gonna blow your wad on a classic, at least get one without an identity crisis," Christian continued. "Dumbass hick."

"You want to fight?" I took a step toward him, keeping my voice down. "Go outside and punch yourself in the head a few times. You'll feel better."

He lowered his face toward mine. The smell of last night's beer soured his breath. "Who's talking to you?"

Zach appeared and got in front of Christian, nudging him back. "Let it go, all right?"

My mom showed up as well, dirty plates in hand. "Not in my diner, guys."

Christian kept his eyes on Alex, not budging.

"Gabi's here," Zach said to him. "We're all hungry. Come on."

"See you around, Billy Bob." Christian wiggled his pinkie finger at Alex before heading back to his table.

Alex tensed against me. I swore I could feel heat coming off his skin. If anything would make him snap, it would be reminding him of that night.

Zach didn't follow Christian. Instead he stood there for what felt like eons. There were shadows under his eyes, as if he hadn't slept in days.

"Sorry about that," he said, avoiding my gaze. "I think he's still drunk from last night."

He turned and walked away before I could tell him I didn't want to hear another excuse.

Christian had his reasons for being an ass, according to Zach. His dad died when he was four. His mom was never around. His stepdad hated him. The list went on. At the end of the day, it was easier for Zach to make excuses than see who his best friend really was.

We all had a choice. Let the hand we were dealt drown us or rise above it. "Did you seriously almost hit them?" I asked Alex.

"Christian walked out right in front of my car. I stuck it in neutral and revved the engine." The corner of his mouth curved up. "Made him jump like a jackrabbit."

"Nova," Mom said, nodding toward the kitchen.

"You should go," I told him.

Mom grabbed my elbow as soon as the door swung shut behind us. "What the hell is going on?"

Gramps eyed us, his thick eyebrows raised.

"Christian is starting crap, as usual." I yanked out of her grasp and handed Gramps my orders. She didn't need to know about Alex's part in it. "Why can't we ban him?"

"He brings in lots of friends, and he doesn't stiff us on the tip. I can think of worse customers."

"He also insults people, loud enough for them to hear. He rates girls based on how many beers he'd need to hook up with them. Believe me, he's not helping business."

Mom sighed, closing her eyes. "If someone complains, we'll do something. Otherwise? We can't risk it. We got another bad review last night. One star because they had to wait fifteen minutes for a table."

"Miserable people are gonna find misery, Angela," Gramps said to her. "There's no point in rolling over and playing dead." He nodded at me. "Tell that boy to go stick it and be done with it."

"*Dad.*" Mom pulled the jaw clip from her bun, letting her dark hair unravel down her back. "If you had your way, this would be a saloon."

Gramps poured pancake batter into a pan and shrugged. "What's wrong with that? I could wear my woolly chaps."

Mom rolled her eyes at me. "I thought I burned those."

"Could you take Zach and Christian's table?" I asked her. "Please?"

Her brow scrunched up as she redid her bun. "I can't, babe. Gavin got another stomachache, so Rhonda took him back to their place. I've got to seat people and work the counter. See if Brandon will switch."

"Zach, the heartbreaker?" Gramps asked. "Let me know which order is his. I'll show him what heartbreak feels like."

"Har, har," I said. Knowing Gramps, he'd dump an entire bottle of cayenne in Zach's eggs. Which might not be a terrible thing.

"Before I forget…" Mom pulled a purple envelope from her black apron pocket, holding it out to me. "This was left on ten."

I'd barely slept the last few nights, waiting in the darkness for *them* to come back. I'd even set up Eric's ancient mini-DV camcorder on a tripod in my room, letting the lens peek through the side of my curtains. Those tapes only had an hour of recording time, though, which made it pretty pointless.

"When did you find it?" I asked, taking it from her.

"Just a couple of minutes ago."

"Who was sitting there last?" My heart thudded—would they be that obvious?

"Betty and her favorite gossip buddy, Pam." Mom's nose wrinkled. "Don't think they're your admirers—at least I hope not." She cocked her head, her eyes combing my face. "You still think this is a prank?"

Gramps appeared to keep himself busy with beating eggs, but his creased brow and pursed lips told me he was listening intently. "Counter order's up," he said.

"We'll talk about it later, okay?" Mom said, hustling to take the plates.

I nodded, stuffing the envelope into my apron pocket before heading back out.

Gabi was sitting in Christian and Zach's booth now, eyeing the menu and sucking on her lower lip. Brandon, who was wiping down a table nearby, kept staring at her, like he wanted to say something. Hopefully he'd want to cover their table.

I walked over to him and leaned toward his ear. "You want to take care of them?"

Brandon twisted his rag, squeezing harder than necessary. "I'd rather jump off the roof." He glanced up at me. "But I will. If you need me to."

"That's okay." I patted his shoulder. "Just know…one of these days I'm going to make you tell me what your deal is with them."

He nodded, his expression softening. "Duly noted."

"What can I get you?" I asked, moving to their table and keeping my eyes on my order pad.

"Look at that," Christian said, loudly. "Service without a smile."

"Just order," Zach said.

They must've been hungry because they each rattled off their orders in record time. I was surprised when I got to Gabi—I'd somehow written everything down without actually hearing it.

I turned and walked away before they could say anything else. But I didn't get out of earshot fast enough.

"Nice rear view," Christian called after me. "Too bad it's so beat."

"Dick," Zach said, in that quiet way of his. The way that said he wasn't going to do anything but clear his own conscience.

I quickened my pace, my cheeks burning. I knew people around us had heard, but I kept my head up, eyes forward, not wanting to see their disbelief, their pity, their judgment.

Alex stood in my path, giving me his concerned look. He could always see right through me, especially when I didn't want him to.

"You okay?" he asked.

"Fine."

"No, you're not," he whispered.

"Alex, please? Drop it."

He touched my cheek, his fingers barely grazing my skin. "Stop listening to them."

I pushed past him and dropped my order off at the kitchen. Then I headed out the back door, letting the gentle breeze cool my face. I closed my eyes until my heart slowed down. Until I didn't have the overwhelming urge to go back in there and deck Christian in front of dozens of customers.

My fingers curled around the envelope in my pocket. I ripped it open this time.

I shouldn't be thinking about you, but I can't stop. Your messy ponytail. Your raspy voice. That crooked, goofy smile you get sometimes when you think nobody is looking. You drive me crazy, Nova.

I bet this tool thought I'd be touched by these oh-so-sensitive observations. They got to watch me, without my knowledge. They got to do all the talking. They got to choose when and where.

But I didn't have to keep listening.

I crumpled the paper into my fist, using all my strength to crush it, and tossed it into the Dumpster.

When I went back to check on my tables, Alex was standing in front of Zach and Christian's booth, his hands flat against their table. He was staring hard at Christian. Challenging him.

Zach's eyes met mine, a warning in his expression.

Alex straightened and backed away, keeping his focus on Christian. Then he turned and headed toward me, his fingers clenched.

"I can fight my own battles," I said as I passed him, keeping my voice in a whisper.

"So can I," he said to my back. "I'll pick you up at nine."

I kept walking.

"What's going on with you two?" Gramps asked after Alex finally left. He'd stuck around for about an hour, having a debate with Gramps in the kitchen about the merits of Black Rebel Motorcycle Club.

"What do you mean?" I didn't know why I was bothering. He could smell bullshit a mile away.

Gramps pointed his spatula at the grilled cheese he was making me. "You want this or not?"

It was three thirty. The diner would be dead for *maybe* another half hour. And I knew him. He really would hold that sandwich hostage until I started talking. Tillamook cheddar. Freshly baked sourdough. My stomach growled. "You suck sometimes, you know that?"

"Yep." He flipped the bread over. "So what'd he do?"

"How do you—"

"I'm sixty-two years old. Can we leave it at that?"

So I told him. Everything. How I felt like I was losing him, at least the Alex I knew. And the scary part was I couldn't imagine my world without *that* Alex in it.

"Well…" he began. "If you knew half the stuff I pulled when I was—" He scrunched up his face, holding up a hand. "Guys do stupid shit. It doesn't matter if we're sixteen or sixty."

"You're old and wise, remember? You're supposed to tell me something I don't know."

"Ohhh…" He chuckled. "Snap. Is that what you say?"

"Don't." I shook my head, breaking into a grin. "Just

don't."

His dark eyes studied my face for a few seconds. "You like him, don't you?"

"He's my friend. Of course I—"

"Don't play that card with me." He pointed the spatula at me this time. "You know exactly what I mean."

I looked away. "I don't know if I can get past this."

"He forgave you for dating that rich joker."

"It's not the same. Zach wasn't his worst enemy. And—"

"Isn't he part of the crowd that pantsed Alex a couple years ago?"

"Yeah, but..." My voice softened. "Zach wasn't there."

I remembered telling Alex if he was really my friend, he'd respect my feelings for Zach and back off. "You got it," he'd said, his voice quiet and icy. He never brought Zach up again.

I was too angry at the time to see how hurt he was. Now it was as plain as day. My stomach knotted up thinking about it.

"He doesn't see me that way," I said, finally.

"Then why's he always around?" Gramps asked.

I rolled my eyes. Gramps didn't believe that guys could just be friends with girls, unless they were gay or "something was wrong downstairs."

Alex had a zillion opportunities to make a move. Say something. Anything. Then again, so did I.

I curled into the wooden rocking chair Gavin always sat in to watch Gramps cook. It was blissfully quiet in here without him.

"I asked him point-blank if he's been giving you those envelopes." Gramps plopped my sandwich onto a cracked "employee" plate and handed it to me. "I told him a real man tells you how he feels to your face."

"You *what*?"

"He seemed genuinely surprised you'd gotten more than one." He raised his eyebrows at me. "Guess those letters are pretty juicy, huh? You're not talking to anyone."

"It's some messed-up prank. You know they came to my bedroom window the other night?"

Gramps stopped buttering the sourdough for his sandwich. "What exactly do these things say?"

I described each one I'd gotten so far, how I set Eric's camcorder to record when I went to sleep, even if it was for an hour.

"You hear them come around again, you dial 911."

"And say what? Help—I have a fake secret admirer?"

"They're on your property uninvited in the middle of the night." His voice rose. "You know who does that? Someone who isn't right in the head."

"You know the cops won't do anything."

He placed his sandwich into the frying pan. "Things are changing with Koza running things now. And with the animal mutilations and that rich girl going missing? You better believe they're under a lot of scrutiny." His eyes flickered up to mine. "I mean it. They come back, start dialing."

Gramps was never one to panic. He was always the first to say we should live our lives, no matter what. *If the bogeyman is gonna come, he's gonna come. All you can do is keep your head out of your rear and your eyes open.*

Humor got Gramps through all those years of cleaning up gory crime scenes. He always told the newbies to crack a joke when it got overwhelming—as long as family members weren't around, of course. The dead wouldn't care.

I chewed slowly, trying to ignore the thoughts that had been nagging at me for a week. Amber went missing the day after those mutilations happened. If this were Portland or some bigger city, those two events would seem like a coincidence. But in a town this size…every bad thing that happened seemed related.

Brandon came through the swinging doors, an order in hand. "It's starting to fill up again out there," he said, eyeing the remnants of my sandwich like a starving man.

"Take five." Gramps thrust his plate in Brandon's direction. "Have at it."

Brandon's eyes widened. "No, it's cool. I—"

"Don't waste time being coy," Gramps broke in. "Take the damn thing."

Brandon smiled and took it, almost cautiously, as if he expected Gramps to snatch it back. "Thanks."

"Guess I'm done." I crammed the remainder of bread into my mouth and dusted off my apron before heading out.

"Nova," Gramps said to my back. "Use your head."

"Always do." At least I tried like hell.

CHAPTER NINE

Brandon offered me a ride home after our shift. He drove an older silver Toyota Corolla, just the car you'd expect a cop's son to drive. Practical and economical, probably a great safety rating. The inside reeked of cigarette smoke and cheap air freshener, the kind that smelled vaguely like melons.

There was a blast of sound when he started the car. Guitar riffs on speed. A guttural voice that sounded more like a long belch.

Brandon turned it down. "You're probably not a black metal fan, huh?"

"Not really." But I used to listen to it with Alex for hours. He heard something inside the noise, something he'd clung to all through eighth grade. He told me I needed to close my eyes and keep an open mind. One day I'd hear it, too.

I never did.

"You live in Green Rock, right?" Brandon asked, inching the car back to get out of the tight spot we were in.

"Yep. On Pluto." I found the name of my street far more amusing than it actually was.

Brandon stuck a cigarette between his lips and lit up. He took a quick drag and then put his hand low on the steering wheel, letting the smoke curl right into his face. I guessed his mom didn't spend much time in his car—or around him, for that matter. My mom smoked far less than Brandon did, and I could always smell it on her.

"So, running and smoking. How's that working for you?" I asked. Then I realized how preachy that probably sounded. "Not judging. Just curious."

He shrugged, the corner of his mouth pulling up. "I like a good challenge." His right leg jiggled. "Honestly, I hate running."

"Then why—"

"Because I'm good at it." He took another drag, holding it in his lungs like he hoped it would stick. "I'm not good at much."

"I feel that way sometimes. I'm pretty good at drawing cartoon versions of people, though. And I can run really fast when a situation calls for it."

He let out a soft laugh, his free hand smoothing back his inky hair. I wondered if he was capable of sitting still. "I like to draw, too. Manga, mostly. I'm storyboarding one right now."

"What's it about?"

"A metal band made up of assassins."

"Nice."

He was blowing rings now, his lips moving like a fish. Brandon Koza was kind of a geek. Who knew?

We were stuck on Beach, waiting for a parade of tourists to cross the street. I rolled my window down, letting the fading sun warm my face. "Time to fess up. What's your deal with the cakes?"

"There's not much to tell. I went to their parties because Gabi did. I'd sit there by myself, like a chump, 'cause they wouldn't talk to me. Then they'd ask Gabi why I was so quiet."

"Sounds familiar." When me and Zach first got together,

he was more than willing to bow out of a party because he knew how uncomfortable I was around his friends. But as the summer went on, he started giving me guilt trips about it.

"You looked pretty miserable at those parties," Brandon said.

I was merely an observer, listening to Zach have conversations about people I didn't know. Share memories I didn't have. All while Amber and her friends sent me death glares and whispered to one another. "You always seemed like you were having a good time."

"After a few beers? Sure. Their idiotic conversations became comic relief instead of…"

"Needles in your eyes?"

He nodded. "They're like a fucking cult. All their inside jokes and nicknames and codes."

"God, I know. Like butter lips. What the hell was that and why was it so funny?"

"No idea." He flicked his cigarette butt out the window. "It's like if you're not one of them, you're the enemy."

"Can't argue that."

"What I don't get is Gabi doesn't even like them. I mean, she…" He trailed off.

"What?"

His lips remained parted, but nothing came out for a few seconds. "She was always complaining, you know? Talking about what dumbasses they all are. So we agreed that this year we'd do our own thing."

"What happened?"

He threw his hands up. "She just stopped talking to me. No explanation. Nothing." His face puckered, like he ate something sour. "I mean, we've been friends since freshman year, and she…"

"Completely shut you out," I muttered before I could stop myself. "You two kind of dated, right?" Sometimes they'd embrace like they were a couple, at parties and at school, but they were never "official." I always thought that was weird.

"We messed around. But…" Brandon squinted out the windshield. "It's never been more than that."

"And you want more?"

"Is it that obvious?"

I raised my eyebrows at him. "What's she like—Gabi?"

"She's… I don't know how to answer that. What's Alex like?"

He had a point—how did you begin to describe your best friend? Alex couldn't be defined by a list of adjectives. "Complicated," I said.

He nodded. "Yep."

"My friend Megan—Alex's little sister—is pretty gaga over Gabi at the moment," I said. "I guess I'd feel better if…" How did I put this in a way that wouldn't be offensive?

"You knew Gabi wasn't a total bitch?"

"Or if I knew anything about her."

He grinned, crinkling his brow at me. "You sound like a concerned parent."

"Yeah, well. Someone needs to look out for her."

Brandon puffed up his cheeks, blowing the air out slowly, as if he was trying to buy time. "She has her guard up around a lot of people, but when you're alone with her she's kind of… amazing."

I rolled my eyes. "Said like a boy in love."

His cheeks flushed a little. "All right, that was lame. She has this way of making everything seem fun, even the little things. She's daring. She got me to do things I never thought I'd do. She's…"

"The shit. I got it."

"I was going to say—unpredictable." His face grew serious. "She always keeps you guessing."

"Yeah. I know that feeling," I said quietly.

We drove over the Deception Creek Bridge. The coral sky turned the creek into liquid rust. It would be drying up soon, leaving a path that snaked up into the Coast Mountains. I'd hike it almost every summer, never fearing anything but a potential run-in with aggressive coyotes.

Now all I could think about was how vulnerable it made me.

"You got any theories on what happened to Amber?" I asked.

"Me?" His eyes flickered to mine. "Or my mom?"

"Both."

"You know, people assume we sit around and chat about cases over dinner. We don't. She's usually locked in her cave." He tilted his head and smiled. "Her home office."

"But you probably hear some things…"

His forehead creased, as if he was debating whether or not to continue. "It's tough because Amber ran away once before. There haven't been any obvious signs of foul play. She doesn't have a car. She didn't leave anything important behind—a purse, her phone, whatever. She basically just…" He rubbed his fingers together and opened his hand.

"They didn't have any luck tracking her phone?"

He shook his head.

For all we knew it was in the middle of the Pacific. Along with Amber.

"What about Zach?" I asked. "Do you know if they got anything out of him?"

"All I know is nobody saw her leave. But people said he

was there a lot longer than she was."

"Dark blue house on the left," I said as we turned down my street.

He nodded and sped up a little. "Remember how she'd go off on her dad whenever she got drunk?"

"I tried to stay as far away from her as possible."

He pulled into my driveway. "She'd go on and on about how he cuts her down. She said she'd make him sorry one day."

"From what I've seen, Amber's all talk…"

"Yeah. Seemed that way, didn't it?"

I could feel his eyes on me, waiting for me to say it.

"Do you think she's alive?" The words felt heavy on my tongue.

"I think a week is a long time to be completely off the grid."

The hiss of a metal song filled the silence between us. The volume wasn't turned high enough to hear the words or even make out a melody. It was static and drums, an erratic heartbeat.

My fingers grabbed his door handle, squeezing it harder than necessary. "Thanks for the ride."

"Sure. Give me a call if you ever need a ride to work or whatever." He dug into his baggy jean pocket, pulling out his phone. "I'll text you my number."

"No cell." I gave him my email address instead, ignoring his bewildered expression.

I always liked coming home to a dark empty house. It meant I could play my music through our home theater system at any volume and belt along. But tonight I didn't want to make a sound. I wanted to make sure every window and door was locked.

At five to nine, I sat outside on the porch steps to wait for Alex. My skin was covered in goose bumps, despite the mild breeze. There was so much I wanted to say to him. So much I was afraid to.

Mom told me I needed to make a decision right here and now. Alex was either my friend…or he was more than that.

I wrapped Alex's army coat tighter around me. Gavin continued to whimper inside, begging Mom for chocolate milk, despite throwing up everything he'd eaten today. That kid had the most sensitive stomach on the planet. Even worse than Alex's when we were kids.

I could still see Alex's face the day he walked into my fourth-grade class. It was early November, right before we were hit with this huge storm that tore the roof off Vista Pizza. I took one look at those big, scared green eyes--they practically swallowed his face back then—and that feathery blond hair and knew he'd be eaten alive.

At lunch Alex and his sister sat at my table, probably because I was the only one at it. Neither of them asked my permission or said hello, but Alex glanced at me, the flicker of a smile on his lips…as if he were saying, *we come in peace*. I didn't let myself get too excited. Sitting with me meant getting harassed by Jenika. Nobody else had stuck around.

Alex put an empty water bottle on the table, touching his fingers to the plastic. A ladybug crawled up the inside, toward the opening.

"What if it flies out?" Megan asked.

"Then we have to let it go," he said.

"But I want to keep it," she said.

"We can't. It needs food, like other bugs."

She covered the opening. "She's ours. We found her."

"How do you know it's a girl?"

"They all are." I remembered the way she looked at him, like it was *so* obvious.

"No, they're not."

She wrinkled her nose. "Yeah-huh. They're called ladybugs. Lay-dee," she emphasized for good measure.

"So?"

They debated the gender until Megan knocked her fist against the table like a gavel. "It's a girl!"

"Fine." Alex put his hands up. "What are you going to name her?"

Megan thought about this for a while. Her eyes found mine. "What do you think?" she asked me.

I froze, not wanting to come up with something dumb. "Um, Dot?" Clearly I failed.

She cocked her head, considering it. Alex gave me a real smile this time—or maybe the name amused him. That was when Jenika tapped him on the shoulder and whispered something in his ear. His eyes met mine. I felt like I might throw up.

He stared up at her, almost expressionless, and said, "That's stupid."

She sneered down at him. "*You're* stupid." Then she leaned across the table and spit on my peanut butter and banana sandwich. A big foamy wad of saliva dripped down the crust. "Eat that, Chipmunk," she said, before walking away.

I still had some baby fat, mostly in my cheeks. She loved pointing that out, especially when I smiled. I didn't stand up to Jenika at all back then. Like nearly everyone else, I was afraid of her. She had this way of finding people's insecurities. Later I realized she was going to hate me whether I kept my mouth shut or not.

"How come you're all alone?" Megan asked me. Not in a mean way. Just calling it like she saw it.

I remember Alex elbowing her and the confusion on her face. He was older than his age, in some ways. He had to be.

"I don't know." It was all I could think to say. I considered warning them about Jenika's wrath. But I didn't want them to go…

Alex picked up half his sandwich and offered it to me, wrinkling his nose. "It's egg salad."

It felt weird to take a strange boy's sandwich, but I was really hungry. "I like eggs."

His face scrunched up more. "My grandma puts pickle relish in it."

"Oh." I took a bite anyway. I wasn't that picky. Turned out I liked the relish.

Funny how Jenika brought us together and ripped us apart. But I couldn't blame her entirely, could I?

Alex pulled into my driveway right at nine, just as he'd said he would. As I got closer I noticed white scratches covering the entire length of the El Camino. Someone had keyed "Junk Me" across the hood in giant, shaky letters. But they didn't stop there. "White Trash" was scrawled on the driver's door, just under his window.

Heat rose up my neck and into my cheeks. I knew who did this.

Alex's grandpa had spent years restoring and pampering that car. It was probably his biggest pride outside his family. He'd roll over in his grave if he saw this.

Alex kept his eyes straight ahead when I got in, his mouth set in a firm line. He was dressed all in black, the hood of his Alice in Chains sweatshirt pulled over his head like it was a rainy day in January.

"When did it happen?" I asked.

"While I was at the diner."

"Where'd you park?" Nobody could key a car on the street and not be seen that time of day.

"Your lot. Didn't have change for the meters."

Our little gravel lot was hidden from everything. Definitely an easy place to vandalize a car, if nobody was out back. I hadn't even noticed the El Camino when I went out there, but I was a little distracted.

"This is all I've got left of him," Alex said, his voice soft.

The anger I felt toward him slipped away for a few seconds. He became my best friend again. The guy who just lost the only real father he'd ever had. The guy who needed me.

I touched his forearm. His muscles tensed underneath my fingers. "What about you? You're part of him." He was a lot like his grandpa, from his soulful eyes to his odd sense of humor.

He shook his head, staring straight ahead. The air inside the car was warm and thick, filled with his simmering anger. That's how it always was with Alex. When he got mad, he got quiet. Eerily quiet.

"You know it was Amber and Holly who painted that crap on my window?" I said.

"Doesn't surprise me."

"The words eat you up inside. No matter how much you don't want to let them. When I heard Amber bragging about it, God... I wanted to..." Kill her.

"I don't miss her," he said. "Do you?"

"No." My voice came out in a whisper. It felt wrong to say it. She really could be dead.

We sat in silence for what felt like minutes. I kept wishing he'd tell me what he was thinking. Look at me. Something.

"I'm ending this," he said, finally. "Tonight."

For a split second I thought he meant us, then I realized

he meant retaliating against Christian. "Let's go for a drive, okay?"

"We can't keep sitting back and…" He didn't finish his thought. "I have to do something."

"It doesn't have to be tonight."

He gripped the steering wheel. The pale skin on the backs of his hands strained against his tendons. "Christian thinks he's untouchable. He thinks he can say and do whatever the fuck he wants." His lips parted again, like he was going to say more. But he didn't.

"I'd love to hit them back—believe me. But it can't be on impulse." I stared hard at his profile, hoping to break through. "When it comes to what we have and what they have…they will always be able to hit harder. Remember?" He should. They were his words.

He leaned back against his headrest, his glare fixed toward the sky. "I'm not talking about jacking up a car, Nova."

"Then what are you talking about?"

He opened his window, draping his arm outside. The only sound was the faint hiss of the ocean a half mile away. "They're having a party at Winchester Beach tonight. Megan said Christian keeps cases of beer in his trunk. Goes back to get more as needed. Shouldn't be hard to get him alone."

"And do what?"

He turned his head, his eyes finally meeting mine. "Let him know we're done taking his shit."

"Sure. You hold him down. I'll get a few punches in. That'll do it."

"It's not just going to be us."

That nauseating feeling came rushing back again. "You can't trust her," I said through gritted teeth.

"I'm not as naive as you think I am," he said, quietly.

"Oh, you don't even want to know what I'm thinking right now." I turned away and stared out the passenger window.

"She hates Christian as much as we do. I trust that."

"She hates everyone."

He exhaled, long and slow. The moments ticked by. He was supposed to be the voice of reason here. The one who stopped *me* from going headfirst into a situation.

I wanted to tell him what an idiot he was being and get out, but I couldn't move. He had nobody to look out for him. If something happened, I'd never forgive myself.

"Let's go, then," I said, my voice tight, my heart pounding. If I stayed, it bought me more time to reason with him.

"Are you sure you want to come?"

"I said let's go."

He put the car in reverse, backing out of the driveway. We careered down my street and took a sharp turn onto Beach, the wind slapping my face through the cracked windows.

"Do you even know what you're walking into?" I gripped the cool leather seat.

"I don't care."

The coldness in his voice told me he meant it, at least in that very moment. "You will when it blows up in your face."

He steered the car to the curb, right in front of Neahkahnie Park, and cut the engine. Jenika was standing on the sidewalk, her arms folded. Just seeing her again made every muscle in my body tighten.

"Don't worry," he said, as if hearing my thoughts. "She's not going to start anything with you."

"Why? Because you told her not to? You *are* as naive as I think you are."

The only response was the sound of his breath, the tapping of the engine.

"Let this go, okay?" I said, facing him. "We have one more summer to get through. We could be out of here next year."

"I'm not going anywhere! Don't you get that?" His fist hit the door. "You think I can leave Megan? Who's going to pay the bills?"

"Alex—"

I wish I'd said something else. Anything else. We'd been planning our escape for so long, it was easy to forget...

"I can still take you home," he said. "Just say the word."

A sharp knock on the driver's side window made us both jump. Jenika peered inside Alex's cracked window, a lit cigarette dangling from her fingers.

"You going to hide in there all night?" Jenika asked, her gaze lingering on me. She was dressed like she was going into battle. A black wifebeater with matching cargo pants and a swamp-green military backpack slung over one shoulder. Her upper arms were thicker than I remembered and ropy, the kind of muscle a half pint like her could only get on purpose.

Alex pushed his door open, climbing out. I did the same. The smell of salt and freshly mowed grass thickened the air, and the sun was a hot pink ball fading into the horizon. We were supposed to be cruising down 101 right now, watching it disappear.

"Are they in?" Alex asked her.

She nodded, blowing a trail of smoke over her shoulder. "Told you they wouldn't miss this."

"Who's they?" I asked.

"Matt and Tyler," Alex said.

I leaned against the hood of his car. "Are they your buddies now, too?"

Jenika smirked. "I wouldn't say that."

"Can you give us a second?" I asked her.

Jenika gave Alex a knowing look before walking off toward the playground. Yellow tape still blocked off the swings. The plastic rattled like a bird flapping its wings.

"Don't do this," I said, keeping my voice low. I had to try one more time.

His expression softened with uncertainty. For a second, I saw the old Alex again. The guy who literally dragged me home after a raccoon nipped my finger and told my mom to take me to the hospital because he was afraid I'd get rabies. The guy who made a lockbox for our secrets and buried it deep in the ground.

"I have to," he whispered.

"*Why?*"

"What's it going to be?" Jenika asked, approaching us again. "You in or out?"

"I'm here, aren't I?" I said, folding my arms. She'd love it if I bailed on Alex. It would give her even more room to wedge between us.

She tossed her cigarette on the ground, grinding it out with the toe of her boot.

"Are they on their way or what?" Alex asked, his hands jiggling inside his jean pockets.

"They're waiting for Matt's mom to get back with the car." She gave him a rough shove, smiling up at him. "Relax. They won't stand us up."

I looked away. It was bad enough knowing they'd hooked up. Seeing her tease him somehow made it worse. He had this whole other relationship outside me now…this whole other life.

He whispered something to her before lifting himself up on the hood.

An older red Honda pulled in behind Alex's El Camino.

Matt's mom had driven that car for as long I could remember, probably since the beginning of time. I didn't know much about her other than she worked the ER front desk at Tillamook General, and she was kind. She'd given me a handful of cherry lollipops after I got my first rabies shot for the raccoon bite and told me I was brave.

Matt got out of the car and started walking toward us, his eyes hidden by that dumb cowboy hat of his. "Look who's here."

I rolled my eyes, like I couldn't be bothered.

Jenika threw her hands in the air. "Where's Tyler?"

"Grounded."

"What the hell for?" she continued.

Matt shrugged. "He forgot to recycle his Mountain Dew? Mama Bear said he couldn't come out and play." He shifted his gaze to Alex. "Can I talk to you a second?"

Alex's brow crinkled, but he nodded and slid off the hood. "Be right back," he said, lightly touching my arm as he passed.

I tried to follow, but Jenika blocked my path. "Don't mess this up for him. He needs this."

I glanced over at the guys. They were standing next to Matt's car, both tense and keeping their distance from each other.

"You've hung out what, a handful of times?" I asked. "You know shit about him."

Her dark eyes bored into me, like she could see right into my mind. "Guess he told you."

"Isn't that what you've been waiting for?"

"Oh, yeah. Because it *has* to be about you." She stepped closer, until she was inches away from me. "Don't you ever get tired of being the victim?"

"You didn't answer my question."

"Here's an answer." Her smile grew. "He doesn't disappoint."

I stuffed my hands in the pockets of my jeans, not trusting myself. My racing heart. The tension inching up my limbs. I didn't want to be one of those girls, the kind that acted like a rabid cat over some guy.

But Alex wasn't just some guy.

"If you hurt him," I said, "I'll come after you with everything I have." I regretted the words as soon as they slipped from my mouth. Backing me into a corner was what she wanted.

"You want to talk about hurting him?" She lowered her voice. "Find a mirror."

My mouth opened, but the words got caught in my throat. She pushed past me, her bony shoulder sending an ache down my arm.

I didn't say anything when Alex and I got back into his car. I tried to bite my tongue. Hold in the explosion building inside me. But I couldn't.

"Remember our box of secrets?" I asked as we continued down Beach Street. Winchester Beach was only five minutes up the road.

"Yeah."

"Remember what we promised the day we buried it?"

He glanced over at me, his forehead crinkling. "We'd never lie to each other."

I nodded, keeping my eyes on him. "And?"

"We'd never tell each other's secrets."

"I've kept my promises. Have you?"

He focused back on the road, his fingers flexing against

the steering wheel. "I try to…"

I'd seen him use this trick on Cindy. He'd become a master at it over the years. Saying what she wanted to hear, but not. I just never thought he'd try it on me. "That would be a no."

"I've never told anyone your secrets. And I never would."

"But you've got no problems talking bad about me to Jenika."

His eyes fluttered shut for a second. "What did she say to you?"

"Other than you don't disappoint?"

He sped up to catch up to Matt. "What does that mean?"

"What do you think it means?" I turned away, focusing on the ocean. The water had turned into a smooth gray blanket, matching the fading sky. Cold and surreal. Like the dead of winter. It made me want to crawl out of my skin.

"It's not going to happen again," he said.

"Why?" My voice came out so quiet I wasn't sure he heard it.

"Because…" He paused for a second. "It's not."

I closed my eyes. Could he see how it was eating at me on the inside? How much I wished I'd had the guts to tell him how I felt. "I still can't believe…"

He waited a few seconds before answering. "Is that all it is?"

"What are you getting at?" My words came out rushed.

"Nothing," he said, his grip on the steering wheel relaxing. "What else did she say?"

"That I've hurt you."

"She didn't get that from me. She decided that."

"Based on something you told her."

He looked over at me, his eyebrows pinching together. "You matter to me more than anyone outside my sister. I've never said a bad word about you."

I swallowed back the ache in my throat. Jenika's words probed at me, echoing again and again in my head. *Find a mirror.* "Why does she think I hurt you?" I was pretty sure I knew the answer, but I wanted to hear him say it.

"It doesn't matter."

"If that were true, you'd tell me."

He exhaled. "She thinks it's messed up that you hung out with Zach and them, all right? But it's in the past. I'm over it."

Was he?

"Why did you do it?" I asked. "Hook up with her."

"I was curious, I guess."

"I don't buy that." He wasn't the type of guy to sleep with a girl just to do it. It had to mean something.

He rolled down the window, sticking his hand into the wind. "I'm not like you, Nova."

"What does that mean?"

"It means…" He glanced over at me. "No matter how hard you try to hide it. There's still a part of you that needs the dream."

I wanted to argue, but I couldn't. He was right. I thought he was the same way, holding out for that special girl.

"I know you don't get why me and Jenika are friends. I don't expect you to," he continued. "But that's all we are. It was just…"

"You wanted to get laid, and you did. Congratulations." My fist clenched in my lap. This wasn't helping. The hole inside me kept getting bigger.

We passed the sign for "North" Winchester Beach. The beach was about three miles long with two main entrances— north and south. The north entrance consisted of several flights of wooden steps, leading to the sand and water below.

Large houses were perched on the hills, overlooking miles of ocean.

This was where Zach spent his summers. A three-story house with brown shingles and white trim. A makeshift garden on the balcony, his mother's obsession. I used to press my hands against the cool glass of his bedroom window, watching the sun dive into the water, while he strummed his acoustic. It seemed like a lifetime ago.

The cakes usually partied near the south entrance because it was farther from town and there were no houses nearby. That part of the beach was also hidden by a hill covered in tall grass and evergreens. A steep, windy trail led down to the water.

Matt swerved to the right, pulling onto the shoulder. We followed suit, kicking up a cloud of dirt around us. Cars lined the side of the road a couple hundred feet ahead.

"Do you regret it?" I asked. It wasn't that I wanted him to. Or maybe I did... Maybe I wanted him to feel sick inside about losing his virginity to the wrong person.

He turned the car off. His eyes combed my face like he was searching for something.

"What?" I asked.

"I regret hurting you."

Jenika and Matt emerged from the Honda, both dressed in dark hoodies with the hoods pulled over their heads. Matt grabbed a tire iron from his trunk, making my heart pound.

"This isn't you, Alex."

He yanked the keys from the ignition and pressed them into the palm of my open hand. "Stay here if you want. Take off if the cops show up."

"What are you going to do?'

He smiled a little, but there wasn't anything happy about

it. "I'm about to find out."

I wasn't a saint. I wanted to smash every window of Christian's little orange Audi, even if it was paid for and fully insured by Mommy. But my gut kept telling me we should leave. Now.

CHAPTER TEN

Nobody said a word as we walked up the road. The three of them moved like soldiers, quick steps, eyes straight ahead. A thudding drumbeat, shouting, and laughter echoed from the beach below, and bonfire smoke sweetened the air. It sounded like any Saturday night in the summer, as if they hadn't even registered that one of their own was gone. If Amber were my friend, I'd be doing everything I could to find her right now.

The summer before freshman year, Jenika, Matt, and their friends got the bright idea to crash a cake party. I heard they'd set off firecrackers, stuffed things in tailpipes, threw some bottles, and generally made a lot of noise. Then they got their asses handed to them by about twenty drunk cakes. Matt got a concussion and the start to his juvie record. The cakes claimed it was self-defense, that Matt had threatened them with a pocketknife. A pocketknife Matt swore they'd planted. But the cops didn't care—it was the word of thirty tourists against known troublemakers from the local trailer park.

As we approached the cars, Matt began looking in windows and trying doors. "Fifty bucks says one of these idiots forgot to lock up," he said.

It had to be at least sixty-five degrees out, but I felt a chill.

That itchy feeling of being watched.

Jenika stroked the shiny black hood of a GT500. "Can you imagine what this feels like starting up?"

Alex gave her this intimate smile, the kind of smile that held secrets. "You don't want a new car," he said. "It's like driving a computer." His grandpa always used to say that.

"What are you—seventy?" Matt asked, trying the handle of an Impreza. "Who cares?"

"Get into the CAN bus and you can pretty much control the car," Alex continued, peering inside the car Jenika was admiring. "Kill the brakes. Disable the ignition."

"Where'd you hear that?" Matt asked. "I-Never-Leave-My-Bedroom dot com?"

"Something like that."

"I've never heard of anyone hacking a car," Jenika said.

"The point is…it's possible." Alex moved toward Christian's car. The orange paint glowed like the harvest moon.

"Maybe you should give us a demonstration, big shot," I said. I was done listening to him try to dazzle them with crap he probably read on one of his techie message boards.

He gave me a fleeting glance, but he didn't respond. Instead, he made his way over to Zach's car—or baby was more like it. A green 1969 Mustang. It was out of commission at least half the time. Zach's mom wanted him to get something more practical, like a Toyota Prius, so she refused to pay for repairs or insurance. He got a part-time job at Guitar Center just to drive it.

Alex dug a mini flashlight out of his pocket and peered in the driver's window. "A Club? That's it?" He aimed the light inside, muttering, "How does he still *have* this car…"

"He can't afford an alarm," I said.

Jenika walked next to Christian's Audi, scratching the side with what looked like a utility knife. The *screech* made my teeth clench. "So what's the big draw with Zach?" she asked. "Is it that he's the world's biggest pussy or that he spends more time getting ready than you do?"

Before I could respond, Matt shushed us, moving his hands up and down. Female laughter echoed from the beach entrance, followed by a guy talking loudly.

Everyone ducked behind the car they were nearest to. Alex squatted behind the hood of Christian's Audi. I kept my head low and moved next to him.

Three shadows emerged from the entrance and headed in our direction. Two girls and a guy from the looks of it.

The guy made big hand gestures as he talked. I knew the voice. Christian. "His jeans are completely in flames, right? And he starts going like this." He jumped up and down, flapping his hands to demonstrate. "Get it off me. Get it off!"

"What a tool," the taller girl said. From the long waves that fell around her shoulders, I was guessing it was Gabi.

The other girl laughed, sweet and hesitant. Megan's laugh.

"Shit," Alex muttered.

They were heading right toward Christian's car. I wondered if Alex was thinking of Megan in all of this. What the cakes would do to her if he jumped Christian tonight.

"Your mom seriously wants you home by ten?" Christian asked, moving in front of them and stopping. "That's crazy. You know that, right?"

"My grandma," Megan said. "And, yeah. She's kind of… nuts." She wasn't wearing much, a blue bikini top and a short jean skirt. A far cry from her gigantic band T-shirts. She kept folding her arms over her stomach, like she was trying to cover herself. My heart ached for her.

"I can give her a ride home, if you want to stick around," Christian said.

I didn't have to look at Alex to know he was tensing. I could feel it.

"Please." Gabi laughed. "You can't walk straight, and it's not even ten."

"Yeah, I can." He held his arms out like an airplane and walked backward.

"Nice try," Gabi said, heading across the street toward her red Honda Civic. "See you in a bit."

"Come on, Megan," Christian said. "Don't go."

"Bye," she said, jogging after Gabi.

"You're breaking my heart!" Christian shouted, before muttering "freak."

He stood in the street, watching them until they pulled a U-turn and took off. Then he unlocked his car, heading for the trunk.

My hand clamped around Alex's wrist. "It's not too late to walk away," I whispered.

His answer was pulling his arm from my grasp and standing. I closed my eyes, my stomach twisting in knots.

"What the…" Christian didn't finish his sentence. "Get off me!" His words were muffled.

I straightened to see Matt gripping him in a headlock. Christian rammed his fists into Matt's rib cage, his face reddening. They grunted as their feet dug into the gravel, both pulling in opposite directions.

Alex closed in on them from the left, moving slowly, purposefully. Jenika took the right side.

They formed a circle around Christian, shoving him, punching him. The sound of their fists hitting his body was dull and hollow, hidden beneath the crunch of the dirt and sand under their shoes.

Christian covered his head with his arms, his breathing

labored. Matt threw him against the back of the Audi. The *thud* of his body hitting the bumper made me wince.

Alex pulled him up by his shirt, his features twisted in a grimace. "Was it worth it?" he asked, his voice low and hushed. "Did you have fun?"

"What?" Christian's voice came out breathless. Red blotches covered his left cheek.

Alex slammed him against the bumper again. "You're gonna pay to fix it. Every fucking cent."

Christian grabbed Alex's wrists, trying to break his grip. "Fix *what*?"

Alex clocked him hard, right in the face. No hesitation. No regret.

I thought about Christian's cruelty. That cocky, I'm-so-untouchable smile. What he and his friends did to Alex on this beach two summers ago. The way he talked to me, like I was nothing but used up meat.

Maybe I should've enjoyed seeing him this way. Wide-eyed and bumbling. Completely vulnerable. God knows, I'd imagined throttling him myself a dozen times.

But I just felt…sick.

Jenika dangled her lit cigarette over his arm. Christian sucked in his breath. "Please, don't," he said, his voice ragged, his eyes squeezing shut. Blood and snot bubbled under his nose every time he exhaled.

Jenika's eyes were like icy puddles. Dark. No depth or soul. I'd seen her angry before, but not like this. This was pure hate.

Matt stood back watching the whole thing. He had this odd smile on his face. A little fascinated. A little surprised. The kind of smile you get when you're on the edge of your seat, waiting for the other shoe to drop.

Christian fumbled in his pockets, pulling out a black

wallet. "You want money?" He tossed a couple bills at Alex. "Here. Take it, okay?"

"You think forty bucks is going to cover it?" Alex said.

"What? I don't know what the hell you're talking about!" Christian shouted.

Alex's expression twisted, like he was preparing to punch him again.

"His car," I said, approaching them. "Just tell him the truth, Christian." I was surprised how even my voice sounded, when I was shivering on the inside.

"I didn't touch your car." Christian's voice cracked. "I swear, okay? It wasn't me."

"Then who was it?" Alex asked.

"I don't know."

"Bullshit," Alex said.

Matt drove his tire iron into the top of the trunk. It sounded like an explosion, leaving a dent inches from Christian's head.

"I swear I don't know," Christian muttered, closing his eyes. "I don't know. I don't know." He kept repeating it over and over, almost like a chant.

Jenika imitated him in a high voice, getting right in his face. Every consonant sounded like broken glass. Her fingers clenched, as if she could barely contain herself.

I believed him. No matter how much I didn't want to. I could think of a couple other people who'd trash Alex's car to get him riled up, and they were standing right here. Jenika was definitely manipulative enough.

"Look at him," I said to Alex. "He'd have told you by now."

He finally made eye contact with me, a defeated expression on his face. I thought I had him. That he'd stop. But he slammed Christian against the bumper again, using his forearm to pin him down. Christian jerked against him, punching, struggling to take a breath.

"You're the trash," Alex whispered through his teeth.

I grabbed his arm, pulling with all my strength. My nails dug into his skin, hard enough to draw blood.

Alex tore himself from my grasp and backed away, running his hands through his hair. His arms shook; every part of him seemed to shake.

The only sound now was Christian's fast, wheezing breaths. He moved away from the Audi, reaching into his pocket.

Matt pushed him back again. "Where're you going?" He stuck his hand inside Christian's jean pocket and pulled out a phone. "You don't need this." He tossed it behind him.

"What the fuck do you want?" Christian's chest heaved up and down, and his eyes watered.

"You guys made your point," I said. "Let him go."

"So he can go call the cops?" Jenika asked. "You're here, too. You're part of this."

It didn't matter if the cops had proof of us being here or not. They'd take one look at Christian's face and bust us, no questions asked. But we couldn't hold him hostage here forever…

Alex was pacing, walking around in circles, fingers curled at his sides.

"Take your clothes off," Jenika told Christian. "Now."

Christian didn't ask why or even hesitate. Maybe he'd given up. Maybe he'd stopped thinking all together. He just started stripping down, until he was in his boxers.

"Everything," Jenika said. "Start recording, Matt."

Christian's hands hovered over the waistband of his boxers. This time he asked why.

I wanted to know why.

"I think you know," Jenika said.

Christian's eyes flitted to Alex, his body shivering. He

looked so pale. So small. Matt walked toward him, holding his phone out and smirking at the display.

"Are you stupid?" Alex hissed. "Turn that off."

Matt raised the tire iron in the air, as if letting us know he was in charge. "Do it," he said to Christian.

Christian slid his boxers off, covering himself with one hand. His breath came out in short, thick bursts.

"You remember this part, right?" Jenika asked Christian. "This is where you say 'I'm a little bitch. A white trash piece of shit.'"

Christian didn't respond. He kept staring at the ground.

"Say it!" Jenika said. She looked over her shoulder at Alex then. He stood there like a stone. He didn't even blink.

I knew I should've been doing something. Trying to stop them somehow. But I couldn't move. I could barely breathe. Was this what Christian and his friends did to Alex? Did they make him say those things?

Christian repeated her words, his voice barely audible.

"We can't hear you," she said.

Christian's face crumpled like a wet dishrag. "I'm sorry, okay? I'm sorry."

Jenika laughed. It was bitter. Vile. "No, you're not."

The two of them stared each other down for what felt like forever. Every muscle in my body tensed.

"Say it."

He said it again. Louder this time. His lips curled up into a snarl. His hands balled up in tight fists.

"How's it feel?" she asked him, her voice oddly calm.

"What?" he muttered.

"How's it feel to have no idea what happens next?"

He didn't answer, but I could see the realization in his eyes. He didn't know how far they'd go.

Neither did I.

Alex kept his head down, his eyes closed.

"Turn it off," Jenika said to Matt. Then she walked up to Christian and kicked him right between the legs.

He collapsed to the ground, on his knees, buckling over. His naked back shivered in the dim light of the moon.

Jenika stood over him, her stare cold. "Tell anyone about this, and I'll make sure that video gets sent to everyone you've ever known." She picked up his jeans and threw them at his head.

He clutched his jeans, his breaths still fast, panicked. We left him there. Crumpled. Broken. Alone.

didn't say anything. Alex didn't say anything. We just got in the car and started driving, the hum of Alice in Chains in the background.

Acid was gnawing at my gut, inching up to the back of my throat. "Take me home," I said. I didn't look at him. I couldn't.

"I'm sorry," he said.

Sorry. Sorry like Christian? "For which part?" My voice came out low and choked.

"All of it."

Was he?

"I didn't know that was going down—the video," he continued.

"Is that what the cakes did to you?"

He inhaled sharply, but he didn't speak. Seconds passed. It felt like hours. I didn't want to hear what came next. It hurt too much to imagine him like Christian, beat down and terrified. Made to say those things, for all to see.

"Yeah," he said, his voice barely above a whisper. "Only they held me down and ripped my clothes off. It was Christian and two older guys. Amber just stood there and watched."

I squeezed my eyes shut, the pressure unbearable. I couldn't hold it in anymore. He was so quiet back then. So skinny. So unseen. "Why didn't you tell me everything? Let me help you?"

Every time I asked for details he said he didn't want to talk about it. He was embarrassed, didn't want to relive it. I respected that. But now... I wished I'd pushed. Maybe we wouldn't be here like this. Maybe he wouldn't be a stranger.

"I didn't want..." He paused. The car accelerated. "I didn't want to give you another reason to feel sorry for me."

I finally turned toward him, my eyes hot with tears. "I don't feel sorry for you!"

"Yes, you do."

My mouth opened, but nothing came out. Maybe I was overprotective sometimes. All I ever wanted was to make things better for him. To see him happy.

"Is that why you went to Jenika instead? Told her everything?"

He rolled down the window, draping his arm over the edge, feeling the air through his fingers. "It came out."

"Yeah? Clearly it came out to the wrong person."

I took in his hard jaw. The way he stared at the road, so intense. As if it might swallow him.

"You scared me tonight." I watched the lights blur by as we drove down my street.

"I'm so fucked up right now." He slowed in front of my house and stopped. "Sometimes I feel everything. Sometimes I feel nothing. Sometimes...I don't want to be here."

I didn't know what to say. I didn't know what to do. "I want you here."

His eyes shut. "I don't want to keep hurting you."

"What are you saying?"

"You can't help me, Nova." He hesitated. "I know you want to, but you can't."

I held my breath, fighting the urge to scream. "What a bunch of defeatist bullshit."

"Nova…" he said.

I got out and slammed the door shut, making his window rattle. If I looked back, I may not have had the strength to walk away.

And I needed to walk away.

SUNDAY, JUNE 29

It takes a long time to strangle someone, even with their hands tied behind their back. Minutes seem like hours. She almost broke away and, for a second, I almost let her.

Then I heard your voice, reminding me again and again.

She is not a victim. She is not

CHAPTER ELEVEN

There was blood on my hands. I scrubbed until my skin was red and raw, but it kept pooling inside my palms. I needed to get it to stop. I needed to get help. But my body was weak. Numb. I could barely take a full breath.

Then I woke up, my skin clammy, the bitter taste of nausea in my throat. Rays of sun blasted through the gaps in my curtains, a harsh reminder.

Last night happened.

A siren wailed in the distance. Other sirens joined in soon after, dozens of them coming from different directions. Long and mournful. Jagged and staccato. It seemed like they went on forever, fading away and getting louder again.

My chest went heavy with dread, and it felt as if ants were skittering down my arms and legs. The only time I'd heard that many sirens was when that ten-car pileup happened on Highway 101. It was a couple years ago, when we had a freak snowstorm right before Christmas. At least a half dozen people were ejected from their cars and lying on the icy pavement.

The house was so quiet I could hear the walls settling. It was after eight. If Gavin were here, he'd be in my room by now, yelling at me to get up. When that didn't work, he'd grab food from the fridge and stuff it under my covers. Usually I had to babysit him on my days off, but Mom always tried to give me at least one Gavin-free day.

I actually wished she hadn't picked today.

The doorbell rang, sending a jolt down the back of my neck. It was followed by four meaty knocks, the sound of someone who wanted to make sure they were heard.

What if Christian went to the cops? I remembered him telling Zach once that there was nothing more lowly than a rat.

I scrambled out of bed and ran to the living room, peering through the cracks in our blinds. What I saw in our driveway was almost as bad as a cop car—Zach's green Mustang. He wasn't one to rise before nine—unless he got hungry. And it would take a hell of a lot for him to show up here.

I moved in front of the door, pressing my hands against the chipping white paint. "What do you want, Zach?"

"To talk."

"About?"

"Just open the door." His voice sounded somewhere between commanding and pleading. "It's about Alex, okay?"

My heart jumped a little in my chest. Christian had to explain how he got beat up somehow. If he wanted retaliation, I was the easiest target. He knew Jenika hated me. And *she* had the video.

I looked out the peephole. Zach was the only one standing on my porch, his nose oddly elongated through the glass. "You'll have to wait a minute," I said.

I took that moment to peek out the living room window again, as well as the windows in our small den. Both gave me a good view of the front yard, his car in our driveway, and our porch. As far as I could tell, he was completely alone.

After throwing on jeans and a T-shirt, I finger-combed my tangled hair into a ponytail. I'd never been one to doll up for guys, but I did for Zach when we went out. As if straightening my hair and wearing retro sundresses and red lipstick actually changed how he saw me.

I opened the front door a crack, enough for him to see a sliver of me. His eyes were bloodshot, and his lips were pale. Even his golden-brown skin lacked color.

"You look like shit," I said.

"Yeah." He pulled his elbows closer to his body, as if he was freezing. "I feel it."

He didn't look like someone hell-bent on revenge. He looked scared shitless.

I opened the door to let him in, and he took a hesitant step inside, taking a few seconds to move past me.

My stomach used to flutter every time I saw him. His long, tangled hair always damp from surfing. That gentle smile.

Now the only tug I felt was regret.

He smelled how I remembered—like the lemon-scented body wash he always used. It was this expensive aromatherapy stuff his mom bought.

I directed him to our old white leather couch. The bright rays of sunlight showed every crack and stain. I couldn't help but feel a little shame…everything in his house was pristine.

"What about Alex?" I asked, sitting on the brown recliner next to the couch.

He leaned forward, clasping his hands and studying my face. "He beat the shit out of Christian last night."

I swallowed back the tightness in my throat, trying not to let my expression falter. "Is that what Christian said?"

"He won't say who did it."

"Then how—"

"Yesterday, in the diner, Alex looked him right in the eye and said he was going to fuck him up."

My thumbs traced circles against my jeans. "That's talk. Not proof." But there *was* proof.

He squinted at me before looking away. "I saw him with Jenika a few days ago. When did that happen?"

"A while ago, I guess." The words came out muted. I wasn't even sure he heard me.

But he nodded slowly. I could see his wheels turning.

"He's going through a lot right now. His grandpa just died. He's…" I trailed off, realizing I sounded like Zach. Listing excuses for my friend's asshat behavior. But I still had this need to protect Alex. I didn't know if it would ever go away.

"He's got serious problems," Zach said.

"You want to talk about serious problems?" I asked. "Let's start with what Christian and *your* friends did. Making him say those things. Videotaping him."

"What things?" His voice rose. "What video?" He and his parents were in Mexico that summer, and he'd always played it like he knew as much as I did. But I wondered if that was even true.

"I don't know what happened that night, okay?" he continued. "Believe it or not, I don't know about every fucked-up thing Christian does."

"But you're his loyal lapdog."

He turned away then, his forehead tensing. "Look, I know you hate me—"

"Then why did you come here?"

"I should've told you the truth. I know that," he mumbled.

"The truth?"

He stared hard at his clasped hands. "My mom found out we spent the night together. She said I couldn't see you anymore."

"Or what—she'd take your car?"

His eyes shut, and the muscles around his mouth tensed.

"That's it? You dumped me for a *car*?"

"It was more than that. A lot more."

It was getting harder to sit still. "Are you going to tell me?"

"You wouldn't get it." His voice was low. Bitter. "You never did."

"That's such a cop-out!"

"I don't live in a trailer. I have two parents. I don't have real problems, remember?"

He used to complain that his parents were on his case, about his grades, his lack of interest in college—even his hair. It was hard to turn that voice off in my head, the one that said he didn't have actual problems. If he wanted to go to college, it was all paid for. He could try it out. See if it was for him. No years of paying off student loans.

One time I got mad enough to tell him just that. I felt bad and apologized later, even told him I didn't mean it. But I did…

"You don't get to do this," I said. "You don't get to make yourself the victim here."

"Wouldn't dream of it. I got nothing on poor little Alex."

"We're talking about me and you. What does he have to do with it?"

He shook his head, his lips stretching up at the corners. As if he was in on some private joke. His finger ran along the leather arm of the couch, slow and deliberate.

"You told everyone I slept around." My heart pounded as I spoke. "Do you have any idea what I've been through because of you?"

"You really think that was me?" He paused for a moment.

"Of course you do."

"You took my virginity and dumped me the next day. Why the hell not?"

His eyes combed my face. "Everyone said you were cheating on me with Matt."

"And that makes saying those things okay?"

His face scrunched up. "It doesn't matter anymore. This isn't why I came here."

I waited for him to continue, but there was nothing. Just the ringing in my ears. The hum of the water cooler in the kitchen.

"I think Amber's dead," he said, finally, his voice tight. "But nobody will admit it. They keep making excuses. They keep saying she ran away."

"And you're sure she didn't?"

He paused, his fingers gripping the couch arm. "I know her. She would've been back by now."

My thoughts exactly, I wanted to say. But was that what he wanted to hear? I'd be holding on to any hope I could find.

"I heard you guys had a fight at the party." I kept my tone gentle, unassuming.

"And?"

"What was it about?"

"That's between us." He looked away, his eyebrows pinching together.

I knew that expression. It was the same one he got every time he saw me after we broke up.

"Alex was there that night," he said. "Amber was yelling all this crap at him. She wouldn't stop…"

"So?"

He was completely focused on me now. "The timing of it all is…interesting."

Zach became convinced that Alex wasn't right in the head within minutes of meeting him last summer. He kept insisting that Alex was obsessed with me, that one day he was going to snap. I'd told him to knock it off or we were done.

"It's also *interesting* that you and Amber had a fight right before she disappeared," I said. "Look, I heard she was really drunk. If she went off on her own... A lot of things could've happened."

"If it was an accident, she would've turned up by now."

"Maybe... Maybe not." I wanted to say something reassuring. But what? Some people got swept out to sea and never came back. Some people walked off the beaten path and got lost, forever.

Zach shook his head, his mouth tensing. "I got an email last night, telling me to *watch my back*. I'm guessing it was from Alex?"

"He wouldn't be dumb enough to threaten someone in an email."

"You sure?" His gaze turned hard and accusing. "He threatened Christian in front of me and Gabi."

It was still their word against Alex's. Sending an email, even anonymously, was undeniable proof. You might as well have written the threat on paper and signed it, unless you really knew how to cover your tracks. Which Alex did...

"I know you're freaked out," I said. "But—"

"Freaked out?" he snapped. "I don't sleep anymore, Nova. I get in my car and drive around all night, every night. I don't know what the fuck else to do."

I took him in again. His hungry, red-rimmed eyes. His hair, caked and ragged with yesterday's gel. As much as I wanted to hate him, I couldn't.

"Why do you think Alex sent it?" I asked.

"Who else would send me that?" His dark eyebrows rose. "Besides you."

"Watch your back" was something Matt said. And he was definitely the type to act first and think…never. But as far as I knew, he hated the cakes in general. Why target Zach specifically?

"Forward it to me," I said.

"Why?"

"Because I might be able to help you figure out who sent it." A lot of email programs still displayed the sender's IP address in the header—you just had to know where to look. It was how I figured out who some of my anonymous email senders were. Sometimes it was as simple as a Google search.

Zach studied me for a few seconds, suspicion written all over his expression. "You know it was Alex."

"I don't know anything until I see proof. You gonna send it or not?" I stood to get my laptop.

"Fine." He dug his phone out of his jean pocket.

I was almost out of the living room when I heard a murmur from him. It wasn't a word or anything recognizable. Just a noise that came from his throat.

He was staring at the display on his phone, his expression contorted. At first I wasn't sure if he was about to laugh or cry. Then he looked up at me, the muscles in his face going slack.

"Is this a joke? What is this?" he asked.

A chill spread across my skin. I moved back toward him, my steps small and hesitant.

He dropped his phone on the coffee table, like it was contaminated, and hunched forward, his hands braced on his knees.

I knelt down, wincing as the wood floor creaked loudly underneath me, and picked up his phone.

The picture on his display was a jumble of color at first.

White. Red. Varying shades of gray and brown. It took me a few seconds to register what I was seeing. A face as white as paper. Half-open eyes rimmed in black. A crimson smile with dagger-sharp edges.

Dark, jagged lines stretched downward from both eyes and stopped about midcheek, resembling mascara streaks.

It was definitely a girl. The clown makeup didn't hide her delicate features or the roundness of her jawline. She was lying on what looked like wet sand, her tangled hair spread out like a fan above her head. One hand was next to her face, palm facing up, fingers slightly curled.

Amber's name was at the top of the message window, as the sender. My heart thudded in my ears.

"Tell me I'm hallucinating. Tell me that's not…" Zach's eyes squeezed shut.

The artificial light hitting her skin and the grainy background told me the picture was taken at night, probably in complete darkness. The color of her irises was too washed out to define, but the whites of her eyes glowed against the black paint on her lids.

I recognized that stare. It was like looking into the eyes of a doll. You couldn't fake that kind of emptiness.

I took a deep breath, trying to slow my heart, stop the buzzing in my extremities.

"I put my phone on silent last night. People wouldn't stop texting," Zach said, running his fingers back and forth through his hair. "Why the hell did I do that? I shouldn't have done that."

I put my hand over his—it was even colder than mine. "Go to the cops and show this to them," I said, keeping my voice steady. "Now."

He didn't answer. His eyes were wide and staring, like he

was seeing me…but not.

I pressed the mail button on his phone and forwarded the picture to myself. There was still a chance this wasn't what it looked like. Blowing it up on a bigger screen would at least give me a better idea.

Then I remembered those sirens when I woke up. Those sirens that seemed to go on forever… What were the odds?

"She's dead. She's really dead," Zach muttered.

Dread tightened my throat. "What time did you get that threat last night?"

"I don't know." He stood up, scanning the room like he expected something to jump out at him. "I don't know," he repeated under his breath.

I pressed his mail button on the toolbar and scrolled through the dozen emails he'd gotten in the last twelve hours. The sixth message down was from "I.M. Nobody" with the subject line "Hey Coward." I opened it up to see WATCH YOUR BACK written all in caps.

"I have to go. I have to get out of here." Zach dug into his pockets, pulling out his keys. He ripped his phone from my grip. "What are you doing?" His voice was sharp, accusing.

I stood slowly, keeping my eyes on his. "I'm trying to help."

He stared back at me like a cornered animal, clutching his phone so tight his knuckles were white. His nose wrinkled. "You'd defend him no matter what, wouldn't you…"

"Alex didn't do this."

"You're as fucked up as he is," he said through clenched teeth. He turned and bolted then, slamming the door behind him.

I didn't know how long I stood there, in the middle of the living room, just breathing. My mind kept telling me this wasn't real. It couldn't be real.

The phone rang, loud and shrill, making the lump in my throat ache even more. I ran toward the kitchen.

"Hello?" I answered. My hand shook so much I nearly dropped the receiver.

"Nova." There was an anxious edge to my mom's voice. "They found a body at Winchester Beach this morning," she continued. "People are saying it's that girl—Amber."

I squeezed my eyes shut, not hearing the rest of what she said. Winchester Beach. The place I was hours before. The place where my best friend assaulted someone. The cops would be gunning for anyone and everyone who was there last night.

"I don't want you going out alone, okay? Even walking to the diner," Mom said. "Not until they've figured out what's going on."

"Oh, stop, Angela!" Gramps yelled in the background. "You can't keep her locked up in her room."

"Dad…" Mom said.

"She's not much safer at home," he continued, his voice getting closer. "Especially with those crap locks you have."

I was hearing their words, but I couldn't process them. This was really happening. Amber was murdered. *Murdered.*

"Put Gramps on the phone," I said. "I need to talk to him."

"Oh, hon, don't let him scare you—"

"Mom, put him on." If I told her what I saw on Zach's phone, she'd go into a full panic. Right now I couldn't even calm myself down.

There was a rustling noise as Mom passed the phone to Gramps.

"What's going on?" he answered.

"Have you been listening to your scanner? What are they saying?" The words tumbled out. My mouth was so dry I couldn't swallow.

"Far as I can tell, it's a homicide. Sounds like the body might've been staged, but people are saying a lot of things right now."

I kept seeing her eyes. Eyes as dead as the January sky. "I saw it."

"What do you mean you saw it?"

"Zach got a picture." My breaths were coming out shallow and fast. "On his phone. He was here, and we were talking and—"

"Hold on. Why was he there?"

I told him everything I could about Zach's visit—except the part about what happened last night. I didn't want anyone to know about last night.

"Gramps, he's talking crazy. He seriously thinks Alex is behind this."

Gramps blew out a dismissive breath. "Well, I wish him luck with that. He's the guy in Amber's life—yeah? They're going to be a lot more interested in him."

"You should've seen the look on his face. He was terrified."

"I don't care what he *looks* like, Nova. I care that his girlfriend just turned up dead. Stay away from him."

I used to think I was damn good at reading people, even people I'd never met. One time I went through my mom's yearbook and accurately described 99 percent of the students just by their picture. The look in their eyes. Their smile. The way they held their head. Every detail gave them away.

Yet the two guys I'd let closest to me, the two people I trusted the most outside my family, managed to betray me. And I never saw it coming.

"I've gotta get back," Gramps said. "Are you going to be okay until your mom gets home?"

I still had the shakes, and the lingering smell of Mom's

coffee was making me sick. But it was Sunday morning. There was no way my mom or Gramps could leave the diner without causing mass chaos. "I...yeah."

Alex. I needed to warn him about Zach. But I didn't want Gramps to go. My fingers gripped the phone tighter.

Mom's voice rang in the background, loud and anxious. "I'll give you a call a little later and check in," he said before hanging up.

I dialed Alex's number, my fingers going faster than my brain. I actually had to *think* about the last four digits—I couldn't remember if it was 3756 or 5637.

"Nova?" he answered, as if he were waiting for me.

"Amber's dead." It came out just like that. I didn't know how else to say it. "Someone killed her."

He didn't respond for a few seconds. Long enough for me to wonder if he was still there.

"They sent the picture of her body to Zach, from her phone." I swallowed, closing my eyes. "And they sent him an email, telling him to watch his back."

"How do you know that?"

"He came by here this morning..."

There was more silence on Alex's end.

I ran my fingers back and forth over my scalp. I had to say it. Get the words out. "He thinks you did it."

"What? Why?" Finally there was some emotion in his voice—something that told me he was still in there.

"Because he's crazy? I don't know! We need to get our story straight," I said, my words coming out fast. "If Christian talks..."

"He's not going to talk." Alex sounded so sure of himself, as if he had Christian under lock and key.

"His friend was *murdered*. Everything is different now."

My heart was starting to pound again. I stood and paced around the kitchen.

"Nothing matters to that guy more than his ego."

"That's not exactly convincing me, Alex."

"Look…" His voice softened to a whisper. "I'm not going to let this land on you. If last night comes out, tell the cops I made you go with us. Threatened you if you didn't stay quiet. I'll back you up."

"And help Zach convince them you're a psychopath? There's no way I'm saying that!"

"They need some kind of evidence, Nova. I didn't send him any email. And I sure as hell didn't kill her. So there isn't any. I dropped you off, I went home, I went to bed. Megan was up—she saw me."

I slumped against the fridge, letting it hold me up. "I don't know what to do…"

"Just take a breath," he said, his voice calm. How could he sound so calm? "We don't know what they're going to find. They might not even need to question us."

"We'll tell them we just drove around. It's half true."

"You don't have to lie for me. I lost it last night, okay? That's on me."

My eyes burned, but I held my breath, fighting the urge to cry. "Megan needs you. Your grandma needs you. You just got that job…"

There was no response on his end, not even a breath. I waited a few seconds. And then a few more. The ticking in my head kept getting closer, louder.

"You should talk to Megan," he said, his voice barely above a whisper. "She misses you."

"I can't. Not now." She'd sent me four emails since I found out about Jenika, asking if I was okay, if I wanted to talk. I hadn't answered one of them. I didn't know how to answer them.

"Do you want me to come over?" he asked.

I kept my eyes shut. "No."

There was another long pause before he said, "You know where to find me."

Something resembling "yeah" came out of my mouth before I hung up.

I sat down at the kitchen table, rocking and counting the scratches and chips in the wood. Gramps swore by saying the alphabet backward in his head. He said it made him think instead of feel.

I couldn't even get past "*T*."

stared at my in-box for at least a half hour, wondering if I'd ever have the guts to open that picture. I'd seen pictures of dead bodies before, plastered to the pages of a homicide investigation textbook I'd bought at a library sale. They were strangers who lived and died long before I was born, their eyes crossed out with black bars. It was easy to look at their bodies clinically, how they were killed, the evidence left behind, even the position they were found in. How all of it led to their killer.

This was Amber, a girl who spent her last day acting ugly, like she had a lifetime to make up for it. A girl I hated with every inch of me. I kept hearing her sneering voice, calling me Diner Skank.

It would be easier if I thought of her like that. An evil villain in my life. Not a real person. But she *was* a real person.

I double-clicked on the attached image in my email, my breath stuck in my throat. Her chipped, chrome nail polish caught my eye first. I remembered how her nails looked that last day I saw her at the diner, all shiny and meticulous.

Now those leftover specks of silver gnawed at my gut. Maybe because they were remnants of who she was, always so self-conscious, so put together. She'd never be put together again.

Her skin didn't even look real, moonlight pale and as smooth as a mask. Her drawn-on mouth was different up close, more of a brassy red, like ketchup. One corner went up higher than the other, forming a crooked smile. All of the lines painted on her face were broken and hasty, like they were created by a five-year-old.

Her lips were slightly parted, but the space between them wasn't completely dark. I zoomed in close, my heartbeat thumping in my ears. There was something partially blocking her front teeth, a sliver of purple.

I'd bet my hands it was a foxglove.

Cold raced underneath my skin until it consumed every inch, until my toes and fingers went numb. I wanted to be wrong about that deer being the beginning of something. God, did I want to be wrong.

I could already hear what the locals would say. They'd blame it on a drifter, some *outsider* who deserved to be hunted down and taken out like a rabid coyote. Hell, if it had to be someone, I wanted it to be an anonymous psycho, too.

But this didn't feel anonymous. It felt close and suffocating, like a warm, unwelcome whisper in my ear.

Most of us were warned about foxgloves as kids, the elegant, vibrant flowers that grew along the beaches and in the woods. Look…but don't touch. We all heard the tale about the young girls who used them to make "fairy stew," hoping it would give them magical powers.

Instead, they never woke up.

MONDAY, JUNE 30

You don't know it yet, but I'm taking everything away from you. One day soon you're going to wake up and your life, your whole big bright future, will be gone. I will never forgive you.

CHAPTER TWELVE

All day at the diner, people said her name in whispers and hushed voices. As if it were disrespectful to say it out loud. As if she'd come back from the dead and haunt them.

A couple photographers on their honeymoon found her. They were probably taking pictures of the morning sun hitting the waves or kissing like fools. Now they had to live with that image for the rest of their lives. Just like I did.

Local stations were spinning a different headline every news hour. *Missing Teen Found Dead on Oregon Coast. Medical Examiner Confirms Amber Connelly Strangled.*

They think she was killed sometime early Sunday morning. The thought made me crazy—where was she for the last week?

They called her a bright girl who wanted to be a Broadway singer. Her friends said she was known for her big voice, but she had an even bigger heart. The latest update online quoted her friend Holly Chapman. "She was my rock. She was my best friend."

Only "good" girls were murdered, if you believed the TV—which most people did. In a day's time, Amber had become a saint, like every other pretty white girl who turned up dead. Maybe some of them *were* saints. But Amber wasn't. She was the one who laughed the loudest at every insult. The one who earned Alex's trust and lured him to the beach that night.

I didn't know how I was supposed to feel, but I couldn't forgive her just because she was dead. Maybe that made me a bad person.

She sure as hell didn't deserve this, her last moment captured and shown to the world, her face drawn on like she passed out drunk at a party. That sloppy red smile was there every time I closed my eyes.

Gramps, Mom, Gavin, and I were huddled around our dinky kitchen table, everyone but Gavin picking at our undercooked pizza crust. Vista served two kinds of pizza— doughy or burned. Tonight was our family night, one of the few nights none of us worked at the diner…or ate food from the diner. Sometimes we'd play poker. Sometimes we'd watch a cheesy movie just to make fun of it. An obnoxious amount of laughter was guaranteed.

Not tonight.

The six o'clock news was on, and they were talking about Amber again. They hadn't really ever stopped.

An image of Steve De Luca filled the screen. The Inn at Emerald Cove sign towered behind him, the cursive green lettering demanding attention. He was dressed in a suit, his salt-and-pepper hair slicked back. A lot of women in town gushed over his blue eyes, but I found them cold. Predatory.

He probably did everything he could to set this interview up. A few tourists were already packing up and leaving, running back to cities where murders were a weekly or daily event. But as Gramps said, the rules were different in someone else's backyard.

"We're a small community," Steve said. "A lot of us knew Amber. She was a friend of my daughter's."

She hated your daughter, I wanted to scream as he went on to express his condolences to Amber's family.

"Emerald Cove has always been a very safe place," he continued. "We watch out for each other here. I know this tragedy will make us stronger and more vigilant. In turn, Emerald Cove will be safer than ever, for residents and visitors."

Translation: Stay put and keep spending your money, tourists. We'll do our best to make sure you don't get murdered.

They cut to a Neahkahnie County Sheriff spokesperson, a younger guy who looked a little awkward in front of the mic. He squinted in the sunlight, as if he'd been locked in a dark room all day.

"Can you tell us if this is a random act?" a reporter asked.

"We're exploring different options. That's all I can say right now."

What kind of answer was that? You explored college options. Job options. Not murder options. Clearly they had nothing.

"Is this connected to the recent animal mutilations in the area?"

"That's a possibility we're looking into." No, it was a certainty.

"I wish you'd turn that crap off," Gramps said, looking in the direction of our TV in the living room.

"I wanted to see if the news had any updates," Mom said, as the tip line flashed on the screen.

"News? That's not news." His bushy brows furrowed. "That's a goddamn made-for-TV movie."

Gramps had been anti media for as long as I could remember. "Sensationalism keeps us neutered and spending," he always said.

Mom shut her eyes. "Dad…"

"Hey, Grandpa?" Gavin asked. He was practicing the dovetail shuffle with a deck of cards.

"Don't *dad* me. If you want to know what's really going on, go outside!" Gramps spread his arms wide. "Take a walk. Look around. Listen."

Mom let her fork fall against her plate. "With a psycho out there? Great idea."

"Grandpa," Gavin said louder. "Watch."

"It's broad daylight right now," Gramps said. "You think someone's gonna chase you down the street with a chain saw? You watch too much *news*."

A small part of me wanted to laugh, but I couldn't. It didn't seem so ridiculous now. Not after everything I'd seen lately. I was starting to question everyone's sanity. Even my own.

"I'm glad you can shrug this off," Mom said, her eyes meeting mine.

I knew what she was thinking. It could've been me. She kept asking questions about Zach, if he had a temper, if he'd ever made me feel uncomfortable.

I'd heard the cops already questioned him extensively. They weren't officially confirming that email threat he got, but it didn't matter. Everyone around here knew. People thought it meant he was next, but that didn't make much sense to me. It was kind of hard to kill someone when you gave them and the cops plenty of warning.

"I'm not shrugging anything off," Gramps said. "But I'm going to trust my gut and my own eyes and ears."

"And what's your gut telling you?" I asked.

He pushed his unfinished plate away. "They took a picture of her and sent it to her boyfriend. Come on. This wasn't a random act."

"Grandpa!" Gavin pounded the table, making my entire

body jerk. He was like an angry bee constantly *zzz*-ing for attention.

"Okay, show me," Gramps said.

Gavin attempted a shuffle, but the cards erupted from his fingers, scattering across the table and onto his lap.

Gramps quirked an eyebrow. "Keep practicing."

"They had her phone," I said to Gramps. "It wouldn't be hard to figure out who her boyfriend was."

"Well, not too long ago, we kept our phones at home and our private matters private. I forget sometimes." He shook his head. "I ever tell you about the Seaside Strangler?"

"Dad," Mom said, her eyes flitting in Gavin's direction. *Not now*, she mouthed.

"Give me a break," he said.

"He's eight years old—" Mom began.

"But not too young to watch the news?" Gramps broke in with a half smile. "If Eric had his way, he'd send the kid to school in body armor."

"This is my house, and that's my son. Do you get that?" The loudness of Mom's voice made us all freeze.

Gramps's lips parted. "Angela…"

"No, I'm done talking about this," Mom said, grabbing her plate and standing. "You had your way. I have mine. Deal with it."

They'd had this argument before. Many times. Gramps thought Eric was trying to make up for Jenika by "sanitizing Gavin's childhood," as he put it. Mom would get irritated and brush him off, but she'd never reacted like this.

Gramps stared down at the table, his forehead creased. Gavin watched Mom rinse off dishes, his hands frozen on top of the cards. The TV got louder by the second, until it seemed like the male announcer was screaming in my ear. I kept hearing the word "body," over and over.

I needed it to stop.

"Gramps," I said, swallowing the lump in my throat. "Feel like going for a walk?"

"Actually, I got something for you," he said. "Need your help setting it up."

Now seemed like a weird time for a present. I glanced over at Mom, who shook her head.

"You should *not* have spent that much money," she said.

"Then you can pay me back," Gramps barked at her, before getting up and motioning for me to come outside with him.

Gramps pulled a large box from the passenger side of his aging Dodge pickup. Digital Security System was spelled out in block letters across the sides. He shoved the truck door shut with his foot.

I rushed over, sliding my hands under one end of the box. A lifetime of physical work had pretty much worn out his back—he was *not* supposed to be lifting anything heavy. Luckily this box was a lot lighter than it looked.

"This must've been insanely expensive," I said, helping him set it down on the front lawn. Phrases like "long range" and "night vision" told me it was at least a couple hundred.

"Have you and your mother ever heard of a thank-you?"

Gramps had this habit of spending money he didn't have on us. It was hard not to feel guilty. "Thank you, but—"

"But I didn't have to. I know, I know. Let's move on." He grabbed his toolbox from the truck and took out a box cutter. "Now you can set these cameras to record only when motion is detected. That way you're not wasting a bunch of space on the tape."

"You mean the SD card?"

"Whatever." He sliced open the box and started pulling out Styrofoam. "I'll let you figure out how it works." He winked. "I'm here to make sure you don't destroy the house installing the cameras."

Normally I'd give him a shove or tease him right back, but I couldn't even manage a smile. Gramps was doing what he did best, trying to create normal out of chaos. But there was nothing he could say or do to take away the constant hum under my skin, this feeling that it wasn't going to be okay.

"If that *admirer* of yours comes back around, he'll be in for a nice surprise," Gramps said.

God, those letters. I hadn't even thought about those letters. They seemed so unimportant right now, like ancient history. "Yeah…" I carefully unwrapped one of the two cameras.

"Your mom told me what those kids wrote on your window last week," Gramps continued. "You guys have been needing this a long time."

"Amber did that." The words came out before I could stop them. "The night before she…went missing."

The two vertical lines in Gramps's forehead deepened. "How do you know it was her?"

"I overheard her bragging about it, in the diner bathroom."

"Did you confront her?"

I shook my head, and his expression softened. I knew what he was thinking—if the cops found out, *I* might be a suspect. Actually it wasn't a matter of if, but *when*. Someone would tell them. They probably already had.

The words of the instruction manual blurred into gibberish. "Seeing her like that. I just… I can't get it out of my head."

"It's a whole different ball game when you know them. Doesn't matter how you felt about them." Gramps got a faraway look in his dark eyes, the one that said he had a story to go with his words. There were parts of his past he didn't talk about, and we knew better than to ask. All we knew was he'd gotten into trouble when he was young. Enough to make a career in law enforcement pretty much impossible.

"How long did you look at that picture?" Gramps asked.

"Way too long," I muttered, assembling the receiver, a remote, and power cords on the grass. "I sent it to myself... from Zach's phone."

"Well, that's insane."

I met his gaze. "You would've done it."

"Yeah." His dark eyes bugged out. "And I'm not sane."

My fingers dug into the cool grass. "She had a foxglove in her mouth, like that deer. I'm almost positive."

"I don't doubt it. You live this long, history repeats itself. This whole situation is familiar."

"The Seaside Strangler?" I asked.

He nodded. "Some of my first cleaning jobs. He started with a couple stray cats and then moved right on to people. Four young women up in Seaside, all in one summer. Their bodies were always staged in public places. Always with a ribbon tied around their necks. And..." He glanced up at me, his lips remaining parted.

"I can take it..." Could I?

"Well, their eyes were cut out. Real hack job, too."

"Jesus." The pizza I ate was burning a hole into my stomach.

"I wasn't gonna mention the eye thing in front of Gavin, by the way. I'm not *that* bad. Anyway, the ribbons around the victims' necks were different colors. Any guesses why?"

I picked up the receiver to the security system, pushing

different buttons. Red lips and black tears. That was all I could see right now. "Each color represented something about the victim?"

"It was their favorite color."

"So he knew them." Or watched them enough to figure it out. My mind went back to those letters I got, all in purple envelopes. *My* favorite color. A chill ran up my arms.

"These women had no known connection to one another," Gramps said. "Two were tourists from different states. One worked at an ice cream shop in town. And the last one was a drifter, homeless."

"Did he stalk them first?" The humming in my hands and feet was worsening, turning into a full-on vibration.

"Good guess, but no. He approached them when they were alone and struck up a conversation. He came off harmless, like any young schmuck trying to pick up girls. But he always worked one question in…"

"What's your favorite color?"

"Nope. He'd ask them out. If they turned him down…"

"He asked them what their favorite color was," I finished. Talk about rejection issues.

Gramps stood, motioning toward his truck. "Let me grab the ladder."

"I can get it," I said, scrambling up and following him.

He waved me off. "I'm not paralyzed."

"At least let me…" He hoisted the ladder out of the truck bed before I could finish. I tried to grab the other end, but he jerked it away as we headed toward the entrance of the house.

What the Seaside Strangler left behind was violent and messy, all about shock value. Same with the beheaded deer in the park.

I didn't see any of that red-hot rage in Amber's picture.

Her pose was almost ethereal, like a princess in a fairy tale washed ashore, waiting for her true love's kiss. The only horror was painted on her face.

"The way they left Amber was so different than the deer," I said.

He carefully leaned the ladder against the house. "I think we're dealing with someone young. They're not quite sure what they're going for yet. Which is good—because they probably left all kinds of evidence behind. The Seaside Strangler was only eighteen—and sloppy as hell. But we didn't have DNA testing back then."

"Do you really think it was someone she knew?" That *I* knew.

"I think it's a good possibility." He kept his gaze on me. "Which is why I want you to be real careful who you hang around with. Especially that ex-boyfriend of yours. Innocent or not, I don't trust that spoiled little putz one bit."

"He thinks Alex killed her, remember? We won't be talking."

"Come on." Gramps backed away from the ladder and squinted up at our roof. "We're talking about a kid who's made it his life's mission to save Fido and Bambi."

I closed my eyes, swallowing back the truth. I hated lying to Gramps more than anything, but telling him what happened Saturday night meant I had to explain Alex's behavior. I couldn't.

"Those rich nitwits can point fingers all they want—it's what they're best at. But at the end of the day, they need real proof. And they got nothing." Gramps gave my shoulder a rough squeeze.

Sweat was forming down my back, the kind that made me weak all over. I was surprised he couldn't hear my heart pounding.

"Have you heard a lot of people making accusations?" I asked.

"Pretty much what you'd expect around here. The locals are saying something bad walked into town—some of them are looking hard at Zach. The out-of-towners are saying it's someone who knows the area well."

"Some of those *out-of-towners* know it pretty well, too."

Gramps nodded. "Yeah, well, people believe the truth they want to believe. There was a fight over at Emerald Market earlier—you hear about it?"

I shook my head. That would require having talked to someone outside family and customers today.

"Some tourist started mouthing off to the cashier about how unfriendly we are here. He said something to the effect of we probably killed that girl for kicks. Bill Johnson was behind him, three sheets to the wind, no doubt—invited him to take it outside."

"Oh God." At first glance, Bill Johnson came off like any other grumpy old man, a little underweight and slightly hunched over. But the two things he loved most in life were beer and using his fists, and he wasn't giving up either any time soon.

"So, the tourist apparently shook his head at Bill and laughed. Finished paying for his stuff and headed outside. Well, Bill goes after him, taps him on the shoulder, and gets him right between the eyes." Gramps chuckled, shaking his head.

"And this is why nobody respects us," I said. "We've got way too many Bills in this town."

"Some of those wealthy, so-called educated people do a lot worse. I've seen a few of their closets." He jerked his head toward the house. "Where should we put these cameras?"

I didn't want to think about installing cameras. I wanted to build a fort with boxes and branches, like Alex and I used to, and assume the duck-and-cover position. "One above the entrance, the other above my bedroom, facing the backyard?"

"I like that plan," he said, watching me expectantly. "Sun's going down soon. Better get to it."

"Do you think—"

"No more talk about that girl. It does you no good to focus on it 24-7." He gave me a gentle shove toward the parts lying in the grass.

"I have no idea what I'm doing, Gramps."

"I know. Isn't it great?"

Did he really expect me not to think about Amber? She was with me every time I took a breath, every time I glanced at the stringy clouds in the sky. She'd never feel air in her lungs again. She'd never see another sunset. At some point early Sunday morning, when I was under a heap of covers, safe and warm, she simply stopped existing because someone wanted her to.

called Brandon a half hour before sunset and asked him if he wanted to hang out. I didn't tell him I wanted to go to Winchester Beach. Or that Alex kept calling and it was getting harder not to pick up the phone.

But I did tell him one truth. I didn't want to go out alone.

"Uh, sure," he said, sounding confused. "What do you want to do?"

"Find some answers."

"Okay?"

I had a feeling if I was too specific, he'd say no. "You coming or not?"

He sighed. "I'm pretty sure I know what this is about, but what the hell... See you in a few."

He pulled into my driveway fifteen minutes later, fast guitar riffs echoing out his open window.

"Where to?" he asked as soon as I hopped in the passenger seat.

"Winchester Beach."

He huffed, rolling his eyes. "Of course. You know it's still closed, right?"

"North Beach, too?"

His forehead scrunched up. "Why do you want to go there?"

"Because there's that little trail that connects the two."

He backed out, shaking his head. "Pretty sure they've got most of that closed off, too."

"I'll make do..." I didn't have a plan exactly, other than trying to quiet these thoughts in my head. How Amber disappeared without anyone seeing her. How they might've gone about dumping her body—it wasn't exactly an easy place to access. I figured maybe just being there, seeing the place in the light of day, would give me some ideas.

"Are you expecting to find something the cops didn't?" Brandon asked.

"There's just a lot that doesn't make sense to me."

We stopped at a red light, and he dug out a cigarette. "Why do you care so much? It's not like you two were friends."

I focused out the window. An Emerald PD car was pulled over on the other side of the road, lights flashing. Bube was out of the car, harassing a couple local guys. I didn't know their names, but I'd seen their faces around school. I was pretty sure they were in Megan's grade.

"Zach was at my house when he got that picture of Amber," I said.

"Shit. Did you see it?"

I nodded. "Can't get it out of my head. They had to get her down to the beach, pose her—at some point draw her up like a clown. They probably did that part before."

He made a left on Beach. "If I got something like that, like of Gabi… I'd probably be thrown in the crazy house. I don't know." A burst of air came from between his lips. "There are some things you can't unsee."

I didn't want to tell him I'd sent the picture to myself. Or that I'd looked at it again and again, because I couldn't *not* look at it.

"I told Zach to go to the cops," I said. "Haven't seen him since…"

"From what I heard, he hasn't left his house." The smell of the ocean filled the car, a mix of salt and sulfur—the sulfur was extra strong today. "Do you think he killed her?"

I opened my mouth and closed it again. His question caught me off guard. I couldn't tell from his tone if he was curious or if he actually suspected Zach. "He can't even kill a spider."

He exhaled a laugh. "I don't think he did it." There was a certainty in his voice, like maybe he'd heard things from a really good source. "Serial killers stage bodies like that. Zach doesn't seem like the type."

"Organized serial killers," I clarified. The type that plans every detail. Makes it harder than hell to catch them. "You're right—planning isn't Zach's thing."

Brandon turned into the deserted North Beach parking lot and pulled into a space facing the ocean. Most of the parking lines were faded and covered in sand. Usually this lot was filled with cars facing every which way, anywhere they could squeeze in.

"What now?" Brandon asked.

"Follow me," I said, getting out.

I scanned the mansions perched on cliffs around us—that was a lot of people who could see what was going on down here. If the killer had half a brain and didn't want to get caught, they wouldn't use the North entrance to kidnap someone or dump a body.

High tide was in, and the waves were high and furious, a low roar vibrating the ground beneath us. I headed down the winding wooden staircase until we reached a trail. One sign directed us toward the beach, and the other pointed to the left. SOUTH BEACH 1M.

I made a left, walking into the shadows of trees. The bottoms of my shoes sank in the wet dirt and crunched on fallen leaves. God, I missed this. I hadn't gone running in days.

We walked for quite a while before I broke the silence. "Have you ever been on this trail?"

He lit another cigarette and blew a trail of smoke away from me. "A few times. Not in a while—too many crowds."

"Yeah. Same here." Like most of the beaches around here, sleeping or camping on Winchester Beach wasn't allowed—but that rule was rarely enforced. "Makes me wonder how they did it without being noticed. I mean, there's always a few people who crash on the beach all night when the cakes have a party."

"Not anymore," Brandon said. "Mom started kicking them out by two a.m. at the end of last summer. They were getting too many complaints about people showing up first thing in the morning and…finding them."

"Huh—is that why they hate you?"

He smiled a little. "Probably a big reason."

"And you know for a fact she's still doing this?"

A squirrel ran across our path, zigzagging into the bushes.

"Every night in the summer. The cakes know if they're not long gone by two, they're getting busted."

That followed the timeline well. Amber's body was dumped in the wee hours of Sunday morning—assuming she was killed first and then dumped. Usually the "planning" type didn't kill in the same place they dumped the body. Too much evidence.

"Why doesn't she just come earlier and bust them?" I asked. "She's gotta know there's a ton of people getting wasted."

He took another drag. "And how would they haul them all in? Besides, their parents would bail them out and complain about the hassle. She'd get shit from the city council. Gotta keep our bread and butter happy. Make sure they have a good time."

I shook my head. What must it be like going through life and getting all these allowances? Zach never even seemed to be aware of it. But Christian knew *exactly* what he could get away with.

"Anyway," Brandon continued, "she sends patrols out to get the ones who try to drive home drunk. But…they can't get them all."

"No, they can't," I muttered, spotting a barricade as we rounded a corner. Crime scene tape, telling us not to enter, was stretched between two tree trunks. There was a narrow path just behind the barricade that led back up the hill, toward the street. It wasn't a real path exactly. More like a hidden, poorly maintained shortcut. Footprints in the mud, human and animal. Flattened shrubbery. "You know where that comes out?"

"The midpoint between the two beaches, I'm guessing."

That path could answer either of my questions, maybe both. If Amber walked out this way, it would've been pretty easy to grab her, force her up the path—if they were strong or had a weapon. But why would she have come all the way out here by herself?

The path looked pretty steep, and it was full of roots.

"Think you could carry a body down that?" I asked.

"Sure, if I had Hulk strength."

"Exactly." Carrying a body down there might not be impossible—but it would be very difficult. Still, it seemed like the most protected way in and out of here. The cops obviously thought so, too.

"What now, Detective Morgan?" Brandon asked. "You wanna search the ground for trace?"

I elbowed him. "Shut it—this isn't a joke."

"I know. Just thought we could use one right now."

"You sound like my gramps." The sun was almost set—soon we'd need flashlights to see. Who knew if they had patrols coming around? Getting caught snooping was the last thing I wanted. "We should head back."

"You get any of your answers?" he asked.

"Not really…"

"No offense, but maybe you should let the actual cops handle this from here on out."

"You're probably right." I kept my focus on the path ahead of us, my thoughts racing again. Amber went missing after a party on Saturday night. Then her body was dumped after a different party on a Saturday night. Same place, same people. Probably not a coincidence.

If I were going to dump a body, I wouldn't do it on a weekend night at the most popular beach in town. Unless I knew the place would be cleared out by 2:00 a.m. That wasn't something a random outsider would know—I lived here and I didn't even know about it. And Amber probably didn't just go wandering off by herself. Her going missing made a lot more sense if she was lured away by someone she knew.

But how?

As we were getting into Brandon's car, an engine came roaring down Beach, sounding like it was doing about eighty. It was Christian's orange Audi, coming from South Beach. He slowed as he passed the parking lot, almost like he was going to come to a stop. My breath caught in my throat. But then he gunned the engine again and took off, tires screeching.

Dread filled my stomach.

TUESDAY, JULY 1

My mom used to walk into the ocean at night, far enough to feel the waves crash into her body. She'd open her arms wide, close her eyes, and pray for it to take her to a better place. She said she'd never felt so alive. So pure.

I tried it tonight and stayed there until my legs went numb, waiting to feel something. But there was no moment. There was just cold and darkness and salt water burning my nostrils and throat.

CHAPTER THIRTEEN

Two detectives showed up at my house first thing the next morning. Mom shook me awake, still wearing her robe, her expression puckered and concerned. I shouldn't have been surprised. But I was.

And completely unprepared.

"Just be polite and give short and direct answers," Mom whispered, as I scrambled into a pair of jeans and threw a dirty T-shirt over my head. "Don't fidget."

"Mom, please. You're making this worse." I combed my hair with my fingers. The mirror reflected a tired and faded version of me. A little more pale. Shadows under my eyes.

A cold sweat broke out across my skin, and nausea hit me, sharp and hard. I held my breath, closing my eyes. What if they asked me about Saturday night? These weren't small-town cops busting grannies with pipes in their glove boxes — Emerald Cove PD couldn't handle a case like this on their own. They could probably smell a lie on me before I said it.

"Want some water?" Mom asked, rubbing my back.

I shook my head. I didn't want to risk having anything in me to throw up.

"Want me to tell them you'll be a few minutes?"

"I want to get this over with."

After giving my teeth a quick brush, I exhaled, slowly, and walked toward the living room. My thigh muscles quivered like they did after too long of a run. Mom guided a sleepy Gavin into the kitchen.

Two men in button-up shirts and ties sat on our white leather couch. I wasn't sure what to expect—I'd only seen detectives on TV. These guys looked like any Joe Smith in an office building. One had gray hair and smiling eyes, like someone's grandfather. He probably *was* someone's grandfather. The other was rounder and much younger—no more than thirty.

The younger detective took a sip from Gavin's yellow hot chocolate mug—probably the first thing my mom grabbed out of the dishwasher. He had a notepad in his lap, and he was already writing something down.

"Nova?" the older detective asked. He gave me a polite smile, but his eyes went straight to my clenched hands.

"Yeah." My voice came out as a squeak. I took a seat in the brown recliner that was Eric's favorite place when he was home.

"I'm Detective Hahn from Neahkahnie County," the older one said. "This is Detective Sandoval from OSP."

He went on to mention Amber and something about being here to gather information. Mostly I heard my heart. Fast, heavy contractions getting louder by the second.

"Thanks for getting up to speak with us," Detective Hahn said. "I know it's early, huh?"

I nodded, trying to smile a little.

"Are you willing to answer some questions?" he pressed.

"Sure."

Mom padded around the kitchen, opening and closing cabinets. Not so slyly listening in. Gavin kept whispering to her.

"Did you know Amber Connelly?" Hahn asked.

Obviously they knew the answer or they wouldn't be here. "Yeah. But not well."

"Did you ever hang out?" Detective Sandoval spoke for the first time, an analytical glint in his dark eyes.

"Not really. I mean, I saw her at parties last summer. She comes into the diner I work at sometimes. Came…"

"The Emerald Spoon?" Sandoval asked, writing again.

"Yeah." Of course they knew that, too. They probably heard all kinds of things about me.

"What about Zach West?" Hahn asked, tilting his head. "Do you know him?" His eyes weren't smiling anymore.

"We dated last summer."

"Do you still talk?" he continued.

It was hard to swallow. Maybe I should've taken that water. "He comes into the diner, too. We say hi… That's about it."

"So you're not friends?"

"No."

Sandoval kept writing, writing, writing. He pressed hard into the paper. The sound was quick and jagged. Accusing. I had the urge to tear the pen out of his hand.

"Zach said he dropped by here last Sunday morning," Hahn said. "Is that true?"

My nails dug into my lap. "Yes."

They waited, probably expecting me to say more. I'd read somewhere they liked to keep their questions general and conversational at first. People talked more when it didn't *seem* like they were being interrogated.

"Was it just to say hi?" Sandoval asked, his lips turning up a little.

I wasn't going to bring up Alex's name. Not until I had to.

"He got this anonymous email. He thought I might know who sent it."

"Do you?" Hahn asked.

"Like I told him—no. I offered to help him find out, though."

Hahn glanced over at Sandoval, and Sandoval shook his head slightly. What the hell did that mean?

"Do you remember what you did Saturday, the twenty-first?" Sandoval asked.

That was the day I'd woken up with "whorehouse" on my window, courtesy of Amber. The day Alex fought with Matt. "I worked most of the day…"

"What about that night?" he pressed.

It seemed like a million years ago. "I came home from work about five. Me and my mom watched *Freaks and Geeks* on Netflix." I also went for a run and thought up creative ways to get back at Amber.

"So you were home all night?" Hahn asked.

"Just went for a half-hour run around seven."

"What about last weekend?" Sandoval's voice was too high, too casual.

I swore I could feel my heartbeat in my toes. If I lied and Christian talked, we'd look guilty as hell. They had to have seen his face, asked him if he'd been in a fight. But if he'd told them the truth, wouldn't they have busted us by now?

"Worked most of Saturday," I said. "Then I went out with my friend Alex. We…drove. Around." I'd done it. I'd just dug my own grave.

Sandoval's dark eyes flickered up to mine. "Alex Pace?"

"Uh-huh." They'd probably already spoken to him. That was why he kept calling yesterday. I should've answered or at least checked my email last night.

Detective Hahn looked at my lap. My fingers were laced together so tight they ached. I flattened my palms against my jeans.

"Did you drop by the party at Winchester Beach?" Hahn asked. "Last Saturday night," he clarified.

What do I say? What do I say? Alex wouldn't admit to what we did, not unless he had to. I needed to choose my words carefully. Really carefully. "We drove around the area, but we didn't go to the party."

My shirt clung to my sweaty back. My neck itched, but I didn't want to scratch it. I didn't want to move.

"So, that's all you did?" Hahn asked. "Just drove around... all night."

"No. Alex dropped me off pretty early."

"What's early?" Sandoval asked.

I was starting to get dizzy. "Like eleven."

Sandoval stopped writing. His full attention was on me now. "He have other plans?"

"No. I wasn't feeling well."

Neither of them said anything for what felt like forever, their expressions blank sheets of paper. If they knew I was lying, they would've called me on it by now. Right...?

"Do you remember the last time you saw Amber?" Hahn asked.

Every second of it. "She and her friends came into the diner Saturday morning—on the twenty-first. I waited on them."

Detective Hahn nodded and stared at me, like he was expecting more. Sandoval was still focused on his notepad.

More silence.

"We heard there might've been some kind of confrontation between you and Amber that morning," Hahn said. "Can you tell me about that?"

Sandoval was watching me now, his eyes narrowed.

"Um…" I licked my lips. "I overheard her talking about me to someone on her cell—"

"Where was this?" Hahn asked.

"The diner bathroom. I was in a stall. She was by the sink." I went on to tell them exactly what I heard her say. "Then I came out of the stall and looked at her. She turned and left."

"There was no exchange between you at all?" Sandoval's brow was furrowed, a cynical expression on his face.

"I think she cussed when she saw me. But that's it. I didn't say a word to her."

"Why not?" Sandoval continued. "If someone did that to me, I'd have something to say."

Because sometimes silence scares people even more. Bad answer. "It's my family's diner. I was on the clock. She's a customer."

"Did you contact the police about the vandalism?" Hahn asked.

I shook my head. "When I saw it, I wanted it gone. And I figured there wasn't much they could do. It would've been my word against hers, right?"

Neither of them answered.

"Is there anything else you want to share? Anything you think would be helpful?" Hahn asked.

"No. I…" My tongue stuck to the roof of my mouth. "Like I said, I didn't know her that well."

Everyone went quiet again, Hahn watching me, Sandoval scanning his notepad. Gavin kept whispering the same question in the kitchen. *Is Nova in trouble?* Mom shushed him every time.

I wanted to ask them if I was a suspect, but I kept my

lips pressed together. They hadn't accused me of anything yet. Asking that might make me sound paranoid...or guilty.

"Okay, Nova. We appreciate your help," Hahn said, reaching into his pocket. "If you think of anything else—something you forgot to mention—give us a call, okay?" He handed me his business card.

Detective Sandoval stood and dug one out for me as well. He gave me another nod and thanked me as I took it from him.

Gavin bolted into the living room then, staring up at the detectives like they were a fireworks show. His mouth hung open a little. "Are you really police?"

"Gavin," Mom said, grabbing his shoulders and trying to turn him around. "Back in the kitchen."

Both detectives grinned.

"We are," Hahn said, his eyes crinkling at the corners. "Promise."

"Is my sister in trouble?"

I gritted my teeth. *Shut up, Gavin. Just shut up.* They both glanced at me, but they didn't say anything.

Mom laughed. "Sorry."

"No worries. It happens," Hahn said.

"Have a good day," Sandoval said, reaching for the door.

As soon as they left, Mom wrapped her arms around me. "You okay?"

"Did I seem nervous?" I asked.

She pulled back, studying my face. "Everyone gets a little nervous in those situations—they know that." She rolled her eyes. "I kind of froze up, too. It's intimidating, you know?"

"What'd they ask you?"

She gave my arm a squeeze. "Just if I knew where you were and what you did the last two weekends. That kind of thing."

"What did you say?"

Her eyes widened. "Pretty much what you said. It's the truth, isn't it?"

I ran my fingers through my hair, grabbing the sides of my head. I needed to find the phone and call Alex. If they hadn't talked to him yet, they were probably heading over there now.

"You told the truth, right?" Mom asked again.

I nodded, moving away from her. "I—I have to..."

"Nova—what's going on? What aren't you telling me?"

"Nothing." I did my best to keep my voice calm. "I wasn't expecting them to show up so soon. It freaked me out."

"I know—this whole week has been a lot to take."

"I'm going to lie back down for a while. I didn't sleep well."

She eyed me with suspicion, but she said okay and herded Gavin back into the kitchen. She wasn't going to push things in front of Gavin, but I knew she wasn't done with me.

I grabbed the portable phone from her bed, dialed Alex's number, and locked myself in my room. It seemed to ring and ring.

"Please be home," I muttered. "Please."

"Hello?" Megan answered, sounding confused.

"Hey, you," I said.

"Why are you calling so early?" Now she just sounded pissed. I wanted to tell her I was sorry, that we'd talk soon, but there was no time.

"Is Alex there?"

"He's asleep."

"Can you wake him up, please? It's an emergency."

"I doubt that."

My hand balled up into a fist. "Megan, I—"

"Hold on." There was a rustling sound, followed by

footsteps walking away from the phone and a muffled knock.

It seemed like a million years went by before Alex picked up.

"Hey," he said, his voice low and scratchy.

"Have the cops questioned you about Amber?"

"No. Why?"

The breath I was holding poured out. "They just came by here and asked a *lot* of questions. Can you meet me?"

"Where?"

"The Rainbow Creek Park. Where the picnic tables are?" It was nice and hidden, but there were always parents and kids there in the mornings, which made me feel safer.

"Okay. See you in a few." He hung up.

I opened my window and climbed out. Otherwise, Mom would insist on driving me and I'd have to explain why I was meeting Alex in a park all cloak-and-dagger-like.

Alex was sitting on top of a table, facing the creek. The hood of his black pullover concealed his eyes, but I knew he was watching for frogs, a habit that never really went away. He used to give people tadpoles as gifts, thinking they'd enjoy raising them as much as he did.

I was wrong about people being here. It was completely dead. Eerie quiet, actually.

I slid in next to him, resting my feet on the mossy bench, but not as close as I usually would. There was this invisible line between us now. It didn't feel right to cross it.

"Hey," he said, keeping his focus on the creek.

I did the same. It was better that way. "The cops asked me what we did Saturday night. If we dropped by the party."

"What'd you tell them?" If he was nervous, his voice didn't show it.

"That we drove around. You dropped me off around eleven…"

He stayed quiet for a few moments. Long enough to make me uncomfortable. To wish I could be inside his head.

"I'm sorry I put you in this situation," he said.

"And I'm sorry I went. But it's kind of late now." My fingers gripped the edge of the table. "They had to have seen Christian's face. Asked him what happened."

"Obviously he lied."

"Or they're seeing if we lie."

He turned my way, finally making eye contact. "Why would they waste time playing games like that?"

"To give them reason to hold us? All they need is Jenika's recording to prove we were there."

"We weren't even on that."

"Your voice was. You told Matt to turn it off, remember?" Goose bumps erupted across my skin. I ran my hands up and down my forearms. "Think about it. They're looking for people with motive. We've got plenty of that, especially if Zach told them…what they did to you."

"You think he'd rat out Christian?"

"I don't know…" Normally I'd say not in a million years.

"You're overthinking this. Even if Zach tells them about that—why would I kill her and just beat Christian up?" He rubbed his palms against his shredded jeans. "She was killed a few hours before her body was found, right?"

I nodded, her blank stare flashing in my mind again.

"Where did I keep her all this time—my closet?" he asked.

Lying made me paranoid. Maybe I wasn't thinking rationally. But Emerald Cove was a desperate town—nearly all of us depended on tourists to keep roofs over our heads. The cakes were probably going stir-crazy locked away in their "Secured by ADT" fortresses. Everyone wanted someone to blame *yesterday*. And the low-hanging fruit would do just fine.

Alex, Jenika, Matt, and me—they didn't even have to reach for us.

I closed my eyes, taking in the hum of the creek. It seemed to reverberate around us, getting louder and softer again. I wanted to ask him if he was as scared as I was. But I doubted he'd tell me the truth.

Two ducks squawked and batted each other with their wings. Alex grabbed a Ziploc filled with bread crumbs out of his pocket and tossed a couple at them. There was a time he never left the house without bread crumbs. But that was years ago…

"You think Zach could've done it?" he asked.

"No," I said quietly.

"You sound sure."

"I saw his face when he got that picture. I've never seen anyone so scared." I couldn't imagine anyone I knew doing this, not even Jenika. I was pretty sure *I'd* be first on her list.

"I can't make sense out of that threat he got," I continued. "Why warn him ahead of time? Why send something the cops can easily trace back? Even if you use a public computer— there are cameras. Witnesses."

"You're assuming they have half a brain."

"Well, they kidnapped a girl, killed her, and staged her body without getting caught."

"Touché." He tossed a few more crumbs at the ducks. "They could've used something like Maze."

He'd told me about Maze a few times. It was software that allowed you to be anonymous on the internet by bouncing data from server to server. Supposedly, it was near impossible for even law enforcement to trace you.

"Or maybe Zach sent it to himself so he could go crying to you about it," Alex said. "Isn't that why he came over?"

I shrugged. It was easier than saying, *He wanted to talk about what a psychopath he thinks you are.* "He knows dick about computers. The cops would've figured that out by now."

He stuffed his bag back into his jeans pocket. "He could've had someone else do it."

"Maybe." I glanced over at him. "What about Jenika or Matt?"

"They wouldn't send an *anonymous* email. They'd just go after him."

My heart beat a little harder; heat rose into my cheeks. "Right. I forgot. You know them so well."

"I never said that," he said.

"You sure think you know Jenika. But do you? Really? Would you trust her with your back turned?"

Alex stared at the bread crumb he was rolling between his fingers. "She didn't kill Amber."

"Did I say she did?"

"I know you've thought about it."

"Then you know shit." I pressed my lips together. "Do you guys actually have real conversations or do you just…"

"I told you—it's not going to happen again." He touched my hand that was clutching the table, his thumb brushing across my skin. My fingers went slack, and my jaw quivered.

"Where's my coat?" he asked after a minute. Like we were us again. Like everything was fine.

I ripped my hand away, balling it in my lap. "I'm not saying I think she killed Amber. But what makes you so sure she didn't? It could be anyone."

He peeled off his hoodie and ran a hand through his hair, smoothing it back. "We live in a cramped-ass trailer park. We're all up in each other's business, whether we want to be or not."

"I'm well aware."

"Then you know Jenika couldn't have stashed Amber any more than I could."

But there were other places. Emerald Cove was at the base of the Coast Range, miles of untouched forest. Miles of places to hide anyone or anything. Still, that involved a lot of hiking in rough terrain. There were several abandoned buildings in town, including the Pacific Sunrise motel, but the homeless had taken those over.

If I were going to hold someone hostage, I'd want somewhere hard to find with no nearby neighbors or major roads.

"Why would she go after Amber, anyway?" Alex continued. "It's Christian…" He trailed off, raking his hand through his hair again.

"It's Christian what?"

"Nothing," he muttered.

I remembered the way Jenika looked at Christian that night, like she wanted to set him on fire and watch him burn. And the way she spoke to him, every word clipped and through her teeth. It was as if the rest of us weren't there.

Alex tossed his pullover into my lap. I threw it back.

"Come on," he said. "I know you're freezing your ass off."

"What did he do to her?"

Alex flicked his last bread crumb toward the creek, his jaw tense, his eyes focused on some invisible thing in the trees.

"The same thing he did to you?" I pressed.

He shook his head, but there was no change in his

expression. Nothing that told me I was right. "It's not my story to tell."

Maybe it wasn't. But I hated that he wouldn't tell me. "Guess you need a new box of secrets."

"Nova…"

"Save the explanations, okay? I get it."

"No, you don't," he whispered.

"You should go," I said, sliding off the table. "Those cops will probably be at your house soon, if they aren't there already."

He sighed before grabbing his skateboard and jumping to the ground. I thought we'd say our good-byes and that would be it, but he reached for me instead.

"What?" I took a step back.

He took two steps forward, this weird intensity in his green eyes.

I took another step away. And then another.

His lips turned up a little.

I bumped into the trunk of a Douglas fir. "Thanks for the warning."

He closed the distance between us and pressed his hoodie against my chest, his gaze never leaving mine. "I want this one back."

"Alex, I—"

"Just take it, all right?"

I gave in and slipped it over my head. It smelled like he hadn't washed it in a while. Soap, rain, and grass mixed together. A little smoky, too. It hurt in the worst possible way.

He lifted his hand, like he was going to touch me, but then he lowered it again. "I'll walk you out."

Neither of us said another word after that, even when it came time to go our separate ways.

FRIDAY, JULY 4

You're right about people. Be the person they want you to be and they'll believe anything you say. It's a rush having this secret, seeing everything going on and knowing you caused it. It's a lot like being God.

CHAPTER FOURTEEN

The Fourth of July sneaked up on me this year. Usually there was a buildup, a change in everyone's mood in the days before. They'd get bolder. Louder. Just like the illegal fireworks our normally quiet neighbors set off every year, waking me up out of a dead sleep for a week straight.

Sunburned tourists would fill the sidewalks, all in a hurry to get around one another but going nowhere. The air smelled like charred meat and sunblock, making it hotter, more suffocating. And, like magic, the ever-present low clouds gave way to a sky so blue it would make Smurfs jealous.

This year the Fourth looked like November. Gray skies. Empty streets. Only the air was thick and muggy, clinging to my skin. Forecasters were talking about thunderstorms tonight. A freak thing around here, especially in the summer.

But what about this summer had been normal?

The diner had been deserted most of the day, our only customers locals who whispered to each other in quiet voices. Some of them were saying it was probably the "boyfriend" who did it, that they weren't going after him hard enough because of who his parents were. And others, like me, felt like it was only the beginning of something. This wasn't just a guy getting pissed at his girlfriend and going way too far.

Megan came into the diner with Gabi around four, right as my shift was ending. They huddled together in a booth whispering, like they'd been best friends for years.

"Hey." I gave Megan a nod, but she avoided eye contact. Guilt swelled inside me. "I'm sorry I haven't written you back yet—things have been crazy."

She shrugged, still looking at her hands. "It's fine."

I wanted to say more, but I could feel the heat of Gabi's stare. Maybe she was judging me. Maybe she wasn't. But this wasn't a conversation I wanted to have in front of her.

"What can I get you guys?" I finally met Gabi's gaze.

"Two chocolate milkshakes," she said, handing her menu to me.

"Taking a walk on the wild side?" I asked. She'd yet to order anything with an ounce of sugar in it.

She shrugged. "Why not?"

"Any chance we can get these on the house?" Megan asked, finally looking up at me, her eyes hopeful.

"Uh…" If I said no, she'd be even more pissed at me than she already was. But I didn't want her to think it was cool to extend those free meals to Gabi.

"It's okay," Gabi said, smiling at Megan. "You know I got you."

Megan mumbled a "thank you," as if she was ashamed, and I felt even worse. "I'll double the chocolate," I said, before giving Megan's shoulder a squeeze and walking away.

About five minutes later, Christian and a guy with a blond fro I'd seen around but couldn't name showed up and invited themselves into Gabi and Megan's booth. Dread welled up inside of me. Christian hadn't come around here since that night, and I didn't think he would. No cake had set foot in here in days.

I wanted to run over there and grab Megan, get her away from whatever venom would come out of his mouth. Instead he gave her a flirtatious smile and asked her what was up, like she was one of them and this was any other week.

"Your brother's not here, is he?" Christian asked, making a show of looking around. "Last time he tried to run me over."

"My whole family is crazy," Megan answered. "I wish I were adopted."

They all laughed, and she joined in, not seeming to grasp that they were laughing at her expense.

I scrubbed hard at invisible dirt on a table two booths away. Sure, Alex was probably shutting her out, too. She had every right to be pissed at him. But he was still her brother. You didn't sell out family—not without a real good reason.

"How crazy is crazy?" Christian asked, his voice turning serious.

I held my breath. The reason for his friendliness toward Megan was painfully clear—he was pumping her for information.

"Crazy like a bad country song," Gabi said with this all-knowing tone, like she had a clue. As if, in the very short time they'd been "friends," she'd earned the right to comment about Megan's family.

"My grandma does three things," Megan said. "Drinks, bakes, and talks to herself."

I turned, glaring over my shoulder at her. Her eyes met mine for a quick second before she went on. "My mom's a junkie. She's probably dead." She tried to laugh, but it got stuck in her throat and came out choked.

Everyone got quiet. Even Christian. His mouth hung half open. Megan had always been a bit clueless socially; it was why she never had many friends. But she never brought up her mom to anyone outside Alex, even to me.

"Seriously?" the guy with the blond fro asked.

Megan shrugged and looked down then, as if finally realizing she'd gone way too far.

"What about your brother?" Christian asked. "Does he talk to himself, too?"

I straightened then and looked directly at him. He stared right back, his jaw tensed, his knuckles banging against the table.

I hadn't slept through the night in days. I was waiting for the cops to come back, accuse me of lying about that night.

"Maybe we should change the subject," Gabi said, catching my gaze. I turned my attention to a newly vacated table behind me.

"What's his deal with Russian Roulette?" Christian asked, louder than necessary. I could feel his eyes burning a hole into my back. "They a thing now?"

"What do you mean?" Megan asked.

"Jenika," Gabi muttered.

I picked up a torn sugar wrapper, crushing it in my palm.

The cakes started calling Jenika "Russian Roulette" last summer. To them, she was just a crazy girl who didn't fall far from the tree.

Her mom had a Russian accent. An accent that grew thick when she was drunk, making her hard to understand. Last August, she'd gotten thrown out of the Hemlock Tavern for losing her shit on a couple frat-boy tourists. One of them recorded a video of her on his cell and put it up on YouTube. It was called "Crazy Russian Lady."

Zach's friends played it over and over. They'd laugh, imitating her mom's big hand gestures and pronunciation of certain words.

"Didn't *you* have a thing for her once?" Gabi asked.

"Hell no," Christian said. The defensive edge in his voice was hard to ignore. But Christian and Jenika? No way.

I could see why he'd go for her. She was cute—as much as it pained me to admit that—and she hated everything he stood for. Apes like Christian got off on that kind of thing.

But until Alex, Jenika liked her guys tatted up and older. Bonus points for starving musicians or anarchists. If she had hooked up with Christian, it would be a secret she'd want to keep buried.

Which…explained a lot.

"Girls in this town come three different ways," Christian went on. "Beat. Crazy. Or half and half."

"Screw you," Gabi said.

"Present company excluded," he added.

She shook her head, like it was all okay, as long he didn't mean *her*.

I set a stack of dirty plates down with a *clank* and found myself walking up to their table. I didn't know what I was going to say. Or do. I just wanted to shut him up.

"You got something to say?" The words came out through my teeth. "Say it to my face."

Christian stared up at me, his face contorted in disgust. The fading bruises on the bridge of his nose and under both eyes made his irises look darker, more menacing. But he didn't say a word. He didn't move.

I turned my attention to Megan. "Can I talk to you?"

"Now?" Her cheeks were flushed, like my presence embarrassed her.

"Yeah. Now."

She shot Gabi an apologetic look, as if she needed her

permission to leave. I almost called her out on it, but I kept my mouth shut. What I needed to say was between Megan and me.

I led her out the back, where we'd get more privacy. She let the door shut behind us, but she kept one hand on the knob and her gaze averted.

"You can let go of the door," I said.

She folded her arms. "What do you want?" Her tone was icy, like on the phone a few days ago.

"What the hell was that, Megan?"

"The truth," she said softly.

"No, that's you selling your family and *yourself* down the river to entertain a bunch of assholes."

"I'm not saying anything they haven't heard!" Megan threw her hands up, her green eyes blazing. "It's just a lot less funny when I'm doing the laughing."

"What are you talking about?"

"You know that old metalhead who sits outside the Hemlock and whistles at girls?"

I nodded. "Joe—something." My mom said he was once that hot bad boy every girl wanted a piece of.

"Me and Gabi walked by him the other day. He whistled at me and said"—her nose wrinkled as she lowered her voice to imitate him—"*Check out little Mary Pace. All legs, just like her mom.* Then he asked me if I party like her, too."

"You should've reported that creep."

"Yeah? Should I report everyone who looks me up and down, like I'm diseased, and tells me I look just like her? Or everyone who asks me and Alex who our dad is?"

Not knowing who their dad was or if they even had the same dad had always been a touchy subject—one I knew never to bring up. But some people in town thought it was their business because Mary got pregnant with Alex while she was still living here. I thought they'd finally gotten tired of asking.

"You know I get what it's like," I said. "We can talk about it. We can—"

"Oh, you mean you'll actually answer my email this time? Or call" —she put her hand against her chest—"for me?"

"I'm sorry," I said. "There's been so much going on. With everything." But she needed me. "We're still friends. That hasn't changed."

"No, we're not. " She glared at me, her voice tight. "We've never been friends."

"What the—"

"Alex is your friend. I just came with the deal."

"That's bullshit. You're like a sister to me."

"Exactly." Her voice softened.

My face felt hot, and there was a lump in my throat. I was losing her, too.

"What do we have in common?" she continued.

I took in her clothes, *Gabi's* clothes, the inches of skin between her jean cutoff shorts and tank top. Her hair, blonder than before, was completely straight now. Even her posture was different. Straighter, almost defiant.

But the uncertainty in her eyes was still there.

I tried to think of a memory, any memory of the two of us. A funny conversation we had. Something only she knew about me. But I couldn't. Alex was always there, a bridge between us.

"Maybe we're not best friends," I said. "But I'm more of a friend than Gabi will ever be."

"How's that?"

"I wouldn't make jokes about your family, for starters." I took a step toward her. "If Alex knew the stuff you were saying in there, to *them*, it…" It would kill him.

"I don't know if you've noticed, but Alex doesn't really care about anything right now."

"I get that you're mad at him. I am, too. But you guys need each other."

"He won't even *look* at me."

I let out a breath, but it didn't relieve the pressure in my chest. "He's a mess right now."

"He's always been a mess."

"Not like this…"

She studied me for a moment, her long, skinny fingers clutching the ends of her hair. "He's different around you. Even when we were kids."

"What do you mean?" There it was again. That ache.

"Figure it out."

Maybe I needed to hear her say it. Maybe then it would finally sink in. I never really knew him.

"I need to get back," she said.

"To what? Christian using you to get dirt on Alex? He's not your friend, Megan."

She squinted, shaking her head. "You think I don't know that? He has a thing for Gabi. He practically stalks her."

"Then why doesn't she tell him to fuck off?"

"I don't know…" She wrapped her arms around herself, making her seem more breakable. "Sometimes it's better to keep your mouth shut."

"Right. And bat your eyelashes. Giggle while they rip other girls to shreds. At least they're not doing it to you, right?"

"That isn't what I meant."

"I'll bet you anything your good friend Gabi is having a laugh at your expense right now." The words tumbled out before I could stop them. I wanted to take them back…and I didn't.

Her eyes rolled up to the sky, and her face turned red, but she didn't respond. Not right away.

"You know what you are, Nova?" she asked, finally. Her voice was quiet, almost calm. "Jealous."

My mouth dropped open.

"You hate that me and Alex have moved on," she continued. "That you're not the center of Alex's universe anymore. That—"

"You should stop right there." My fingers curled into fists. I kept having to remind myself this was Megan talking. Not some cake. "You can't take it back."

She turned and grabbed the doorknob, looking back at me once more. "You're wrong. Gabi's a better friend than you ever were."

And with that, she was gone.

I stood there, my hands shaking. Heat behind my eyes. I wanted to cry, but the tears wouldn't come. It was like I was trapped inside myself…all I could do was breathe.

"Ouch," a guy's voice said behind me. "That was harsh."

I spun around to see Christian. He was coming from the side of the building, where he'd probably been hiding out.

"You're not supposed to be back here," I said.

He moved toward me, closing the distance between us in seconds. "Uh-oh—better sic Granddaddy Garcia on me. Maybe he can beat me with his bong."

"What do you want?"

He leaned over until his face was inches from mine. His pupils erased most of the blue in his eyes, and the muscles in his jaw were tense. Ready for a fight. "You wanted me to say it to your face, right?"

My heart pounded, urging me to run. But my pride

wouldn't let me back down. He was a coward. I didn't run from cowards.

Christian didn't give me time to think. He grabbed my arm, his jagged nails digging into my skin, and threw his fist into my stomach, the soft spot right beneath my rib cage. My knees gave out; the sky turned brown. I was on the ground, hugging my torso, the gravel cutting into my shins.

I couldn't breathe in or out. Nausea took over then, freezing me in place. My eyes squeezed shut.

"Feels like you're gonna die, doesn't it?" Christian's hot breath hit my ear.

I still couldn't move. I couldn't scream or even speak. If Amber's killer was someone she knew—and every bone in my body told me it was—Christian would be at the top of that list. And I was in the worst place I could be right now, no witnesses.

A burning sensation inched up my esophagus. The strawberry milkshake I'd had for lunch stung the back of my throat.

"You're not getting away with it," he continued, keeping his voice low. "None of you."

I didn't know if he meant his beatdown or Amber. Or both.

He grabbed my hair, snapping my head back. Forcing me to look at him. He was squatting next to me, his cheeks flushed.

I balled up my fist. One swing. That was all I needed.

"Don't try it," he said. "You'll lose." Then he spit at me. The wad landed right between my eyes.

The back door screeched open behind us. Christian scrambled to his feet and took off running.

"Hey!" Brandon's voice called out. Footsteps crunched behind me. "Nova—you okay?" His hand warmed my back.

"I think so." It was as if Christian's fist remained in my gut, twisting and squeezing. I wiped his spit from my face with the end of my T-shirt.

"Here. Let me help you up."

I put my arm around his shoulders, and he kept his hand on my lower back, steadying me. I felt weak all over, but my legs managed to keep me upright.

"Thanks. I got it." I made my way over to one of the white plastic chairs and lowered myself into it.

I took slow breaths for a few minutes, waiting for the dull sky above to come back into focus. Wishing I'd had the strength to take a swing at Christian. His words rang in my ears. *You're not getting away with it. None of you.*

"What happened?" Brandon asked, sliding into the other chair.

"He sucker punched me."

Brandon stared at me like he had more questions. Questions I didn't really want to deal with. "You want me to call my mom? I'm a witness. I could—"

"Please don't." No way did I want to talk to the cops. I was already too much on their radar.

"Why not?"

I couldn't think of a good answer. I couldn't think at all. He knew the detectives came by to question me earlier this week...he just didn't know I'd lied. "I should go home. Put some ice on this."

"Your mom told me I could take off—it's dead in there. I can give you a ride."

I stood, rubbing the sore spot on my abdomen. As if that would somehow stop the throbbing. "I can walk. Thanks, though."

"Really?" he asked.

I wasn't exactly in top form at the moment. It would be

easy for Christian to corner me again…or someone else. But I was used to getting places on my own, especially when I wanted to be alone. It pissed me off to feel like a prisoner in my own town.

"Actually, I think I'll take that ride."

He scanned me for a few seconds, his mouth turned down at the corners. I got the feeling there was something else he wanted to say. "Okay. Let me get my stuff."

We passed Gabi and Megan on the way to Brandon's car. They walked slowly, their bare arms pressed together like they were conjoined twins. If I didn't know better, I'd think they actually were sisters. Their coloring was night and day. But at first glance they were tangled locks of hair and delicate features. Long legs and bony knees.

Megan kept her head down, but Gabi's dark eyes focused on Brandon. She whispered something to Megan that made them both smile.

Brandon jammed his hands into his jean pockets, and his pace quickened. I had to jog a little to keep up with him.

"Think it's about to rain," he said, looking up.

The clouds had grown charcoal bellies, and they were starting to move east with the wind. The western sky was unsettling, almost the color of mud. I usually liked big storms, but today I wanted the sun. I wanted normal.

After we got into Brandon's car, he rolled down his window and slid a cigarette between his lips. He stared in the direction Gabi and Megan went while grabbing a lighter out of his pocket.

"She talking to you yet?" I asked. "Gabi."

"Nope. She comes to the diner every chance she gets, though."

"I noticed. Maybe she misses you?" I offered this mostly for his benefit. I didn't want to say what I really thought. She was a spineless princess who dropped him because the cakes deemed him unworthy.

He took a first drag and shifted into drive. "She likes playing games."

The bitterness in his voice took me by surprise. "You sounded like a boy in love just a week ago. What happened?"

"Nothing," he said, before exhaling. "I called her. Asked her what the hell I did."

"And?"

He shook his head. "I never got a real answer."

"She had to say *something*."

His finger tapped against the steering wheel as we drove. "Yeah. A lot of bullshit."

Clearly he wasn't going to offer more, but I needed to know more. "Well, Megan thinks Gabi is her new best friend. And I'm not buying it."

"What's not to buy? Everyone at school thinks like you," Brandon said. "*She's De Luca's daughter. She's the enemy.* You think she has an easy time making friends around here?"

Now he was defending her? Maybe bringing up Gabi was too raw of a subject for him right now.

We stopped at a red light. He scanned our surroundings, keeping his cigarette low and out of sight, as if his mom were waiting to jump from the shadows.

A group of teens were gathered on the sidewalk about ten feet away, a cloud of exhaled smoke above them. Matt and Jenika in their matching black hoodies. Tyler in his trying-too-hard studded leather jacket. Alex with his skateboard tucked under one arm. And Haley St. James, her hair as blue and bright as the desert sky.

Haley and Alex had their arms wrapped around each other. It could've been a friendly gesture. But as far as I knew, she'd never given him the time of day before.

Matt smiled a little and gave me a salute. I rolled my eyes, telling myself to ignore them. But my gaze went right back to Alex.

He saw me and dropped his arm from Haley's waist, like he was doing something wrong. He hadn't called me since Tuesday afternoon, after the cops showed up at his house. They asked him the same questions about that night, and he gave them the same answers. He told me not to worry.

I told him to worry more.

"This light can turn green any time now," I muttered, the pain in my stomach getting worse again.

"Want me to run it?"

I wished. "Sure."

Brandon glanced in the rearview mirror and both ways before gunning it into the intersection.

I gripped the sides of my seat. "I thought you were kidding."

He just smiled.

"Ever feel like this place makes you stupid?" he asked after a few seconds. "Like, if you stay here, you'll never do anything worth doing?"

Putting it that way sounded bad, like I thought I was better than my family. Or my friends…if I still had them. But I knew what he meant. "I'm leaving the first chance I get."

"Me, too."

Quarter-sized raindrops smacked the windshield. One flew inside the car, hitting me in the eye. I rolled up my window.

"Hear anything more on Amber's case?" I asked.

He glanced at me. "Do you think about anything else?"

It was true. I'd been asking him if he'd heard anything nearly every day since we'd gone to Winchester Beach. But if he knew about any major leads, he wasn't sharing. He just said they hadn't found Amber's cell phone, that the killer probably destroyed it or tossed it in the ocean.

"Do you think Christian's capable?" I asked, remembering how he happened to be passing by that day we went to the beach to check out the crime scene. Killers often liked to come back and check up on the police.

"Honestly? Yeah." He rolled his window down and smacked a new pack of cigarettes against his palm. "He's a vengeful fuck."

"No kidding…" I rubbed my stomach again. "He doesn't strike me as the organized type, though."

"I heard he set some guy's car on fire."

My breath got caught in my throat. "What?"

He looked over at me, his forehead creasing. "You didn't hear about that?"

"Uh, no."

"Supposedly, he was in love with this girl his freshman year, and she cheated on him with an older guy." He paused to light up.

Christian in love? I wasn't buying it…

"Two days later," Brandon continued. "The guy's car is a bonfire in his driveway."

There was a rumble behind us, the sound of a restless ocean. But we were too far away to hear the waves crash against the rocks. It had to be thunder. "Did Christian get busted?"

"Nah, they couldn't pinpoint the cause. Arson is harder than hell to pin on someone."

"Who told you this—Gabi?"

He nodded, flicking ash out the window.

"Why does she hang around him?" I asked.

He rested his head back against the seat, his light brown eyes somewhere other than here. "I don't know," he muttered.

The hardness in his stare said otherwise. I opened my mouth to call him on it, but he spoke first. "I'm guessing you know what happened to his face?"

"I know I didn't do it."

He watched me like those cops did, reading every tic. I felt like a specimen in a jar. "But you know who did…"

"Is this an interrogation?" I forced a smile.

He took another drag, his expression softening. "Just curious…"

The wind howled through his cracked window, spraying us with rain. It made the sticky heat inside his car a little more bearable.

"I don't run home and tell my mom everything," he said.

"I never said you did."

"You don't have to. Everyone thinks it." He ground his cigarette butt out in the car ashtray.

"I should go put ice on this." I patted my stomach. "Thanks for…well, for being there."

"Look, this might sound weird. But whatever." He kept his gaze down as he spoke. "We're both kind of low on friends. If you ever want to hang out or talk for real…" He raked his hands through his inky hair, wincing. "Man, that sounds lame. It's been so long since I…"

"I get it. Believe me. And I'd like that." I'd give anything for someone to confide in, someone who wasn't Alex. But trusting anyone right now felt impossible. "You do know at least half the girls in this town would kill to hang out with you, right?"

He smiled a little, shaking his head. "If you say so." His expression turned serious. "Too bad there's only one girl I want like that."

"Well, I hope she wakes the hell up." Actually I hoped he'd realize he was way too good for her. I'd tell him that when he was ready to hear it.

He looked up at me then. "I hope Alex does, too."

I turned my focus out the passenger window, heat pouring into my face. "I'm that obvious, huh?"

"Yeah."

I winced a little. "Great. And with that…" I reached for the handle. "I'm really going now."

He touched my arm lightly. "Hey, wait…"

I turned toward him, hoping he wasn't going to push the topic.

Instead he said, "Whatever's going down between you and Christian. Watch out, okay? The guy has more than a few screws loose."

There was genuine concern in his eyes, enough to give me chills.

Christian wasn't going to rat on us to the cops. He was going to come after us his way, on his terms.

CHAPTER FIFTEEN

The phone rang at 10:36 p.m. I was lying on my bed, listening to the apocalyptic sound of fireworks being set off in a thunderstorm. The sky could've been falling for all I knew. Part of me wouldn't mind if it did.

Mom opened my door, a beer in one hand, our cordless black phone in the other. She'd been camped out on the living room couch, attempting to hear an episode of *CSI* over the explosions.

"It's Megan," she said, holding the phone out to me. *She's upset*, she mouthed. Her eyes were full of questions.

Alex was my first thought. Something happened to Alex. "Hello?"

"Nova?" Megan's voice was weak and shaky.

"What's going on?"

"I keep trying to call Alex. He's not home. He's not at work. I don't know what to do." Her words blurred together.

"Megan—take a breath."

She exhaled into the receiver. "I'm at the Shell station near Oswald Beach. On the highway. Can you pick me up?"

Oswald Beach was a few miles south of Emerald Cove. It was more like a wasteland than a beach, and it was big with tweakers, the homeless, and people who just didn't want to be found. It was also a great place to set off illegal fireworks.

"Is there a party down there?" I asked. Of course the cakes wouldn't miss another party, murdered friend and all.

"It was supposed to be, like, a tribute to Amber." She sniffled. "Nova, I know you hate me. But please. I need help." She whispered the last part, like someone was listening in.

"I don't hate you. Is someone—"

"I'm using the attendant's phone," she continued. "I have to go. Please come." There was a *click* and then silence.

I hung up and let the phone drop against my bed. If Christian wanted to make us hurt, going after Megan was the way to do it. They could've ganged up on her, done who knows what.

"What's wrong?" Mom asked.

"She needs me to pick her up." I got out of bed and reached for the first clean T-shirt I could find. "Can I borrow the car?"

Mom grabbed my elbow and yanked. "Where is she?"

"Down near Oswald Beach."

"What's she doing there? Why is she alone? Where's Alex?" She did this whenever she got worked up—asked one question after another without even a blink in between.

"Party. And I don't know. She can't get a hold of him." I tried to reach for my jeans in the hamper, but she tightened her grip on my arm.

"How long do you think I'm going to let you *not* talk to me?"

"Mom, I…"

"I get that you've been wanting space, and I've been respecting that. But I've reached my limit."

"I can't do this right now."

She studied me for a second before dropping my arm.

"You're not going down there by yourself."

"Then let's go."

"I wake Gavin up now, he'll be up all night." Mom exhaled, running a hand through her tangled dark hair. "I'll go get her. You stay here with him."

I nodded at the half-empty beer bottle in her hand. "How many is that?"

"Four." She scrunched up her face. "Shit."

The Emerald Cove Police Department's main focus on the Fourth of July was to bust anyone driving over the legal limit. It was usually the most excitement they got all year.

"It's only ten minutes away," I said. "I'll drive right there, drop Megan off, and drive right back."

"It's not a good night. The storm. Everyone's drunk…" She'd gone from laid-back Mom to hovering Mom in a week's time. Now I knew how Gavin felt.

"She has nobody else. You know Cindy can't drive, and I'm sure she's passed out by now." And she probably had no clue Megan was gone. "I'll be careful. I promise."

"Being careful isn't enough. Not with a psycho targeting young girls."

"We don't know for sure if it will happen again." I tried to keep my voice calm, rational. If she knew how afraid I was, she'd never let me go.

"Have they caught the guy? No!" She whispered through her teeth. "It'll happen again."

"Then we shouldn't leave Megan stranded at a gas station." I pulled on my jeans. They were still damp from the washer, cold against my skin.

"Call Brandon. Ask him for a ride."

"I don't have time for that." I threw on Alex's army coat.

"Don't go anywhere." Mom left the room and came back

a minute later with two things she'd normally never be caught dead with. A cell phone—the one Eric gave her and insisted she keep for emergencies. And a small black Taser.

She handed me the phone. It was ancient and as basic as they got. "Eric set up speed-dial. Press two for home. And then hit the—"

"Mom, I know how to use a cell phone. What are you doing with a Taser?"

A *boom* outside made us both tense. It was loud enough to rattle the windows, which meant our neighbors had given up on waiting for the storm to end.

"I ordered them online. Just got them yesterday," Mom said.

"Them?" She really *was* freaking out.

"We needed something, you know? I could only afford the cheap one, but it'll help me sleep better at night." She held it up and pressed a button on the side. "Turn the safety off. And then push this." A blue flash of electricity appeared. The zapping sound made me cringe. "You'll have to make contact. It's not like those ones on the cop shows that shoot out at people."

"I know. I have eyes."

She handed it to me. "Fine, expert. You try it."

"I have to go."

"Not until you show me." She was blocking the doorway, and she may have been a couple inches shorter, but she could hold her own.

I pointed it at the ceiling and demonstrated. "Okay?"

She finally stepped aside. "Turn the safety on," she said to my back. "And call me if anything comes up. And I mean anything."

The drive to Oswald Beach was surreal. Smoke gave the sky a pink cast, and flashes came from every direction. The air blowing through my window smelled like burning trees, salt, and wet pavement. At least the rain had stopped.

Haze subdued the lights of the gas station and the High Tide aka Bedbug Motel next door. The motel's dull green sign still boasted VCRs and phones because the only amenities their guests cared about were sex, drugs, and a bed. Times must've been hard, though. They'd raised their weekly rate from $100 to $120.

I dialed Alex's number and waited. The longer it rang, the more I wanted to reach through the phone and punch him.

"Alex—get down to the Shell station in Oswald Beach now," I said to their old answering machine.

The parking lot was a graveyard, except for a couple arguing by a rusted pay phone. They were all furious arm movements and slurred insults. I could smell the alcohol on their breath before I even got near them.

There wasn't any sign of Megan inside the gas station. Just someone stocking shelves in the back and the cashier, a young guy who watched the eleven o'clock news the way most guys watched football. Nothing else existed.

"Excuse me?" I asked.

"Yeah?" He kept his eyes on the TV. A picture of Amber flashed on the screen, and the announcer was talking in a too-chipper voice about evidence connecting her murder to the animal mutilations.

"There was a girl in here. Long blond hair, about—"

"You Nova?" He finally looked at me. His eyes were bloodshot, and he smelled faintly of skunk.

I nodded.

"She's in the bathroom." He nodded behind him. "In the

back to your right."

I made my way to a scratched-up blue door. The restroom sign was crooked, nearly ready to fall off.

"Megan?" I jiggled the loose knob. "It's me."

There was a clicking sound, the turn of the lock. But she didn't say a word. Part of me was afraid of what I'd find on the other side.

I pushed the door open, scanning the dirty sink, the dizzying black-and-white tile. Megan was sitting on the floor, her back against a writing-covered wall, her face in her hands. NEVER FORGET 6403 was scrawled in red marker above her head.

"Hey..." I said.

She lowered her hands, revealing black makeup smudged around her eyes. Scratches and dirt covered her knees, as if she'd fallen on the pavement.

"What happened? What did they do?"

Megan wound a lock of hair around her finger, pulling tight. She didn't look at me. She stared straight ahead, into nothing.

"We were out on the beach—there were just a few of us. Most people didn't want to come out." She spoke in a soft monotone. "Christian said he needed to talk to me..." She paused, but her lips remained parted.

I squatted down and reached for her hand. She jerked it away.

"Then what?" I wanted to ask her why the hell she'd go off alone with him, but I held my tongue.

"We went back to his car," she said. "He even opened the door for me, like we were on a date or something."

My heart started to pound. I didn't want to hear the rest. I was *this* close to losing control and going after Christian myself.

"As soon as he got in, he…" Her nose scrunched up, and her hands formed tight balls. "He grabbed my arm and squeezed really hard." She stroked a spot on her upper arm through her hoodie.

I closed my eyes for a second, remembering the sting of his jagged nails.

"He started saying all this stuff," she continued. "That Alex is a killer, and we're protecting him. He said someone saw Alex with Amber, on Beach Street, right before she went missing."

"Who?"

"He didn't tell me."

"Because it's a lie," I said, anger tightening my throat.

"I haven't told anyone this," she said in a voice barely above a whisper. "But the night she went missing…Alex sneaked out. He tried to be quiet, but I heard him."

He could've been going anywhere. To see Jenika most likely. "Alex had nothing to do with what happened to Amber. You know that."

She wove her fingers together, her gaze shifting to the floor.

"What happened next?" I asked.

"I got the door open and screamed as loud as I could. Zach was standing right outside."

"*Zach* was there?" I couldn't see his parents letting him out of the house.

She nodded. "He was a mess. So drunk he could barely stand." She sniffed. "I tried to punch Christian, anything I could hit." She touched the side of her head. "He got me right here."

My heart was racing so fast it felt like a jackhammer.

"Then Gabi showed up, asked what was going on. And he let me go." She rubbed her banged-up knees. "I ran so hard I fell."

We could go to the police, but then what? We'd *lied* to homicide detectives. The proof was on Christian's face, in that stupid video. All he had to do was tell them. They wouldn't believe a word we said after that.

The bathroom door was shoved open. Alex glanced from me to Megan, his expression tensing. With his black hood pulled over his head and black cargo pants, he reminded me of a ninja.

"Are you okay?" he asked her, coming inside and squatting down next to me.

"Does she look okay?" I asked. "Where were you?"

"I went for a drive."

"Hope we didn't interrupt anything," I said.

"You didn't." There was an edge to his voice, but then his gaze softened. "I'm sorry."

"You've been saying that a lot lately…" I muttered.

Alex touched Megan's arm. "What happened?"

"What do you care?" She jerked away from him. "I called and called and called…"

"Megan—" Alex began.

"Shut up!" she screamed, new tears forming in her eyes. "Just shut up!"

Alex got back on his feet slowly, but I froze in place. I'd never seen Megan like this. I was pretty sure I'd only seen her cry once…the day her grandpa died.

"She had another epic fit tonight," Megan continued, her voice low and shaky. "Dumped all of Grandpa's stuff out and cried and cried. She left it everywhere. The hallway, the living room. The kitchen counter."

Alex knelt in front of her again, his forehead creased. "I told you to leave it next time," he said. "I'll take care of it."

"How? You're never there!"

I swallowed back the urge to reach out to her, to tell her she could've called me. It sounded shallow after the fact, a way to ease my own conscience. I hadn't been there for her either. What *could* I say?

Alex put his arm around her, trying to pull her close, but she shoved him away.

He hung his head, shutting his eyes. His back rose and fell without a sound. There was just Megan's jagged breaths, the occasional drop of water hitting the sink.

"I'll be outside," I said, knowing they needed a moment. Or a few.

The air outside was still stale and as thick as chowder, but it was a lot less charged. I could take a full breath, let my eyes well up and wipe away the evidence. The phone rang in my pocket, making my body jerk.

"I'm okay, Mom," I answered, pacing back and forth in front of the entrance.

"Alex stopped by about twenty minutes ago, looking for you. I told him Megan was in some kind of trouble and where you were."

"He's here. He's talking to her."

"Well, he can talk to her on the way back."

I shut my eyes. "I'll leave in a minute. Promise."

"Is she okay? What happened?"

"Yeah, she's…" An orange Audi pulled into the gas station. My heart about stopped. "She's okay. We're leaving now. I'll talk to you when I get back."

I was hoping they were just pulling up for gas, but Christian gunned the car into a parking space facing the motel. Their timing couldn't be more perfect.

Alex came out the gas station doors with Megan in tow, his

face like stone. As soon as he saw Christian's Audi, he nudged Megan toward me. "Get her out of here."

The light was on inside Christian's car, but nobody was getting out.

I handed Megan my keys. "Go. Lock the doors," I told her.

"I'm not—" she started to protest.

"Go!" Alex and I said in unison. She backed away, slowly.

I moved in front of Alex, blocking his path toward Christian's car. "Don't." My eyes pleaded with him. For all we knew those detectives were watching us right now—or maybe I'd seen too many movies.

"He attacked her," he said in a harsh whisper.

I put my hands on his chest, giving him a less-than-gentle shove. "They're spreading rumors about you. They're saying someone saw you with Amber on Beach right before she went missing."

"That's bullshit—I picked up Megan and went home."

You didn't stay home, I wanted to shout. But now wasn't the time. "To the cops, it's your word against theirs. And if you come at them right now, in public? Your word's going to mean a lot less."

Car doors opened and closed. Alex's fingers curled into his palms. I pushed him harder this time, making him stumble back. "Walk away."

Voices echoed across the parking lot. There was something raw and feral rising inside me, an ache in my chest that wouldn't subside. I shoved him again, using my fists this time. "You want to help Megan? Then fucking be there for her."

He caught my hands, his eyes wide, searching my face. His grip was shaky, clammy. "Okay."

It was all he said. But it was enough. I'd reached whatever rationalism he had left.

We headed toward our cars, our steps fast and quiet on the wet pavement. Megan was standing outside, her face turned in the direction of Christian's car. Because it would kill that girl to listen, just once.

"Hey!" a guy yelled. It wasn't just a yell, though. It was ragged and broken. I knew it was Zach's voice without even turning around.

Footsteps echoed across the parking lot, fast and uneven.

"Get in the car," I told Megan, breaking into a jog. She finally listened.

"Hey, I'm talking to you," Zach said, his voice closer.

Alex slowed, but I grabbed his arm, yanking him forward. He pulled away. "Get Megan home," he said.

But they were right up on us. Three of them. Zach looking all wrong, his eyes red and wild, his jaw slack. A beer bottle dangled from his left hand. It was just like Christian, getting his grieving best friend crazy drunk.

Christian and the guy with the bleached fro who came into the diner earlier were a few feet behind him.

"You call me a coward," Zach said, his words slurred. "You're the coward."

Alex was still facing me, his back to them. His eyes flickered up to mine. "Go," he mouthed.

I shook my head.

Zach reeled back and hurled his beer bottle at us. It grazed Alex's arm and shattered around our feet, making my ears ring. We both froze for a few seconds, the air going completely still.

"Look at me, you psychotic fuck!" Zach's voice cracked.

Alex turned and got right in his face, opening his arms wide. "I'm here. I'm looking at you. What do you want from me?"

Zach stared at him, his eyes watery slits. "Killer."

It wasn't the word itself that made me hold my breath; it was the way he said it, so sure of himself, so justified. The way it sat in my chest and clung to me.

The tendons in Alex's hands strained against his skin. I was sure he was going to take a swing. Instead, he said, "The last time I saw your girlfriend, she was at that party. With you."

Arms wrapped around me, squeezing me so tight I could barely breathe. "Do it," Christian's voice rang loud in my ear.

Alex took a step toward us, but the guy with the fro shoved him into Zach.

Christian's lips pressed against my ear and his fingers probed at the sore spot beneath my rib cage. "How's your tummy?"

The few fights I'd been in had left me sore for days, and I'd never been jumped by three people. Christian was the one holding me back for a reason.

I didn't fight or squirm like he expected me to. I went limp, hoping it would distract him for a second. All I needed was a second.

It worked.

His arms loosened just enough for me throw my body forward and back. I slammed my elbow right into his gut, twice, and twisted out of his grasp. He lurched for me, clutching his stomach and wincing.

I pulled the Taser Mom gave me from my pocket, turned the safety off, and held it out toward him. He glared at me, his hand still on his stomach, teeth clenched.

The commotion was enough to disrupt Fro and Alex's shoving match. Zach was on his knees, completely checked out. His features twisted all up like he was about to cry.

"Where'd you get that—7-Eleven?" Fro asked me.

"Who cares? It works," I said, pushing the button to activate it. The crackle of electricity sounded like a mini firecracker. I couldn't feel my toes or my feet. Sheer willpower kept my hand from shaking.

Zach was rocking now, his breaths quivering and fast. A small part of me felt sorry for him. He probably couldn't even process what was happening. In the morning, it would seem like a vivid dream.

Fro and Christian exchanged a look, but they didn't budge.

An old pickup had pulled up to one of the station pumps. The gas station attendant came outside, his face turned in our direction.

I scanned the parking lot, looking for witnesses. A guy in a dirty red hoodie stood near the pay phone, having a cigarette. A couple was standing outside their car in front of the motel, groping each other.

"Someone's going to call the cops," I said. "If they haven't already." I'd be surprised if that were true. People came here to hide from the cops, and the attendant probably didn't want to explain his bloodshot eyes.

After what seemed like another eternal minute, Christian and Fro each grabbed one of Zach's arms, helping him up.

"Tell Jenika I said hi," Christian said, his eyes fixed on Alex.

Alex watched him, his chest heaving.

They didn't get very far before Zach sagged back to the ground, his palms hitting the pavement. He made a retching sound, and brown liquid poured from his mouth.

Megan had gotten out of my car at some point. She was watching him, her lips forming a snarl.

"You okay?" Alex asked, touching my arm.

"Get your sister home."

I didn't say another word. I just got in my mom's car and left.

CHAPTER SIXTEEN

After I got home. After I let Mom squeeze me and whisper in my ear that she was never letting me out of the house again. After I'd given her the PG-13 version of what happened—*the cakes were being asses to Megan. She wanted to go home.* After I got in the shower and stood under the lukewarm water for a half hour, in a daze…I opened up Amber's picture again.

She was exactly how I left her, horrific and beautiful, any useful detail obscured by phone-camera grain. Yet I kept staring, as if a hidden image would appear, giving me the key to everything.

Alex told me he'd picked up Megan from that party and went home. But going home didn't mean he stayed there. He knew I wouldn't think to ask that, though. Most people wouldn't.

Chances were he *was* with Jenika, doing things I didn't want to picture. But what if he wasn't?

Despite everything I'd seen lately, Alex would always be that skinny nine-year-old who sat at my lunch table and offered his sandwich. A kid with a "heart too big for this world," as his grandpa always said.

He might have a mountain of issues. He might be acting like

someone else entirely. And they might say some psychopaths were made, not born. But Alex wasn't a killer. He just wasn't.

A knock sounded at my window, making me suck in my breath. One-two. One-two. One. Alex's knock.

My muscles relaxed. It was like this every night now; even small noises made my hair stand up. I glanced at the time on my laptop—12:31. It was officially July 5, Alex's birthday. In the almost eight years we'd been friends, I'd never forgotten that. Until tonight.

The rain was coming down again, fat, sturdy drops that burrowed into the ground and made the air smell like soil and honey. Alex peered up at me through dripping wet bangs, his lips forming a weak smile.

"You got cameras," he said, motioning to the roof above my room.

"They obvious?"

He shook his head. "Nah. You know me. I notice every-thing."

"Come to get your hoodie?"

He looked down, his foot making dragging sounds on the grass. "I was hoping you'd talk to me."

"Isn't that what I'm doing?"

"Can I come in? Please?"

His gray pullover was soaked through, which meant he'd walked here. "You realize there's a killer running around, right? Walking around by yourself in the middle of the night is a completely idiotic thing to do."

He shrugged. "Killers break into houses, too."

There was a part of me that wanted to step aside and let him in. Like always. But *like always* didn't exist anymore.

The wind picked up again, blowing rain on my face, cooling my sauna of a room.

He came closer, putting his hands on the window ledge. "I miss you…"

A lump pushed at the back of my throat. Saying "I miss you" was so simple; it didn't make up for what he'd done. But I needed to hear it from him like this, with fear in his eyes.

That was how I knew he meant it.

"If I let you in this room," I said, "there's no shutting me out."

His eyes stayed on mine. "I know."

I stepped aside while he hoisted himself up and climbed over the window ledge. Water from his cargo pants and pullover started dripping all over the carpet—good thing it was old and ragged.

His gaze traveled down my body and lingered on my legs. Long enough to remind me I wasn't wearing pants and the old Filter T-shirt I had on barely covered my butt.

He averted his eyes when I grabbed a pair of homemade cutoff shorts from a pile in my closet and slid them on.

"It's hotter than hell in here," he said.

"Yeah, well. I haven't really wanted to keep my window open lately."

I grabbed a towel and threw it at him. "Take that wet crap off. I'll get you something of Eric's."

I waited, scanning my room, as he stripped off his pullover and pants, leaving on a black T-shirt and a pair of blue-and-white patterned boxers.

"Um…" He held his clothes in a ball, his eyes darting from me to the floor. "What do you want me to do with these?"

"I'll hang them up over the bathtub—the dryer will wake everyone up," I said, grabbing them and hustling out of the room.

When I came back from tiptoeing in and out of my mom's

room, a fairly easy thing considering the volume of her snoring, Alex was standing in front of my nightstand with one of my "secret admirer's" letters in his hands.

"How many of these have you gotten?" he asked.

"Four. I tossed one, though." I threw a pair of black sweats at him. "Those two were taped to my window."

"No wonder you got the cameras," he muttered, setting it back on my nightstand and pulling the sweats on. "Have they been back since you installed them?"

I shook my head. "Haven't gotten one since...last Saturday. They left it on one of the tables at the diner, while you were there."

"Why didn't you say anything?"

"Uh, you had your mind on other things."

He turned toward my open window, staring out into the darkness.

I walked over and slammed it shut, yanking the curtains together. The breeze felt amazing against my sweaty skin, but I wasn't taking any chances. Especially not with the cakes out looking for blood.

"We're going to get heatstroke in here," he said. It was something the old Alex would say—he never did like the heat much.

"So sit in front of the fan," I said, settling on my bed and scooting up against the headboard.

He lowered himself to the floor by the window and leaned his back against my wall, draping his arms over his knees. He couldn't have been more than a few feet away, but it felt like miles.

I swallowed back the ache in my throat. "The night of the first party, when Amber went missing. You said you picked up Megan and went home."

"Yeah?"

"Did you stay home?" This was it. If I got even a whiff of a lie, I'd probably lose it on him.

His lips parted, realization hitting his eyes. "You believe them?"

"Just answer me."

He exhaled, looking down at his knees. "Jenika came by. She wanted to see how I was doing, after the fight with Matt."

"How nice of her. She couldn't do that before midnight?"

"She doesn't sleep much."

"Then what happened?" My words came out small. I wasn't sure I wanted to hear what came next, but Megan said she'd heard him sneak out.

"What usually happened. We went for a walk on the Deception trail, got wasted, and finished off a jumbo bag of pretzels."

"What *usually* happened?" I tilted my head back, rolling my eyes to the ceiling. "Wow. Okay." This from a guy who, just months ago, preached to me about the effects of too much pot like he was filming a DARE commercial. "Do you have multiple personalities? I mean, how does a person change so much in a few weeks?"

"It's not that I've changed..." He paused, his fingers playing with a loose thread on Eric's sweats. "I've just stopped running away."

"What the hell does that mean?"

He twisted the thread around his index finger, pulling tight. "There's always been this part of me I don't trust. Like, if I let it out, I won't be able to stop myself..."

"From what?"

"From losing it...I don't know." He muttered the last part. "My mom never had any self-control. We'd be in the car with her and something would set her off. Me and Megan talking too loud. Someone on the road. It never took much. She'd step on the gas and drive crazy fast, like she wanted to hit something."

He'd talked about how his mom took anything she could get her hands on and how she'd run hot and cold with them, but he'd never told me this. I couldn't imagine what that must've felt like, not knowing if she'd stop. Not being able to do anything about it.

"Sometimes I feel that way," he continued. "I want to keep going until I crash."

Fear knotted up my stomach. "But you don't... Something inside you must click."

"So far. Yeah."

"That's the difference between you and your mom. You have that voice. I don't think she ever did."

He rested his head against the wall, his gaze going somewhere else. "There's stuff I buried so deep it's like it never happened. And then Grandpa died, and my mind wouldn't turn off. I'd be up all night thinking." His fingers banged an erratic beat against his knee. "Remembering all this shit..."

A shiver ran down my arms, despite the air in my room growing thicker by the minute. I waited, letting him decide if he wanted to say more.

"Most of it I can deal with," he continued. "Move on. Hopefully forget again. But there's this one memory... I didn't get what was happening then. But I do now."

My hands clutched my sheet, a million worst-case scenarios running through my mind. "What is it?"

"I can't..."

"Why?"

He didn't respond for a few seconds, but his lips remained

parted.

"Alex?"

"If I tell you, you'll wish I didn't."

"I'll worry about me, okay?" My fingers throbbed with my pulse.

He ran his hand back and forth through his damp hair. The more he hesitated, the faster my heart pounded.

"It was when we were living with Tim in Reno. Right before Mom...dropped us off here."

I didn't know a lot about Tim. Only that he had a horrible temper, and he'd been busted for assault a few times. Alex said his mom always chased the bad boys, hoping one would treat her right and protect her from the world. As if *that* guy existed outside the Western romance books she apparently liked so much.

"Mom was working graveyard, so she was gone most nights." He focused hard on his hands. "Tim would watch TV all night, drinking. Usually he'd pass out. But a few times...he came into our room and woke me up."

I held my breath, hoping this wasn't going where I thought.

"He'd make me go out into the living room, saying Megan was having nightmares. Then he'd lock the door." His expression twisted with disgust. "When he let me back in, she'd be curled up in a ball, buried under the covers."

He was right. I wanted him to take his words back. Tell me he wasn't a hundred percent sure it actually happened.

"She said he told her stories about his horses. He grew up on some ranch in Sparks." Alex shook his head, his mouth tensing. "I remember asking him if I could stay once. He laughed and said I was too old for bedtime stories. Called me a pussy." His tapping fingers went still, and the muscles in his forearms tightened. "He was right. I never argued. I sat out in that living room like he told me to, every time."

"You were a little kid," I said. "You didn't understand what was going on."

"I knew something wasn't right. I remember thinking it was weird he shut the door."

"He probably would've hurt you, or worse."

"So?" His face scrunched up, a shine in his eyes. "She's my little sister."

Everything I thought to say seemed wrong. There was just the dull *thump* of his fingers hitting his knee again. The wind moaning through the gaps in the window.

I got up off the bed and joined him on the floor, sliding my fingers between his. His hand remained stiff, like it was frozen solid.

"How could I forget?" he whispered.

"You said you buried a lot of things. You had to cope somehow."

"I promised I'd take care of her. No matter what."

"Whatever happened to Megan in that room wasn't your fault." I stared at his profile, hoping some part of him heard me. "It wasn't."

His dazed expression didn't change. I wasn't even sure he blinked.

"She's never said a word about it," he said after a minute.

"Would *you*?"

His eyes searched the room. "What if she doesn't remember? If he did what I think he did, I can't make her relive that."

The same questions were running through my head—should he bring it up? Should he let her come to him? I didn't have any answers. Fact was—whether she remembered or not—Megan may never tell a soul what happened in that room.

I wasn't sure I would.

"Do you think your mom had any idea?" I asked.

"I remember telling her about Megan having nightmares and Tim going in there and kicking me out," he said, his voice turning bitter. "Not too long after, we were on Grandma and Grandpa's doorstep."

Anger filled my chest. "So she knew?"

"Running was the best thing she ever did for us." His tone was flat, like he'd rehearsed it a million times.

"No, it was the best thing for her. She could've—"

"Nova…" he broke in. "I can't talk about this anymore, okay? Not tonight."

I kept my hand in his, my mind still scrambling for the *right* thing to say. Why did we do that? Try to fix everything with words, despite knowing it was impossible.

I was here. That was all that mattered.

We stayed on the floor, listening to the rain fade in and out, in and out. Until it stopped altogether and the silence became overwhelming.

"Music?" I asked.

"You read my mind."

I set my laptop on the "desk" I'd made out of cardboard boxes—the only productive thing I'd done in the weeks after Zach and I broke up—and plugged in my speakers. "Shoegaze mix?" I asked.

"Whatever you want."

I hit play. The dreamy, rhythmic guitar of Chapterhouse's "Autosleeper" whispered out of my speakers, just soft enough not to carry through my walls. It was like a dark lullaby. Creepy, yet oddly comforting. I'd been falling asleep to it almost every night.

"You got Chapterhouse," Alex said, his voice close behind

me.

I pulled the Whirlpool album from a stack of import CDs I'd bought last month and turned, handing it to him. "Happy birthday."

He took it, a flicker of a smile crossing his lips. "You always know what to get."

"Glad that hasn't changed…"

We stared at each other, no more than a foot apart. He had that intense look in his eyes again, like he was daring me. My stomach knotted up. I wanted to run. Hide. Stay. Touch him.

"What?" I asked.

He reached out, his fingers drawing a line down my forearm. My body jolted with an embarrassing shiver.

"Come here," he whispered.

I let him pull me into a hug, his arms wrapping lightly around my waist. I closed my eyes, listening to his heart. It was forceful and steady, unlike mine, which was racing again.

He stroked the nape of my neck, his fingers combing through my hair. My muscles relaxed, even with the stifling heat, but I fought the urge to press closer, to tilt my head up and face him. Everything I missed about him, every bit of anger rose up in my throat, forming a tight ball.

It was hard to breathe. But it was harder to let go.

His fingers tensed against my skin. "You're a better friend than I deserve right now," he whispered.

It was true…and it wasn't. I edged out of his grip, but he took his time letting me go, his hands lingering on my waist.

"Post-breakup me was pretty brutal," I said.

"Nah. Just your nightly chocolate peanut butter milkshakes."

"Shut up. You loved those." I brushed past him and leaned against my wall, too keyed up to sit.

"The first ten or so. Yeah."

I smiled because, for a few seconds, everything was normal. Our normal. Then the awkward silence returned. His fingers drumming against his legs. Me still trying to process what he told me. The day. The week.

"Do you have plans for today?" It felt so strange to ask him that. His birthday had always involved the three of us.

"Depends if you let me stay."

"And if I don't, you'll what? Go over to Jenika's? Haley's maybe?" I regretted my words as soon as they came out. It seemed silly to bring that up now. But the hurt hadn't gone away. Not even a little.

He moved closer. "How long are we going to do this?"

"Do what?"

"You know what."

I looked away, heat rushing into my face. The muscles in my legs tensed, urging me to run.

"Just for tonight, can we pretend out there doesn't exist?" He motioned toward my window. "Can we be…us?"

I wanted that so bad it ached. It was natural, uncomplicated. Safe. But it didn't give me the answers I wanted to hear.

He rested his hand against the wall next to my head, leaning in close. I could smell firecracker smoke in his hair. "What are you doing?" I asked, my skin buzzing.

He inched closer, his eyes staying on mine, like he was asking permission. The palms of my hands pressed into the wall, but I didn't move. Didn't breathe.

His lips touched mine so lightly it tickled. I closed my eyes, ready to kiss him back, but his mouth moved toward my ear.

"This," he whispered.

His lips brushed against my neck, just below my earlobe. He kissed a trail down to my collarbone, making my thighs go weak.

I wanted to feel his hands on my bare skin. I wanted to kiss him hard enough to forget…everything. But my brain was screaming at me to stop. I couldn't do this. Not without knowing what it meant.

I grabbed his shoulders and nudged him back. It was only then I could see the uncertainty in his expression, his trembling hands.

"I'm not going to be some escape, Alex."

He squinted at me, opening his mouth and then closing it again. "You're not."

"Then what is this?"

"Do you really have to ask?"

I folded my arms. "Yeah. I do."

His eyes went from the Pixies poster on my wall to the plastic stars on my ceiling, to the floor. Everywhere but me. Seconds crawled by. My fingers and toes still hummed with anticipation.

"Remember when your mom made us watch that old movie, the one where they built their dream girl on a computer?" he asked, finally.

"*Weird Science*?" It was ages ago—seventh grade, maybe.

He nodded. "You asked me—no, you *demanded* to know what my perfect girl was like." His lips curved up a little. "You wanted every detail."

"Even her cup size. I remember."

"Most of it I made up, 'cause…" He shrugged. "I didn't know what to say. Then I asked you about your perfect guy. You must've gone on for an hour. It was this impossible list."

There were many things about my twelve-year-old self I was happy to bury. My obsession with romance was one of them. I didn't just assign a specific haircut and shoe size to my fantasy guy. He had a name.

"I started trying to be that guy," he continued, shaking his head. "Then I realized how dumb that was, waiting around for a girl who'll never see me…"

His words broke my heart and made me wonder, once again, how much of the real Alex I knew. If the person I had all these feelings for even existed. I had to believe he did… Nobody could spend as much time together as we did and completely hide who they were. "I do see you that way. I have for months."

"Months…" A sad smile crossed his lips. "What changed?"

"I don't know." My mind grasped for words—something that made sense. "One day these feelings were just there. I wish I could explain it better. I wish…"

"You wish they'd go away," he said.

I knew saying yes would hurt him, but it was the truth. "They freak me out."

"It doesn't matter. I'm not that guy." His voice softened. "I'm never going to be."

"It was a dumb fantasy I had when I was twelve. It's not what I want now."

"I know you pretty well, remember?"

"Then you know how much having you, as my friend, means to me. I don't want to lose us."

"Your version of us." He put his palms against the wall again and leaned down until our faces were inches apart. "I've always wanted more."

My eyes stung and my throat ached. "Is that why you hooked up with Jenika?"

"Was I supposed to wait forever?"

Yes, I wanted to shout. But that wasn't fair.

I lifted my chin, keeping my voice steady. "Give me a real

reason, not some *I was curious* bullshit. You're not that guy either, no matter how hard you're trying to be."

He stared at me, his breaths short and tense. "Who am I, then?"

"Someone who cares too much."

His gaze shifted to the floor, but he stayed close. So close I wanted to touch him.

"Tell me why," I repeated.

"Why did you hook up with Matt?" His voice was gentle, almost calm.

"I don't know…"

"Yes, you do."

"I wanted to forget. I…" *Just wanted to forget.*

He lifted his head, his eyes meeting mine again. "Did it work?"

"You know it didn't. Is that what you wanted—to forget me?"

He touched my cheek, his thumb wiping away the dampness on my skin. "I don't want to fight, okay?" he said. "Not tonight."

"Not tonight—you keep saying that. Why?"

He touched his forehead to mine. "Because it's my birthday. Because we can't figure it all out right now." His fingers hovered over the fine hairs on my arm, making them stand up. "We don't have to talk. I'll sit across the room if you want. I just want to be here with you."

I grabbed his hand, weaving my fingers through his. "I don't want you across the room."

"What do you want?"

I let out a shaky breath, tilting my face toward his. Our lips met, both of us gentle and hesitant at first. His hands moved down my back, following the curve of my waist. My fingers tangled in his hair.

He kissed me harder, his tongue teasing mine. I could barely inhale, but I didn't care. I just wanted more.

With Zach, every kiss was like our first. Long and sweet — sometimes we'd go until our lips got sore. Matt's hands went everywhere, rough and hurried, as if he were afraid I'd disappear.

But I'd never felt anything like this, our bodies shaking, my legs struggling to hold me up. Every time Alex's fingers grazed the skin between my bunched-up shirt and cutoffs, a jolt ran down my spine.

He buried his face in my neck, his damp palm running up the side of my thigh. "You smell so good," he mumbled.

All I could smell was sweat and the rain and smoke in his hair. With my fan blowing warm air on us, it was stifling, so impossibly hot, but I wanted him closer.

His body pressed into mine, making the place where Christian punched me ache. I nudged him back until we were inches from my bed, and then pushed him onto the mattress.

His eyes widened, and he gripped the edge of the bed. "Damn…"

"What?" I asked, straddling his lap. It was supposed to be like one of those movie scenes where I was this ultra-confident girl taking charge. But my legs still shook, and I didn't know where to put my hands.

"Nothing." He drew in a breath, inching up my shirt and pulling it over my head. Then he took his off.

I stared at him for a few seconds, focusing on the ring of gold around his pupils, way too aware of the moment. I was on top of my best friend, naked from the waist up. There was no going back from this.

"What's wrong?" He stroked my shoulders, making me

shudder.

I kept thinking about Jenika, how she most likely tore his clothes off and got right to it. No hesitation. No weirdness. He was probably waiting for me to take the lead—I'd always taken the lead in our friendship.

But I had no idea what to do right now.

"I'm burning up," I said just to say *something*.

His gaze went to my breasts and back up to my face. "Yeah, you are."

I shoved him, my lips breaking into a smile. "Worst line ever."

"You said it."

"Shut up." My body was trembling even more now. Too much to play it like anything other than the truth—I was scared shitless.

His smile faded. "Lie on your stomach and close your eyes."

"Why?"

"You'll find out."

Lying on my stomach wasn't an option. "How about I sit?"

"Sure…"

I got up off his lap, keeping one eye slightly open. He put his hand in front of my face and turned off my light.

"I hate you," I muttered.

"No, you don't."

I heard him pick up my glass of water from the nightstand and stiffened as he moved in behind me. "If you dump that on me, I swear…"

The sensation of his wet finger on my back made me suck in my breath. He traced what felt like the number one and then a V shape. A drop of water slid down the base of my spine, making every nerve come alive.

We used to write secret messages on each other's backs when we were little, only we were fully clothed and it didn't feel like this.

"First word?" he asked.

I smiled. "You'll have to do it again."

He wrote it slower this time, each stroke lasting seconds.

"You…" I said.

He painted three more letters.

"Are…"

The third word took a couple of tries—it was long with a lot of rounded strokes. Or maybe I didn't want to try that hard to figure it out. Maybe I wanted this moment to last forever.

"Beautiful," I whispered. I'd been called cute, sexy, *exotic* (which I hated)…but never beautiful, unless you counted my mom. "So are you."

I leaned into him, reaching for the water, but I found his lips instead. In the dark, our hands went everywhere, places we might not have had the guts to go with the light on. I pulled his sweats off, and he unbuttoned my shorts, tugging them down over my hips.

We ended up on our sides, my legs tangled with his, both of us sticky with sweat. It was like the time Mom took us sledding in the Cascades. I'd go for the steepest hills, and I didn't want to slow down. Even when I knew I should.

"Do you have a condom?" I asked. The only barrier between us was his boxers and the thin cotton of my underwear. It felt like nothing.

"No. Do you?"

"Maybe…" I'd gotten a three-pack last summer and kept it in my room, just in case. But I had no idea where it was now.

"Are you sure you want to?" he asked.

My body was aching to, willing me to close my eyes and

lose myself entirely. But I wasn't sure. Far from it. "I…"

"It's okay." His breath tickled the crook of my neck. "I'm good with this."

He kissed the space between my breasts, moving lower until he reached the place where Christian punched me. The muscles in my stomach tensed.

"What happened?" he asked.

"What do you mean?" It was a stupid answer, but it was all I had.

"I saw the bruises…"

Bruises? I didn't even know there was a bruise. "I ran right into a table at the diner. It was brilliant."

"A table. Really?"

"Yep." I hated lying to him. God, I hated it.

He exhaled, running his fingers over my stomach gently, like he was afraid I'd break. The song playing faded away, and it seemed like a century went by before a new one started. I stiffened, waiting for him to call me out as the hypocrite I was.

But he started kissing me again, my belly button, my hip bones…lower. I drew in a breath when his lips brushed against my thigh. His fingers tugged at my underwear.

"This okay?" he asked.

My heart started racing again, making my fingertips and toes go cold. I'd never done this with Zach. I thought about it—a lot. But I felt weird bringing it up.

"Yeah," I said, closing my eyes.

It was weird at first. Ticklish, a little uncomfortable. The muscles in my thighs tensed. My hands gripped the sheets.

But then every inch of my body tingled, and I went somewhere else. Somewhere warm and safe.

A place I never wanted to leave.

SATURDAY, JULY 5

We had a plan, a beautiful plan, but everything went to hell tonight. It's my fault. Everything I touch turns to shit.

CHAPTER SEVENTEEN

When I opened my eyes, Mom was standing over me, a golden beam of sunlight across her forehead. Cool breeze hit my back, making me shiver. I yanked the sheets over my naked chest and reached for Alex. But my hand met air.

"What's going on?" I asked, my voice hoarse. That was when I saw it. My curtains parted. My window wide open. I sat up, keeping my sheets pressed against me.

Mom motioned to the window. "Are you insane?"

"When I went to bed, it was closed." I scanned the room, my hands turning to ice. "Where's Alex?"

"You tell me." Her gaze went to the floor, where my discarded clothes lay. If I weren't so freaked out, I probably would've hidden under the covers. "Did you guys…"

"No." It came out too quickly. "I mean, we…stuff happened." The last thing I remembered was Alex holding me, the warm stickiness of our skin, his breath tickling my ear. He wouldn't take off and leave the window open. Everything about this scene was wrong, bad-dream wrong.

"Tell me you used a condom," she said, in an exasperated voice.

"We didn't need to."

Mom's mouth opened.

"We didn't do that," I clarified.

She exhaled and sat on my bed, massaging her forehead. "The cops just called," she said. "They're bringing Jenika over here."

"What? Why?" I pinched my leg, hoping I'd wake up for real. Alex would still be here, stroking my arm like he was when I fell asleep. Then I started to wonder if last night actually happened.

"There was a fire in their house last night," Mom said. "They said there was a lot of damage."

It took me a minute to process what she was saying, to understand this was reality. A reality I wasn't waking up from.

"Are they okay?" I asked. It could've been an accident, one of their cigarettes left to burn. A firework that landed on their roof. But the timing was too right.

"Anya's in the hospital with smoke inhalation and some burns. They said it wasn't life-threatening. Jenika is okay—I guess she pulled Anya out."

Not many people around here had AC, and it was way too hot last night to keep the windows closed, unless you were paranoid like me. Christian wouldn't have even needed to get inside. He could've walked by and tossed something in. "Do they know how it started? Were they asleep?"

"I don't know, hon. They didn't give me details."

Maybe that was why Alex took off in such a hurry. But there was no way he could've heard about it. He didn't have a phone… Unless he heard the sirens. Even then, he wouldn't be able to tell exactly where they were going.

My head felt like it was going to explode. "There's no way she's going to want to stay here," I said.

"Well, Eric is all she's got in town."

"Did you call him? Is he coming home?"

She nodded. "As soon as he can, he said."

"How about now? He needs to be here—"

"I know, Nova. I know." She gripped the edge of my bed. "They said Jenika took off after she got her mom out. They had to track her down. She must've been terrified."

Or she was going after Christian. Maybe she came here, looking for Alex. But that would mean I'd slept through her knocking *and* Alex getting up and taking off.

"Where did they find her?" I asked.

"They just said a friend's." She blew out a breath. "We need to do what we can to make her feel comfortable, okay? I know it won't be easy."

"Easy? Mom, she *hates* us. It won't matter how nice we are."

"It matters to me." She met my gaze, a glare in her hazel eyes, the one that said the only answer she wanted was a nod.

I pulled the sheet higher on my chest. "Where is she going to sleep?"

Mom threw her hands up. "Best I can come up with is Gavin's room. He can sleep with me until Eric gets home."

"And then what?"

"I don't know."

The doorbell rang, making us both stiffen. Mom got up, stepping around my clothes, like they were contaminated.

She turned, her mouth turned down at the corners. "I could've been Gavin coming in here this morning…"

Heat rushed into my face. "The door was locked."

"No. It wasn't."

Alex must've forgotten to lock it after he grabbed his clothes out of the bathroom. Just like he *forgot* to close my window. "I'm sorry…"

"I hope you guys enjoyed last night," she said. "Because he's not sleeping in here again." With that, she left, shutting the door quietly behind her.

Normally I'd tell her how ridiculous it was to enforce that rule now. But all I felt was the strong, fast beat of my heart and a knot in my stomach. If Christian really did set that fire, with people inside, he was willing to do anything.

I got up, keeping my sheet around me, and shut my window. As I backed away, the heel of my bare foot sank into a piece of paper. It looked like it had been ripped out of my spiral notebook and torn in half.

I picked it up, relieved, thinking Alex left a note and the wind must've blown it onto the floor. Then I read the jagged, hasty writing.

GUESS YOU REALLY ARE A WHORE, it read. LOVE, ALEX

I stopped breathing.

Alex's writing was small, round, and absurdly neat, even when he was in a rush. These strokes were long and pointy, almost illegible. The *U*s looked more like *V*s, and the *O*s were oblong. There was something unnatural about it—nobody I knew wrote like this.

A cold sweat broke out across my skin. Alex didn't leave the window open. Someone else did. Someone who was in my room, standing over me, when I was lying there naked and completely vulnerable.

I imagined Christian the way he looked last night, his tangled hair and red-rimmed eyes. That note sounded like it came right out of his mouth. But he'd have no problem calling me a whore to my face. Or possibly setting my room on fire.

I threw on a dark green cami and the cutoff shorts on my floor. The camera outside my room should've picked up everything that happened overnight...and anyone who was here. I needed to grab the SD card from the receiver and see what it recorded. But instead, my hand froze on the doorknob.

Either someone other than Alex was in my room or they weren't. There were no other explanations. No easier-to-swallow scenarios. There was only the truth, a truth I wasn't sure I wanted to know. Because no matter how many times I told myself Alex didn't write that note, there was this small, nagging doubt. Maybe he'd really lost it.

Even from the end of the hallway, the air felt thick. Mom was talking in a low voice, silence her only response. The receiver was in the living room, between the two cameras—probably right where she and Jenika were standing.

I tiptoed past Gavin's room and peered into the bathroom. Alex's clothes were gone, which meant—whatever happened—he'd definitely had time to grab them. He must've been extra quiet to make sure I didn't wake up.

Mom and Jenika were standing in the entryway, several feet apart. Jenika was still in front of the door, her military backpack slung over one shoulder, one foot behind her. Soot tinged the ends of her blond hair, and there was gauze around her right hand.

"Do you want to take a shower?" Mom asked.

"Not here." Jenika's voice was low, almost emotionless. Her face was in the shadows, but I knew she had her chin tilted up and that stone-cold glare.

"Where are you going to go?" Mom asked.

"Matt's."

"Did his mom *say* you could stay with them?"

"Sure." Jenika didn't miss a beat.

Considering Matt told me he slept on the couch because his younger brother and baby sister were in the other rooms, I doubted that was the case.

"We both know you've got nowhere else to go," Mom said, softly.

I tiptoed toward the living room, staying close to the wall, but Jenika's face turned in my direction. I kept going, focusing on the blue lights of the receiver.

"Look, I know this is awkward," Mom continued. "But you're welcome here. Eric really wants to see you."

"Yeah? Where is he?"

"He'll be here as soon as he can."

"I bet."

I reached for the SD card. There was no way around this. I couldn't unsee whatever was on here.

"You going to join the conversation or are you just going to spy?" Jenika called out.

My hand squeezed the card, part of me wishing I could crush it. "I was grabbing something," I said, meeting them in the entryway.

"Right," Jenika muttered. Her eyes were bloodshot and smudged with mascara. She looked every bit as small as her five-foot-three, hundred-pound-and-change frame right now. Even with her knee-high steel-toe boots and stick-straight posture.

Mom gave me a questioning look. If I told her I thought someone other than Alex was in my room last night, she'd freak out and want to call the cops. I needed to see what was on that video first. I needed to prepare myself.

"The cameras recorded something last night," I said. "It was probably just…" I paused. "Alex."

"Is he here?" Jenika asked, her eyes darting between me and the hallway.

"He was gone when I woke up." I knew her. If she even got an inkling of what happened between Alex and me, she'd use it against me somehow. "Did you see him at all? This morning?"

"No." Her mouth tensed, and she folded her arms.

My nose caught a whiff of old burned carpet and cigarettes. "I'm sorry about your house," I said, knowing it was lame. It was also the most sincere thing I could say to her.

"Why?" she asked. "Did you set the fire?"

A door opened behind me, and Gavin padded out in his blue Avengers pajamas and green socks. His hazel eyes widened when he saw Jenika, and he froze, as if he wasn't sure it was safe to come closer. He'd only met her a few times—and it wasn't for very long.

Jenika stared back at him like he'd stepped out of a portal. Her fingers tensed around the strap of her backpack.

"What's she doing here?" he asked, his voice uncomfortably loud in the morning light.

"She's going to be staying with us for a little bit," Mom said.

"Why?"

Grateful for the distraction, I headed back to my room, my heart getting faster with every step.

It took five minutes of staring at the "7-05" folder on my computer to have the guts to open it. Eight video files sat inside, each titled with the time of the recording and the camera that recorded the footage—003046_1, 003105_2, when Alex showed up at my window last night, 021704_1, 023211_2, 023213_1, 024055_2, 025445_2, and 025454_1.

Pins and needles ran up my arms. Either the feral cats around here decided to have a party in our yard or someone else was definitely here last night. Camera One recorded the entranceway and the driveway. Unless Alex left out the front door, which he never did, there was no way he could've triggered the recording at 2:17 a.m. because Camera Two would've picked him up crawling out my window first.

I opened the 2:17 file, my chest full and tight with dread. A figure, silhouetted by the streetlights, stood at the edge of our driveway, almost out of frame. They swayed side to side like an anxious little kid waiting their turn. They were too far away to make out details, especially since I'd picked lower-quality recordings to save space on the SD card, but the body definitely looked male—tall, square shoulders, narrow hips. He was wearing a baggy dark-colored T-shirt.

I turned up the volume on my computer speakers, but there was just white noise and the occasional hum of a car on the main road. After about ten seconds, a fire truck siren bellowed in the distance, gradually getting louder. More sirens joined in seconds later. As they got closer, the figure bolted out of frame and the recording ended.

I double-clicked on the first 2:32 a.m. file, the camera outside my room this time. There was the low rumble of my window sliding shut before a figure fully appeared in the frame. Alex, dressed in his gray pullover and jeans, tilted his face up toward the camera and gave a quick wave. His expression was odd, not smiling but not noticeably upset either. He turned and went left, disappearing from the picture.

An ache formed in my throat. Maybe he didn't know how to deal with what happened between us. Maybe he was having second thoughts. But that didn't give him a free pass to sneak out like I was some chick he hooked up with. He knew what a big deal last night was to me. I couldn't believe he'd just leave...

I opened the second 2:32 a.m. file, expecting to see Alex heading down the driveway. But it wasn't Alex walking past my mom's Subaru. It was the same figure I saw at 2:17. Only this time he came much closer to our entrance. Close enough to see his dark, spiky hair and WE ARE NUMB spelled out in white letters across his shirt. We Are Numb was Zach's favorite band.

I held my breath. Zach froze, his face turning toward the direction Alex would be coming from. Then he ran to the other side of mom's car, ducking out of sight.

A moment later, Alex cut across our front lawn and headed down our driveway. He was jogging, almost like he couldn't get out of here fast enough. I bit my tongue, waiting for Zach to reappear. But the video clip ended.

Alex always did have a sixth sense—he was impossible to sneak up on. Maybe he sensed that someone was out there, lurking around. Maybe he was running because he heard Zach's footsteps as he got closer to the front of the house.

The next clip was recorded almost eight minutes later. Zach appeared from the right side, which meant he'd gone all the way around my house to get to my bedroom. A sick feeling settled in my stomach as he moved toward my window and I heard the gentle rattle of the glass. Based on the sound, he took his time opening it, inch by inch.

I already knew what came next. He crawled inside, saw me lying naked in bed, and wrote that note. But he'd been in my room for eleven minutes. That note could've been written in a minute or two. What else did he do in here?

A prickly itch shot down the back of my neck, the sensation I always got when I felt like I was being watched. I went still, my hands gripping the arms of my chair.

"That doesn't look like Alex," a voice said behind me.

I jumped, whipping my head around to see Jenika standing inside my doorway.

"What are you doing in here?"

She motioned behind her. "Door was wide open."

"No, it wasn't." I remembered pushing it shut behind me.

"Okay, maybe more like a crack. But open is open."

"That doesn't give you the right to walk in here."

She took a couple steps inside, scanning my walls. "This was going to be my room. Eric ever tell you that?"

"No…" When Eric and my mom started seeing each other, we were still living with Gramps in his three-bedroom rambler in the woods off Cascade Creek Road. Eric had gotten this house for a steal because it was a dilapidated mess and the old lady who lived here died in the master bedroom closet. His plan was to fix it up and sell it for twice as much. But he'd changed his mind after he met my mom, and we moved in.

At least that was what I was told.

"Did he mean if you decided to live with us?" I asked.

"Nope." She looked down at her feet, pursing her lips. "He used to take me with him when he was fixing the place up. Said it was a *surprise* for Mom."

"He never told us that."

"Eric only tells you what you want to hear."

Maybe it was true, maybe it wasn't. With Jenika, you never really knew. But I didn't have time for her games.

Jenika's gaze moved from my disheveled bed to my clothes on the carpet. "Underwear on the floor. Classy."

"Yeah, well, nobody invited you to come in here and look at it." I walked over and collected my dirty clothes, throwing them in the hamper. "How's your mom?"

"She'll be okay." She said it deadpan, like I'd asked her if she was enjoying the weather. I opened my mouth to ask for more details, but she spoke before I could. "Is Amber's body even cold yet?"

"What are you talking about?"

"What do you think?"

Heat rose into my face as I realized what that video probably looked like. "Zach let himself into my room, without my permission. While I slept."

"Was Alex here?"

"No, the cameras picked him up racing out of here around two thirty, like he was going to…" I trailed off.

Her eyebrows rose. "A fire?"

"Yeah." I sat back at my desk, turning away from the intensity of her stare. I didn't want to say too much—not to Jenika—but the words still came out. "It's not like him. He never…takes off like that."

"Without getting your permission?"

There was the snark I expected. If I'd just lost the roof over my head and my mom was in the hospital, I'd probably be a mess. But Jenika was never one to show feelings, other than anger. "Look," I said. "I can't do this right now. I'm trying to figure out what happened last night."

"So am I."

I hovered over the 2:54 a.m. file with my mouse, but I didn't open it. "Then shouldn't you be doing that?"

My bedsprings squeaked behind me. Apparently, she wasn't planning on leaving anytime soon.

"What time was Zach here?" she asked, after a few seconds.

"He first showed up at two seventeen. Sirens scared him off, though—is that around the time the fire started?"

"It didn't start. Someone started it."

I swiveled my chair around to face her again. She was sitting on the corner of my bed, the note signed by "Alex" in her lap.

"Zach write this?" she asked.

"Only other person here was Alex."

She squinted at me. "You seriously think Alex would write this?"

"Did I say that?" I swallowed back the tension in my throat, the ache of guilt. It was a small voice that doubted Alex. But it had been there just the same.

"I always knew Zach was a twisted little fuck," she said.

"Yeah. I'm realizing that…"

"Him telling everyone you're a nasty skank wasn't enough?"

I didn't respond. The last thing I wanted to be reminded of was how much I'd trusted him. How I ignored every red flag.

My eyes went to the purple envelopes on my nightstand. The excuses I made for Zach not being behind those letters were just that—excuses. Probably because a big part of me still didn't want to believe I'd given it up to a creep. But it was as plain as day now. Leaving anonymous letters, whether they were a joke or not, was a cowardly act. And Zach was the biggest coward I knew.

"Why would he write this as Alex, though?" Jenika held the torn piece of paper up.

"He's always been dead set on convincing me Alex is a psycho."

Her eyebrows rose, like she wasn't quite buying it. I used that moment to turn around and double-click on the last video the camera above my bedroom recorded. Zach backed away from the window, like he wasn't sure he was ready to leave. He was clutching a piece of spiral notebook paper.

My heart pounded with anger this time. Alex *wouldn't* take off without leaving a note. That was probably it. But still, of all times for him to take off on me. Why after that? It didn't make sense.

The entrance camera showed Zach walking up my driveway, the paper a ball inside his fist.

"What time was that?" Jenika asked, making me jump a little.

"Two fifty-four." I faced her again. "You never answered me about when the fire started."

She studied me for a few long seconds, pursing her lips. Finally her shoulders sagged a little, and her expression softened. "I don't know exactly. I wasn't there."

"Where were you?"

"Does it matter?"

I resisted the urge to snap back at her. If I were in her situation, I'd feel guilty for not being there, and I probably wouldn't take kindly to anyone bringing it up. "I'm trying to figure out the timing."

"Me and Haley were out taking night shots of the fireworks," she said. "We got back after two—it wasn't more than ten minutes after. I saw the smoke. A few of our neighbors were standing there, being useless."

"I heard you pulled Anya out."

"Yeah, cause she's a dipshit. I crawled in through my window, and…" Jenika shook her head, her lips lifting into a bitter smile. "She was trying to put it out with bath towels and bottled water because she was so wasted she…" Her eyes lifted to mine. "Whatever. That's what happened."

I didn't know how to respond to that. It was a lot like when Megan was making fun of her family yesterday. You could laugh with them or pity them, both equally insulting. Or you could sit there uncomfortably, saying nothing at all.

"How much damage was there?" I asked.

"Enough." She flicked Zach's note to the floor. "We didn't have much to lose, though. Perks of being poor."

I wasn't buying the devil-may-care act. I'd heard the rage in her voice when she said someone started that fire. And I saw it that night with Christian. Inside she was probably screaming.

"Did they say it looked like arson?"

"They wouldn't tell me shit. They have to *investigate*." She used air quotes. "And this is Emerald Cove. That'll take a while."

"My house is a five-minute drive," I said. "It's possible Zach was involved. But he seemed startled by the sirens…"

Before she could respond, Mom tapped lightly on the door, her eyes going back and forth between Jenika and me. Her expression said exactly what she was thinking—*how long until they kill each other?* "Are you guys hungry? I was going to make Gavin some blueberry pancakes."

Yeah, right. Mom made pancakes only about once a year, usually for someone's birthday. But my stomach was so knotted up I doubted I could choke down a banana.

"I'm good," I said.

"You got real maple syrup?" Jenika asked, like Mom was her server. "I won't eat the fake shit."

"I can pick some up." She flashed a tight smile. "I've got to get eggs, anyway." She started to retreat, but then she turned around again. "What did the cameras get?"

I really wished I'd inherited Gramps's poker face. "Just Alex coming and going." I could sense the heat of Jenika's stare. All I could do was hope she didn't say anything.

Mom's brow crinkled. "He have somewhere to be?"

I shrugged. "I'm going to give him a call and find out."

With that, she left, telling me to keep an eye on Gavin.

Jenika waited until we heard the jingle of Mom's keys to speak. "I thought you guys told each other everything."

"What would you know about it?"

Her black nails traced patterns on my sheets. "Enough. So, why'd you lie?"

"Because she'd want to get the cops involved." And then I'd never have the chance to find out what he did in here, why he was writing me those letters.

"That's right. She'd rather rat than fight her own battles. How's that working out for her?"

I knew she was referring to the time Anya pushed my mom in the Emerald Market parking lot. "What was she supposed to do? Throw down in public, like she was on some trashy talk show?"

"'Cause screwing a married guy is real classy."

I could've argued that Eric had tried to separate from Anya a few times, even before he met my mom. That he only stayed as long as he did because she said she'd kill herself if he left. But that would probably end with a fistfight between the two of *us*. And unlike my mom, I'd have no problem defending myself.

"Your mom should've sucked it up," Jenika continued, keeping her gaze outside. "She deserved it."

"She did suck it up that day. And she's sucked it up every day since."

She turned, motioning to the walls around her. "Yeah, looks like it."

We stared each other down for what felt like an entire minute before she said she was going to take a shower. The tension in my chest dissipated as soon as I heard the water turn on.

After checking on Gavin, who was glued to some cartoon on TV, I grabbed the phone and dialed Alex's number. I cringed when his grandma answered with a curt tone.

"Hey, Cindy. Is Alex there?"

"It's barely eight in the morning."

"I know. I'm sorry—"

"You left a message at eleven o'clock last night," she continued over me. "It is extremely rude to call at all hours like this."

I closed my eyes, gritting my teeth. "It's really important I talk to him."

"If it's about the fire at that girl's house, I'll tell him when he gets up. He was working 'til late—didn't even come out of his room when those sirens were blaring."

Alex was really lucky her arthritic fingers couldn't pick locks anymore. "So, you haven't seen him yet? I mean, since yesterday?"

"No, why?"

The queasy feeling inside me intensified. "Just wondered. Is Megan up by chance?"

"She's right here. But if you keep calling like this, I'm going to start unplugging the phones."

"I understand." It seemed to take forever for her to hand the phone to Megan. With each passing second, my skin grew a little colder.

"Hey," Megan whispered. "You need to stop calling so early."

It was hard not to want to reach through the phone and hug her. But I couldn't let her see what I knew. I couldn't act differently.

"Can you get into Alex's room—make sure he's in there?" I asked.

There was a rustling noise on her end. "His car's here."

I told her he'd been at my house and took off in the middle of the night. "I want to make sure he got home okay."

She let out a breath of a laugh. "Oh my God. You're like

his mom sometimes."

I winced at that analogy.

"Hang on," she whispered.

As I listened to the clicking of her sliding something through his lock, I kept my eyes closed, hoping she'd say he was there, completely conked out. At least then this kicked-in-the-stomach feeling of dread would turn to anger that he couldn't face me in the morning. I was so ready to call him out.

It was silent a little too long, just the sound of her breathing.

"Megan?" I asked.

"He's not here."

"Is he in the bathroom, maybe?"

"I'm looking at it," she said, softly. "It's open."

My lips pressed together. I didn't want to freak her out, too…but maybe she needed to be freaked out.

"Nova, what's going on?" Megan asked. "Do you think the cakes did something?"

"I don't know… Did you hear him come home?"

"No. I had my earphones on to block out all the noise outside. The people next door were having a party and shooting stuff off."

Cindy's voice rang out in the background, asking where Alex was. Megan went silent—I could see her just standing there, looking at Cindy wide-eyed.

"I'll go out and look for him," I said, my mouth so dry I could barely move my tongue. "Call my house if he shows up."

"Okay," she said in a small voice before hanging up.

Jenika was standing in my doorway, running a towel through her hair. "Look for who?" she asked.

"Alex never made it home last night." I said the words, but they didn't feel real. My mind was too busy trying to find reasonable, safe explanations. He'd taken off early for a reason. And knowing Alex, that reason was he couldn't sleep and he needed time to think. Maybe he went to one of his spots to be alone and decided to sleep there, like he did when he was a little kid.

My gut was telling a much different story.

CHAPTER EIGHTEEN

"Let the cops handle it," Mom said, when I told her I wanted to look for Alex. She'd never buy my and Jenika's going out together otherwise.

"I don't even know if Cindy called them."

She turned on the sink, washing off a colander full of blueberries. "If Alex truly is missing, it's not a good idea to go looking for him on your own. I shouldn't have to tell you that."

"Thanks for the concern. But I don't really need your permission." Jenika laced up her boot at a rapid-fire pace.

Mom spun around, her lips in a firm line. "Actually, you do. We're legally responsible for you until your mom is out of the hospital."

"So, if I get eaten by wild bears or psycho killers, you can tell them I snuck out," she answered.

"That's not funny," Mom said.

Jenika hoisted her backpack over her shoulders. "They might never catch this killer. Are we supposed to hide under our beds for the rest of our lives?"

Mom wrapped her left hand around her right arm. It was her go-to move whenever she was in defense mode. "I'll say it again—maybe you'll hear me this time. It's not safe."

"Nothing's safe," Jenika said. "Just ask my mom. She was asleep in her house, minding her own business, when someone torched our living room."

Mom's mouth opened and closed again, her eyes widening. "Did the investigators say it was set on purpose?"

"They don't have to. I know it was."

"How?" Mom pressed.

"I just do."

Mom's eyes flickered to me, doubt in her expression. A house fire on the Fourth of July wasn't all that uncommon, even around here. Plus, Anya was a chain smoker. As much as I wanted to tell her that Jenika wasn't paranoid, I couldn't. She'd only want to pull the reins tighter.

"Look," Mom said. "I've got to go in to the diner for a few hours. If Alex hasn't turned up by this afternoon, I'll take you wherever you want to go."

"I can't just sit here, waiting around," I said. "And I'm not going to."

"My friend Matt can borrow his mom's car," Jenika said. "I'll have him pick us up and escort us around like it's 1857, okay?"

Mom's jaw tensed, as if she was holding back her own snippy comment. There was defeat in her expression. She knew I was going, short of her chaining me to a door. "Take the phone and the Taser. I call, you answer. Got it?"

I nodded. It was bad enough being alone with Jenika. Adding Matt to the mix made me nervous. But the only other person I could call was Brandon and he was working today.

Is your mom always this insanely overprotective?" Jenika asked as we waited on the porch for Matt. "I mean, there's little old ladies out power walking right now."

I had my doubts about that. It wasn't as if the entire town went into hiding, but I'd noticed subtle differences. More people walked in groups, even if they weren't actually together. There was less eye contact and more silence. "She's been like this ever since they found Amber."

"Have you heard that rumor, about Alex being seen with Amber before she went missing?" she asked, lighting a cigarette.

"He told you?"

Jenika shook her head. "It's been making the rounds." She tilted her head up, exhaling smoke toward the low clouds in the sky. "Why Alex? I don't get it."

"Because, like I said, Zach is convinced he's the devil incarnate…"

"He's convinced or he wants to convince?"

"Both." The chilly marine air was back, making my bones ache. I was wearing Alex's pullover, the one he gave me a few days ago at the park. His scent had faded, but every now and then I'd pick up a whiff that made me clutch the rough black fabric tighter.

"Strangulation is a slow way to take someone out," she said, spitting over her shoulder. "You really have to commit."

"I wouldn't know."

"You think Zach could go through with it?"

I felt like I'd answered that question a million times this week, but my answer hadn't changed. Even with how hell-bent he was on pinning this on Alex. Even after seeing how disturbed he truly was with my own eyes. I wasn't afraid of him. Not even a little. Right now my only fear was not finding Alex.

"Zach needs someone to do his dirty work for him," I said.

"He broke into your room, didn't he?"

"Yeah. While I slept. He probably would've pissed his pants if I woke up."

She took another drag. "That's tough talk for someone who looked like she was gonna piss *her* pants when she saw that video."

"You don't agree?"

"Taking Zach at face value? Sure."

"You don't think Christian's a lot more capable?" I watched for even the slightest twitch in her expression.

She lifted her cigarette to her mouth, but she didn't take a drag. Her eyes narrowed at something in the distance. "If he was gonna off someone around here, it'd be one of us."

My chest tensed again, my fingers growing cold. "You think he set that fire?"

"Think?" she asked, her cigarette-holding hand still frozen in place. "I know he did."

I remembered the last thing Christian said to us, with that mocking tone. *Tell Jenika I said hi.*

Matt pulled into our driveway, coming to an abrupt stop. His beloved hard-core punk screeched out the open windows of his mom's old red Honda, a mash of jittery guitars, shouting, and rabid drum beats.

His face scrunched up as he watched me walking toward the car. "This is different," he said with a smirk.

"I'll take the backseat," I said, ignoring him.

"Nah." Jenika opened the back passenger door before I could get to it. "It's way more comfortable up front." She got in without even giving me a chance to protest.

There was a baby seat next to her, leaving the front my only option. I didn't trust getting in the car with them, much less having my back turned on Jenika.

Matt turned the music down. "You coming or not?"

"Relax," Jenika said. "We're not going to kill you." Her eyes widened in faux innocence. "Your mom would know who did it."

I got in, keeping my hand on the Taser in my pocket, not that it would do a whole hell of a lot.

I told Matt to drive to Rainbow Creek Park first; it was the closest, and it was the place Alex ran away to most often when he was a kid. His grandpa would find him in his sleeping bag on the grass next to the creek.

The park was almost as quiet as it was when I met Alex here the other day. Only this time we passed a couple walking their dog and a guy sitting alone, feeding the ducks. He looked about our age, even had light brown hair, like Alex's. I kept hoping if I blinked enough it would turn out to be him.

"Why are you guys so sure he's missing?" Matt asked, trailing behind Jenika and me.

"She is," Jenika said. "I'm not ready to panic yet."

"Is that why you wanted to bolt out of the house with me?" I asked.

"I wanted to get the hell out of there."

I wasn't buying that. Jenika would sooner wear a pink dress in public than willingly go anywhere with me.

"When's the last time you saw him?" Matt asked.

"Two thirty this morning," I said, knowing full well how paranoid I probably seemed.

Matt snorted. "The guy can't take care of himself for a few hours?"

"Christian cornered Megan at Oswald Beach last night. And then he, Zach, and this other guy tried to jump us when we picked her up. If they saw him walking alone…" I closed my eyes, trying not to go there. A lot of the cakes were probably convinced that Alex killed Amber by now. *Any* of them could've done something to him.

"What do you mean he cornered her?" Jenika said, her voice sharp.

I told them briefly what happened. They went quiet for a minute, Jenika falling into step behind me. I could feel the heat of their stares and the weight of their thoughts on my back.

"Ray Munoz told me he saw a newer Ram 3500 right before the fire started," Matt said. "He thinks it was a Laramie Longhorn."

"Why's that significant?" I asked.

"Because it's a fifty-thousand-dollar truck." He said it like I was an idiot for not knowing the ins and outs of pickups. "Ray said it was circling around the lanes—drove past his house twice."

I wanted to tell him *that* was the more significant detail, but I held my tongue.

"What color was it?" Jenika asked.

"He just said dark."

"That's kind of a cowboy truck for a cake," she continued.

I couldn't think of anyone in Christian's circle who drove a big pickup, but that didn't mean anything. I didn't know most of their names, either.

"Did you guys try tracking Christian down after the fire?" I asked.

"His house was dark and his car was in the driveway," Matt said. "The jackass has motion lights and cameras, though. We couldn't get too close."

We headed down the narrow gravel trail until it curved away from the creek. It eventually connected to the Neah-kahnie Mountain Trail, a path that ran all the way up into the foothills. But Alex liked to be by the creek.

"What are you going to do when you find him?" I asked.

"Don't worry about it," Jenika said.

The shadows of tree branches extended across the path like fingers lacing together. I was too aware of the fading light, Matt and Jenika's measured footsteps behind me, and the complete lack of any other sound.

"Alex isn't here," I said, turning and facing them.

"Do you have some kind of Alex detector on you?" Matt asked, a half smile on his face.

"I just know him."

Jenika threw her hands up. "Where to next, then?"

"How many places we going?" Matt asked, glancing around like he heard something. "I've gotta get the car back by eleven."

"I'll keep looking by myself," I said. I'd stick to the public streets in town, instead of taking shortcuts on the trails.

"It's not eleven yet," Jenika said. "Where else are we going?"

"Why are you—" I began.

"I'm not doing this for you," she said. "I'm doing this for Alex."

Matt bumped his arm into hers. "What, are you in love with him now?"

"Oh, yeah. That's it." She turned and walked the other way, her shoulders stiff.

I'd never considered that Jenika might have real feelings for Alex. Probably because I couldn't imagine her having real feelings for anyone. But what if she did?

We checked the parking lot of the old Pacific Sunrise motel, a place where he skated sometimes, Neahkahnie Park, the old Emerald Bay Dock, where you can watch sea lions without the twenty-dollar cover charge, and the Deception Creek Trail behind their trailer park. Each time, I held my breath, hoping I'd see him sitting or wandering around, his hoodie pulled over his head so he could hide from the world. I even called up his Uncle Joel in Portland.

But he was nowhere to be found.

After walking down the Deception Creek Trail, Jenika and I went to Alex's house, trying his window first. When he didn't answer, I already knew...he wasn't there. We knocked on the front door anyway, and Megan answered, her eyes wide and expectant.

"Did you find him?" she asked.

"No." My voice came out cracked. It felt like someone was pushing on my chest, applying more pressure every time I inhaled.

"It's his birthday..." Megan trailed off, noticing Jenika for the first time.

"I know," I said.

Jenika shifted her weight, keeping her gaze down. It was the first time I'd seen her look

even remotely uncomfortable.

"Grandma's making him a cake right now."

Even though he never came home last night. She really was losing her mind. "You guys should call the police," I said.

Megan looked over her shoulder and came outside, pulling the door shut. "They had a huge fight yesterday, about getting the car scratches taken care of. He told her he doesn't have the money yet. She was like, 'If you had any respect for your grandfather, it never would've happened in the first place.'

Then he tore out of here."

"She knows where to hit, doesn't she…" I said.

Megan exhaled, folding her arms. "Yeah. Well. *She* thinks he's staying out to spite her."

"So she's baking him a cake?" Jenika asked.

Megan shrugged, keeping her focus on me. "It's probably one more thing she can hold over his head."

"Let me talk to her," I said.

"It's not going to…" she started to protest, but I was already pushing past her and opening the door.

Cindy was in the kitchen, stirring batter in a mixing bowl by hand. Flour peppered her arms and heat-reddened chest. It wasn't all that warm inside, but her forehead and neck were glistening, and her breaths were heavy, like she was jogging in place.

A pang of guilt hit me in the stomach. I wanted to yell at her, but defeat was in her every movement, from her limp wrists to the way she'd fruitlessly blow at the stray hairs in her face.

"Mrs. Pace," I said, approaching the counter.

"Oh. Hello." Her sharp blue eyes roamed from me to Jenika. "I'm sorry about your home," she said. "Did you have insurance?"

Most people would ask if she was okay, if her mom was okay. But that was Cindy.

Jenika nodded, but she didn't respond otherwise.

Cindy turned her attention to me. "Alex still isn't home."

"And we can't find him," I said. "We've looked everywhere he likes to go."

She stopped stirring, her mouth puckering, and turned to get some vanilla out of the cabinet. "He thinks he's teaching me a lesson, stayin' out like this."

"If that were true, *I'd* know where he is."

She poured the vanilla into a teaspoon. "Really? Can't say I've seen much of you this summer."

"Something is wrong," I said, ignoring the sting of her comment. "I know it."

The spoon fell through her swollen fingers. It sank into the bowl, bit by bit, until the handle disappeared into the brown sludge. "He used to do this all the time, remember? Give him a few more hours. He'll be back."

She said it so calmly, too calmly, like she was trying to convince herself.

"You know that girl who got murdered?" Jenika cut in. "She was missing a week, and she was alive—right up until the morning they found her body."

I winced at her words, both in anticipation of Cindy's reaction...and the reality of it. When Amber went missing, she disappeared into the night, just like Alex.

"I know that," Cindy said. "The police have been here twice to question him. You'd think *he* was a suspect."

Twice? That was news to me... I looked over at Megan, but her eyes were fixed on the ground, her hair wound tight around her fingers.

"I told him to clean up his act or this kind of thing would happen," Cindy continued, her gaze resting on Megan. "You two already have enough to overcome."

Megan lifted her head. "He's missing," she said between her teeth. "We should fucking do something about it."

Cindy lifted her finger, her mouth dropping open. "You don't—"

"There are people who want to hurt him!" Megan yelled over her.

"Who? Why?" Cindy ran her fingers over the dry skin on

her elbow, her cheeks a few shades paler than they were a minute go.

"Some rich kids," I said. "They're the ones who messed up the El Camino."

Cindy's face scrunched up, and she turned her back to us, picking up a towel and wiping off her hands. "I need to talk to Megan," she said. "I'm going to have to ask the two of you to leave."

Megan held her hand up and gave me a nod, saying it was okay.

"If she doesn't report this, you need to do it," I told her, not caring that Cindy was well within earshot.

Then I left, letting the door slam shut behind me.

We stood in front of Jenika's house, taking in the damage in the light of day. Yellow tape that said FIRE LINE DO NOT CROSS blocked off the entrance. Scorch marks reached outward from the window like sun rays, and the air reeked of melted plastic and burned fingernails, the kind of smell that embedded itself deep in your nostrils. I couldn't see inside the window; it resembled a cave, black and infinite. It went with the stillness of the day. The dread in the pit of stomach. The anger gouging at my throat.

I pulled my mom's emergency phone out of my pocket and dialed Zach's cell number. Like I expected, he didn't pick up.

"I have video of you breaking into my room last night," I said to his voicemail. "Meet me at Vista Pizza by noon or I'm taking it to the cops."

"That's real fucking intimidating," Jenika said when I

hung up. "*Meet me at Vista Pizza by noon*," she imitated me in a low voice. "We'll chow down and catch up."

"It's open, and it's public. That's all I care about."

"We'll get a lot more out of him if you have him meet you at the creek, and I call some people."

"What are you, the mob? He has his own *people* he can call. A public place tells him he's safe. He's a lot more likely to come alone. And I want him alone."

She shook her head. "He's not going to tell you dick."

"If you and your friends want to try to lure him out to some deserted place afterward, go for it. I wish you luck with that."

"No, moron." She moved in front of me. "The key is having you set it up. He won't know we're there until it's too late."

"If I tell Zach I'm waiting in the woods all by myself, he'll *know* something's up and he'll bring company. Maybe it'll just be Christian. Maybe it'll be five of them. We don't know. Are you guys going to have my back if you're outnumbered?"

Jenika stared up at me, her dark eyes showing no signs of backing down.

"I didn't think so," I said, before turning and walking away.

"I didn't say no," she called after me.

I kept going.

Mom called as I waited inside Vista Pizza. I'd picked a booth by the window, so I could see Zach approaching and anyone who might be with him.

"I'm okay," I said, before telling her that Alex was still missing.

"Are you going home soon?"

"Just grabbing some pizza. Jenika got hungry," I threw in. Mom knew me well enough to know I'd have zero appetite right now. I'd only been here a minute, and the thick smell of canned tomatoes, cheap pepperoni, and Parmesan was already making my stomach turn.

"I still think he'll turn up soon," Mom said. "It's not the first time he's wandered off for a while, you know?"

Yeah, people said that about Amber too. If it were me, she would've already assumed the worst and called the cops hours ago. But she was going to try to reassure me right up until the moment she couldn't anymore.

Zach's green Mustang pulled up along side the curb. He was alone in the car, at least.

"I have to go," I told Mom. "Call me right away if you hear from Megan."

Zach took his time getting out of the car, and I could tell, as he ambled toward the entrance, he hadn't been to sleep yet. Last night's T-shirt and jeans were loose and rumpled, and his hair looked dry and frizzy.

A jolt shot up my spine, springing my mind into action. I put my shaking hands in my lap, lacing my fingers together. If he saw me flinch, it was over. He'd know he had the upper hand.

As he approached, I took in his bloodshot eyes and hollow cheeks. I hadn't noticed it last night, but he'd lost weight—at least five pounds. When he slid into the booth, I could tell he'd put on fresh deodorant, but it didn't cover the scent of old sweat and last night's booze.

He stared at his fingers, his breaths faster than they should've been. "Is there really a video?"

"I installed cameras—one above my room, one above the entrance. But I guess you're not very observant."

A server approached us, the forced smile on her face all too familiar. "Can I get you guys something to drink?"

"Lemonade," I said, not taking my gaze off Zach.

He ordered coffee, still without looking up.

"Why didn't you call the cops?" he asked, running his fingers back and forth across the table. Dirt was embedded under all of his nails, as if he'd been digging in the mud.

"Where's Alex?" I asked.

He finally looked up with a squint. "What?"

"You heard me."

"How the hell would I know?" His eyes were like dark pools of nothing right now. I couldn't tell what he was feeling, *if* he was feeling anything.

We sat there for a good minute, staring each other down. He'd violated my trust. My privacy. I hoped every ounce of hate I felt was showing on my face.

The server came back with our drinks, eyeing us warily. She set the glasses gently in front of us and then scampered away.

"I know it was you leaving me those ridiculous letters," I said.

"You mean the ones piled up next to your bed, like some kind of shrine?" He said it in a low, intimate voice, the way he used to talk to me when we were alone.

I squeezed my fingers together in my lap and kept my chin up, reminding myself not to falter. He was still Zach, spineless. "Why'd you write them?"

"Because, at the time, I meant it. I don't anymore."

"Your girlfriend was missing. And you still kept it up."

His lips moved, but his words were inaudible.

A figure moving in my peripheral vision caught my eye. Jenika, appearing out of seemingly nowhere, slid in next to

Zach, forcing him to scoot toward the window.

"How's it going?" she asked him.

Zach straightened, his eyes darting between the two of us. "Why is she here?"

I shrugged.

"Tell me what you want," he pressed.

"You're the one stalking me," I said. "What do *you* want?"

He studied me, his face scrunching up in disgust. "Did you enjoy it?"

"What kind of question is that?" Jenika asked.

His words made my heart pound. I knew what he was asking, and it wasn't as if I enjoyed being stalked. What happened between Alex and me last night was one of the most intense things I'd ever experienced. The kind of moment you kept in a lockbox inside your head because it wasn't meant to exist anywhere else. It wasn't anyone else's business.

"You're legally an adult now," I said. "You think you're going to get a slap on the wrist for breaking into my room?"

Zach's chest rose and fell, but he didn't blink. He glared at me, like he was trying to burn a hole between my eyes.

"I didn't touch you," he said, finally. "If that's what you're thinking."

If he'd laid a hand on me, I would've woken up—that I knew for sure. But that wasn't what I wanted to know. "You were in there for eleven minutes. You could've done anything."

"I was going to talk to you, all right?" he said. "But then I saw him leave. And I saw you…" He looked out the window, his nose wrinkling. "You know what I saw…"

Jenika leaned toward him, her fingers tracing circles on the table near his elbow. "Where's your master?" She craned her neck to view more of the sidewalk outside. "I know he can't be far."

"If you mean Christian, I don't know. Nobody does." He turned to face me. "Maybe he's wherever Alex is."

"He's missing?" I asked, a shiver running down my neck.

"He was supposed to meet up with our friend Ben at midtide this morning. He didn't show, and he's not answering his phone."

My gaze went to Jenika, but she didn't even flinch. "Arson is tiring," she said. "He's probably passed out somewhere."

"What the hell are you talking about?" Zach's voice rang out, loud enough to get the attention of a family sitting several booths down.

Jenika leaned even closer, her mouth inches from his ear. "You know. You were probably there."

"Where?" he shouted again.

"Lower your voice," I said. "You want everyone to know your business?"

His lips curved up, showing his teeth, but his eyes were rabid and vacant at the same time, the look I imagined addicts had when they couldn't get their next fix. "Everyone already does." He leaned toward me, his fingers digging into the table. "They've interrogated me. My family. Turned my house upside down. Took my things. My fingerprints. My spit. I couldn't even mourn my girlfriend's death"—his fist hit the table—"because I was too busy convincing people I didn't kill her."

"They'd need a warrant to take those things," I said.

"They asked. I let them."

"Then you can't really complain, can you?" Jenika said. "They have to rule you out somehow."

Zach's breaths were getting shakier, and his fingers were curled into fists. "Why can't you see it?" he asked me, his voice low and tense. "Even his own sister is afraid of him."

Sweat was forming down my back, making an unreachable

place under my shoulder blade itch.

Zach stared at me, shaking his head. It felt like minutes passed, but it was probably more like five seconds. "He left you a note."

"I know. I want it back."

"I burned it."

I considered shoving this table right into his chest. "Then I guess I'll have to go to the cops."

"Do it," he whispered. "I don't give a fuck anymore."

In a flash of movement, Jenika grabbed his hand, bent it back at an awkward angle, and used her other hand to pull his pinkie to the side, away from the rest of his fingers. "What about now?"

Zach winced, sucking in his breath. He pried at her death grip with his other hand, but she bent his pinkie more.

"The more you fight, the more it's gonna hurt," she said.

I looked around the restaurant, seeing if we had any witnesses. Luckily the only server in the place was busy talking to the cook. The family a few booths down had left.

"Go ahead," Zach said. "Break it." He let his arm and hand go limp, a dare in his eyes. "Do it in front of everyone."

The server's face turned in our direction. I leaned over, like I was picking something off Jenika's shirt.

"We have an audience," I whispered.

Jenika dropped his hand, and Zach rubbed at his pinkie, his brow crinkling when he tried to move it. She got up then, letting him out of the booth.

As he stood, she grabbed his arm and whispered, "Just remember. I know where you live, too."

He tore his arm from her grasp and walked out, shoving the door open. Seconds later, his Mustang jerked away from the curb, the tires squealing down the street.

SUNDAY, JULY 6

I don't understand people who are afraid to die. To me, life is a cage. You're stuck in your body, in the limits of your own mind. No matter how fast you run or where you go, you can't escape the noise. You can't escape them. You can't escape yourself.

Death is a journey. One day, those doors will open and you can be whoever you want. Go wherever you want. The options are endless. But you have to walk into the unknown, or you'll be stuck here forever, as yourself. I may choose my time. I may not. But when it comes, I will go willingly, with my head held high. I hope you come with me.

CHAPTER NINETEEN

The sirens in my head jolted me awake, dozens of them, like the morning they found Amber. My skin was covered in sweat, and my heart felt as if it were coming out of my chest. Only when I focused on the dim light glowing behind my curtains, the sirens kept going, getting louder until it seemed as if they were turning down my street. But they didn't. They passed by on the main street and kept going for another ten seconds before their wails cut off, leaving only the sound of a bird's laugh-like call.

I tore my covers off and threw on a pair of jeans and the first sweater I could grab. As I shut my bedroom door quietly behind me, Jenika emerged from the living room, where she'd decided to sleep, fully dressed.

"You heard them, too?" she whispered.

I nodded.

"Where do you think they went?" she asked.

I tiptoed toward the front door, motioning for her to come with me. It was just after 6:00 a.m. Mom would be up any minute, since we both had the opening shift.

The fog was thick this morning, so thick I couldn't see the houses across the street. I hated fog as a kid, the way it would swallow up and mute everything around me. Sometimes I'd cry because I was terrified that, one of these times, the world would stay gone. And I would be alone.

That was how I felt as Jenika and I ran down my street. No matter how fast I went or how out of breath I got, it seemed like I was going nowhere. I'd never find a way out.

But the fog wasn't as dense on Seal Point, the main road. The flashing blue and red lights were able to cut through, illuminating the pavement a couple blocks down. I knew where they were. Rainbow Creek Park.

It wasn't until we got closer that I saw Neahkahnie County sheriff cars, at least three unmarked cop cars, and a white van that resembled an ambulance...but it wasn't an ambulance. CORONER was painted on the side in blue lettering.

Nausea came on sharp and hard, and the muscles in my legs got weak. It felt like the world was growing dimmer.

Somehow my legs kept going.

Crime scene tape was already blocking off the entrance, and Officer Bube and Officer Mackey stood just behind it, facing each other. There were only a few onlookers gathered around. A woman in a jogging suit, her arms pressed in tight to her sides, one hand over her mouth. Mr. Kruse, who lived a couple doors down from us, gripping his dog's leash. A transient couple with dirt-stained clothes and tired eyes who were probably sleeping in the park.

We couldn't see much past the entrance, since the trail curved and went through a bunch of trees before reaching the creek.

"Let's try getting in another way," Jenika whispered, her eyes wide and searching our surroundings.

The only other *way* was taking the Neahkahnie Mountain Trail, which had an entrance over five miles from here. And this was clearly a suspicious death scene—they had every good way in blocked off.

"We'll never get close enough," I said. I tapped Mr. Kruse on the shoulder, making him jump and his dog growl.

"Oh, you scared me, Nova." He put a hand on his chest. "Did the sirens wake you up?"

I nodded. "Do you know what happened?"

"No, I was on my way over here… Glad I didn't make it." He motioned toward the woman in the jogging suit, lowering his voice. "I think she's the one who called it in."

I heard Jenika asking the young transient couple if they saw anything.

"No," the girl said. "We were out on the trail. This cop came running at us—I thought we were getting busted."

I turned, facing them. "Did you see anyone—before, I mean?"

"What are you guys, like, junior detectives?" The guy let out a nervous laugh. "Nah, we were comin' from the hills." He shook his head, running his fingers through his scraggly blond beard. "This is some fucked-up shit. If we'd come down any earlier…"

"We didn't," his girlfriend said, resting her head against his arm. "That's what matters."

A couple guys wearing plain clothes emerged from the trail, one of them carrying what looked like an iPad. Detectives, most likely.

I approached the woman in the jogging suit, who was standing away from the rest of us. She was still huddled up, her arms folded tight, so I spoke in a soft voice.

"Ma'am?"

She dabbed a Kleenex under her eye with quivering fingers. "Yes?"

"Did you see the body?" I hadn't meant for it to come out like that, but my thoughts were a jumbled mess.

She eyed me up and down, her mouth open, like I'd just asked her to hand over her purse. "A young man was killed."

My breathing stopped. "A young man? Like a teenager?"

"Leave me alone," she said.

"Look, my best friend went missing yesterday. And..." Every part of me was trembling now, even my voice. "I just... I need to know it's not him. Can you tell me what he looked like? His hair color? Clothes..."

The lines around the woman's eyes softened. "Oh, honey..." Her voice was about an octave lower than it was a few seconds ago. "I'm sorry. I shouldn't..."

"Was he wearing a hoodie, like a gray hoodie?"

She stared at me and put her hand over her mouth, her dark eyes growing shiny.

I could see the woman's face, her skin flashing red and then blue, the trees towering behind her like giant, lurching shadows. I could hear shoes crunching on gravel, the hiss of radios, murmuring voices, and birds chirping. But I wasn't here. I couldn't be here.

A hand touched my back, and there was a guy's voice but I didn't register what he said.

"Nova," Jenika's voice broke through.

I turned to see Detective Sandoval, the younger detective who was at my house, staring down at me.

"Hi," he said. "It's Nova, right?"

The white noise was still in my ears. "Is it Alex?" The words tumbled out of my mouth, choked and frantic. "Please say no. Please." I wasn't talking to him. Not really. I was begging some God I didn't even believe in.

"Take a deep breath for me, okay?" Sandoval said, his

dark eyes studying me. It wasn't in a concerned or human way. More like I was a broken clock he needed to put back together.

I did as he asked because it was the only thing I could do. There was no running away from this moment. No rewind button. No second chances.

"Why do you think it's your friend?" he asked, his voice gentle.

"Because he's been missing since the night before last."

Cindy had finally reported Alex missing after we left yesterday, but if Sandoval knew that, his expression didn't give him away. It didn't give anything away. I might as well have been talking to a statue.

"Why are you out here right now?" Sandoval asked.

"The sirens, they woke me up." My hands gripped at the fabric of my sweater. "Is it him?"

Sandoval's gaze softened, the first sign of emotion I'd seen on his face. I couldn't tell if it was sympathy for my fear...or something worse. "I'm sorry. I can't share anything right now."

"You just have to say no," I said. "Shake your head. Something."

"Can I have someone take you home?" he asked.

"We're okay," Jenika said. "We can walk." She sounded so sure herself, like the possibility of that body being Alex's hadn't even crossed her mind.

"Nova!" My mom called out. She was silhouetted by the police lights, jogging toward me.

She threw her arms around my shoulders, her long dark hair hitting me in the face. "I heard those sirens and...God, you scared the hell out of me." She pulled back, cupping my face. "What's going on?"

"There's a body—a young man."

Mom's eyes crinkled at the corners, and her mouth trembled. She drew in a shaky breath. "Is it...?"

"I don't know."

She pulled me to her again, squeezing me so tight I could barely draw in a full breath. I closed my eyes, waiting for the tears to come. To lose it. To break down.

But nothing happened. There was just that horrible humming in my ears and the smell of my mom's hair, jasmine and menthols.

couldn't work my shift, but Mom didn't want me to be alone, either. So I sat in the diner kitchen, rocking back and forth in the old brown rocking chair, tensing every time we heard voices on the scanner. Not that they ever said anything useful on the channels we could hear.

It was hard to sit still. I wanted to be out there, turning the town upside down. I wanted to be here in case something useful came in over the scanner or Megan called. I wanted to be at Alex's, in case... In case... I couldn't even say it. It wasn't him. It *couldn't* be him.

"There's just as much chance it's someone else," Jenika said. She stood in front of the back door, her arms folded.

"She's right," Gramps said, chopping onions and peppers. "You can't let your mind go there—not until you have to."

I kept seeing that woman's eyes when I mentioned the gray hoodie. It played like a loop, over and over. "What other 'young men' are missing right now? How can I not go there?"

"Christian is..." Jenika said.

"We don't know that for sure," I said.

Jenika glanced at the display on her phone, her left leg

jiggling. "So sit there being scared and useless. That's gonna help."

Her words felt like a flame inside my chest. "We can't all be sociopaths like you, Jenika. He's my best friend. I've got every right to be scared!"

"What'd you call me?"

I stood, moving toward her. There was a voice inside telling me to stop, but I couldn't. I wanted to keep going. I wanted to hurt her. "You barely know him. All he is to you is…"

She came at me, stopping inches from my face. "Go on. Tell me what Alex is to me. Tell me who *I* am."

I opened my mouth, but the words didn't come out this time.

"Say whatever makes you feel better about being weak," she continued, her voice barely above a whisper. "Because that's what you are. A weak, self-righteous bitch."

"Hey!" Gramps hollered, smacking his meaty hands together. "Go outside and duke it out. You'll do less damage."

Neither of us moved or even blinked. If she wanted to have it out, I was game. Right now I wanted to tear the world apart with my bare hands.

The kitchen doors swung open, making us both turn toward the entrance. Brandon walked in, his brow furrowing at Jenika. "Hey," he said, his gaze shifting between us.

"They found another body," I said. "Have you heard?"

He ran his hand through his hair, smoothing it back. "Yeah… My mom took off early this morning. Told me I'm no longer allowed to walk anywhere alone."

Everyone went still and quiet, even Gramps, who'd stopped chopping. I rubbed my fingers across the goose bumps on my arms. "Alex is missing," I said.

The lines in Brandon's forehead deepened, and his lips

parted, but nothing came out for a few seconds. "I know…"

"The sirens woke me up, so I went to the scene." My voice was starting to quiver again. "And I heard it was a young man—the body. But they wouldn't tell me who…"

"I'll call my mom, okay? See what I can find out."

I nodded. "Thank you."

He pulled out his phone and went out back. Jenika followed him, letting the door slam shut behind her.

"Tell me it's going to be okay," I said to Gramps, walking in circles around the rocking chair. I almost wished Gavin were here instead of with Rhonda; it was too quiet, too calm.

"Alex is a tough kid," Gramps said, dumping the chopped peppers into a silver bowl. "It's not him."

"Then where is he?"

"Probably best I don't know. 'Cause when I find him, I might kill him myself."

Distorted voices echoed through the kitchen, making me jump. More codes and letters. I watched the back door, waiting to see the knob turn. Waiting to see Brandon come through.

Gramps pulled me into a hug, squeezing me so tight his arms quivered. Jenika was right—I should be out there doing something. Not rolling over and playing dead.

The back door opened and Brandon came through, his head down. I pulled away from Gramps, my stomach in my throat.

Brandon knew something, because his fingers were twitching at his sides.

"Just tell me," I said.

He looked up then, and I stopped breathing. My skin went cold. A second lasted a minute. *It isn't Alex*, I told myself over and over.

"It's Christian Barnett," he said.

I exhaled, my muscles turning to jelly, the odd sensation of being relieved and horrified at the same time. Gramps turned then, cracking eggs into a pan, but not before I saw his shoulders relax and his eyes slowly close.

"Where's Jenika?" I asked.

"She took off after I told her." Brandon stared at the wall behind me, like he was in a daze. "This is insane…"

"Do you know if he was painted up, like Amber?"

"Between us?" Brandon said. "Mom said the scene is similar."

"Strangled?" Gramps asked, his back still turned to us.

Brandon looked down at his feet, shifting his weight. "His throat was slit, but you didn't hear that from me."

"Hmm…" Gramps said. Usually he had a lot more to say than that, but I had a feeling he was just as stumped as the rest of us.

I didn't believe in a coincidence at this point. Someone was targeting the cakes. In the eyes of the cops or *anyone*, that could be me, Alex, Jenika, or Matt, especially if they got a hold of that video.

And if anyone had a motive, it was Jenika. She didn't even ask those potential witnesses if they saw the body; she asked if they saw *anything*. She knew where our security cameras were, so she could've sneaked out the back door and hopped the neighbor's fence while we all were asleep.

Still, it was all too obvious. The killer was meticulous, trying to make a point, not get caught. Jenika straight up told Zach she thought they'd torched her house.

My hands and feet were buzzing again, begging to move. The damp heat in the kitchen clung to my skin and made my insides feel like they were melting.

I bolted for the back door, dug my feet into the gravel, and took off, letting the cool air sting my face. I ran until my lungs burned and there was nowhere to go but into the fog and the gray waves crashing in front of me.

I felt like I'd been split in two. There was the girl watching from above, wanting to press the stop button and make this all go away. She told me I should be scared. I should cry. I should feel *something*.

Then there was the girl inside me. She felt nothing other than the need to get answers.

Answers were the only way out of this.

went home first and called Mom, telling her I'd stay there. She made me promise. I closed my eyes and said *I promise*. Then I looked at the footage the security cameras recorded last night. The camera above the entrance recorded something at 4:26 a.m., a shadow darting across the driveway. I went through it frame by frame, only to see a bushy tail and four legs.

I kept going over the other night with Alex, seeing that weird intensity in his eyes. When he'd leaned in and kissed me the first time, it seemed like slow motion. But it was sudden, almost rushed. At least for the Alex I knew up until a couple weeks ago. He would've danced around the moment forever, the tips of his ears turning red.

"Just for tonight," he'd said. "Let's pretend out there doesn't exist."

It was like he knew everything would be different in the morning. Like he knew he'd be gone…

But he wouldn't bail on his job and Megan, not unless he had to. Cindy did say the cops had been by to question him twice. Maybe between them circling around and that rumor, he got scared. Still, other than his Uncle Joel's in Portland, he had nowhere else to go. He barely had any money. Even with the wilderness survival skills his grandpa taught him, he wouldn't last long out there without supplies.

I needed to find out what he'd said in that note, not that Zach would ever willingly tell me. And it would be almost impossible to get to him now. His mom probably had him under twenty-four-hour surveillance.

There was one way I could get to him, though. His email. Knowing Zach, his password was probably one of five things.

The phone rang, making me tense. A local number I didn't recognize showed up on the caller ID, and the chill down my arms told me it wasn't good news.

"Hello?" I answered.

"It's Jenika. Your mom said you went home."

"What's going on?"

"There was just a bunch of cops at Alex's place. It looked like they were doing a search."

A full-on house search around here usually meant a drug bust or some wanted felon who was hiding out at his relative's place. Or, in this case, someone who was suspected of a lot more than running away.

"You there?" Jenika asked.

"Did you see them carry anything out?"

"Some bags—I couldn't tell what. They have to have something on him, right?"

The apple tree leaves fluttered outside my window, reminding me to stay calm. Think, don't feel. "Or Cindy gave them permission."

"Why the hell would she do that?"

Because she was Cindy. She probably didn't think she had a choice. "I'm going to head over there now. See you in a few."

If I were one of those detectives, I'd probably be looking at Alex, too. The victims had bullied and humiliated him. That stupid rumor about him being seen with Amber was spreading like a cold on an airplane.

And then he disappears, right before Christian turns up dead.

It all fit together in a nice little box. But life wasn't a nice little box.

On the way to Megan and Alex's, I walked the route Alex usually took, keeping my eyes open for anything that could explain what happened to him that night. There were the usual things—cigarette butts, fast-food containers, and Band-Aids. There was a pair of jeans lying in a crumpled heap on the side of the road, which made my heart jump in my chest. But they weren't Alex's.

How would the killer be able to kidnap three people without ever being seen? Emerald Cove had no traffic cameras and plenty of remote areas, but it was almost impossible to avoid people during tourist season, even in the middle of the night.

Megan answered the door, her thumbnail in her mouth, her blond hair wild and tangled, like she'd been running her fingers through it constantly. "The cops were just here."

"I know," I said, moving past her. "What happened?"

Jenika followed me in and headed down the hallway, straight for Alex's room.

"They tore his whole room apart," Megan said. "Took our computer."

"Did they have a warrant?" I asked, following Jenika.

"No. Cindy let them because…"

I turned, facing her. "Because why?"

She folded her arms, focusing on the floor. "Grandpa's A-5 is missing. She noticed it last night."

"What?" Their Browning Auto-5 shotgun was a family heirloom, passed down from Alex's great-grandfather. Alex's grandpa had left it to him, but Alex wanted nothing to do with it.

"Where did you guys keep it?" Jenika asked, standing in Alex's open doorway.

"In its case, in the living room."

"You said Cindy tore the house apart the other day," I said. "Are you sure—"

"Yes!" Megan broke in. "We went through everything last night looking for it." Her face scrunched up like she was about to cry. "It's not here…"

"It's okay," I said, trying to keep my voice calm. "We're going to figure this out."

"How?"

I didn't even believe my words right now—why should she?

Still, neither Amber nor Christian was shot. The detectives couldn't tie it to the murders. If he did take it, the only reason I could think of was for protection.

"Where's Cindy now?" I asked.

"In her room, crying." Megan's voice softened to a whisper, as she motioned for us to go into Alex's room. After we were all inside, she shut the door and locked it.

"She's starting to believe he's involved in the murders," Megan said. "Like, really, truly believe."

Jenika threw up her arms. "What kind of person turns against her own blood without proof?"

"Cindy," I muttered, her name leaving a sour taste in my mouth. She'd always expected Megan and Alex to "go bad" as she put it, like they were nothing more than cartons of milk. It wasn't surprising to me that she'd turned her back on Alex already. She'd done it to both her kids.

I opened Alex's closet, looking for anything that might be missing. Not that I could remember every item of clothing he had. He did only have two pairs of shoes, though. Blue-and-white running shoes and his Vans. Both were missing.

"What else did you see them take, besides the computer?" I asked Megan.

"I couldn't tell," she said. "They told us to stay out on the couch, and the stuff was in bags."

I scanned the room for his backpack. Usually he kept it in the corner next to his desk, but it wasn't there. His skateboard was propped against the wall, next to his bed. Jenika sifted through the piles of books, socks, and papers scattered on his floor. It looked like the police had come in here and literally thrown everything into the center of the room.

His iPod was gone, too, but he took that thing everywhere with him. It could've been in the pocket of his jeans that night he came to my house. I should've found a way to search his room yesterday. At least then I might've been able to tell if he'd made it back here or not.

"If people were accusing me of killing someone and came after my little sister, I might not stick around," Jenika said. "Maybe he thinks it's better to stay away."

She was right—that did sound like Alex. But it still didn't make sense. "So, he thought taking off with a shotgun would make things better?"

"Who says he even took it?" Jenika asked. "When's the last time you actually laid eyes on it, Megan?"

"I can't remember."

"So it could've been gone for months, right?" Jenika pressed.

"Maybe." Megan ran her fingers through her hair, her forehead scrunching up. "I don't know…"

I touched her back, moving my hand in gentle circles. She stiffened at first and then leaned into me, resting her head against my shoulder.

"What if it's true?" she said, softly. "What if he killed them?"

"He didn't," Jenika shot back, glaring at her. "How the hell can you even ask that?"

"This is Alex," I said in a whisper, swallowing back the lump in my throat. My own tiny sliver of doubt. "Look me in the eye and tell me you think he's capable."

"I can't."

I put my hand on her arm, pulling her into a hug. "I'm here for you, okay? Whatever you need."

"I know," she whispered.

A phone rang, making us both jerk a little. It took me a few seconds to realize it was coming from my pocket. I'd taken the emergency cell in case Mom decided to call home while I was gone.

"I'm fine, Mom," I said without letting her talk.

Megan moved away from me and sat on the bed, pulling her knees to her chest.

"Those detectives came to the house looking for you," Mom said, her voice tense. "Nobody answered, so they came here. Where *are* you?"

"Alex's."

"Get back to the house now. I'll tell them to follow me," she said. "They want to talk to Jenika, too. Do you know where she is?"

My gaze met Jenika's; her frown told me she could at least hear some of what Mom was saying. "She's here."

"See you soon," she said, hanging up.

My heart was pounding again, sweat forming down the back of my neck. "Get rid of that video of Christian," I told Jenika. "Now."

"What video?" Megan asked.

Jenika shrugged, not even a flicker of concern in her expression. "There never was a video. I'm not that stupid."

"Why the hell didn't you say something?"

"It kept your mouth shut, didn't it?"

My mouth, as in I was the only one in the dark. "Did Alex know?"

She motioned to the window. "We should get back, don't you think?"

"Answer me." He knew how worried I was, how I couldn't sleep over it. If he'd lied about that, too, I'd never forgive him, whether he was dead or alive.

She tilted her chin up, her eyes narrowing. "No."

I let out a breath. She could've been lying—but why? If she wanted to mess with me, saying yes would be the way to go.

"He have any idea how little you trust him?" I asked.

She didn't comment either way. She stared back at me, her eyes nearly black in the dim light.

I opened Alex's window and stepped back. "You first…"

CHAPTER TWENTY

Detective Hahn and Detective Sandoval sat on our old white leather couch, just like the first time they came over. Only Hahn's grandfatherly smile was gone, and Sandoval didn't have my little brother's yellow mug in his hand. Their attention was fully on Jenika and me. I could feel them studying my shaking hands, the fact that I couldn't decide how long to look them in the eye. Too long made me nervous. Too little made it look as if I was hiding something.

I motioned for Jenika to take Eric's recliner, but she settled on the floor instead. *She* looked perfectly calm, like she did this kind of thing every day.

"Why do I need to be here?" she asked straight off.

"Do you know Christian Barnett?" Detective Sandoval asked.

Jenika's dark eyes darted between them. "Yeah…"

"What about Alex Pace?" he continued.

"Yeah."

"That's why you need to be here," Sandoval said.

"It's a small town. A lot of people know them," she said.

I pressed my lips together, wishing she'd shut up. She was going to get us both harassed even more.

Sandoval squinted at her, his thick fingers tensing around his knee. "Two teens, one of them you say you know, have been murdered. That concern you at all?"

"Of course it does," Jenika answered without missing a beat. "I'm just not sure how I can help."

Hahn stayed quiet and expressionless, watching us both.

"Answer a few questions, and we'll see," Sandoval said. "That's not a big deal, is it?"

"What do you want to know?" I asked.

Jenika shot me a dirty look and shook her head.

Detective Hahn straightened, motioning to Jenika and me. "You're both friends with Alex, yeah? Would you say you're close?"

"He's my best friend," I said, without even thinking about it.

"We've hung out a little the last few weeks," Jenika said. "Wouldn't say I know him that well."

No, you've just seen him naked. Sandoval started writing on that pad of his, keeping his head down.

Hahn focused on me. "How long have you been friends?"

"Since fourth grade."

"That's a long time," he said. "You must be pretty upset about him being missing."

"I'm terrified."

Sandoval looked up from his pad then, his dark eyes softening. He had seen how scared I was when I thought that body might be Alex's. That alone should tell them I had no idea where he was.

"Is this about Alex or the murders?" Jenika asked.

"We want to find him, make sure he's safe," Hahn said to her. "Don't you?"

Jenika folded her arms, her lips set in a firm line. She was probably thinking the same thing I was. They thought we'd talk more if it seemed like they were only concerned about his welfare. But giving them attitude wouldn't help, either. They wouldn't buy anything we said.

"Does Alex have an interest in firearms?" Sandoval asked. And there it was—the question I'd been dreading.

"No," I said. "That was his grandpa's thing. He hates guns."

"His grandfather left him one, didn't he?" Sandoval pressed.

"Yeah, but he wanted nothing to do with it. Cindy, his grandmother, keeps moving stuff around and then forgetting where she put it. It might not even be missing."

"So, you know it's missing?" Hahn asked.

"His sister told me."

Hahn studied my face, my hands, long enough to make me fidget even more. I was messing this up, probably making Alex look even guiltier by answering questions they didn't ask.

"Any idea where he might be?" Hahn asked.

"You mean if he hasn't been taken against his will?" I asked. Hahn gave me a nod in response. "We've looked everywhere for him. Everywhere we thought he might go."

"Who's we?" Sandoval asked.

"Me and Jenika."

"Where'd you look?" Hahn asked.

I rattled off the list of places, knowing that if Alex *did* take off on purpose, he wouldn't go to any of them. He'd be somewhere none of us knew about.

"He go to Rainbow Creek Park a lot?" Hahn asked.

"Not any more than other places," I lied. "He likes to feed the ducks, catch tadpoles."

Hahn's lips turned up a little. "Really?"

"He loves animals," I said. "Called the police once because his neighbor yelled at her cat."

"Huh…" Hahn said, glancing over at Sandoval.

Yeah. Not the kind of guy to behead a deer.

"When's the last time you saw him?" Hahn asked me.

"He came by my house about 12:30 a.m.—on the fourth. Or the fifth, technically. He stayed until…" I paused, remembering Alex waving at the camera. "He stayed until about 2:30."

"I noticed you got a camera above the entranceway now," Sandoval said. "Any chance that picked him up?"

"It did. I have it on an SD card."

"Would you mind giving that to us?" Hahn asked. "It would be helpful."

"Okay."

"Can you walk us through that last night you saw him?" Hahn said. "Why'd he come over so late?"

My fingers were grasping at the end of my T-shirt. I didn't want to walk anyone through that night. "He comes over late sometimes—just to talk. Listen to music. I gave him his birthday present."

"Did he seem upset at all?" Sandoval asked. "Say anything unusual?"

I swallowed back the lump in my throat. "He's been going through a lot with his grandpa dying. He didn't say anything about taking off, though. He left a note, but…Zach broke into my room that night and stole it."

Sandoval's head jerked up, and Hahn's eyebrows rose. "What do you mean he broke in?" Hahn asked.

I told them what happened, including Zach forging a note from Alex and how Zach had been leaving me anonymous letters before that. "The cameras got him going to my window."

"How do you know he wrote them?" Hahn asked.

"Because he admitted to it."

"Is that why you both threatened him yesterday, at Vista

Pizza?" Hahn continued.

"Threatened?" Jenika broke in. "Nova said if he didn't give her the real note from Alex, she was going to turn that video over to the cops. You call that a threat?"

Sandoval was flipping through his notepad. "So, you didn't accuse him of arson and say you were going to break into his house and mess him up?"

"No!" Jenika said, keeping her eyes on me.

I shook my head in agreement, part of me wishing I'd slugged him yesterday—while I still had the chance.

"Why didn't you contact the police right away?" Hahn asked me. "He could be charged for trespassing at the very least."

"I thought he might know where Alex was. It was the only way I could think of to make him talk."

"Why would he know where Alex is?" Sandoval asked.

"Because Zach has this vendetta against him," I said. "Because he saw…" I closed my eyes. I didn't mean for that to come out.

"He saw what?"

I took a breath, trying to slow my heart. "When he broke into my room, he saw that me and Alex had… We'd been messing around." I could feel Jenika's gaze on me, burning into my skin.

Sandoval's lips parted, but he didn't say anything. Instead he busied himself with writing.

"You and Alex are more than friends, then?" Hahn asked.

"I don't know what we are."

Hahn nodded slowly, his blue eyes going from me to Jenika and back. "Is it safe to say there's been ongoing problems between you and the summer residents? And by you, I mean the two of you, Alex, and some of your friends?"

I didn't know how to answer that—we were damned either way. "I'd say it takes two sides to make a problem."

Hahn held his hands up. "I'm not making any assumptions about who started what. But there's definitely been some bullying, yeah? Some physical fights, too?"

"What are you getting at?" Jenika asked.

Hahn nodded at me. "We heard that you and Alex got into an altercation with Christian Barnett on the night of the Fourth. Is that true?"

I told them what went down at Oswald Beach, including how they'd scared Megan and came after us. "Zach's making a lot of crazy accusations without anything but his mouth to back him up," I said. "You might want to keep that in mind."

Hahn's eyes narrowed at me, as if I was a sign he couldn't quite read. "We're not accusing you of anything. We're trying to get the whole picture, okay?"

I nodded.

"Let's back up a week," Sandoval said. "It was clear Christian had been in some sort of physical altercation when we spoke to him prior to the Fourth. Now, he claimed he didn't know who attacked him. But when we spoke to other people, both your names, Alex, and Matt Delgado came up as possibly being involved." He made a shrugging motion with his hands. "Any reason they'd single you out?"

I didn't want to lie again. I was sick over all the lying. But there was no choice. With Christian dead, that night made us look guilty as hell.

"Like we just went over," Jenika said. "We don't get along. Of course they're gonna point fingers at us."

Sandoval nodded, cocking his head to the side. "It's kind of strange, because witnesses said Christian left to walk a couple girls to their car, but he never came back. When they saw him the next day, he had bruises on his face and his car had been vandalized."

"I'm sure he was drinking," Jenika said. "Maybe he cut the wrong person off."

"Maybe, but," Sandoval continued, "multiple witnesses heard Alex threaten to physically harm Christian a few hours before the party." He shifted his gaze to me. "This was at your family's diner."

"You mean Gabi and Zach, Christian's friends?" I asked. "I didn't hear him say it."

"Okay," Sandoval continued. "But didn't you say that you and Alex were driving in the area that night?"

"Yeah, and I also said we didn't go to the party."

"This feels a lot more like an interrogation than a few questions," Jenika said.

Sandoval glanced at Hahn and motioned to the room around us. "If we were interrogating you, you'd be in a much less comfortable place—believe me. Right now, we're asking questions, and you're answering at your own free will."

"Okay. Then I'm done answering questions," she said.

"That's your right," Detective Hahn said. "Look, I know you want to look out for and protect your friends. Even I was a teen once. I get it. But this isn't just a 'your side against their side' situation anymore. Two kids are dead here." He kept his focus on me as he spoke, probably because he figured I'd be more likely to break. "So if the two of you are lying or holding back any information, even if you don't think it's relevant, you're potentially endangering someone else's life."

I tried not to let his words get to me, but they were, slowly nipping at my gut. I wasn't just protecting myself and Alex; I was protecting Jenika and Matt, too, people I didn't trust at all.

"In my experience," Sandoval cut in, "people have a hard

time keeping anything but the truth straight. They're not too good at keeping secrets, either. If you're not being completely honest here, there's a good chance we're going to find out about it." His stare made me feel cold to the bone.

Gabi and Megan did leave right before the fight broke out. Gabi could've seen both our cars parked down the road. But if the cops had any evidence we'd been at Winchester Beach that night, they wouldn't be trying to intimidate it out of us.

Instinct told me not to talk—not yet. I couldn't throw myself and three other people under the bus until I dug a little deeper.

"I understand," I told them. "If I think of anything else, I'll let you know."

Jenika stayed silent, her arms folded tight across her stomach.

"Do you mind getting us that SD card and the letters, as well?" Detective Hahn asked.

"Sure," I said, getting up.

After handing everything over, they gave us their cards again and left, saying they'd be in touch again soon and to let them know if we hear from Alex.

Mom emerged from her room as soon as they were gone. One look at the fear in her eyes told me she'd heard every word.

"Nova?" she asked. "I want to talk to you." She nodded toward her room. "Right now."

After shutting the door behind us, she sat beside me at the foot of her bed. "You're going to tell me everything," she said.

"Mom…"

"I'm not asking this time." Her voice rose. "Start talking."

I wrapped the edge of her floral patterned comforter around my hand, wondering how much to tell her. If I should tell her everything. She'd already heard plenty… "Where do you want me to start?"

"Did you lie to them?" She lowered her voice, as if she feared they could hear her somehow.

I stayed focused on my hands. I couldn't lie anymore, not to her; it was taking all I had just to function. "Yes…"

She cussed, putting her hands on her cheeks. Then she let out a breath, staying silent for a few seconds. "About what?"

I had to tell her. So I did. About Alex's car being vandalized and what he, Jenika, and Matt did to him later that night. "Christian and his friends did the same thing to Alex a few years ago."

"And that makes it okay? You should've told me, Nova. You should've—"

"I know."

"If those detectives find out…" Mom closed her eyes, shaking her head. "This isn't something I can bail you out of!"

I couldn't think about that. Thinking in what-ifs would break me down more. "Zach's been planting these rumors, getting people to think Alex is behind these killings. I had to protect him. Nobody else is going to do it."

"Why didn't you tell me Zach broke into your room?"

"Because you'd call the cops right away."

"Yeah!" She threw her hands up. "That would be the logical thing to do."

"I thought he might know where Alex is—"

"What about *you*?"

I wrung the comforter in my hands like a sponge. "What about me? I'm not the one missing."

"Look…" Mom paused, her hazel eyes searching my face. "I know you love him. I love him, too. I don't want to believe for a second that he's involved in this, but—"

"Don't say but," I said. "You know him."

"He's gone. His grandpa's gun is gone." She touched my arm, but I jerked it away. "Those kids have bullied him for years…"

"He didn't do this!" My voice reverberated around the room, making me wince.

Mom grabbed my hand, forcing me to let go of the comforter. "I'm not saying he did. But these are the things people are seeing."

"They're seeing wrong."

"And if we're talking about the Alex I know, I agree," she continued, her voice softening. "But you told me yourself, he's been changing. He's been getting into fights…"

"Mom, stop." My leg jiggled, urging me to run.

"Honey, sometimes even the best of us break. I'm just asking you to prepare yourself for the possibility."

I knew the possibility was there—but I wasn't going to accept it. Not until I had to.

"What about Jenika?" I whispered. "She thinks Christian started that fire, and now he's dead."

Mom breathed out, tilting her head up. "I couldn't sleep last night. I must've checked on her three times, just to make sure she stayed put on that couch. She was there every time."

"Doesn't mean she didn't leave at some point," I muttered. If she *was* involved, she'd need help dumping his body. Matt could've done it. But still, Christian was a big guy—even Matt would probably need help.

"Eric is leaving Seattle real early tomorrow," Mom said. "Should be here by noon." She lowered her voice. "It's not soon enough."

"How's her mom?"

"She should be out tomorrow—Eric is going to help her

get a motel room. Get settled. But we can talk about that later. Right now—"

I pulled my hand out of her grasp and stood. "I'm not giving up on him—I'm sorry you have."

"My first priority is looking out for you, because you're not doing that." She watched me for a few seconds. "Maybe you're better off telling the detectives the truth. Tell them you were scared to come forward." Her voice softened to a whisper. "You didn't do anything that night."

"I lied about it—twice. You think they're going to care?"

"I think they're going to keep putting pressure on all of you until one of you talks. And if that person isn't you…"

"Then I'll deal with it *if* that happens. Until then, I'm going to keep my mouth shut. You heard them. They're looking at all of us, not just Alex."

Mom stared up at me for what felt like eternity. "You need to lie low, keep your head down. Promise me you'll do that."

I crossed my fingers behind my back, knowing there was only one way out of this conversation. "I promise."

"Why don't I believe you?" The phone rang, making her huff out a breath in frustration. She checked the caller ID. "I've got to get back to the diner."

"Then go. I'll be fine."

She got up and pulled me to her, giving me a quick hug and kissing me on the head. "Keep Gavin out of the ice cream. The doctor thinks he's got lactose intolerance."

"Okay…"

"I love you, sweetie," she whispered into my ear, giving me another squeeze.

After she left, I peeked into Gavin's room to see if he was in there. He wasn't. Instead, I heard his voice down the hall—coming from my room.

Jenika was sitting at my desk, staring intently at my laptop, and Gavin was on my bed, going on about his hate for spinach.

"What are you doing?" I asked, moving in behind her. She had the video footage from the night Alex went missing up.

"Had to check my email. Gavin said I could use it."

"It's my computer, too," Gavin said.

I put one hand on the desk, and the other on the back of my chair, leaning within inches of her face. "That doesn't look like email."

If me being in her personal space bothered her, she didn't flinch. Instead, she kept her gaze on the screen. "Relax. Your ranty diary entries don't interest me." She clicked on the video of Alex waving good-bye to me, dragging the playhead back and forth.

"I don't keep a diary."

"Why's that?" She stopped the video before he moved out of the frame and replayed it.

"Because diaries are meant to be read."

Her lips lifted in the corners. "Like you've got anything to hide."

"What does that mean?"

"Exactly what it sounds like." She turned the chair away from me and got up, motioning to it. "All yours."

"Hey, Jenika?" Gavin asked. "What do you think of asparagus?"

"I don't."

"I like to dip it in peanut butter," he continued with a grin. In a matter of hours, he'd gone from being terrified of her to barraging her with questions. Shockingly, she didn't seem to mind.

"What were you looking for?" I asked, sitting down and replaying the video.

"Anything useful. Didn't find it." She sat next to Gavin, folding her arms.

I opened up my in-box, hoping if Alex did take off on purpose, he'd found some way to send me a message. Some way to give me an answer. Instead, there was a message from Christian Barnett, sent at 4:23 a.m. this morning, file attached.

Subject: Thought you might like this…

My blood turned to ice.

"Gavin?" I said, trying to keep my voice steady. "I'm pretty sure there's an *Animal Cops* marathon on today. Wanna check?"

"Ooh!" He slid off the bed, running toward the living room. Luckily Gavin wasn't picky—there was always something on that captured his attention.

"Trying to keep him away from me?" Jenika asked.

"I got a message from Christian…" I read his name over and over, hoping it would disappear.

She moved next to me, squinting at the screen.

I'd deleted my old email address last fall, when I got all those nasty anonymous emails. Zach didn't even have this one, so the chances of Christian having it on his phone were slim. Still, whoever sent this could've gotten my email from someone who knew me.

But that wasn't what made every hair on my skin stand up. It was the subject line. *Thought you might like this…* As if they knew I kept that picture of Amber's body on my computer. As if they knew, no matter how hard I tried, I couldn't bring myself to delete it. I couldn't tell if they were bragging or taunting me—maybe both.

"You gonna open it or not?" Jenika asked, like it was no big deal. She had no idea what was attached.

Or maybe she did.

I clicked on the message, my stomach muscles tightening, preparing for the worst. But there was no preparing for what loaded in that email.

Even Jenika's breaths stopped.

CHAPTER TWENTY-ONE

Red was everywhere, in varying shades and tints, from the maroon gash across his throat, to the bright streaks through his long blond hair, to the murky stains on his gray sweatshirt.

He was lying on top of a picnic table, the same one Alex and I sat on days earlier. His arms were open wide, like he was surrendering to the sky above, a scarlet grin painted across his face. The fake grin stretched from the middle of his chin to the sides of his cheeks. A jagged black line had been drawn inside, giving the effect of sharp, white teeth.

A message above the picture read: He won't be bothering you anymore.

Jenika cussed under her breath. She leaned closer, her lips parting. Her finger hovered over the center of Christian's mouth, where a sliver of purple could be seen between his actual lips. "Is that…"

"A foxglove."

His lids were slightly open, showing only the whites of his eyes. For me, that was the most horrific part.

A prickly feeling swept across my skin, and my fingers curled inside my palms. That could've been Alex, and next time…maybe it would be. I swallowed, trying to shove my fear deep inside. Fear wasn't going to help me.

"Can you blow it up more?" Jenika asked, still studying the screen like it was a beautiful work of art.

"Would you like me to make you a poster?"

"That'd be great—thanks."

"You are beyond sick," I said, increasing the zoom value.

"I don't see you looking away."

She was right, and I hated her for it. Just like with Amber, I wanted to look away, needed to look away. But I couldn't do it.

"Look how clean that is." Jenika ran her finger across the gash on Christian's neck. "It's like they used a scalpel."

"How do you know that?"

She shrugged. "I read a lot of forensic books."

"Why?"

"Why do you have so many books on homicide investigation?" She shook her head, keeping her eyes on the computer screen. "If those detectives see that bookshelf, they'll love you for this."

"They'd love you a lot more—if they knew everything."

She straightened and stared down at me. "I get accused of shit just for breathing around here. If I were going to kill someone, I'd do it somewhere else." She threw her arms up. "Don't you get it? Who's been doing a knockout job of making Alex look guilty?"

"Zach… But—"

"But nothing." She paced back and forth in front of my bed, her fingers tapping together. "Mama's boy, repressed anger. He fits the bill."

"According to what—Hollywood?" I looked at Christian's white-eyed stare and the blood on his throat. There was no way Zach had the stomach for that, not without being possessed.

"If you spent any time with him, you'd know—"

"Let's see. He's obsessed with you. He hates Alex. The victims are the two people closest to him."

"Why the hell would he kill his girlfriend and his best friend?"

Jenika stopped pacing. "Crazy doesn't need a reason. I should know. I live with it."

I thought back to the night someone put those scratches all over Alex's car. I'd never even considered Zach being behind it, but it made sense. It was just the thing to do if you were a coward and wanted someone else to pay the price—he knew Alex would make a beeline for Christian. And Alex played right into his hands.

Then there was that threat Zach got, the one that came just at the perfect time to make him look like a potential victim.

Sure, if someone was trying to set Alex up, Zach looked good on paper. But Jenika didn't see the terror in Zach's eyes when he got that picture of Amber's body or the anguish on his face the night of the Fourth. Unless she was right about the crazy part. I'd read about a guy with dissociative identity disorder once. The killer was just one of his many personalities.

But Zach was rarely alone. If he had multiple personalities, people would notice. Especially his mom.

"We're talking about a guy who didn't notice the security camera right above my window," I said. "Not exactly a mastermind."

"Or maybe he's having a good time playing you," she said. "It wouldn't be the first time."

The eleven minutes he spent in my room was plenty of time to snoop through my email and my hard drive. But none of this explained what I still felt in my bones—Zach wasn't the one killing people.

"He could've planted evidence in here," she continued. "Have you done a search?"

"You saw him yesterday. He was coming apart at the seams." I pointed at the cut across Christian's neck. "That takes calculation. A steady hand. I'm telling you—there's no way Zach did that."

"Okay, fine." Jenika sat on my bed, her left leg jiggling. "Let's pretend you know what you're talking about. Who the hell is it, then? 'Cause clearly they know you. It almost sounds like they did this *for* you."

"I have no idea…" But I needed to figure it out. I needed to figure out now. I hit the forward button on the message and dug out the detectives' business cards from my pocket.

"What are you doing?" Jenika asked, her voice tense.

"Forwarding it to those detectives."

"So they can be even more suspicious? That message implies you're involved."

"That's partly why I'm sending it." I knew forwarding this would make them circle me all the more, but not sending it was far worse. There was always the chance it would help the case. And like Detective Sandoval said, these things had their way of coming out, even though I was sure the killer got rid of Christian's phone, too.

"They're going to think Alex sent that," Jenika said.

"If they have half a brain, they should be wondering why he'd be so obvious."

She went quiet, but I could hear her shifting and tapping the floor with her heel.

After forwarding the message, I signed out of my account and typed in Zach's email address for the username. He had multiple email addresses, but this was the one he used the most for personal communication—at least with me. I probably had three guesses at a password before his account would get locked, and he'd get notification of someone trying to break in.

"Who else has your email address?" Jenika asked, startling me.

"My family, Alex, Megan, some other people at school, like Brandon."

"That's right. You and Koza have gotten…close."

I turned to face her again. "Not like that."

"Like what?"

"You and Alex," I blurted out.

She stared back at me for a few long seconds, no hint of emotion in her dark eyes. "I've heard things about Koza…"

"What things?"

"That he's a pretentious pothead. Likes to do massive bong hits in his backyard when Mom's not home."

I shrugged, focusing back on the password field. "All I know is he's a nice guy. And he's into Gabi De Luca."

"Into or obsessed? Because I heard obsessed. Like, he stalked her."

My fingers froze on the keys. She was definitely at the forefront of his mind a lot, but I could say the same thing for me with Alex. Still, he hated the cakes at least as much as I did. They'd stolen Gabi away, in a sense.

Yet when I closed my eyes and tried to imagine him slashing Christian's throat, I couldn't see it. Maybe that was my problem. I didn't want to put a face I knew on the killer; a stranger was easier to swallow. A stranger didn't know me.

"Brandon's a joke to them," I said. "Just like the rest of us…"

"But you don't think it's him, either."

"No," I said, automatically. As if I knew him that well…

I typed in Gotham, what Zach named his favorite guitar. That was his PlayStation password. "Invalid" appeared in red above the field. Strike one. Since most email services recommended numbers being included in a password now, he might've done his birthday or something else easy to remember.

"That leaves Megan, I guess," Jenika said.

"Right. And she transported and dumped the bodies how?"

She snorted out a laugh. "I was kidding, but thanks for the mental image."

I spun to face her. "How the hell can you make jokes right now? Nothing about this is funny."

"I'm a sociopath, remember?"

I faced the computer again, ignoring her.

Getting Amber's body down to South Beach seemed like it would be difficult for one person, given the steep incline. But Christian had to weigh close to two hundred pounds. Two hundred pounds of dead weight—not something just anyone could lift.

Maybe I'd been thinking of this all wrong. I'd been assuming they killed Amber and Christian before dumping their bodies—because that was what most "organized" killers did. But nobody fit into a neat little box in a textbook. Either the killer had help or Amber and Christian were brought to their dump sites alive. It made sense—both were killed shortly before they were found, in the wee hours of the morning. That would be how I'd do it, if I were a raging psychopath.

"Is it better to be scared like you?" Jenika asked. "Hide out in my room and dick around on my computer?"

"I'm not dicking around. I'm trying to get into Zach's email."

"Why? You know the cops have probably been through

it."

She had a point, but how could we know for sure? "Maybe. Maybe not."

"And if you don't get in, then what? You going to leave him another voicemail? Ask him to meet you for ice cream this time?"

My fingers dug into the armrests of my chair. "You are scared like me. You just don't have the balls to admit it."

Her eyes narrowed into a squint, and she shook her head. "That'd make you feel better, wouldn't it? If deep down, I'm just like you. All fragile and insecure."

"At least I'm real."

"Yeah?" She hunched forward, resting her forearms on her legs. "Were you real with Alex? Stringing him along, year after year, until he finally decided to try to move on."

"You don't know what you're talking about. So stop talking."

"Or what? You'll try to guess my password and hack into my email?"

I couldn't get into this. Not now. But I couldn't say nothing either. "You've never cared about Alex. You put him down every chance you got. Now all of a sudden, you want to fight his battles? You're full of shit."

She held my gaze. "Alex knows where I stand. That's all that matters to me."

"Where's that?"

"I don't owe you an answer." She straightened, her chin tilting up slightly. "I don't owe you anything."

"But right now you're sitting in my room, asking *me* for answers. And I don't have a single reason to trust you."

The tension around her mouth faded, and her gaze went from my face to the wall behind me. "He's become a good friend."

"A good friend you don't know that well?"

"That was me shutting those cops down. Something you should've done. But, no"—she threw up her hands—"you had to blab. Tell them all about your big old crush on your best friend."

"It's better than acting like you've got something to hide."

She shook her head. "I think it's safe to say I've dealt with the cops a lot more than you have."

"And?"

"They go after the weak links, the people who spill their guts 'cause they're scared and they think they have to."

"All you did was piss them off. They'll be looking for any reason to bring both of us in."

Her shoulders lifted and fell. "So what? They'll talk a big game and throw out their best scare tactics. They need actual evidence to hold us."

My stomach muscles tensed thinking about being in some windowless room with fluorescent lights humming and flickering above me. I'd always imagined those interrogation rooms smelling like sweat and cold coffee.

"You want real?" Jenika asked, her eyes boring into mine. "Here's real. I'm not here, in Eric's little dream house, because I have to be. I'm here to find Alex. You know him better than anyone else. And if you haven't noticed? We're about the only people he's got on his side."

"I—"

"I don't care what you think of me," she continued, her voice taking a harsher tone. "Or how you feel about my relationship with Alex. You treated him like dirt, too. Only it's worse because you're his best friend. You were supposed to have his back."

"I've always had his back," I said the words, but my voice

came out weak, barely audible.

"You can't honestly say that, can you? You spent all last summer chasing after the privileged piles of dog shit who tortured him *for fun*."

Sweat was forming down my back, under my arms, behind my knees. Every part of my skin seemed to burn and itch. "I didn't know everything they did to him."

"Didn't know or didn't want to know?"

As always, she knew just where to hit. I was good at that, wasn't I? Seeing only what I wanted to. Only what I could handle…

"I'm done talking about this," I said.

"Of course you are. You don't want to tarnish that perfect little image of yourself in your head."

I tried to block her out, typing in "Gotham" with the first four digits of Zach's birth date. Would he really be dumb enough to use his birthday? Maybe.

"You don't deserve him," she said.

I hovered over the log-in button, telling myself to just click it. "Neither do you."

"I won't argue that. But I'm not the one in love with him."

"You sure?" My finger tapped the mouse button, and the screen went white. Waiting…waiting.

"I don't have to love a guy to hook up with him. I don't even have to like him."

The screen popped up with another invalid username/password message. "Glad you've got standards."

"You calling me a slut?"

"I'm saying that's a good way to get hurt."

"And what are your standards?" she asked, her voice low and pointed. "Spineless. Psychotic. It's all good, right? As long as he's pretty, and he spends Daddy's money on you."

I closed my eyes, reminding myself I didn't give a damn what she thought. She had no right to judge me, not after everything she'd pulled.

"You put on this little hard act," Jenika continued. "But you're about as naive as it gets."

I stood, shoving my chair hard enough to send it into my wall. The *thud* echoed through my room. "You really want to sit here and have a pissing match right now? Then let's go outside and get it over with."

She glared up at me, her fingers picking at the material of her black jeans.

"People are being killed, Jenika. Alex might be..." I couldn't say it. If I said it, I might start to believe it.

She didn't answer. Instead, we were both motionless, listening to the muted sound of dogs barking on the living room TV. There was no other sound. Not even the wind gently rattling my window, like it did almost every minute of every day here.

"He's not dead," she said, softly. "I can feel it."

"You can feel it? Are you psychic now?"

The corners of her eyes crinkled, and the tension in her expression returned. "I trust my instincts."

I folded my arms, wishing I could say the same. But I felt like I was in a dream, waiting for the fog to lift. I was doubting everyone and everything, even my own thoughts.

"Will you do something for me?" Jenika asked.

"What..."

"Look me in the eye and tell me you're sorry Christian's dead."

A chill ran across my skin. I wouldn't have minded seeing Christian rot behind bars—because that was where he belonged. Was I sorry he was dead? The right answer would be yes.

"I'm not going to miss him," I said, remembering Alex saying those same words. "But I'm sorry someone took his life. It wasn't their decision to make."

She broke eye contact, gazing at the small gap between my curtains.

"I know something happened between you and Christian... before," I said.

Her head snapped back toward me, her eyes wide and defensive. "Did Alex—"

"He didn't have to," I broke in. "It's obvious."

She shrugged, her lips pursing. "Christian and his friends screwed with me a few summers ago. So what?"

"A *few* summers ago?"

"I was thirteen." Her voice was both calm and tense, like a storm waiting to happen.

"That's the same summer you guys crashed that cake party, isn't it?" I waited for her to say more. She didn't. "What happened?"

"Ask Zach. He was there. Watched the whole thing go down."

My veins hummed with what felt like electricity. "Watched what?"

"At the beginning of the summer, Christian invited me to a party at his friend's house. I was dumb enough to show up," she said.

"Did they attack you?"

Her gaze moved to her hands. "Christian was dared to lose his virginity that night and film it. He picked me to be the lucky girl. But I didn't know that until my top was off, and I noticed the open laptop with the little green light on."

My chest felt tense, making me realize I was barely

breathing.

"I got out of there, eventually," she continued. "But not without them blocking the door. Giving my body a good critique. Making threats."

"I'm sorry you had to go through that."

She shrugged, her eyes lifting to mine again. "If I were going to kill Christian, I would've done it a long time ago."

I kept going back to the one thing I knew about the killer—they couldn't pull off what they did without extensive planning. Organized killers usually made sure nothing pointed in their direction. Part of the "fun" was the rush of getting away with it, again and again. If that was Jenika's goal, she was failing miserably. The same went for Alex and Zach. Even Matt. We were all under a spotlight now. Those detectives would be watching every move we made.

I leaned down in front of my computer, staring at the empty password field. Last chance. If I didn't get it right this time, Zach would know someone was trying to get in. I'd probably be the first guess on his list.

I typed in "Gotham" one more time, hoping I at least had that part right. He could've used his entire birth date or some other part of it. But even for Zach—it seemed too easy. He didn't have a lucky number or a date he was particularly attached to. There was the year of his Mustang—1969. He'd said once if he could time travel to any year, it would be 1969, so he could go to Woodstock and see Jimi Hendrix play.

I typed it in, hit log in, and held my breath. A list of emails popped up on the screen with a "Welcome Zach!" message in the left-hand corner.

"You're in?" Jenika asked, sounding as surprised as I was.

I nodded, skimming the subjects in the emails. Save 10% on Fender! Are you okay? Thinking of you. The list of "condolence" emails seemed miles long, and every single one was unread. I checked his "sent mail," but he hadn't sent anything in a week. There was a response to someone about Amber's funeral. There was another response to a girl or woman named Katie Song. She'd written a lengthy letter, encouraging him to come back to Seattle and letting him know she was just a call away. His reply was "thanks." Nothing he'd written showed anything more than what he appeared to be—a guy who just lost his girlfriend.

His draft box had two letters in it. One was started on July 5 at 12:02 a.m.

> Katie,
>
> I think I'm going crazy…i can't remember the last time I slept. The ambien the doctor prescribed didn't do shit but make me dizzy and forget things. I drank so much tonight I can't remember half of what happened. My heart is pounding I

The other letter was also addressed to Katie, and it was written at 4:04 a.m., just over an hour after he broke into my room.

> I went to Nova's house. She's screwing that psycho now. when I got there he was sneaking out of her room. It was the middle of the night..wehre was he going in the middle of the night?

It left off there, right where I needed it to continue most.

"That's a stream of crazy…" The sound of Jenika's voice next to my ear made my entire body jerk. I'd been so focused on the letter I hadn't heard her come up behind me. "Does Katie know she's his psychiatrist?"

"I don't know who she is—he never mentioned her when

we were together." I let out a shaky breath.

"What were you expecting to find?" Jenika asked. "A jpeg of Alex's note? His exact location?"

At least I had an idea of what Alex's note *didn't* say—where he was going. Why he was taking off in the first place. "Right now I'll take any new information."

"What's new? He's crazy, obsessed with you, and he *claims* he doesn't know where Alex went."

I went back to Zach's in-box, scrolling down for the threat he'd gotten the day before Amber's body was found. It might not have even been sent to this email address—I hadn't noticed which mailbox it was in that day on his cell.

"He clearly wrote those drafts without a filter," I said. "It's a safe bet what's there is the truth."

"Really? He doesn't talk about breaking into your room. Or forging a letter. I'd say there was plenty of filtering."

"He didn't finish it." The oldest email in his in-box was from a week ago, which meant he'd deleted anything before that.

The damp air in my room felt as charged as my nerves, and the floor kept creaking behind me. I knew Jenika was shifting her weight.

"The other night with Alex," she said. "Was that the first time you guys…"

I straightened and faced her. She didn't need to know the details. "What's that got to do with anything?"

"He holds you up like you're some kind of saint. What you think matters to him more than anything else." Her lips parted and her eyes narrowed, as if she wasn't quite sure what to say next. But Jenika always knew what to say next. "Sex is a big deal to you, right?"

My hands gripped the edge of my desk. "He told you

that?"

"No. You did with your judgy little standards comment."

"That isn't what I—"

"My *point* is—you finally give him the keys to your precious kingdom and he takes off on you? He wouldn't do that without a real good reason."

She could've been implying that I'd chased him away. But there was no hint of amusement in her expression.

It still didn't make sense, no matter how many ways I spun it. He wasn't under duress. He had time to write a note—just not tell me where he was going or why he left. He'd looked at my camera and waved, like it was any other night. It *wasn't* any other night.

"He wasn't exactly himself that night…" I said.

"How so?"

I hated that she was probably the only person—outside Megan—who knew him at all. The only person who might be able to help me make sense of that night.

"I always thought if anything was going to happen between me and Alex, I'd have to make the first move," I said.

"Why? I didn't."

My mouth opened and shut. I'd assumed Jenika did the pursuing. For the last two weeks, the unwelcome image of her seducing him like some kind of dominatrix invaded my head again and again.

Maybe she was messing with me. But the questioning look on her face was genuine.

"Who was he with you?" I asked, after a few seconds of silence.

She settled back on my bed, her brow crinkling. "What do you mean?"

"I thought I knew him better than anyone. But he's been

hiding so much… I don't know what's real and what isn't anymore." My words came out louder and angrier than I'd meant them to. But I needed to get it out. I needed to say it out loud.

Jenika watched me, clutching a handful of my blanket. "He's crazy about you," she said. "That's real."

"But *who* is he? Because the guy I knew was such a do-gooder sometimes it drove me crazy. He was painfully shy. And sweet. And way more together than he should've been." I closed my eyes, willing myself to stop before I couldn't hold back the lump in my throat anymore.

"I think you answered your own question," she said. "Nobody can pretend everything's okay forever."

I rubbed my hands up and down my arms, as if that would somehow ease the buzzing inside me. "I keep making excuses in my head about that last night with him. But the more I think about it, the more… It really did seem like he was saying good-bye."

"Was there a specific thing he said?"

"It was everything…"

She let out a breath. "So maybe he really did take off."

I walked back and forth in front of my desk, multiple scenarios running through my head. "But why? He's got no money. Nowhere to go. All running away does is make him look guilty."

"We don't know what those cops said to him. Maybe they threatened him. If he's being set up, maybe some kind of evidence was planted and they found it…"

I threw my arms up. "Like what?"

"I don't know! You're the one with all the fucking homicide manuals."

I'd read about a case once where a suspect's license was

found on the victim, but they couldn't arrest the suspect because—technically—the evidence could've been planted. The cops would need fingerprints, hair, or some other DNA evidence that showed Alex had contact with the victims. That wouldn't be so easy to pull off.

"I can't sit around here anymore." Jenika got off the bed. "We need to be out there, looking. Asking around about him."

"I can't leave Gavin here alone. And even if I could, there's an infinite number of places to look. We need to narrow it down."

She put her hand on the doorknob. "That's why we talk to people. It was the Fourth of July. Someone had to have seen something."

"And you think it's a good idea to approach a bunch of random people right now?"

"I'm not you, Nova. I can take care of myself just fine— done it my whole life." With that, she left, slamming my door hard enough to make my walls rattle.

I grabbed the first thing on my desk I could reach, my U.S. history textbook from last year, and threw it at my wall, missing the window by only a few inches. The *bang* was loud enough to make my ears ring.

My breath came out fast, and there was warmth building behind my eyes. I couldn't lose it now, not yet.

"Nova?" Gavin had opened my door partially. He was peeking at me through the gap. "What's wrong?"

I wiped under my eyes and opened my door all the way. "We had a fight."

He stared up at me, still not moving. "About Alex?"

"You want tater tots? Mom got us a massive bag."

"Okay," he muttered, sounding uncertain.

I bent down and wrapped my arm around him, giving him

a one-armed hug. If I had to be okay for Gavin, I couldn't focus on all the thoughts racing through my head, pulling me in a hundred different directions. I couldn't doubt myself or feel guilty. I couldn't shut down.

MONDAY, JULY 7

What if I can't do it?

CHAPTER TWENTY-TWO

Detective Sandoval wanted to come by first thing in the morning and talk about Christian's picture. He showed up ten minutes early, before I'd had a chance to put on a pair of jeans or get down a couple bites of cereal. Jenika had already torn out of here, suddenly deciding that she couldn't miss her summer school class.

Mom let Sandoval in, and I turned off the news in her room. They'd just shown a picture of Alex for the second time this morning, saying he was missing and might be armed. It was surreal, seeing my best friend's face plastered on the TV. There weren't many pictures of Alex in existence, but this was one of the worst. His grandpa had taken it last New Year's Eve, after he and Alex had an argument. Megan was actually sitting next to him, but they'd cropped her out, leaving Alex glaring at the camera. He was wearing one of his old metal band T-shirts with skeletal remains and bloodred writing on the front—that was what the argument was about. Cindy had threatened to throw all his band shirts in a box and burn them.

And now that moment was being broadcast to millions of people. People who'd take one look at that scowl and black clothing and figure he had to be a murderer. They'd never know the context behind the photo or even want to ask.

Detective Sandoval took one end of the couch, and I took the other. My eyes burned and the room seemed foggy from lack of sleep. Like Zach, I was beginning to feel crazy.

"How are you doing?" Sandoval asked, a hint of concern in his voice.

"As good as I can be…"

"I'm sorry you had to see that picture." He let a few seconds of silence pass, probably trying to gauge my reaction. "Any idea who might've sent it or why they may have sent it to you?"

I shook my head, hoping he wouldn't stay long. I couldn't trust what came out of my mouth at this point.

"Have you heard from Alex since we talked yesterday?" he asked.

"No. And he didn't send that picture."

Sandoval cocked his head, his eyes narrowing. "How do you know?"

"I'm not stupid, okay?" My mind was screaming at me to stop, but I kept going. "I know you're looking at him as a suspect—"

"Right now he's a person of interest. Person of interest doesn't mean suspect."

My fists clenched in my lap. That wouldn't be how the entire town saw it. "Alex isn't a killer. But if he was, hypothetically, he wouldn't be this obvious."

Sandoval's expression softened. "Like we told you last night, we're not accusing anyone of anything right now. Our job is to ask questions and gather all the information we can."

"Okay, then." My voice cracked. "I've told you everything I know about who sent that picture. Nothing."

"Have you gotten any other emails or messages that

concern you?"

"No."

He nodded and wrote something down on his pad. "Would you mind getting your mom for me?

I called out to her, knowing I didn't really have to. She'd been listening. Mom emerged from the kitchen and stood in the middle of the living room, arms folded.

"Is it just you and the kids in this house?" Sandoval asked her.

"A lot of the time, yes." She let her arms drop to her sides. "But Eric, my boyfriend, lives here, too." She babbled on about him working in Seattle and coming back to help out with Jenika. "He said he should be here around noon."

"Can he be here with the kids when you're not?"

Mom's eyes darted back and forth between me and Sandoval. "Definitely. I was planning on that... Do you think that picture was meant as a threat?"

Sandoval shook his head slightly and made a shrugging motion. "We don't know what the intention was at this point." He turned his attention to me. "I highly suggest you avoid being alone, especially going out alone. We can't offer you twenty-four-hour protection, but we can have a patrol car drive by the house regularly."

"We'll take you up on that," Mom said. "Thank you."

"If you get another message or if you hear from Alex, contact us right away—okay?"

I agreed.

Sandoval rose, handing Mom his card, as if he'd assumed we tossed the last two. "My cell is on there, if you have any concerns or questions."

Mom nodded and asked something about the patrol car. I didn't know what exactly—I'd already tuned them out.

Maybe I should've been more worried about my safety. But in my dazed, sleep-deprived state, all I cared about was finding the truth. And that would be impossible with a babysitter twenty-four hours a day.

When we pulled up to the diner, Gramps and Brandon were out front with buckets and rags, scrubbing at the entrance window.

"Shit," Mom muttered under her breath.

Ask About Our Killer Special was painted in sloppy bright red letters across the glass—clearly by someone who hadn't used a spray paint can much. My money was on a cake.

There was glass on the ground as well—someone had thrown something through the front door.

Guilt burrowed itself deeper inside my stomach, even though I knew it wasn't my fault. My family was still going to lose business they couldn't afford to lose because of who my best friend was. Some people probably figured I was involved, too.

I offered to help Brandon, so Gramps could go inside and start preparing the kitchen. Gramps gave my hand a quick squeeze and kissed my forehead, but he didn't say a word about the vandalism.

"Mom and Brandon are going to handle all the tables," he said. "You can hang out in the back and help me, okay?"

"Thanks." Part of me wondered if I should wait tables, like normal. The distraction might help hold me together. But all it would take was hearing the wrong conversation, getting one bad customer…anything could set me off.

Brandon gave me a nod and a quick smile. His dark bangs

hid his eyes, so I couldn't tell if it was sincere. "How are you?"

"I don't know how to answer that."

"It was a dumb question—sorry." He handed me a razor scraper. "Me and your grandpa already washed it down. Now we have to scrape."

I took the razor and scratched at the paint, the feeling all too familiar. Glass. Red letters. Humiliation. Only this time I didn't have the energy to be angry.

Brandon joined me, working on the other end of the window.

"They sent me a picture of Christian's body—whoever killed him."

His scraping stopped, but he didn't look in my direction. "That's... You must be freaked."

"You could say that. Whoever sent it obviously knows me—which means I probably know them." I glanced over at him, watching for any reaction. He resumed picking at the paint, his hair still hiding his eyes. "It's kind of hard to wrap my head around."

"Yeah..."

I put more pressure on the glass, making larger chunks of paint disappear. Organized killers were often socially "normal," charming even. They tended to blend in without a problem. That could be Brandon. That could be a lot of people around here. But Brandon had been openly expressing his hatred for the cakes since the day he started here. He kept his cards close to his chest. And he was the police chief's son, which gave him access to information the rest of us didn't have.

God, I really was losing my mind. This was *Brandon*. Geeky, awkward Brandon who'd shown me nothing but kindness this summer.

"Careful," he said, interrupting my thoughts. "You don't want to scratch the glass."

I loosened my grip on the razor and took in a deep breath.

"Did you hear about Zach?" Brandon asked, his voice cautious.

My heart immediately reacted, making my fingertips go cold. What now…? "No…"

"He had a full-on breakdown. It took, like, four cops to hold him down."

That sick feeling was swirling inside me again. "Where is he now?'

"Psych ward at Tillamook, last I heard."

A little relief washed over me hearing that. It really was the best place he could be right now.

My body tensed every time a car passed us, especially if it slowed down. I kept expecting something to be thrown at my back.

"Do they have any leads yet?" I asked.

"I don't know." There was something about the way he said it, a hesitance maybe. It didn't sound like the truth.

I stopped again and faced him. "You must've heard something…"

The fingers of his free hand tapped against his leg. "I can't talk about it."

"Can't talk about it or can't talk about it to me?" My eyes stung, and my chest felt heavy. "I already know they think it's Alex."

He finally turned toward me, but he focused on everything but my face. "My mom isn't on the case, so she doesn't know much. The detectives talk to each other and the DA, and that's about it."

"But you know something."

"I can't," he repeated more forcefully this time.

I ground my teeth together to keep from crying. If I started now, I wouldn't be able to stop. "I don't know where he is... I don't even know if he's alive."

He let out a breath, his pale brown eyes finally meeting my gaze. "Those aren't answers me or my mom have."

"Brandon. Please. Just give me something." I felt pathetic, begging like this. But there was still that doubt in me, the doubt that said I was only seeing what I wanted to see.

"My mom could lose her job, Nova."

Another car slowed as it passed us, a newer black Mercedes. I could feel the eyes of the occupants on us, making the muscles in my legs stiffen. The driver gunned the engine and the car took off, turning the corner onto Second Street.

My paranoia had reached epic levels—it wasn't as if the entire town was out to get me. But it sure felt like it.

"I'm not going to tell anyone," I said.

He went back to work on the glass. "I'm sorry. I wanna help. But don't put me in this position."

I remained frozen, the razor scraper dangling from my fingers, waiting. For what, I didn't know. It wasn't like he'd suddenly change his mind. "See you inside," I said, swinging the door open before he could respond.

Monday mornings were never our busiest, but we'd at least be half full during tourist season. By 10:00 a.m., we had only a handful of customers. An older couple who Mom said were making their way up to Alaska. Joan and Linda, who'd only miss Gramps's $2.99 salmon omelet and pancake special if they were dead. And Jack Cervantes, owner of the only pet store in town—they were closed on Mondays.

"Tourists are fleeing like there's a damn tsunami coming,"

Gramps said, frying up Joan's and Linda's salmon omelets. "The Inn's only a quarter full."

"Can you blame them?" I added fresh blueberries to the pancake batter, the smell of sugar and cinnamon making me even more nauseous.

Gramps shook his head. "This town's going to have a hard time recovering from the stink. If it ever does."

I glanced behind me to make sure Gavin was still reading his Harry Potter book in the back office, out of earshot. "I'm going to ask you a question, and I want you to be completely straight with me."

"Okay."

"Do you think Alex is doing this?"

He flipped the omelets onto a plate and turned off the gas on the stove. Then he looked over at me, pursing his lips. "I think there's a whole lot that doesn't make sense. So I don't know. That's the best answer I got right now."

A sinking feeling hit me hard and fast. I wanted him to be sure of Alex's innocence and list all the reasons why. I wanted someone I trusted to tell me I wasn't crazy.

"I'm going to give Megan a call," I said. "See how she's doing."

Gramps nodded. "Ask her if they need anything."

On my way back to the office, Brandon's gray-and-blue backpack on the floor underneath our coatrack caught my eye. He had this black sketch pad inside that I'd seen him writing and drawing in on breaks and during lulls. I'd never thought much about it—I figured he was working on his manga storyboards. But what if it was more than that…

It didn't matter how much I liked Brandon on the surface— there was so little I actually knew about him. He'd never told me exactly what happened with Gabi, only saying she'd stopped talking to him for no reason. I'd bought it because of whom she chose to hang out with. People who chose to hang out with Christian were either weak, like Zach, or assholes—usually both. Still, Brandon and Gabi had been friends since freshman year. Why cut him off now?

Then there was what Jenika said—about Brandon stalking Gabi.

Gramps was busy pouring pancake batter onto multiple skillets, Gavin still had his face buried in his book, and Brandon had just taken a smoke break about fifteen minutes ago.

I glanced over my shoulder to make sure Gramps's back was still to me and took soft footsteps, keeping my eyes on Gavin. Without stopping, I picked the backpack up by the handle, making sure to lift it slowly. It was heavier than I'd expected. Keeping my steps light and steady, I went straight for the back door.

Once outside, I unzipped the backpack gently, as if Brandon could somehow hear through walls. This felt wrong on many levels. But so did not doing anything at all. I remembered a documentary I'd watched where some big-shot New York City homicide detective said you only find the guilty when you've excluded everyone else.

Brandon's backpack was filled with graphic novels and comics, mostly manga. Two packs of cigarettes were in his front pocket, along with two fancy-looking Zippos. One had a smiling pirate on the front. There was an abundance of pens with chewed lids and empty granola bar wrappers. Nothing even remotely surprising.

Then there was the black spiral-bound sketchbook he hovered over every chance he got. Even if it only contained art, it would at least give me a peep into his mind.

A male voice hollered something, making me freeze.

Then I heard the unmistakable *thwonk* of skateboard wheels hitting cement. The skaters around here loved the parking lot of the old Pacific Sunrise motel almost as much as they loved showing off their battle scars.

I flipped through the pages, mostly half-finished sketches and random scrawls. Almost every female "character" he'd sketched had the same face. Gabi's. One in particular sent goose bumps down my arms. Brandon had given her giant pupils, making her eyes look almost completely black. Red lines ran down both cheeks, as if she was crying blood. Her lips were a hypothermic blue.

It wasn't exactly like Amber. Brandon's strokes were neat, measured, and full of erase marks. But the effect was eerily similar.

Underneath he'd scrawled, *Pull the trigger.*

The breeze suddenly felt like ice on my skin. I couldn't bring myself to flip the page, to see what came next.

But I had to.

The door to the diner flew open, and I thrust the sketchpad behind my back. Not that it would do any good.

Brandon emerged, and his eyes went straight to his backpack at my feet.

I had no idea what to say. There was no good excuse. All I could do was keep breathing.

He walked toward me and grabbed his backpack by the handle, rummaging inside. "What'd you expect to find?"

I held his sketch pad out to him, keeping my distance. "I'm sorry…"

He snatched it away, making the cardboard scrape against my thumb. His nose wrinkled, and there was a glare in his eyes. "Fuck you."

With that, he headed back inside, letting the door slam

behind him.

I stayed outside for a few minutes, the image of Gabi's face and her bloody tears flashing in my mind again and again. It was still just a drawing. And the words on the page were only words. *Pull the trigger* could've been a title. I couldn't exactly go in there and accuse him of murdering two people. Gramps would tell me just that and go off on me for invading Brandon's privacy. And he'd be right.

I needed more.

The back door opened again, but this time Gramps poked his head out. I let out an audible breath.

"You doin' okay?" he asked. "Brandon said you needed some air."

"He's… Is he still here?"

"Why wouldn't he be?" He came outside to join me. I wanted to run into his arms and hide, like I did when I got scared as a kid. His bear hugs always made me feel safe from anything.

"We had a fight. He wouldn't tell me what he knows about the case."

"Well, he shouldn't be giving that information to anybody. And you got no right ask." Even with everything going on, the disappointment in his voice still got to me.

"I think he might be involved." I knew I sounded idiotic, but I had to warn him somehow.

"I think you're trying to find demons wherever you can right now."

"He hates the cakes. He's obsessed with De Luca's daughter—he draws all these pictures of her and writes these weird things."

Gramps held up his hand. "Bein' a lovesick fool doesn't make him a killer, Nova."

I described the drawing to him, including what it said underneath.

His face scrunched up. "He showed you this?'

The wind picked up, making me shiver. I rubbed my hands together to warm them. "Not exactly."

"Ah…" He exhaled a long breath, and for a minute we stood in silence, watching the skateboarders fly off their homemade half pipe and fall on their rears.

"Are you going to say anything else?" I asked.

"About you nosing through his stuff? I don't have to."

"Gramps…"

His dark eyes followed the skaters across the parking lot. "He's a young guy into macabre art. They grow 'em on trees these days. It's not a smoking gun."

I folded my arms, hoping to stop the shivering. But it seemed like the cold was coming from within now.

"I don't know what to do," I said, after a minute. "What am I supposed to do?"

He reached out and pulled me into a hug, mashing my nose into his chest. I squeezed my eyes shut, but the tears came out anyway. Warm and uncontrollable. My body went limp and breath escaped my lips in short, quick bursts. Every time I thought I was done, another little explosion came out of me, my lungs filling with more air than they could handle.

He rubbed my back, staying quiet until my muscles stopped quivering. "Me and your mom are here for you. No matter what, okay?" He squeezed me a little harder, kissing the top of my head. "No matter what."

I wished I could say his words comforted me, made me feel a little safer in my own skin. They didn't. Because he didn't have an answer for me. Gramps always had some kind of answer.

After I went to the bathroom, put myself back together, and cleaned up, I called Megan. The phone rang until the answering machine popped on. I started to leave a message when there was a click followed by Megan's voice.

"Nova?" She sounded almost panicked.

"Hey—what's going on?"

"We've been getting these calls from some guy. He said he's going to hunt…" The machine beeped, blocking out half of what she said.

"I missed that—he said what?"

"He said he's going to hunt Alex down and shoot him on sight."

Knowing some of the gun-toting crazies around here, he probably meant it, too. "Did you call the police?"

"Yeah, they said they're going to trace it." She let out a breath. "We probably won't have a phone for much longer anyway."

"Why?"

"Phone company left a message, saying we're two months behind. They're going to shut it off any time now. Alex was going to pay it, but…"

"We'll take care of it." I glanced over at Gavin. He was watching me, his hazel eyes filled with curiosity. "I'm going to come over, okay? I need to talk to you about something."

"You probably shouldn't…" Her voice got softer. "There's been news trucks outside. I mean, they're staying back for now, 'cause we don't want to talk. But I don't know. Our house is a mess and—"

"I don't care. I'm coming over." I hung up, not giving her a chance to answer. She had to know something about Gabi and Brandon's relationship. And if she didn't, hopefully she could get me in touch with Gabi.

"Mom isn't going to let you go anywhere," Gavin said, still watching me.

Sneaking out would end with her calling the cops at this point. But it was dead enough that she'd probably be willing to drive me.

On my way out of the kitchen, I passed Brandon, who was delivering an order. He acted as if I weren't there, keeping his gaze straight ahead. I swallowed back my guilt—I'd feel guilty when I knew he wasn't involved.

Mom was pouring coffee for Paul Cross, one of only two customers in the whole place now. I motioned for her to come talk to me by the bathrooms.

"What's up?" she asked, still carrying the pot of coffee.

"Can you drop me off at Al—Megan's?" I could still say his name. He still lived there.

"Hon, you should stay here. Why don't we pick her up?"

"Their house is a mess. Their phone is about to be shut off. Cindy's distraught… I told her I was coming by to help."

Mom sighed. "I'm not comfortable with—"

"Megan says there's cops driving around," I said, figuring it was probably true. "Probably just in case Alex shows up."

Mom scanned the diner, sucking on her lower lip. The woman who had been in a corner booth left a couple bucks on the table and headed out, leaving only Paul Cross. "Let me get my keys."

Today belonged in the *Emerald Cove Visitor's Guide*. No fog or clouds. Just an azure sky that went on forever and large turquoise waves crashing ashore. Beach Street was a wide-open stretch. No traffic. No people darting out in front of our car, holding up their hands in a lame apology, as they waddled, hustled, or ran across the street.

I'd never seen a beautiful day this empty. Alex would've loved it. He'd insist we get massive cups of Adele's chocolate raspberry ice cream and sit out on the beach until we saw stars.

There was a news truck from Portland sitting outside Megan and Alex's neighborhood when we pulled in. Jenika and Matt were standing outside Matt's house, puffing on cigarettes. They both stopped talking and watched as we passed and turned down Megan and Alex's lane.

"Shouldn't Eric be here soon?" I asked.

"He hit traffic—said it probably won't be until two now." She pulled in behind the El Camino. "Maybe I should come in for a bit—help out."

"I think that would make Cindy uncomfortable. You know how she is."

"Yep," she said.

I thanked her and went to open the door, but she grabbed my wrist.

"Make sure all the doors and windows are locked," she said. "Don't open the door for anyone. And stay put. I'll be calling to check."

"You can try, but Megan said their phone was getting shut off."

She huffed. "Great. Do you have the emergency phone?"

"I gave it back to you."

She opened her purse, rummaging through it. "Damn it…"

"I'll be okay. It's only for a couple hours." I motioned to the dozen tiny homes around us. "There's plenty of people nearby. And Megan says there've been news trucks—you saw the one coming in."

She wrapped her arm around my shoulders, giving me a

quick hug. "'Kay, I'll be back around two."

"Thanks." I popped open the door.

"Promise me again you'll stay put."

"Promise." I made sure not to break eye contact as I said it.

CHAPTER TWENTY-THREE

As I walked past the El Camino, something shiny and blue on the ground caught my eye. It was lying next to the rear wheel, half buried by the gravel. I knew that blue because I'd seen it a million times.

I squatted down and brushed the rocks away, digging it out. That cold, prickly feeling of panic ran under my skin again. It was exactly what I thought it was—Alex's lucky guitar pick. He'd gotten it when we saw Why Can't I Be You? live in Portland, one of our favorite bands. Jackson Lathrop, the guitarist, threw his pick right at Alex and signed it for him after the show.

Alex kept it in only one place—inside a plastic insert in his wallet. It was probably his most treasured possession. If this pick was on the ground, it was because he put it there. Or someone else did.

Mom's car door opened. I'd forgotten she was sitting there, waiting for me to go inside. "Nova?" she said, getting out. "I've changed my mind. I want to come in for a minute. Make sure everything's okay."

"Mom, Cindy will—"

"I'm not real worried about being polite right now." She

shut her door, her boots crunching on the gravel. "What was on the ground?"

"It was just a quarter." I shoved the pick in my jeans pocket. Telling her would lead to more speculation, more questions. She might insist on staying or taking Megan and me back to the diner. These couple hours were probably all the time I had to get out and do anything. I still had that crappy Taser, and I could take Alex's El Camino, which was better than nothing.

Megan answered the door, her eyes buggy and red-rimmed. The TV was blaring inside—the noon news, it sounded like.

"Hi, sweetie," Mom said, in the most soothing voice she could probably manage at the moment. "Can I come in with Nova for a quick second? I need to use the bathroom."

"Um…" Megan glanced over her shoulder toward the living room. The smell of burned toast and musky candles wafted outside.

"Come on in," Cindy called out. I'd expected her to still be locked away in her room.

Megan stepped back and opened the door wider. Riff ran up to us first thing, making a whimpering sound. He nuzzled his cold, wet nose against my shins, as if I were the first human he'd seen in years. It was hard not to crumble right there.

Cindy watched us from the couch, her blue eyes sizing Mom up head to toe. "Bathroom's down the hall to the left," she said.

Mom gave her a stiff smile and a wave. "Thanks." She not too slyly looked at the mess around us before continuing on.

The ingredients Cindy used to bake Alex's cake were still all over the counter, and there were at least four bags of trash waiting to be taken out. Dirty dishes, glasses, and mugs covered the coffee table in front of Cindy, along with piles of mail and random things like matches and batteries.

Mom emerged from the bathroom not thirty seconds later, wiping her hands on her jeans. That was when I noticed Riff's empty bowls against the wall in the hallway.

"Megan—where did you put Riff's food?" I asked, heading over to grab his water bowl. The bag wasn't where Alex usually kept it, on top of the fridge.

"Ran out last night," she said. "We made him eggs this morning…"

"I'll pick some up for you," Mom said. "What kind does he eat?"

"He's not choosy," I told her.

"We're fine," Cindy said, rising off the couch. She had to hold on to the arm to steady herself. "My friend Louise is dropping some by later."

I mouthed to mom to get the food anyway. Cindy would say almost anything to avoid a "handout."

As I filled up Riff's bowl with water, Mom explained to her that she'd be picking me up at two—if that was okay.

"Sure," Cindy said, making her way into the kitchen. "I know Megan could use the company."

"Megan said your phone might get shut off. I'm happy to—" Mom began.

"It's fine," Cindy said as she fished for another glass. "I've got it taken care of. Thanks."

Mom gave me a questioning look, but I nudged her toward the door, reminding her that I would be okay.

"Lock the door behind me," she said on her way out.

As soon as I turned the dead bolt, because I knew Mom was right outside, waiting to hear the *click*, Cindy said, "Tell your mom we're not a charity case. We've got things covered."

Yeah, looks like it, I wanted to say. Instead I gave her a nod and touched Megan's arm, motioning toward Alex's room.

Once we were inside with the door shut, I started tearing through his things again, hoping there was something we missed last time. Something maybe even the cops missed.

"What are you looking for?" Megan asked. She was wearing an oversize gray sweatshirt with cuffs that dangled below her fingers, as if it weren't about seventy-five degrees in here.

I pulled Alex's guitar pick from my pocket. "I found this on the ground outside."

Megan lips parted and closed again. "That's…"

I untangled his blanket from his sheets and shook the blanket to see if anything fell out. "I feel like it's a sign, you know? Like maybe he wanted someone to find it."

"Okay… But why?"

"To let us know something was wrong?" A couple CD cases fell onto the floor. I got on my knees and peeked under his bed. Nothing.

A knock sounded at the window, two quick taps. My first thought was Mom, but she'd at least try the front door first. I tiptoed toward the window and tried to peek around the side of the blinds.

"It's Jenika and Matt," Jenika said, as if she could sense my hesitation.

"Can I let them in?" I asked Megan.

She shrugged, her expression uneasy. "I had to beg Grandma just to let you over."

"We'll keep quiet, then." I opened the blinds and cracked the window open, putting a finger to my lips. "Cindy can't know you're here," I whispered.

"So what else is new?" Jenika mumbled, climbing inside. She made it sound like she'd been in here a lot…

Alex's room suddenly felt like a tiny closet with four of us inside, Matt and Jenika by the window, Megan with her back against Alex's closet, and me, standing on a mound of sheets next to his bed.

"Have you heard anything?" I asked Jenika.

"We talked to Crazypants across the street," she said, referring to Paul Cross. "He saw a dark pickup that night, too. Only he saw it around three a.m., right in front of his house. Wouldn't Alex have been home by then—if that's where he went?"

I nodded. That was almost an hour after the fire—when Matt's neighbor saw a dark pickup circling around. But there were a lot of dark pickups in the world. "Did Paul see anyone inside?"

"Yeah." Jenika folded her arms, shaking her head. "A hooded devil."

Matt snorted.

I let out the breath I'd been holding. "So he didn't have any useful descriptions?"

"He said he heard voices," Matt said. "Guys *and* girls."

I turned to Megan. "You sure you didn't hear anything that night?"

"I had my headphones on because of that stupid party next door. The sirens didn't even wake me up."

"Which side was the party on?" I asked.

Megan pointed in the direction of the biker couple. "Maybe they were the voices Paul heard."

"The pickup could've belonged to one of the partygoers," I said. "We should talk to—"

"Already did that," Jenika said. "The party was over by one, and they said they passed out soon after." She focused her gaze on me. "See? It helps to talk to random people."

"You didn't say neighbors," I shot back, mostly angry at

myself. It was such a blatantly obvious, common-sense thing to do. I should've done it the morning after Alex went missing. But I was too focused on the idea of Alex missing.

"I think he made it back here," I said, holding up his guitar pick and explaining its significance. "Maybe they were waiting for him to come home?"

"His car was here," Jenika said. "How'd they know he wasn't?"

Matt glanced around the room and headed for Alex's computer desk chair, taking a seat.

I paced back and forth between his bed and the bookshelf. Moving was the only way I could keep my brain going. "Maybe they were waiting for an opportunity to break in, but then they saw him come home and…" No. Forcing Alex into a car would've made too loud of a scene. Unless they had a gun—or it was someone Alex trusted. But who would Amber, Christian, *and* Alex trust?

"And they what?" Matt asked, throwing up his hands. "Hog-tied him, threw him in the back of the pickup, then busted into his house and stole his gun for kicks?"

The A-5. I wasn't even thinking about that.

"Ever try to get through a dead bolt?" he continued. "It's loud. And, you know, noticeable after the fact."

"His window would've been unlocked," I said. He wouldn't risk coming through the front door and waking Cindy. "Maybe they were waiting for him in his room."

I looked over at Megan, who was still pressed against the closet, her arms folded across her stomach.

"You really think someone was in the house?" she asked, her voice a bit above a whisper.

I didn't know what to tell her. There was nothing I could say to comfort her right now.

"You sure you looked everywhere for the A-5?" Jenika asked her. "What about Cindy's room?"

"I told you," Megan said. "We tore this place apart. Every room."

"Let's say you're right," Matt said. "They crawl through Alex's window, but Alex isn't here. So they wait inside, not knowing if the guy's coming back or whatever. Was the A-5 in his room?"

"Living room," I mumbled, knowing where this was going.

"So, they snoop through the house, in the dark," he continued. "Find this old shotgun…"

"Maybe they had a flashlight." Jenika sneered at him.

He was right—putting it that way made the entire scenario sound convoluted and silly. But it wasn't impossible.

"If I broke into a house, I'd look for weapons," I said.

"It sure is a great way to frame him," Jenika said.

"Jesus." Matt tipped his head back, letting out a breath. "Who do you think they took first—Christian or Alex? 'Cause that's a busy night."

"I don't know!" Jenika shouted.

"*Shh.*" Megan moved her hands up and down, her eyes wide.

"Look, I know the two of you are blinded by"—Matt lowered his voice—"whatever you're blinded by. But Alex took that gun and ran. Because he's guilty. Fuckin' accept it."

"I'll accept it when I have real proof," I said. "You have any, Matt?"

The room got quiet enough to hear the weather guy on their TV. High pressure was parked over Oregon. Eighties in the Portland metro area. Seventies on the coast. What a gorgeous day.

A lot of things happened during the early morning hours

of the fifth. Zach breaking into my room, the fire at Jenika's house, Alex and Christian disappearing. Each event seemed unrelated, but my mind wanted to connect them, as if someone were looking down on us, pulling strings.

"These killings seem to be about pitting us against the cakes," I said. "Anyone gonna argue that?"

Matt gave a one-shoulder shrug.

"Think about everything else that's gone on—the rumors, anonymous email threats, Alex's car"—I motioned to Jenika— "the fire. You think it's all a coincidence?"

"I'm still pretty sure Christian started that fire," Jenika said.

"And it had you going after him, right before he turned up dead," I said.

Matt shook his head, running a hand through his unruly blond hair. "So, they're trying to frame Alex, now they're trying to frame Jenika. Which is it?"

"I don't know. I'm not in their head."

"Well," he continued, "you've got them kidnapping two people and starting a fire, all in one night. That's some superhero shit right there."

"Can we just stop?" Megan's voice cut through. She was sitting on the floor now, her knees pulled against her chest. "We're not getting anywhere."

"It's true," I said, gazing outside, at that cloudless blue sky. I was too hung up on trying to convince everyone that Alex was innocent, even myself. "We can argue and come up with scenarios forever, but it's never going to make sense. There's too much we're missing…"

The room went quiet again, except for Jenika shifting her weight and the floor creaking underneath her. It was almost like the ticking of a clock, reminding me I was running out of time. I wasn't going to tell her about Brandon until I knew more. She'd go after him full force. But the more I thought about that sketch pad, the more it ate at me. He was the one who told me about Christian being a firebug, too.

"I went through Brandon's backpack at the diner today," I said, keeping my gaze on Jenika.

"And?" she asked.

I told them about the drawing and all the dots I'd connected so far. His hatred of the cakes. His obsession with Gabi. He was one of the few people who had my email, and he knew how much I hated Christian.

What didn't make sense was why he wanted to frame Alex, or any of us. Then again, psychopaths had reasons most of us could never understand.

Matt shook his head, his brow furrowed. "The guy's a string bean. He couldn't take Christian or even Alex—not on his own."

"Doesn't matter if he's got access to a gun," I said, turning to Megan. "Has Gabi said anything about him?"

"That he's needy, like a puppy. Used to call her constantly."

"So, why does she come into the diner all the time?" I asked.

She picked at her thumbnail, waiting a few seconds before answering. "I don't know. I mean, the last time we went it was my idea."

"Do you think you could get her on the phone?" I asked.

"Screw the phone," Jenika said. "Let's go to her house."

"Why?" I had a feeling she was more interested in intimidation than talking.

"It's harder to lie face-to-face. And there's a decent chance she knows if Christian torched my house."

"This needs to be a casual thing," I said. "If she thinks

we're there to interrogate her—"

"She's not going be okay with all of you showing up at her house," Megan said before standing and motioning to Jenika. "You freak her out."

"Good," she retorted. "Don't tell her I'm coming."

It *would* be better to talk to Gabi in person. Body language gave most people away. "Fine," I said. "We'll go to her house. But it'll just be me and Megan."

"I'm going over there, whether it's with you or not." Jenika's voice rose.

"At least let me do the talking," I said.

"I'll behave, okay?" she said. "We don't want her calling the cops."

"Where's the phone?" I asked Megan.

"I don't think…" she began.

"Megan, please." I moved toward her. "You know we have to do this."

She let out a breath, her eyes filled with worry. "I'll go get it," she mumbled, pushing away from the closet.

We waited in silence until she returned, which seemed to take forever. I sat on the bed and gently rocked back and forth to try to calm myself.

"Phone's dead," Megan said when she came back.

I gave her a questioning look, thinking it was awfully convenient they'd decided to shut the phone off right now.

"It is," she repeated.

Jenika dug her phone out and gave it to Megan.

Megan took it with hesitance, as if she thought it would explode in her hand. "What am I supposed to say?"

"Tell her I was hoping I could talk to her about Brandon— keep it vague," I said.

Her face scrunched up in confusion. "And when she asks

why you can't talk on the phone?"

"This is gonna go well," Matt muttered, fishing a cigarette out of his pocket and sticking it behind his ear.

"How about we just show up?" Jenika asked. "Problem solved."

"Tell her it's something I'd rather do in person," I said to Megan.

She blew out a breath and started dialing. I crossed my fingers hard enough to make my knuckles ache.

"Hey, it's me," Megan said, her eyes meeting mine. "Where are you right now?" Her voice sounded too high to be natural, but I gave her an encouraging nod. "So, I'm with Nova and she wants to talk to you about Brandon. She was hop—" The tinny sound of Gabi's voice interrupted her, but I couldn't make out what she said.

"I don't know," Megan answered. "She saw this drawing…"

I stood and waved furiously for her to stop, reaching for the phone. I'd get into the details once I got Gabi to meet me.

"Jesus," Jenika mumbled.

"Is it okay if she talks to you?" Megan asked. She passed it to me a second later.

"Hi, Gabi," I said, trying to sound casual but not overly friendly.

"Hey…" she answered.

"I know this is out of the blue, but can we come over for a few minutes? It's important."

"We can talk now, if you want."

"Well, I'm on a friend's phone, and I don't want to tie it up. And this is really a conversation I want to have in private."

She paused for a few seconds. "Okay. I guess."

I remembered Megan saying they had a security gate. "Is there a code we need to know?"

"Megan knows it," she said.

I thanked her and hung up before she could change her mind.

Megan told Cindy the two of us were heading to the Beach Bum across the street, a pit with really bad burgers and great milkshakes. Then we all piled into Matt's car, after he wrestled with getting the baby seat out.

"We need to be back by two," I told them, wiping away probably a year's worth of baby food crumbs off the seat.

Jenika rolled down the front passenger window, lighting a cigarette. "Let's drive by Brandon's first."

"It's a cop's house, Jenika," I said. "I'm sure they have—"

"You deaf? I said *drive by*. I wanna see if they have a pickup."

I knew his mom drove a blue SUV when she was off duty. I wasn't sure about his dad. I'd seen his smiling face on ads for his vet office, but I never really saw him around town.

"Would you use a family car?" I asked.

"I'd have no choice," Matt answered.

Matt slowed to a crawl after we turned down Brandon's gravel street. It was a narrow lane with houses on each side. Brandon's house belonged on a bed-and-breakfast brochure, a pale yellow Victorian-style cottage with a white porch and blue flowers in the yard. The driveway was empty, but it led to a separate garage with a couple windows on the side.

"Stop," Jenika said, slipping on a black hoodie. She opened the door and jumped out before Matt came to a complete stop.

He let out a sigh and cussed under his breath.

Jenika walked in front of the house and disappeared around the side that didn't have a driveway. She didn't reemerge for what felt like minutes. Part of my view of the garage was obstructed, but I didn't see her peeking in the windows.

"What if someone comes home?" Megan muttered.

A minute later, Jenika reappeared, sprinting across the street. She dived back into the seat with a huff. "It's empty."

I wasn't sure if I was disappointed or relieved to hear that. It wasn't like I expected there to be a shiny dark pickup in the garage. That would've been too easy.

CHAPTER TWENTY-FOUR

The De Lucas didn't just live in a mansion; they lived on a plantation. The driveway led us uphill, winding through tall grass and lurching Douglas fir trees. Their redwood house was even larger than I'd imagined, sitting in a tamed meadow overlooking miles of the Pacific. The sun bounced off the rows of windows, making blobs of color dance in my vision.

We pulled up next to Gabi's Honda in front of the detached garage, which appeared to be bigger than my house.

Matt glanced over his shoulder at Megan. "Can we park here or is there a lot for commoners?"

"Here's fine," she answered, undoing her seat belt.

"One of you should probably stay in the car," I said to Matt and Jenika. "All of us at her door will be too much."

"Oh, no. We don't want to scare the princess." Jenika flicked her still-lit cigarette butt out the window. "That should be our top concern right now."

"I'm just saying—" I began.

"I know what you're saying," Jenika snapped, looking over at Matt. "You mind waiting out here?"

"Fine by me," he said, turning up what I'd assumed was a Dropkick Murphys song because it had bagpipes, and they kept singing about whiskey.

A stone path, lined with brightly colored flowers and shrubs shaped like mushroom tops, led to the De Lucas' entrance. A statue of a black panther glared at us from their porch, its eyes a supernatural shade of green.

"Gabi got that after she found the raccoon," Megan said. "Pretty creepy, huh?"

"Yeah…" It fit Steve De Luca, his cold, regal presence.

There was a camera next to the front door, a red light glowing underneath the lens. I was guessing that was installed after the raccoon, too.

Megan rang the bell, and I kept my head down instinctively, feeling watched. We waited in silence, the hiss of Matt's music in the distance.

After about thirty seconds, I looked at Megan, a question in my eyes. She shrugged, winding her blond hair around her finger again and again.

"Is she—" Jenika was interrupted by the front door swinging open and Gabi staring at us. I'd expected to at least hear her approach, especially since she was wearing heeled sandals.

"Hey," she said, her dark eyes lingering on Jenika.

"She's staying with me," I told Gabi. "My mom doesn't want us going anywhere alone, so…"

Gabi nodded, her lips tugging up at the corners. "I get it. My dad doesn't want me to leave the house…"

Nobody said anything for a few too many seconds. And she didn't invite us in.

"We're parked in front of your garage," I said, just to say something. "Is that okay?"

"It's fine. My dad practically lives at the hotel in the summer, especially now. With…everything."

"So, can we come in?" Jenika asked, motioning at the camera. "You've got our close-ups, in case we decide to rob the place."

Gabi let out a laugh that cut off almost as soon as it began and opened the door wide, waving us in. I was surprised by the gesture. If I were in her shoes, I wouldn't let us in.

Walking into their house was more like entering the lobby of a fancy hotel, the kind that had rooms starting at five hundred a night. The downstairs was all wide-open spaces, archways, and polished cherry hardwood floors. Paintings of old brick buildings, cathedrals, tundra landscapes, and abstract portraits covered the pale brown walls. They must've had the air-conditioning on full blast, because goose bumps traveled down my arms and legs.

I couldn't imagine having a house like this to myself. Too many rooms. Too much empty space.

Gabi led us to the living room, which had a massive gray couch and views of the ocean out every window. That was when I saw the deer. It was mounted above their stone fireplace, staring at us with empty brown eyes. Icy fingers moved underneath my skin as I sat down on the couch.

I'd always thought that mutilated deer in the park might've been directed at the De Lucas. And if Brandon was behind this, it made even more sense.

Gabi took a seat on the pale green love seat across from us, her hands gripping the cushion, as if she was ready to jump up at a moment's notice. With her dark hair twisted up in a messy bun, hardly any makeup, and a red tee with "feisty" spelled across the front, she looked younger than she normally did. Megan's age, even.

"I'm sorry about your...friends," I said.

She let go of her grip on the cushion and clasped her hands

in her lap. "We weren't super close, but... It's pretty hard to process right now."

I glanced over at Megan, who was staring at her lap, not blinking.

"Thanks for talking to us," I said, trying to ease the tension. "I know it's weird."

"Yeah, I won't lie." Gabi shifted back a little, crossing her legs. "It seems like you have bigger things to worry about? With Alex, I mean."

I ignored the judgment in her tone—there wasn't time to get angry. "That's why we're here. We think Alex is innocent."

"We know he is," Jenika added.

"Sure." Gabi's gaze shifted to Megan and back to me. "I mean, you guys have been best friends forever."

"You think he's guilty," Jenika said.

"I don't know what to think. People are saying a lot of things." Her manicured brows pinched together. "What does this have to do with Brandon?"

"He talks about you all the time," I said. Realization flashed across Gabi's face as I spoke about his feelings toward her and the cakes. "Anyway, I saw these drawings in his sketch pad—"

"Wait," she broke in. "He showed you his sketches? He never shows people his sketches..."

Instinct told me not to admit I'd snooped through his backpack. "He accidently left them at the diner, and I got curious. I flipped through it." Gabi nodded, her brows still pinched together. "Have you ever seen inside it?"

"Just a picture he showed me..." she trailed off.

"Well, it's filled with drawings of you."

"What kind of drawings?"

I described the one with the bloody tears and "Pull the

trigger" written underneath. "Any idea what that means?"

"No. I…" Her lips parted and closed again.

I looked over at Jenika. She kept her focus on Gabi, her eyes narrowed.

"Brandon said you stopped talking to him," I said. "That you didn't give a reason…"

"That's not true. I said I wanted space, but he kept calling and calling." Gabi rubbed her palms against her legs. "He'd show up at my house, wait outside the gate in his car. I figured responding to him would make it worse. So I cut him off— completely. Told people I knew about it in case he…took it further."

That would make sense if she'd stayed away from him. But she didn't. "You come into the diner all the time. That's not really cutting him off, is it?"

Her expression tensed, as if she was offended. "No. It's not. But I wasn't going there to see him." She let out a breath. "I mean, I wanted to see if he was okay. We've been friends for a long time. And Christian and some of his friends gave Brandon a hard time after I told people what happened— called him up, threatened him. I felt bad, you know?"

She never appeared to feel all that bad, but I let it go.

"Did Christian and his friends ever attack Brandon?" I asked.

"What do you mean?"

"Rip off his clothes," Jenika said. "Jump him. Torch his house. You know. Shit like that."

Gabi's gaze went from me to Jenika, her lips parted. "You guys think Brandon might've killed Amber and Christian."

"Nothing gets past you," Jenika said.

Gabi's eyes widened, and her lips turned up at the corners, as if she didn't quite know how to react.

"Sorry," I said. "We're all pretty worked up right now."

"I'm not sorry," Jenika said. "I'm waiting for you to cut the dumb Bambi act and tell us what you actually know."

Gabi stared at her, her forehead crinkling. "What is it you think I know?"

I tried to think of a way to diffuse the situation, even though Jenika was right. Gabi had to know more about Brandon than she was letting on—they'd been friends way too long for her to be so clueless about his sketches.

But then I kept going back to Alex. How clueless *I* was.

A cell phone alert dinged, echoing through the living room. Gabi reached into her pocket, pulling out her phone, and Jenika folded her arms. The air in the room felt like it was moving again.

Megan leaned into me, her arm pressing against mine. "We should go," she mumbled.

Gabi stared at her display, her mouth tensing. "Excuse me," she said, getting up and disappearing down their long hallway.

"What are you doing?" I hissed at Jenika. "She's not going to tell us anything now."

"Wake the hell up," Jenika said, not bothering to lower her voice. "She wasn't going to tell us anything."

"I was getting somewhere before—"

"No. You weren't." She looked over her shoulder at the hallway before continuing. "That chick is sketchy, just like her dad. She'll say anything to come out smelling like roses. If there's even a small part of her that thinks Brandon is behind this, she's going to say"—Jenika crossed her hands over her chest, batting her eyelashes—"*I had no idea he was capable of such things.*"

"She wouldn't do that," Megan said.

"I know you think you're supertight," Jenika said to her. "But—"

"Stop," I said, lowering my voice. "We can have this conversation later."

"She doesn't know you," Megan spoke over me. "Why should she trust you?"

We went silent then, waiting with nothing but the hum of the air-conditioning keeping us company. Jenika paced the length of the couch, her arms folded. Megan sat at the edge of the cushion, drumming her fingers on her knees.

I couldn't take another dead end. Another question mark. Who knew when I could get out like this again?

"I'm going to check on her," Megan said, getting up and heading in the direction Gabi went.

"Look at this place," Jenika said after a minute, motioning around us. "How easy would it be to hide someone away?"

Too easy. They probably had rooms they didn't even use. Not to mention all the acreage. "What—you think she's involved somehow?" I whispered.

She huffed. "No. I don't know. I'm thinking all kinds of crazy right now."

"Me, too…"

Quick footsteps echoed down the hall, getting louder. Megan appeared, panic on her face.

I stood, chills rushing to my hands and feet. "What's wrong?"

"We need to go," Megan said. "Right now."

"Why?" I asked, peering into the hallway. All I could see were shadows and picture frames lining the walls.

"Gabi's freaked out," Megan said, looking at Jenika. "Like, actually scared to come back out here. She thinks you're… going to do something to her."

"Oh, fuck that," Jenika said, loud enough for Gabi to hear. "Are you kidding me?"

"Knock it off," I said.

"She said if I can't get you to leave," Megan continued, "she's calling the cops."

It seemed like an extreme reaction, but I couldn't exactly blame her. She was outnumbered in her own house, and Megan was right—she had no reason to trust us.

"Let's go," I said.

Jenika stayed next to the couch, shaking her head. "I'm not going anywhere. I don't care if I've gotta go back there and beat some truth out of her." She lowered her voice. "I know she at least knows who torched my house."

My fingers curled into my palms. "And then we'll get locked up. Where we can't do anything. Use your head for once."

"Grow a pair," she answered, a challenge in her eyes. "For once. My mom could've died. And what about Alex?"

"We're going to figure something out," I said, willing myself to believe my own words.

"You guys," Megan whispered, her expression pleading.

I wrapped my arm around Megan's shoulders, leading her toward the front door.

"We're leaving, princess!" Jenika's voice bounced off the walls. "You're safe now."

I went for the door, clenching my teeth. She couldn't resist making a bad situation worse.

When we got outside, Matt was standing next to his car, puffing on a cigarette. His dark eyes widened when he saw us, and he flicked his cigarette onto the driveway.

"You guys need to see something," he said, scanning our surroundings as if he'd heard a noise.

"We need to go," Megan said. "Gabi's going to call the cops."

"Let her," Jenika said, catching up to us. "We didn't do anything wrong."

Matt looked toward Gabi's house again and motioned for us to follow him. He jogged toward a dirt path that cut between the towering trees all over their property.

"See what?" I called after him.

"Just come on!" he said, disappearing into the shadows of the trees.

Jenika followed without looking back.

I hesitated, that heavy feeling of dread swelling inside me. The breeze was still enough to hear the roar of the ocean below and the call of the gulls.

"What's down there?" I asked Megan.

"I don't know." She folded her arms across her stomach like she was cold. "I've only ever been in the house."

I tried the passenger door handle of Matt's car—luckily it was open. "Get in. I'll be right back, okay?"

"Nova." Megan's voice was urgent. "Let's get out of here. We can walk back."

"Get in," I repeated, heading toward the path Matt and Jenika went down. The rational part of me knew this was a bad idea, running blindly into acres of woods on private property. But my legs kept moving, propelling me faster into the darkness. I couldn't sit around and wonder anymore. I couldn't wait for the next shoe to drop.

Tire tracks stretched across the mud, going as far as I could see, and there was a small pond to my left with a tiny wooden bridge going over it. Two brown Adirondack chairs, covered with dried leaves and petals, sat on the cement surrounding the water. Beams of sunlight filtered down through the trees, adding to the stillness around me.

You could hide anything out here.

Matt's and Jenika's voices seemed to be coming from every direction, but I couldn't make out what was being said.

A blast of sunlight hit my face as the path curved to the left, blinding me with jagged streaks of light.

"Nova," Jenika said, her voice much closer now. "Hurry up—you need to check this out."

I shielded my eyes with my hand and saw a clearing up ahead. There was a structure, an older cabin with a green roof. In front of it was a large vehicle covered by a gray tarp. Matt lifted the tarp, showing a silver bumper and black paint. It was definitely a pickup.

My breath caught in my throat.

"It's a Laramie Longhorn," Matt said. "Like the one Ray saw."

My eyes focused on the cabin. Green moss covered the base and the roof, and the wood was cracked and warped in places, showing signs of rot. The front door looked new, though, with flawless green paint and one of those fancy keyless entry locks.

Dark curtains hid whatever was inside, but there was a tiny blue light, glowing just behind the glass of the front window. I moved closer to see a round black lens on the ledge, pointing right at us. It was a SpiCam, a popular security camera I'd looked into online but couldn't afford. It let you watch live footage on your phone and sent text alerts when it detected motion.

The trees and the ground seemed to move around me, and a knot formed in my throat. "You know when you said it'd be easy to hide someone away here?" I said, keeping my voice low. "It wasn't a crazy thought."

Jenika opened her mouth, as if to protest, but then closed it again, scanning the scene around us.

"Who puts a lock like that on some old shack?" I continued.

"Rich people?" Matt answered.

"There's a wifi cam in the window, pointed right at us. Why do they need that here?"

Matt's forehead scrunched up like I was crazy. And maybe I was. There was no smoking gun here. But there were too many things to ignore.

Brandon could pull this off a lot easier if he had help. And he and Gabi would make the perfect team, especially since everyone thought they'd stopped talking to each other. He had more access to the case than just about any civilian in town. She had the perfect place to stash the victims. They probably had to take Alex by force. But it would've been so easy for Gabi to lure Christian out here. Amber, too, if she was as drunk as everyone said she was.

I looked back at the cabin, wondering if Alex was in there. If he was alive. Instinct urged me to smash a window and get inside. But they were most likely watching us right now, coming up with a plan in case we did just that. Or maybe they'd already decided we'd seen too much.

Megan. I needed to get back to Megan.

"We have to get out of here and call those detectives," I said, my mouth going dry as I backed away from the house. "Tell them…"

Matt grabbed my arm, stopping me. "They've got a lock and a security camera—so what? That doesn't prove anything."

I jerked my arm out of his grasp. "Why do you think this truck is back here, all covered up? They've got a garage the size of Texas."

"There's a dog kennel and hunting supplies in the bed," he

said, nodding toward the house. "That's probably where they keep their gear, like—you know—guns."

Hunting. I hadn't even put Steve De Luca's love of hunting into the equation. Mostly because—up until now—I'd assumed the De Lucas were being targeted like the cakes. "So, if they wanted to behead a deer and dump it in a park, they'd be all set, right? Come on, Matt. Tell me this is nothing."

"All I'm saying is the cops aren't gonna do shit," he said. "Not based on this."

Jenika glanced in the direction of the camera. "I can't see Gabi offing anyone…"

"Maybe not alone," I said.

Jenika shoved her hand in the pocket of her cargo pants, as if she was searching for something. "Let's walk away and go back to the car, like nothing's wrong."

"That might've worked if we weren't all gawking at the truck," I said. "I'm betting that alert she got was Matt nosing around the first time."

"So, we were admiring it," Jenika answered. "That's all she needs to know."

I inhaled, trying to slow my heart. It was true—the more we showed panic on the outside, the more it would look like we suspected something.

It was hard to put one foot in front of the other, possibly leaving Alex behind. But there was no guarantee he was in there. The only thing I knew for sure was that Megan was alone.

CHAPTER TWENTY-FIVE

My skin hummed, urging me to run back to Matt's car. But I focused on the birds singing. I counted to ten in my head. I did everything I could to stay alert and keep my pace steady.

A small voice inside told me I might be losing it. I was convincing myself that Gabi and Brandon were behind this because it was the best answer I had right now. It was the only answer.

But there wasn't any *actual* proof.

"Nova!" a voice called out. Megan's voice.

The hairs on the back of my neck stood. I heard panic, fear.

As we rounded the curve, I could see her walking toward us, her arms up in the air, palms forward. Gabi was about two feet behind, aiming the black barrel of a handgun at Megan's back.

"Holy shit," Jenika said under her breath, freezing right where she stood.

Matt stopped, too, looking over his shoulder and back at Gabi and Megan again.

"Stay where you are and put your hands up," Gabi called out as they continued walking toward us. "Or I'll shoot her and anyone else I can hit."

Megan walked stiffly, her eyes wide and dazed. I'd gotten her into this. I'd left her alone. If she died today, it was on me. But I couldn't waste time feeling guilty. I needed to find a way to make sure that didn't happen.

"Don't move," I said to Jenika and Matt. I could hear their breaths quickening, sense their desperation. Matt's shoe kept rubbing against a dried leaf in the mud.

I put my hands up first, holding my breath. There were still four of us and only one of her. If Matt and Jenika took off running, there was very little chance she'd get us all.

Matt and Jenika both put their hands up, and I let myself exhale. If Gabi got close enough, we could take her down, wrestle the gun away from her. But something told me she was going to keep her distance.

Her hand didn't shake, even a little, as she kept the gun trained on Megan. Her plan to get us out of here failed and now she had to fly by the seat of her pants. Alone. Yet her face was a blank slate, almost calm.

Brandon's emotions were all over his face when he'd caught me going through his backpack. Maybe I had this backward. Maybe *Gabi* was the mastermind behind this.

I'd never actually seen a handgun up close and in person. The outside didn't shine like metal—it looked like a plastic toy. But some real guns had a plastic frame. It was difficult for even cops to tell the difference between real and fake. I didn't have a chance.

"Empty your pockets and turn them inside out," Gabi said to us, no hint of urgency in her voice. It was the same tone people used to order food at the diner—casual, matter-of-fact. Her gaze lingered on Jenika. "Take your hoodie off first and drop it on the ground."

Jenika did as she said, shrugging it off, all while holding Gabi's stare. Challenging her. I wished I could be inside Jenika's head right now, tell her—just this once—to think before she acted.

I turned the pockets of my jeans out, which meant exposing the Taser. The one thing I thought might get me out of this.

"Drop it," Gabi said to me.

I let it fall through my fingers. That was when I noticed the quivering muscles in my legs. My whole body felt weak, detached from my head.

Matt took out his wallet, a pack of cigarettes, and a lighter. Jenika threw down her phone and two folding knives, both tactical.

Gabi gave Megan a nudge forward with her hand. "Pick up the phone and the weapons."

Megan didn't hesitate. She knelt down in the mud, gathering up our stuff and hugging it to her chest. Her eyes met mine for a brief second as she grabbed Jenika's knives. It felt as if someone was wringing out my insides.

Megan stood slowly, facing Gabi this time.

"Throw all of it in the water." Gabi pointed the barrel of the gun at me, her finger tense against the trigger.

Megan headed toward the pond to our right, her steps small and careful. If I told her to run and she did, it might distract Gabi long enough for us to take her down. But Megan might freeze up. Or she might get shot in the process. I couldn't risk it.

"Where's Brandon?" I asked. Maybe she'd let a little fear peek through. A little uncertainty. Anything that gave me a glimpse into her head.

Her lips curved up the tiniest bit. It was the kind of smile you'd give to a child who didn't know better. "Shh," she said, her eyes following Megan.

Our stuff splashed into the water, making a couple birds flee their hideaways in the trees. It was so damn quiet. I swore I could hear everything sink.

My thoughts raced as Megan made her way back to us, wondering what being shot would feel like. How much it would hurt. If this was the last time I'd see blue sky. If there was life after death.

But if Gabi were going to shoot us right away, she probably wouldn't have bothered making us empty our pockets. She needed to buy time. She needed a plan, some way to get rid of or explain four dead bodies on her property.

That could take a while.

"Turn around, keep your hands up, and walk," Gabi said after Megan rejoined us. "Don't stop until I tell you to."

Matt took the lead, and Jenika followed. I nudged Megan ahead of me, so the gun would be at my back, but Gabi grabbed her arm, holding on to her.

"Move," she said to me.

It was like marching in slow motion toward the edge of a cliff. Our footsteps were hesitant, our breaths quick and shallow. A small plane roared somewhere above, getting louder and softer again—but never disappearing. My body was covered in sweat, but I was freezing, even with the warm air sticking to my skin.

When we reached the cabin, Gabi told us to stop. I glanced over my shoulder at her. She was pressing on the screen of her phone. Something clicked. The door lock, I assumed.

"Open it and go inside," she said to Matt.

The air in the cabin was stale and ripe with antiseptic, sweat, and a skunky odor I couldn't identify. We walked through a small entryway with a coatrack and rain boots, toward a larger room.

"Oh my God," Jenika said, her voice soft.

My heart stuttered. Alex was in the middle of what was probably once a living room, sitting in an old wooden chair. Each of his wrists was cuffed to an arm of the chair, and shackles bound his legs. A black sleep mask covered his eyes, there was duct tape over his mouth, and his head slumped to one side.

He didn't move at all.

"Alex!" I called out, my voice piercing in such a small space.

He lifted his head, mumbling something. Then his whole body jerked and he sat up straight, his fingers clutching the chair arms. A small part of me felt hope. For now, he was alive. I hadn't lost him yet.

And I wasn't wrong about him. He was innocent.

Alex's brow scrunched up, and his breaths came out fast and hard, his cuffs clinking against the chair. He tried to speak, an *O* sound, either "no" or "Nova."

I scanned the room, which was more like a studio. A taxidermy studio. Deer heads lined the walls. There were also fish, birds, and squirrels scattered across metal shelves. A SpiCam was wedged between a duck and a small bird, pointing at Alex. But the blue light was off.

A large owl sat in the far left corner of the room, near a tiny bathroom and a freezer. It stared back at me with yellow eyes. I didn't know much about hunting, but I was pretty sure owls were illegal to hunt in the U.S.

Gabi stood in front of a long worktable that was soiled with deep red stains and dirt—my stomach tensed just seeing it. Behind her was an entire wall of tools—knives, scalpels, shears, calipers, things I couldn't even begin to identify. I only knew they were meant to tear once-living things apart and put them back together again.

Gabi told Megan to stay next to her, but instructed the rest of us to stand side by side in front of Alex's chair and keep our hands up.

"Pat them down," she said to Megan.

It was a smart move, using the most vulnerable person here to get close to us, do her dirty work. But it was also risky. Megan could lie and say we were clean when we weren't.

Megan moved behind me first, and Gabi followed, keeping the gun trained on both of us but always staying out of reach. Maybe she was banking on intimidation.

"You really think you can pull this off?" Jenika asked.

"Be quiet," Gabi said, as Megan patted my sides and my pockets. She did it quickly, her hands barely touching me.

"Or what?" Jenika continued. "If you were gonna shoot us here, you'd have done it already."

My muscles tensed. Letting Gabi know we'd figured that out wasn't going to help.

"Keep talking and find out," Gabi said, her voice still eerily calm.

My eyes went back to those tools on the wall. Shooting people obviously wasn't Gabi's thing. She liked to take it slow, be more "hands on." Or maybe that was Brandon's thing… Where *was* he?

My heart pumped harder just thinking of what she might be planning.

A chair, rope tangled around the legs, leaned up against the wall to my right—probably from when Christian was here.

The trash can next to the table was filled with empty water bottles, tape, and cloths. There were boxes of plastic gloves. Shoe covers. Bottles of bleach. Antiseptic wipes. Everything needed to leave as little evidence at a crime scene as possible.

Matt stared straight ahead as Megan patted the pockets of his jeans, his jaw stiffening. His chest moved up and down noticeably, as if he was gearing up for something.

Gabi backed her way around the long table, keeping the gun pointed in our direction. Her other hand gripped Megan's arm. She was still wearing those sandals, leaving her toes exposed. All Megan had to do was stomp her heel down, as hard as possible. It might buy us enough time to reach them — we just needed a second or two.

I met Megan's gaze and moved my eyes down toward Gabi's sandals, twice. Three times. Megan stared back blankly, like a zombie.

Gabi opened a drawer and riffled through it. "Get on your knees," she told us.

The old wood dug into my knees, making them ache and sting. As Jenika knelt, she slipped her fingers inside her combat boot and pulled something black and silver out. A pocketknife. She dropped it into her back pocket. My eyes flickered up to Gabi, but she was handing a plastic bag to Megan right then, not looking at us.

A little bit of relief fluttered through me.

"Tie their hands behind their back," Gabi said, guiding Megan toward us again.

Megan pulled out a clear zip tie from the bag. They looked like the kind you'd get at a hardware store — cheap. The kind that may not be too hard to get out of, especially if we had time on our side.

Megan did Matt's hands first, while Gabi supervised, watching every movement. "Tighter," she instructed, as if Megan were her student.

Matt winced, his mouth tensing.

"My mom knows where we are," I said. "And we were supposed to be home by two."

Gabi didn't respond.

I overlapped my hands, but I kept my wrists apart, so Megan couldn't fasten the plastic as tight as necessary.

"Nice try," a voice said. But it wasn't Gabi. It was Megan. She shoved my wrists together, squeezing so tight her nails dug into my skin. "She knows you're lying."

My lips parted. I couldn't breathe. This couldn't be happening. This wasn't real.

Megan stood then and folded her arms, staring down at us.

"You're fucking *helping* her?" Jenika shouted, her face going slack.

My mind wanted to deny it, make excuses. She was doing this out of fear. She had no choice. But those missing pieces of the puzzle began to come together. Who besides Alex would've had the easiest access to that gun...

It was something I hadn't even considered because it was unthinkable. This was Megan.

This was *Megan*.

"Get the shotgun," Gabi told her.

"What are you doing?" The words tumbled out of my mouth. "Why are you doing this?"

"You weren't supposed to be here," Megan said. "You put yourself here."

"I wasn't talking about me," I said, heat rushing into my face. "He's your brother—"

"He's your brother, do it for your brother," Megan mocked me in a high voice. "I am so *sick* of hearing you say that!"

Alex made another sound, his fingers curling up inside his palms.

"Megan," Gabi said. She was still behind us, so I couldn't

see her face. But Megan looked at her the way a little kid looked at their mom when they were in trouble. Averted gaze. A mix of fear and shame.

Gabi told me to sit on the left side of the room. Then she sent Jenika to the right side and had Matt stay where he was, in front of Alex. Why were we being separated?

"Brandon's not even involved, is he…" I said.

Nobody answered.

I kept going back to the night Alex went missing. Why take him at all? Sure, his disappearance raised suspicions. But kidnapping him and holding him hostage indefinitely seemed rash for someone as calculating as Gabi. A lot could go wrong. They'd have to kill him *and* frame him.

Megan had easy access to his comb, his clothes, his shoes, his computer—anything they needed. It would've been a lot less risky to plant a little evidence at each scene. Let him take the fall that way.

Maybe Alex saw something he shouldn't have that night.

Megan opened a closet and came out with her grandpa's gun case, carrying it to the table. Gabi joined her, her focus straying from us for a few seconds.

Jenika's arms moved up and down behind her back and she shifted slightly. She gave me a small nod, her gaze shifting between me and Gabi and Megan.

Even with a knife, it would take her some time to cut through the plastic of the zip ties without being obvious. Too much time.

Jenika's forehead was creased and her eyes narrowed. It was an expression I'd never seen on her face before. Fear. Desperation. She was probably putting together the same thing I was.

They were going to shoot us, right here and now. With

Alex's shotgun.

Megan pressed the stock against her shoulder, aiming the long black barrel toward the ceiling. Then she adjusted her grip and pointed it at Jenika.

"Nova first," Gabi said, quietly.

My throat felt like it was closing up, and my heart pounded so fast I was sure it would explode soon.

Alex tried to speak again. He was pleading with them, banging his fist against the chair.

Megan tensed, her eyes darting between Gabi and me. Her face crumpled, and she looked like the Megan I knew again—unsure of herself, scared of life.

"Aim at her head," Gabi told her. "She'll lose consciousness immediately—she won't feel it."

Who knew if that was actually true? I didn't want to find out. God, I didn't want to find out.

"You don't have to shoot anyone, Megan," Matt said. His cheeks were flushed and sweat was dripping down his neck. "You could run."

She kept her focus on Gabi, tears welling up in her eyes. "I don't think I can do this."

"You have to." Gabi kept her voice gentle, kind even. "It's the only way."

"Not the only way." Megan inhaled, wiping under her eye. "We could go. Right now. We'll do it just like we talked about."

I could see Gabi filling Megan's head with Bonnie-and-Clyde fantasies—them on the run. Them against the world.

"We can still fix this," Gabi said.

"But—"

"This whole situation"—she motioned to all of us, including Alex—"is on you."

"I know!" Megan's voice pierced my ears. "I'm sorry." Her

body shuddered, but her finger stayed on the trigger. One wrong twitch and it could go off.

"You promised," Gabi said.

Megan adjusted the shotgun against her shoulder again, walking toward me. Aiming at me.

"She's manipulating you, Megan," I said. "Can't you see it?"

She took another step closer.

"Your fingerprints are all over these zip ties," I said, my words coming out fast. "All over that gun. Your family's gun."

Her arms stiffened, and her finger rose the slightest bit off the trigger.

"Don't worry about that," Gabi said. "We'll wipe it all down—after."

"She's got an answer for everything, doesn't she?" I continued. "Ask her this. Why does it have to be you? Why do *you* have to shoot us?"

Megan's eyes went to Gabi and back to me. "Because it's my fault."

"Megan," Gabi said. "It's you and me, okay? I'll take care of you. I'll always take care of you. All she cares about is Alex."

"That's not an answer." The words came from between my teeth.

Megan put her finger back on the trigger and tilted the barrel, pointing it at my forehead. Her chest heaved up and down.

I wanted to squeeze my eyes shut. Duck. Cover. But I froze.

The voices of Jenika, Matt, and Alex blurred together, like conversations in a crowded restaurant. The thoughts in my head went silent. There was no life flashing before my eyes. No last words I wanted to say. There was just staring into the tiny hole of that barrel. Waiting for everything to go black.

"Turn around," Megan said, cutting through the noise. Her cheeks were red and damp with tears.

"No." My wrists strained against the plastic that bound them. "You're going to look me in the eye."

She went still. I was pretty sure she'd stopped breathing. I couldn't feel my hands or my feet.

"Don't think about it," Gabi said. "Just do it. Like before."

An icy sensation rippled through me. Picturing Megan strangling Amber until her body went still. Slitting Christian's throat. It tore me up inside.

Megan's nose scrunched up and air exploded from her lips. I held her gaze, refusing to look away—it was the only move I had.

My eyes started to burn. Her entire body stiffened, the muscles in her forearms flexing.

A second went by. Two more seconds went by.

Then her shoulders relaxed, and she lowered the gun. "I can't. I can't," she repeated it over and over, her voice high and childlike.

I let out an audible breath, nausea swelling inside me.

Megan faced Gabi, her eyes vacant and staring. "It's time to go. We have to go."

Her only response was silence. An entire minute of nothing but the occasional drop of water in the bathroom sink.

"Come with me…" Megan said.

Gabi's expression was like steel—there was no seeing through it. "Finish this. And I will."

"Promise?"

"I promise."

Megan lifted the barrel of the gun again and repositioned it against her shoulder. Only this time she pivoted, aiming it at Gabi.

There was an explosion in my ears. It seemed to reverberate forever, making my head vibrate like a bell. I was pretty sure I screamed, but all I could hear was ringing.

Megan fell straight back, her head smacking into the wooden planks with a dull *thud*. She lay there, stiff as a mannequin, the shotgun across her chest.

It took me seconds to process what happened. To see the hole in Megan's forehead. The dark liquid seeping into her blond hair. Pale red bits and chunks scattered around. The parts that used to be Megan. The parts that were alive and thinking seconds ago.

"Don't look at her," Jenika said to me. "Don't look."

The back of my throat closed up, making me gag and heave. But nothing came out. I didn't know whether to scream or cry. Megan was sick. A killer. But in my mind, she was still the girl I'd known most of my life.

Alex was screaming, his wrists pulling up the cuffs. Someone needed to tell him.

"She's gone, Alex," I said. "Megan's gone."

He went still then, his breaths quick and shallow. At least he couldn't see her. It was a small comfort, but a comfort just the same.

Gabi hadn't moved. Her gun was still pointing at the place Megan had been standing. Her eyes went from Megan's body to Jenika to me. There was no remorse on her face. No sadness. No fear.

Nothing.

But I could tell her wheels were turning, trying to calculate her next move. She lowered her gun and grabbed a pair of gloves from the box, slipping one on. She snapped the rubber against her wrist, as if she enjoyed the sound.

My pulse rose again, heat building inside me. I could keep sitting here, waiting to die, or I could stand up. Run at her. It really didn't matter anymore. At least I'd die trying.

Jenika caught my gaze and gave a slight nod in Gabi's direction. *Distract*, she mouthed and wiggled her left arm.

Gabi walked toward us, her handgun pointed at Matt this time. She squatted down and lifted the shotgun off Megan's chest, keeping her eyes on us.

I needed to get her to turn her back on Jenika. Which meant I needed her attention completely on me.

"What's the plan?" I asked. "Shoot us all with Megan and Alex's gun. Plant it on Megan. Or maybe Alex. Have you thought that far yet?"

She stood and focused those cold dark eyes on me, but she stayed right where she was.

"You can say you shot Megan in self-defense. Maybe they'll buy it." I felt like I was out of my own body, watching myself speak. "But you'd have to move our bodies somewhere else—there's way too much evidence in here. And how are you going to do that? You gonna ask Daddy to help you?"

She shoved her handgun into her jeans pocket and stepped over Megan's body, gripping the stock and the barrel of the shotgun. There was still no reaction in her expression, but her focus was completely on me. I needed to get her to turn a little more. Then Jenika would be out of her line of sight.

"Where is he, anyway?" I continued. "Doesn't he ever come in here?"

"Only during hunting season," she said. It was almost startling to hear her voice again.

"You could try to clean this place up." My thoughts were going faster than I could talk. "But there'd be a lot to explain. Why were we all here? Did you have the gun on you? If you did, why didn't you use it sooner? Why are *you* the only survivor?"

Gabi took two steps forward, aiming the shotgun at me. Just like I wanted her to.

Jenika brought her arms forward, clutching the pocketknife with one hand. She rose slowly, her legs shaking. If she stumbled even a little or a bone creaked, it was over. Adrenaline rushed under my skin.

"There's going to be cuff marks on Alex's wrists," I said, raising my voice slightly. "Probably his ankles, too."

Gabi's grip on the barrel relaxed and she lowered the gun a little. Still no response. Just that empty stare.

Jenika took a step toward us, lowering her foot slowly onto the floor. Her arms were spread wide for balance. I shifted my knees against the wood, like I was adjusting my position. It didn't make a lot of noise, but hopefully it was enough.

"Even if you kill us now, it might still be possible for them to tell that Megan died first. What about gunshot residue? How are you going to get around that?"

Jenika was closing in, only a couple feet behind her now. Matt's eyes closed, and his chest expanded with air.

"Why don't you face it," I said. "You're screwed."

Gabi stiffened, as if she could sense Jenika, and whipped around, tightening her grip on the shotgun. Jenika lunged at her with the knife, slashing her arm before trying for the handgun in Gabi's pocket. Gabi hit her in the side of the head with the stock of the shotgun.

I stood. Matt stood.

We both slammed into Gabi, taking her down to the floor. She landed on her stomach, and pain shot across my chest as I landed on her back. I shoved my knees into her hips, her rib cage, anything I could hit. Matt was on half on top of me, using his body weight to keep her pinned.

Jenika pried the shotgun out of Gabi's grip and shoved it away from us. Gabi moved her left arm down, probably trying to reach the pistol in her front pocket, but Jenika stomped on her hands, repeatedly, and I dug my knee harder into her rib cage.

Gabi made a feral sound, something between a scream and a growl.

"Get the handgun." I rolled my top half off Gabi, still using my legs to pin her. Matt moved up, his chest forcing Gabi's head down.

Even with Gabi pressing her body into the floor, Jenika managed to slip one hand underneath her hips and yank out the gun.

"Grab the bag of zip ties," I said. "Then break ours."

Jenika ran to the worktable, clutching the side of her head with one hand. She returned with the bag and scissors and knelt next to me. The cold blades slid against my skin and then I felt a pop.

I was free. I was going to make it through this.

I moved my sore arms in front of me, flexing my fingers to get the circulation back into them.

We forced Gabi's arms behind her back and pressed her ugly red hands together, securing a zip tie around her wrists.

"We should get her legs, too," Matt said.

"That was the last zip tie," Jenika said, holding up the empty bag.

I ran to the chair against the wall and untangled the rope from its legs. We wrapped the thick black rope around her ankles, again and again. More than we needed to.

Then we rolled her over and grabbed her phone out of her pocket. Nobody said a word. Gabi remained stiff and silent, except for the air moving in and out of her nose.

Jenika dialed the police.

Matt paced back and forth, keeping his eyes on the floor.

I went to Alex.

"It's over," I told him, pulling the duct tape from his mouth. "We got her."

His lips parted and he gasped, but he didn't answer. His skin was red and blotchy where the tape was.

I put my hand over his, my thumb gently stroking his skin. "Do you know where the keys are?"

He shook his head. "Take this mask off me." His voice was hoarse—more like a whisper.

"You don't want me to," I said. "Trust me."

He didn't protest, but his hand remained tense under mine.

I wrapped my arm around his shoulders and lowered myself onto his lap, resting my cheek against the top of his head.

Neither of us moved. We just waited in silence.

TUESDAY, MAY 1

Everyone screws me over. Overlooks me. My mom. My dad, whoever he is. My perfect brother. The bitches at school, who act like I don't exist. Even my grandpa. Alex is his favorite. Alex always came first. Alex has always gotten off easy. My whole life I've felt like I don't belong here.

But you make me feel like I belong. When I talk, you actually hear what I'm saying. You don't think I'm weird. You don't think I'm crazy. You get me like nobody else ever has. I always hoped I had a soul mate out there. But I never thought in a million years it would be you. I guess it makes sense, doesn't it? We're both alone. Totally and completely alone.

SATURDAY, MAY 10

There was a time I thought I was your number one. But I never was... As soon as Nova came along, she became the most important person in the world to you. I'm something to pity. Something to leave behind like a bad nightmare. I'll never be anybody's number one.

I heard your conversation today. You thought I was still at the cemetery with Grandma, but I walked home before you did. You didn't notice. I was in my room when you got home. You didn't bother to check, though. You rarely do anymore.

I heard your big plan, the whole thing. You're going to run away with Nova. Disappear. You're going to leave me alone with Grandma, let me clean up the mess. How could you do this to me? You said you'd always take care of me—no matter what. You said you'd always be here.

You're a fucking liar. But of course...I already knew that.

TUESDAY, MAY 20

I asked you about him today. If you remembered what he was like. If you think Mom is still with him. And I could tell by the look in your eye that you remember. You know what he did to me. But you didn't say a word. You've never said a word. You don't care. You'd rather just run away and forget I ever existed.

Guess what? I'm not going to let you.

FRIDAY, JUNE 13

I wish you'd believe me when I say I won't disappoint you like he did. I love you more than anything in this world. I will do anything for you. It's us against the world. We're going to make them pay.

EPILOGUE

Two months later…

Alex loaded the last of his boxes into the bed of his El Camino. I stood a few feet away, an ache building in my throat.

We wouldn't be walking together to school tomorrow.

I wouldn't be making him laugh in class with my cartoon portraits.

He wouldn't be taking notes for both of us, so I could tune out.

There would be no "us." No Megan…

Alex would be in his Uncle Joel's Southeast Portland duplex, trying to forget this town. His life here. All the ghosts waiting for him every time he opened his eyes.

I knew he needed to leave more than I needed him to stay. I'd encouraged him to do it. But seeing him now, ready to drive out of here for good, made me want to take it all back.

"Five more minutes?" I asked.

His lips curved up a little and he sat on the El Camino's tailgate, patting the space next to him.

I sat on the cold metal, my arm pressed against his. Stars

were breaking out across the dimming sky, but the remnants of the day still glowed in the distance, turning a small tuft of clouds pink. There wouldn't be many more nights like this. In a few weeks, the low clouds would roll in, and the wind would bite at my fingertips. Then the rain would come, washing away all the color.

Alex wove his fingers through mine, tilting his face up and closing his eyes. We hadn't done a lot of talking these last couple months. Mostly we'd lie side by side, listening to the Chameleons on repeat—our new obsession. Or we'd go for a run, deep into the woods, until our muscles gave out.

I still had so many questions. We all had so many questions. But Alex had given me some of the missing pieces, when he could bring himself to talk about it without shutting down. He said Megan had been acting sketchy for weeks, never coming out of her room, freaking out whenever he'd knock on her door. One night, he'd even caught her sneaking out—she'd said she was waiting for Gabi to pick her up.

After they'd gotten home from Oswald Beach on the night of the Fourth, she took off her hoodie and a phone fell out. Alex picked it up and asked her where she'd gotten it. She snatched it out of his hands and said Gabi had "given" it to her. When he asked her why and who was paying the bill, she told him to mind his own business and locked herself in her room.

He heard her talking on the phone afterward, so he stood outside her door, listening. He heard something about a fire, but he couldn't make out the whole sentence. *I can't wait until they arrest him*, she said. *I can't wait to see the look on his face.* Then she told whoever was on the other end that she "loved" them and she'd "see them soon."

Later, when he was with me, he kept waking up. He couldn't

stop thinking about Megan, wondering who was getting arrested and why she knew about it. There was even a part of him that thought she might be talking about him. He knew she was angry with him, that he'd let her down—but did she really think he was capable of something like this? Obviously she was seeing someone—keeping it secret. He started to wonder if it was some cake, playing games. Or worse.

When he heard all those sirens, he got a bad feeling. So he left me a note, saying he loved me, and rushed home.

That was when he saw all the fire trucks in front of Jenika's place. He picked the lock on Megan's door, because he didn't want to knock and risk waking Cindy up. But Megan wasn't there. He started going through her stuff. Under her bed. Every drawer. Her closet. And then he found a notebook under her mattress.

Alex told me some of it was like a manifesto, as if she wanted to brag about all the details. Other parts were more about her feelings. Her fears. She blamed him for letting "it" happen to her. Called him selfish. A coward.

She talked about some of their plans to frame Alex. Gabi was the one who keyed Alex's car. Even the Fourth of July, at Oswald Beach, was a setup, a way to get Alex and the cakes together. Fuel the fire. It didn't go down quite like she expected—Alex was supposed to answer his phone.

She wrote about Amber's murder too, details Alex couldn't get out of his head. She bragged about how they'd tricked Amber into believing they hated me, too. They told her I'd convinced Zach to dump her, and together they came up with a plan to "get me" that night—but swore one another to secrecy. Amber met up with them later, on the trail between North and South Beach, to execute their plan. But they pulled a gun on her instead.

That was as far as Alex had gotten.

Since the cops took Megan's notebook, we didn't know how they got Christian or if he or they started that fire. We'd always be guessing.

Megan must've seen Alex through her window when she went to sneak back in, because she came in the front door. With Gabi. They were wearing hoods and masks.

Gabi held a gun on him and told him to come out to her truck. When he refused, she said they'd kill Cindy. Megan even got out their grandpa's gun and aimed it at Cindy's door.

So he went.

He wouldn't say much about his time being held hostage. Only that Christian was there, that first day, and then…he wasn't. They gave him small amounts of water and unlocked his handcuffs a few times so he could go to the bathroom. Sometimes Megan would talk to him, but he wouldn't tell me what she said.

A few weeks ago, we were lying on my bed, listening to music, when he made this gasping sound. He sat up, grabbing the sides of his head. And he said it was his fault. All of it. I rubbed his back until his breathing went back to normal, and he didn't say another word.

This doctor in Tillamook said we were at high risk for PTSD, that we'd all need therapy. So Mom and Eric sent me and Jenika to this therapist a couple times—it was all they could afford. But talking didn't help me. Talking just put me back into that room, looking into the long barrel of that gun. Talking made me see Megan die, over and over again.

I still hadn't been able to process that day. I didn't know if I ever would, but I knew I had to try if I was ever going to be able to move forward. If I ever wanted to have a good night's sleep again. Or laugh without feeling guilt.

I should've been there more for Megan. I should've made sure she knew how much she mattered to me, not just because she was Alex's little sister. But because of who she was. Who the three of us were together. Those moments we spent together, playing in the woods, making each other laugh when we'd been through hell at school, were some of the best memories I had. It wouldn't have been the same without her. Not even close.

Would it have changed anything if she knew that? I honestly didn't know. I just knew that question was eating me alive.

It helped to know Gabi was locked up, being held without bail. The murder trial was still months away, but she was getting tried as an adult. Daddy couldn't get her out of this— but he was trying. He pointed out again and again that Gabi hadn't actually killed Amber and Christian, and she'd shot Megan in "self-defense." She grew up without a mother, he said. He wasn't around as much as he should've been. She was troubled. Vulnerable.

Every time I saw him on the TV, telling those lies, I wanted to smash my fist through it.

From what I heard, Gabi wasn't saying a thing. She wouldn't even speak to her lawyer. And the more she held out, the more attention she got. They loved flashing her doe-eyed picture on the news, trying to "unravel the mystery." She and Megan even had a name now—the Foxglove Killers.

I didn't know exactly why she did what she did, but I had a theory. She got off on manipulation, seeing how far she could push people. And it wasn't just about getting Megan to kill people. Or framing Alex. It was about all of us. Seeing how far we'd all go. That was what I'd tell them when I testified. That was what we'd all tell them, including Brandon.

He was going to show that picture he'd drawn of her and talk about how she used to give him "dares." *Pull the trigger* was what she said whenever she tried to get him to do something. Like drive down Highway 8, a road that curved through the Coast Mountains, while she covered his eyes. Steal something just for the hell of it. Jump into the ocean to cure his fear of water.

She told him things about the cakes, too. How they'd done things to her. Cruel things. She was always cryptic about what, never specific. She made it seem like she was afraid to tell him, which made him all the more concerned.

Then one day she told him about how Christian set fire to some guy's car and bragged about getting away with it. "We should set his Audi on fire," she'd told Brandon. "Can you imagine the look on his face?"

Brandon laughed it off, thinking she was kidding. It never dawned on him that she was serious, even though she got quiet afterward. It wasn't long after that she cut him out of her life.

He said he should've seen this coming. He should've seen her for what she was. But like I told him, some people have darkness inside them that most of us can't comprehend. Not until we're face-to-face with it.

Megan had shown plenty of signs, but I never saw the darkness in her or how truly unhappy she was. I only saw my idea of who she was.

"Did you see that?" Alex asked, bringing me back to the here and now. His eyes were open now, watching the sky.

"What?"

"Shooting star—it was bright, too."

"Did you make a wish?"

He shook his head, still gazing up. "I don't have one."

I gave his hand a squeeze. "Want some of mine?"

He looked at me then, and wrapped his arm around my shoulders, pulling me against him. "You know I'm not leaving you, right?"

"I do… Doesn't mean I'm not going to miss you like hell."

"Why? You've got Jenika to keep you company." A playful spark flashed in his eyes. A spark I hadn't seen since…before.

"Oh, yeah." Jenika was staying with us until her mom was out of rehab—Eric had convinced her to go after she got out of the hospital. "I should get back soon—we're trying to decide what to wear to school tomorrow."

Alex's smirk turned into a soft laugh.

The tension between Jenika and me hadn't gone away—we still argued and pushed each other's buttons. But there was a connection between us now, an unspoken understanding. Sometimes it was a look we'd exchange when Mom or Eric tried to get us to open up. Sometimes we had conversations about "regular" things, like how sexy Dean Winchester was and how cool it would be to spend the night in a haunted castle.

Sometimes I even liked being around her. She said things I didn't have the guts to say. As everyone else was tiptoeing around me, saying what they thought I wanted to hear, she kept it real. Made me feel normal…

"How about you just come with me?" Alex said. "We'll figure out the rest later."

"God, I wish." I traced the lines on his palm, willing time to slow down. "I'll be up there every chance I get. Don't want to lose you to some Portland girl with a better music collection."

He closed his hand around my fingers, warming them. "Doesn't matter. They wouldn't be you."

I looked at his house one more time. At the fading sky-blue paint his grandpa had picked out just for Megan and

Alex. This was probably the last time I'd be here. Cindy had moved in with a friend in Astoria, so she'd cleared everything out yesterday. It would go on the market at some point—maybe when this blew over. If it ever blew over.

Until then, it would just sit here. Empty.

Alex leaned in and pressed his lips against mine, lingering for a few seconds, before pulling away. "You're going to be okay." He ran a finger down my cheek. "You're the strongest person I know."

"I could say the same to you." He was right when he said I couldn't save him. I couldn't make this pain go away. I couldn't stop his nightmares. But I could have faith in him. And I did. He'd had so much thrown at him, even before this, and he'd always found a way to survive.

It may take a lot of time, and a lot of space—but he was going to find a way to be okay. And I'd be there for him, whenever he needed me.

Alex looked back up at the sky, exhaling. "I should probably get going…"

"Five more minutes?" I said.

He rested his head against mine. "Five more minutes…"

I closed my eyes, taking in the moment. Alex's warmth. The wind rustling the leaves. I had a long road ahead of me, dealing with my guilt, my anxiety, getting through this without Alex at my side—at least in the way he'd always been at my side. I had to figure out what my life was without the two people I'd seen almost every day since fourth grade. The two people I thought would always be here, fellow outcasts, helping me face this town…this world.

But for now, I had these five minutes.

ACKNOWLEDGMENTS

Thank you to Jesse McCune, my amazing husband, for giving up his time with me and listening to me vent while I wrote and rewrote this book. You are my rock every single day. Thank you to my cat Maestro for giving me hugs when I needed them most. Thank you to my friends, family, and beta readers for being there through my ups and downs and giving me some great feedback—Stephanie, my twin in so many ways, Paula, Denise, Trish, Vivi, Kristen, Julie, Kari, the "Myke", Mel, Stephie Oi, Luke, and Shveta (for listening and offering up a great meditation). Thank you to my fantastic editors, Alycia Tornetta and Stacy Abrams, for their insight and infinite patience with me this last year. And last but not least, thank you to my agent, Jennifer Laughran, who has always believed in my writing and just "gets" my characters and my style.

Check out more of Entangled Teen's hottest reads...

THE BODY INSTITUTE

by Carol Riggs

Thanks to cutting-edge technology, Morgan Dey is a top teen Reducer at The Body Institute. She temporarily lives in someone else's body and gets them in shape so they're slimmer and healthier. But there are a few catches. Morgan can never remember anything while in her "Loaner" body, including flirt-texting with the super-cute Reducer she just met or the uneasy feeling that the director of The Body Institute is hiding something. Still, it's all worth it in the name of science. Until the glitches start. Now she'll have to decide if being a Reducer is worth the cost of her body and soul...

MODERN MONSTERS

by kelley york

Last night, something terrible happened to a girl at a party. And now she's told the police that quiet Vic Howard did it. Suddenly Vic's gone from being invisible to being a major target. He's determined to find out what *really* happened, even if it means an uneasy alliance with the girl's best friend, Autumn Dixon. But while the truth can set Vic free, some truths can destroy a life forever...

NAKED

by Stacey Trombley

When I was thirteen, I ran away to New York City and found a nightmare that lasted three years and left me broken. Only now I'm back home and have a chance to start over. And the first real hope I see is in the wide, brightly lit smile of Jackson, the boy next door. So I lie to him, to protect us both. The only problem is that someone in my school knows about New York. And it's just a matter of time before the real Anna is exposed...

LOLA CARLYLE'S 12-STEP ROMANCE

by danielle younge-ullman

While the idea of a summer in rehab is a terrible idea (especially when her biggest addiction is organic chocolate), Lola Carlyle finds herself tempted by the promise of spa-like accommodations and her major hottie crush. Unfortunately, Sunrise Rehabilitation Center isn't *quite* what she expected. Her best friend has gone AWOL, the facility is definitely more jail than spa, and boys are completely off-limits...except for Lola's infuriating(and irritatingly hot) mentor, Adam. Worse still, she might have found the one messy, invasive place where life actually makes sense.

AWAKENING

by Shannon Duffy

The Protectorate supplies its citizens with everything they need for a contented life: career, love, and even death. Then Desiree receives an unexpected visit from her childhood friend, Darian, a Non-Compliant murderer and an escaped convict. Darian insists that the enemy is the very institution Desiree depends on. That she believed in. The government doesn't just protect her life—it controls it. And The Protectorate doesn't doesn't take kindly to those who are Non-Compliant...especially those who would destroy its sole means of control.

Lun
oct/15